First meeting . . .

No, not large, Sarah thought with wild fascination. *It's huge! Like a grizzly bear.* Only it wasn't like any kind of bear she'd ever seen before. It roughly had the form of a large gorilla.

Her first sensation was gratitude there were plenty of automatic weapons around her. That thing looked like it could probably tear someone's arm off – literally! It was covered in a grayish hair mottled with some darker hue that was almost black. Its coat had a beautiful sheen and its apparent softness belied the obvious power so poorly hidden underneath. The creature stood seven or eight feet tall. *It's like looking up into the face of a mountain. Or a tempest.*

Books by Greg Borman

The Sasquatch Trilogy: Alliance
The Sasquatch Trilogy: Schism
The Sasquatch Trilogy: Confrontation
The Bionic Zombie Werewolf from the Second and a Half
Dimension

ISBN: 13- 979-8457096196

The Sasquatch Trilogy: Alliance

by Greg Borman

CHAPTER 1
Change of Scenery

Peering around cautiously for potential predators, Sarah Scott breathed in the cool, damp air. She didn't expect a wolf or mountain lion to appear but experience had taught her that the forests of the Pacific Northwest were not places for carelessness. She found the beauty to be cathartic, yet fittingly savage given how a normal life had been stripped away from her and everyone she knew-possibly everyone in the world.

Inhaling the crisp, mountain air through her nostrils she smelled everything—the earth, the trees, the shrubs. That manifold menagerie of scents had a delightful effect on her mind.

Moving along a game trail, the sandy blond-haired woman was always on the lookout for wild animals that she could snare.

Having already spent one night sleeping under the stars while gathering food for her tribe, Sarah paused along her trail to look at an animal track. Her mind wandered momentarily, remembering how she had loved her job of working as a forester because it had kept her where she'd wanted to be. However, she'd endured a few challenges to reach her employment goal. Everything had turned out so perfectly.

Before the War, that is.

Sarah peered down at the bag of foraged food that she'd acquired since leaving her tribe the previous day. With a sigh she thought, *This is my job now.* Almost reflexively, she silently acknowledged that few people had "real" jobs any more.

Despite the beauties around her, she began moving forward again with her head downcast. As she walked toward her small town of Drain, Oregon, she remembered how things were before the War. Drain wasn't all that far from Portland and so she had enjoyed a vibrant culture with her fellow citizens. Looking over her shoulder for a potential threat, she knew that she and the other members of the tribe, possibly people all over the world, were in survival mode. She found it hard to believe that the War was only six months old. She surprised herself when she quietly spoke aloud.

"So many dead."

However, she was grateful that she had survived this long. Like most people who still lived, she was well aware that her life was as "good" as it was because she didn't live in a large city, many of which had been the first to be targeted.

A jackrabbit bolted across her path and she wished she'd had a snare set to catch him. It was one thing for her to bring back to her tribe a large assortment of bitter herbs and vegetables, but it was an entirely different prospect to everyone's taste buds when someone was able to provide meat.

As always, she'd volunteered to go into the forest to forage for food and any other kinds of supplies she could find. She did so, in part, to make sure the rest of her small community was aware of her value to their survival. However, she also enjoyed taking any chance she could to be in the woods. On this particular excursion, she had found some kinnikinnick, chickweed and cattails to use as food. She knew they weren't tasty and that some people would complain, but they would help keep her people alive. She was also able to acquire some willow bark and leaves to use as medicine. That would receive a more cheerful response.

Sometimes I wouldn't mind being able to use the jeep, she thought. Like most people, she knew that fuel for operating vehicles was scarce, so was electronic communications. The satellites were still mostly in orbit and functioning, but the decimation of so many major cities had so vitally disrupted the ebb and flow of all kinds of goods and services that very few businesses still operated in a quasi-traditional way.

As Sarah moved down the path she thought, *At least I live near a forest. Some people don't even have that.* With money being nearly valueless, her tribe would be able to barter and trade with other groups to get a few items that they found more difficult to acquire. No one in her tribe knew how to make blankets or rope from scratch. There were other things they traded for but those two were always near the top of their list.

As Sarah drifted along the game trail, her sky blue eyes noticed something different. Her senses focused and went on alert. The words of a friend moved through her mind automatically, "Anything different is dangerous." She noticed that peppered about here and there were trees that bore evidence of having been disturbed by a force that appeared to be unnatural, or at least not quite like anything she recalled having seen before. Intrigued, she took a closer look. Some of the trees in her vicinity had thick limbs broken off near the trunks of the trees. Add to that the fact that the broken limbs were several inches thick and she found herself wondering at this mystery. She realized that it felt good to have a possibly innocuous conundrum to occupy her thoughts, as opposed to the ever-present concerns of survival. *What could've caused such a thing except humans?* she wondered. *Or possibly the Enemy.* Yet, as she looked around at the ground, she couldn't find any human tracks and, though she'd never actually seen the Enemy's tracks, she knew what they looked like and she didn't see any spoor that suggested one of their kind.

She stepped closer to the trees and fallen limbs and began to conduct a cursory examination, her sense of curiosity getting the better of her. She rubbed her finger across the breakpoints of the branches and noticed that the breaks were not made by a man-made tool. As she stood there, analyzing the few visible clues, she couldn't help but notice the oddly pungent odor that emanated from them. She looked around and wondered what would have left behind such an odd scent. Finally, she moved on, never fully forgetting the new mystery that was wrapped up in those broken limbs.

It had taken some time to get deep into the forest and so, as was typical for her, Sarah spent the night in the woods. At her campsite, she made a small stew and ravenously devoured it. It was a little bit of squirrel and a lot of cattails, oyster plant, and other things she'd foraged. Though simple, it tasted wonderful to her, *Especially after a long day of traipsing around a mountain.* After supper, she piled more wood on the fire and then settled into her old, tattered sleeping bag. She started reading a book, "The Swiss Family Robinson." She had chosen this particular book for some leisure reading because its story took place on a tropical island and appeared to be of a rather feral nature. After reading a couple of chapters by the flickering light of her campfire, she turned in for the night.

Although she was tired, she couldn't get those strange tree-breaks out of her mind. She kept telling herself that she was just being foolish. *They were probably made by an old windstorm.* Finally, in order to get some sleep, she promised herself that she would conduct an additional investigation the next morning.

So, after she awoke, Sarah made a steaming hot bowl of semi-stale oatmeal and wolfed it down. She packed up her gear and made sure the fire was completely extinguished. "Well," she said out loud to no one, "time to make good on my promise." She then set out to explore and understand her quarry. As she began examining the prominent breaks on the trunks and the thick branches resting quietly on the ground nearby, she noticed that they seemed to come in groups, two branches broken per tree, with one branch having pointed east, before it had been snapped, and the other having pointed north. At first, she figured they were made by a bear, perhaps a rabid bear, but something didn't fit. She noticed that they didn't seem to have the wild, non-sentient pattern of a bear. They appeared to be more...calculated. Besides, there weren't any claw marks that a bear would have left behind. Then she also noticed something obvious that had eluded her the night before: the breaks were all at least seven feet off the ground!

As Sarah sat there, trying to work out this puzzle in her mind, she was so absorbed that she didn't notice the quiet, gentle sounds of cracking twigs and the rustling of leaves coming up the hill behind her. The sounds got closer and closer. Sarah was oblivious to everything but the puzzle. Then, just as she thought she had it figured out, a hand reached out and grabbed her shoulder. Her instincts kicked in and she spun around swinging her fist, but all she hit was empty air. The cause of her alarm was standing just out of range.

"I never make the same mistake twice."

"Thanks, George," Sarah said panting, her voice dripping with sarcasm. "I remember the last time you did that."

"So do I," George said, rubbing his jaw for emphasis. He noticed her tan was bringing out her characteristic freckles on her cheeks. "It took several weeks for the bruise to go away."

"So, what's the leader of our tribe doing all the way out here?" Sarah chided. She and George were good friends and she knew that the man enjoyed her treating him like "one of the guys."

George Bates had brown hair that was turning to gray and thinning on top. His small pot belly somehow matched his hair. Between that and his cracked glasses that he was not able to fix or replace, he always struck a comical figure. George put his hands on his hips and looked around the landscape at the breathtaking beauty. He stood there for several moments and then let out a long, slow whistle of admiration. When he turned back to Sarah, his face was serious. This worried Sarah. Despite their precarious circumstances, George rarely looked <u>this</u> serious. What could have happened? Fortunately, George didn't give her too long to worry. "We got a call from the Army. They're taking over this part of the forest for the time being. All civilians have been ordered out of the area."

Sarah felt her jaw drop. Before she spoke a host of questions flooded her mind. *How could this happen? What was the Army thinking? Just take over thousands of square miles of land? Civilians had so little to use already; they would starve to death!* It was unconscionable.

Sarah straightened up and asked the obvious question. "Do you think it has something to do with the War?"

"Who knows? Probably. Isn't everything affected by it these days?"

Out in the forest, she could pretend the War was so far away that it might not exist, but now that illusion came crashing down. Her one true refuge had been taken away, violated. "Well, they'd better have one whopper of a good reason!" she exclaimed.

Seeing the look on her face George offered, "How about we head back to town? After we get there, we can try to make sense of all this and see what we can find out."

Sarah consented. "Thanks George. Let's go."

CHAPTER 2
This Land Is My Land

It was a long hike back to town. The path wasn't a direct one. It wound back and forth along switchbacks and the occasional steep grade. As they walked they talked about the weather, how wet a season they expected, and so on, anything but the Army's takeover of the forest. Sarah found herself just staring ahead, wondering why this would happen. Out of necessity, the government and the various branches of the military had done some very extreme things in this War. The country was looking less like a republic and more like a state of perpetual martial law.

She remembered when the War began. *Was it really only a few months ago that all the horror and uncertainty began?* she pondered. Sarah remembered being so completely surprised by how quickly—and tragically—some things could change. The revoking of certain freedoms came first. Most people hadn't been particularly surprised that it initially included mandatory curfews, but when it soon entailed a rescinding of the third amendment— "no soldier shall, in time of peace be quartered in any house, without the consent of the owner, nor in time of war, but in a manner to be prescribed by law"—then people began to take issue. But it was a war, a war worse than any ever before—a war of complete annihilation and genocide.

Then the government instituted martial law, Sarah thought dejectedly.

Instead of voicing her concerns Sarah asked, "By the way, how did you find me? And why didn't you just contact me on the cell phone?"

"As you know, we only have two that still work, and you didn't take either of them."

At that remark, Sarah looked down at the path, a little sheepishly, but grateful that George seemed to ignore the expression on her face. This was not the first time she had left the cell phone behind on purpose.

"As for finding you, that was more difficult than it would've been had you taken a phone." He tried to make his voice sound stern but, as usual, failed miserably. "I contacted a friend who was flying his chopper on a recon assignment for the military. I knew he'd be over the zone where you were foraging and asked him to spot you for me."

Sarah made a mental note to stay under the cover of trees more often and make fires that were less smoky. It would've been hard to make a fairly smoke-free fire this time, what with all the rain they'd had lately, but she knew she could do it.

When they got back to town, George made them a quick lunch at their tribe's communal food area. They called it the "soup kitchen," though the soups they ate rarely tasted anything like what they had been accustomed to eating before the War. With the news of the military coming in and commandeering a big chunk of their land, George knew Sarah would need some cheering up. All he could offer was a soupy broth made from some of the plants she'd collected and a few thin trimmings of rabbit meat.

As they sat and ate, Sarah finally began talking. Between mouthfuls she said, "So what happened? The military just waltzed right up and said 'this land is my land, it isn't your land'?"

"Actually, I don't know much more than you do," George replied. "We simply received a shortwave broadcast early this morning that said, 'All personnel have by nightfall to exit the region'." He took another bite and pensively stared out the window of the quickly-eroding building in which they sat.

They continued to eat their lunch, but more subdued. She tried to think about something else and all that came to mind were those strangely broken tree limbs that she'd seen. She thought about mentioning them to George, but changed her mind.

Sarah thought on that, as she continued to attempt to savor her soup. Then she thought, *Being in my forest is wonderful, but I sure do like some of the comforts of civilization, what few we have left to us, that is.* With that idea nestled cozily in her mind, she luxuriated in eating the last bite of her meal. Then, with forced cheerfulness, George said, "Well, whatever is going on, it's probably some isolated incident, like a recovery mission for some military plane that crashed."

"Yeah, you're probably right." She figured he was just humoring her and trying to be cheerful. She was right.

Finally, George decided it was time to get back to other tasks that needed doing, like looking after the other people of their tribe and making sure everyone had food, clothing, shelter, and medical supplies. He took his leave, but not before adding, "I'll let you know if I hear anything more about all this."

As he walked away, Sarah took a good, hard look at their small town. A few people had moved away to other places when the War began. Some gravitated to the big cities but that had been a mistake. Others had migrated to be near family. Once things had settled down, only about half of Drain's small population had stayed.

She looked down Cedar Street from what had once been Deb's Diner. The owner had vacated with the advent of the War and it still remained vacant. The restaurant had been harvested for supplies, some by brigands, others by the tribe. As she cast her eyes down the road, she couldn't help but notice that a casual glance suggested that nothing had changed. The trees were still there, lazily blowing in the gentle breeze. The buildings still remained in their allotted positions, but the more subtle details told a different story. There were few people outside, what with fear of the Enemy descending upon them at any moment. Peppered along the road were buildings in varying states of disrepair. With the rapid evaporation of societal conventions like property values and fashion statements, few saw any reason to dedicate their resources to maintaining the appearances of man-made structures.

Though there were still a few people living there, Sarah had to admit that Drain looked a bit like a ghost town.

Old Man Guzman came walking down the lonely street and Sarah asked him, "What's new, Al?"

Al was an old hermit that had taken to living in town once the War had begun. He stopped and answered, "Well, I suppose you heard about the military coming in?"

"Yes," Sarah replied through gritted teeth.

He just smiled and continued, "Did you hear the rest?"

A slightly bewildered expression came over Sarah's face, as she replied in the negative.

"The shortwave broadcast also said that they were expecting that the Enemy was getting more boots on the ground here and there around the world, like they were digging in or something. I don't know what to make of that. I'm no tactician." The old geezer looked up at the clouds, as if to garner some wisdom from above. "I suppose that could be good...or bad."

Sarah smiled at his unique form of optimism. Al continued walking on his way, leaving Sarah alone with her own thoughts. Like a weight crashing down upon her, she couldn't help but think of things that were ultimately important to her. She sighed. *How long will it last? Will I have a chance to get married some day? Will I ever have children of my own?*

She decided to try to take her mind off it and think about something she could affect. Those thick, broken tree limbs she'd seen. She thought, *It couldn't be the military. They'd have taken down the whole tree.* She peered up at the sky like Old Man Guzman and thought, *It couldn't be the Enemy. They're not that tall and I can't imagine them doing anything that's not related to conquest.* Soon, she was lost in thought, trying to figure out those breaks that seemed to be shrouded in mystery. What could have made them? Some animal? Hunters? She tried to put it out of her mind which wasn't easy, so she decided to go straight to her last resort: listen to a radio.

She pulled a small wind-up radio/flashlight out of her pocket. Winding the armature, she quickly had enough power to listen to the few incoming radio signals. Though much of the day carried no radio signals or broadcasts, she hoped she'd find something. After several moments of carefully adjusting the old fashioned radio dial, she found a signal.

As she listened, once again the broadcast invariably gravitated to the War. She heard a quick snippet discussing where the battle lines currently were, and she felt herself getting choked with fear and sadness all over again. Her sky blue eyes looked at the ground. Was this a war they'd win? Could they actually beat back *this* enemy? A hundred questions and a thousand fears permeated her mind.

Just then, Al came bursting out of a building. He was carrying one of the cell phones that still worked. He looked like some kind of crazy madman what with the way his arms and legs were gesticulating with excitement—or, perhaps, fright.

"Sarah!" he hollered. "I just heard from a friend. They finally did it."

"What?" Sarah asked, more than curious.

"The Enemy." He took a moment to spit to the side to show what he thought of them. "Our defenses failed and the Enemy has sacked D.C.!"

He continued running to share the terrible news.

Sarah wasn't sure how much more bad news she could take that day. She felt like the wind had been knocked out of her. She couldn't believe it. The capitol of the United States of America. It was unthinkable. How could this have happened? But she knew how. The Enemy was powerful, fast, and well-equipped with orbiting ships.

In shock she wished this could be the typical day of foraging, eating bitter foods, and just surviving.

Desperate to think about something different and not allow herself to succumb to depression, she forced herself to change her thoughts to something else.

CHAPTER 3
Close Encounters

The next day, Sarah found herself at the United Methodist Church. The town had never really had its own medical facility and when the War started, the church had naturally evolved into a sort of hospital. Each member of their tribe had a responsibility to help out at the hospital. She was helping some of the sick and injured. She was grateful that there weren't many people needing attention.

She was in the middle of helping a young girl who had eaten some kind of plant that happened to be mildly poisonous. Sarah wasn't surprised. Food was already scarce and people were looking for whatever they could find, and she had to admit, most people were woefully inept when it came to identifying edible plants.

After she finished getting some water for her patient and giving her the best bedside manner she could muster, Sarah looked at her watch and realized her shift had ended fifteen minutes earlier. *I wonder what I'll do about a watch when the battery dies. It'll be hard to find a replacement*, she thought to herself.

With nowhere else to go in her primitive, War-time life, she headed back over to the soup kitchen. She figured she'd check on the tribe's food supply. She was always looking for a reason to go back out into <u>her</u> woods.

As she was doing a rather cursory inventory of their supplies, she was surprised to see a man in uniform at the other end of the building. He obviously wasn't from around there. Everyone knew everyone else. Besides, anyone who had a military uniform didn't live in Drain. They were off somewhere fighting the War.

Sarah figured he was one of the men the Army sent in to take *her* forest away from her. She immediately took a disliking to him.

As she moved around their stores of food she resolved to put him out of her mind. But as she finished and made her way for the door, he too was on his way out.

"Excuse me," he said. "Go ahead."

Without saying a word, she grabbed the door roughly and opened it with all the pent-up emotion from the last day or two.

"Are you all right, Ma'am?" he asked.

"What do you care," she responded rather threateningly.

The man just stood there, his piercing gray eyes taking everything in. He then stuck out his hand and said, "I'm new in the area. My name is Major Garrison. Pete Garrison. I do hope I haven't offended you. Is there something I can do for you?"

The sandy blond-haired woman noticed the man had a fine head of brown hair and, though he wasn't a bodybuilder, he obviously kept himself in good shape. His eyes seemed to display kindness, but that was the last thing she wanted from him at that moment.

Sarah knew what she wanted to say, but just couldn't say it. Instead she quivered with anger. However, she quickly suppressed her temper, barely. Finally, she spoke. "I'm sorry. I heard about you and your friends coming into town and taking over my forest. I just found out and I'm kind of upset about it."

"I'm sorry about that. I suppose it wouldn't matter if I told you that I'm only..."

"...following orders? Yeah, I know." He had said it calmly, like the most natural thing in the world. When she finished his sentence, her words spewed venom.

He just smiled and waited patiently. Sarah wasn't sure what he was waiting for. She eventually shook her head and walked away in a huff.

When she arrived at her small apartment, she was still fuming. She wished they still had running water, or at least electricity. She knew some places did, but Drain wasn't one of them.

After dropping herself into a ragged bean bag chair, her fury-fueled mind couldn't stop thinking. *What was the military doing there? Why did I have to meet one of them in my town near my woods?*

She twisted a little in her chair, trying in vain to get comfortable, and again turned on her small, portable radio. She left the radio on despite the fact that the discussion being broadcast was more depressing news about the accursed War.

After a while, she calmed down. She turned off the radio and stared at the ceiling. Breathing slower made it a lot easier to see things in their true light. She knew that Major Garrison wasn't there as a personal affront to her. Remembering that helped a little. It was like getting stitches, but not having anything to kill the pain. A frustrated laugh erupted from her throat.

Sarah lay on her back for a while, and began thinking about why the Army would be in <u>her</u> forest. The more she thought the more she had a difficult time avoiding the likely possibility that it must be an indication that the Enemy was closing in on her town and the surrounding areas. *Is my forest going to be overrun by the Enemy?* she thought with fear and dread.

Fortunately, thinking of the forest brought her mind back around to the riddle she'd been considering. She was still curious about those broken trees she'd found. She decided to go back out and examine that mystery. *As an added bonus,* she thought, *I'll be thumbing my nose at that Major Garrison.*

Tomorrow, one way or another, she knew she'd be getting some answers.

CHAPTER 4
Oscar-Romeo-17

Sarah arose early the next morning. She grabbed a jeep and surreptitiously filled it up with some of the town's meager supply of gasoline. She then quickly went home to pick up her backpack, some food, her good knife, and a few other supplies. She didn't spend much time there. She had more important things to do, like finding answers to her questions.

On her way out of town Sarah made sure she avoided the more populated areas. She didn't want to be seen, since what she was planning to do would most certainly be frowned upon because of the unnecessary use of fuel. She also knew that she'd have to navigate around the Army. However, she knew these mountain roads like the back of her hand, so she figured if she took things slow, she'd be fine and the Army would never know she'd trespassed on "their" land.

Initially, she headed into the mountains via a seldom-used back road. It was narrow from lack of use, but passable. Somehow the yearly rain and run-off hadn't yet managed to turn the road into a muddy quagmire. As Sarah drove along, she had to force herself not to think about the point of her "mission." For one, the road certainly wasn't perfect, and, jeep or no jeep, she didn't want to walk back to town for assistance. She also tried to control her thoughts, so that she could approach her mystery in a more scientific fashion, without preconceived notions.

Sarah continued to drive slowly and cautiously, her sky blue eyes taking in the many beauties around her. However, as she came around a blind turn in the dirt road, she saw them. Before she had time to back up and get out of sight, they'd seen her. She tried anyway to beat a hasty retreat, but she knew the effort was futile. *If anything,* she told herself, *at least they'll have to work just a little harder to capture me.*

It only took about a minute and the soldiers were upon her. They carefully helped her out of her vehicle and began asking questions.

"Ma'am. You realize this is a restricted area?" It was more of a statement than a question.

"I got lost," she replied lamely.

"Ma'am, for your own safety, you need to be out of this area posthaste."

Who uses the word "posthaste" anymore? Sarah wondered. Aloud she continued, "Look, I'd love to get back to town just as soon as I finish my picnic."

"Your picnic?" the second officer replied skeptically.

"Sure. I was just coming up here for a nice, quiet afternoon picnic alone."

The first soldier looked incredulous. Sarah didn't know what to say and decided this wasn't going anywhere. So she said, "Look, I'll just be on my way and get out of your hair." She could take a different road once she was out of sight and then continue her excursion.

As she was climbing into the jeep, the second soldier said, "I think you'd better come with us."

Sarah couldn't believe it! Now they were arresting her? *Just how martial have our laws become?* she marveled.

"Since you got lost, we'd better take you to our camp. You can look at a map and figure out how to get down the mountain from there."

She experienced only a partial sense of relief. At least they weren't harassing her, she hoped.

The first soldier climbed into his own vehicle and led the way while the second hopped in alongside Sarah as an "escort."

When they arrived at the camp, Sarah was pleasantly surprised to find that everything was clean and in good order. It didn't look like a slovenly camp of miscreants that her pride hoped she'd find. These men were obviously professional. They knew their job and they were good at it. She climbed out of the jeep and the second soldier, Sergeant Jameson, led her to a large tent. Sarah noticed the man had red hair and was a lanky six feet, one inch tall with plenty of red freckles. He asked her to wait outside and soon returned with what Sarah immediately recognized as a map of the area, *her* forest. The sergeant laid the map down on a folding table and began to point things out. Sarah knew the area as well as a mother hen knows each of her baby chicks. However, for appearances, she pretended to study the map.

"We're right here," he said, as he pointed to a nondescript spot on the map. "Here's the town. The best route to take would be along this road here," he said, as he traced out a road with his finger. It was a relatively major road that they were using for the movement of personnel, supplies, and other things.

When she felt like the man was convinced that she wouldn't have any trouble getting back to town, she walked back to her jeep.

"Now, Ma'am," began Jameson, "we really don't have any men to spare right now to see that you head straight back to town. So, I'm asking you to give me your word that you won't 'get lost' again."

Without a word, Sarah turned away and stepped up into her jeep. Just then a loud screeching of brakes permeated the relative tranquility of the camp. A newcomer was arriving and, judging by his clothing and attitude, he was in charge. She scarcely paid him any mind until he was close enough to make out. The slightly good mood that she was just beginning to experience quickly burned away like the morning dew before the heat of the sun. It was Major Garrison.

The first thing Pete Garrison noticed when he drove into camp Oscar-Romeo-17 was the jeep that obviously did not belong to the U.S. Army.

He immediately dismissed it from his mind, knowing that his troops would've already taken care of their guests and that if they needed him for anything, they'd let him know. He walked toward his tent to deposit some of his equipment he'd taken with him. On his way over he spotted someone he thought he recognized. He stopped and stared, trying to place her. At first he couldn't quite remember the sandy blond hair. When her sky blue eyes met his and she scowled at him, it all came flooding back to him like a tsunami. He gave her a slight smile and then walked over to talk to her, all the while wondering why he would unnecessarily put himself through talking to this young woman again. He was pretty sure of the reception he'd receive upon speaking with her, but his sense of duty got the better of him.

"Good morning," he said. "What brings you out this way?"

Sarah paused and then guardedly said, "Oh, I just thought I'd go for a picnic in the hills."

"Really?" he replied. Obviously she hoped he'd buy into this completely ridiculous excuse, but what puzzled him, and got his curiosity going even more, was what *would* she be doing up here, this far away from town? He didn't figure she was foraging for food.

She could've been doing that closer to town and she clearly knew that this was now a restricted area. But she came up here anyway. Why?

He decided to gently pry a little more. "Well, it is a beautiful place for...just about anything. Is there some additional reason you might've come up here?"

She just stared at him and this time, her response was more accurate. "I'm not at liberty to say."

Surprised, he again could only respond with, "Really?"

"Well, after all, isn't that basically the same reason you gave me when we first met? I mean about why you're here?"

"Touché," Pete replied. He smiled in spite of himself. "You know, my orders are that any civilians I find up here are to receive a stiff fine and a few days in jail."

Now it was her turn. "Really? Then why don't you slap the cuffs on me right now, Sheriff?"

Major Garrison paused for a moment and thought about it. She could be rather annoying, but as far as he knew, she hadn't done anything malicious or with ill intent, but most importantly, his gut was telling him to not only let her go, but to also extend an olive branch to her.

"Listen, we didn't get off on the right foot," Pete responded. "My name is Pete. What's yours?"

"Sarah."

"Great. Listen, Sarah. Can you keep a secret?" He didn't wait for a response. "We're up here in your woods to..." he hesitated and pretended to look around for unwanted, eves-dropping ears. After a moment he continued, "...to keep an eye on the Enemy."

Major Garrison noticed the look on Sarah's face. It was like the blood had drained away and she was soon as white as a ghost. Even her freckles seemed to be turning white. Up until very recently, the Enemy hadn't put any boots on the ground in this vicinity. He prepared himself to catch her if she were to faint but she showed herself to be made of sterner stuff.

She politely, but anxiously, replied, "We'd hoped they were further away, somewhere else, maybe around the big cities like Portland and Salem." She took a breath to compose herself. "Are they here? Now?"

He didn't want to answer. She already looked terrified. Then he understood. For himself and his men, the War had been something they'd been dealing with in a very real way, all the time. For her, she'd never seen the Enemy, except for pictures and the Enemy had never been in this area before. He offered her a chair and brought her a glass of water. She sipped it slowly, just staring off at the woods, as if they might suddenly come alive with Enemy combatants. He felt bad for her but knew that she would eventually have had to face this reality.

After a while, she began to look less shocked. Her gaze purposefully wandered over the trees and far-away mountains. He could tell she was looking at things that were out of his sight, but that were peaceful and special to her. He recognized that look. He'd had that look in his eyes, too, when the War began six months ago.

Finally, in a very subdued tone, she said, "I'm sorry I've been so rude to you. You've been nothing but kind to me." She looked around, as if taking one last look at a world that she would never be able to truly visit again. "I found some strange things when I was last here a few days ago. I wanted to analyze them and see what I could figure out. That's why I'm here."

Major Garrison just stared at her and smiled. He never would've suspected that they had anything in common, but, of course, it was the sense of curiosity that they both shared. He felt it would be pressing his luck if he mentioned this, so instead, he said, "Well, if you promise to go straight down the mountain and back into town, I'll see what I can do for you. Who knows?"

She assented, if only partially convinced of his offer, her old reticence returning a bit. She sat a while longer, quietly. Major Garrison began to feel uncomfortable because of the silence and finally gave a cough to get her attention.

"Oh," she said. "I'm sorry. I guess I should be going." She got up and headed for her vehicle. "Thanks for the water."

She started up the jeep and was soon driving away, thinking about this new revelation, about the War, about the Enemy.

The Enemy!

Now that she thought about it, she didn't think she'd ever seen one of the Enemy, at least not in real life. She'd seen pictures and that had been enough. The Enemy was mysterious, foreign, alien, and incredibly deadly, and now they were here. They could be anywhere.

As she drove down the mountain, she began looking around in a very paranoid fashion, jumping at shadows and seeing things in the shape of a tree or a rock. She desperately wanted to get back to the safety of her pathetic domicile, her town, safety. Would she ever feel safe again? Or was she destined to go on feeling the cold fingers of death clutch at her racing heart in an icy hand of horror?

Her full attention suddenly snapped back to the present, as she barely kept from driving off the road on a soggy hairpin turn, and that's when she realized that she was lost. She'd been imagining so many horrific things that she'd taken a few turns without thinking. Even worse, it was beginning to get dark.

Maybe I don't know the roads just like a mother hen knows her chicks, she silently chided herself.

She stopped the jeep and pulled out her own map of the area. She wasn't panicking. She'd been lost before, *but never like this*, she thought. She forced her anxious thoughts and feelings down so that she could think calmly. Aloud, she said, "Well, it's just a different challenge." She laid out her map on the hot surface of the hood. Its warmth felt good on her skin in the cool mountains. With night coming, she was just starting to feel the desire for that comfort. Unconsciously, her hand slid down to her large bowie knife hanging on her belt.

She looked around and peered at the map. She took a few moments, getting her bearings until she felt confident of her position. She then traced out a route that should get her out of the mountains. She climbed back in the jeep and, as she turned the key, she thought she heard something, a strange, high-pitched sound, almost like a wailing, but somehow more raw. It didn't repeat itself and, since it was apparently a long way away, she ignored it and headed along her path. *What was that? First those strange tree markings and now that unnatural sound.* She paused in her reverie. *It's almost like I don't know my own woods any more. Could those markings and whistles be from...the Enemy?* She quickly got the jeep moving again, forced herself to calm down and avoid driving recklessly. That would only get her hurt, or killed.

She had traveled about two-thirds of the way out of the forest when she stopped suddenly. She sat there in the jeep for a few moments, letting it idle, and felt like screaming. A mud slide had washed out the road. She knew that such things were not uncommon in these mountains, but it was already dark and she didn't have a lot of fuel left, certainly not enough for much backtracking anyway. With a gasp and a sigh of frustration, Sarah pulled out her map and the windup flashlight from the glove box. She repeated the process from last time, laid the map on the hood, determined her position, found another route, and was just beginning to feel proud of herself when it happened: the jeep shut off on its own.

She thought, *You've got to be kidding me!* She plopped herself back into the jeep, noticing how old it suddenly appeared to her. She turned the key and listened to the engine sputter and take life. Her spirits rose with elation and then came crashing back down again as the jeep coughed and died. She looked around the vehicle for a clue of what the problem might be. That's when she noticed a small pool of liquid under the jeep. Kneeling down next to the liquid, she gingerly smelled it. She immediately exclaimed, "Gas!" It didn't take Sarah long to figure out that she must've hit a rock or something that ruptured the gas tank. "Of all the rotten luck! This *can't* be happening to me!" In the back of her mind, she knew it would be preferable to allow her anger to take her for a few moments, since the alternative was mind-numbing fear. She knew she had to focus on something other than the fact that she might be stranded on the side of the mountain with the Enemy quite possibly nearby.

She thought of the gas tank sealant that she kept in her emergency pack, *but what good is that going to do me right now?* she thought. *My fuel is already all over the road.* She sat down in a heap and sighed. After a moment, she screamed in frustration. Immediately, she stopped, not wanting to draw attention to herself from something that might be lurking in the dark.

After a few moments, Sarah pulled herself together and began to think. She knew she shouldn't try to make it out of the mountains on foot in the dark, not when she still had so many miles to go. So she pulled out the tent and prepared to hunker down for the night. She ate her emergency kit rations and then began setting up her shelter.

After pitching the emergency tent, setting up her thoroughly uncomfortable, but warm, sleeping bag inside the tent and then burrowing into it, she tried to get some rest. She slept for perhaps three hours, when she was ripped from her sleep by a noise. Snapping awake, she immediately sat up in her sleeping bag. She felt confused, uncertain of what had woken her. She noticed that she felt a little dizzy. At first, she figured that she was just groggy from waking up in the middle of the night, but then she began to notice that she was also experiencing difficulty focusing on anything, not only visually, but cognitively as well. She was having trouble hanging on to a thought, and not just any thought, but *all* thoughts.

At first, she looked around and saw that things around her looked hazy. She wondered at that and then began to try to think about what it was that she was wondering at. After a few moments, her sight and thoughts began to coalesce into a semblance of normalcy. Finally, she was able to completely form the thought that she had tried to make when she first awoke. *My thoughts are...slippery? Yes, that was it. They were slippery and hard to retain. Why would that be?* she wondered. Sarah noticed the puzzle solver in her coming out as she, in the middle of a cold night, began to attempt to figure out what was happening.

As she sat there, musing, she heard the noise again, only this time it was much closer. For just a moment, she heard a piercingly-loud shriek. An instant after hearing the noise, she began feeling the sense of thoughtless bewilderment that she had before. This time, the sense of mental disjointedness was greatly magnified. Sarah couldn't even form a question regarding what was happening. Her thoughts were more elusive than they were the last time. Had she been able to think, she would've said composing thoughts felt like using her bare hands to grab oil. After perhaps thirty seconds, she slid out of this thoughtless stupor. She was scarcely aware that anything had occurred and was only barely conscious that the experience had been preceded by some kind of noise. Sarah tried to discern what, if anything, had just happened to her. She finally concluded that, since she was still sitting there, she must've had a dizzy spell or something like that.

As she continued pondering this peculiar experience—*Had anything actually happened or was I just imagining it?*—her exhaustion got the better of her curiosity and she finally lay back down.

While was drifting off again, she heard the snap of a twig. This time, she became alert more slowly, figuring that it was an animal walking by. Knowing that it could be a bear or even a raccoon, she knew that she should probably scare the animal away. So, she grabbed her flashlight, switched it on, and began waving it around inside of her tent. Moments later, she carefully climbed out of the tent, grabbed a cooking pot, and banged it against the side of the jeep, creating a dent or two.

She used the flashlight and cooking pot for a few moments longer and then stopped. She listened for further noise coming from the woods, expecting none. She was not disappointed. The forest was as quiet as a tomb. She stood there, peering into the darkness, hoping that everything was fine. Though she knew the Enemy was out there and infinitely more dangerous than any wild animal, she worked hard to abstain from thinking about it.

She headed back to her sleeping bag, bringing the flashlight and pot with her, just in case any other animals came prowling about. As soon as she lay down again, she heard another twig crack nearby, but from a different direction. Poking her head out of her tent, she flicked her light on again and aimed it at the origin of the sound.

Just then, three things happened at the same time. A large, arachnid-type creature, about three feet tall, came running out of the brush, illuminated by the beam of her flashlight. It ran toward her with such lightning-fast speed that she barely had time to notice the pair of inordinately-large razor-sharp fangs that it brandished. She'd never seen one of the Enemy in real life, but she recognized this being from another world the instant she saw it.

Second, she heard what sounded like explosions fairly close. At that moment, a third thing happened: the creature collapsed in a heap. It was dead. Some of the creature's blood got on her.

Far off in the distance she could just make out that stupefying, shrill, shriek-like wailing again.

CHAPTER 5
Out of the Frying Pan...

Sarah ran, blindly, allowing panic and terror to paralyze her mind. She didn't know what had just happened and she didn't want to think about it. All she knew was that she wanted to get as far away as she could. She only wanted to run.

Run!

As she bolted through the brush, she only partially felt the bushes and tree branches slapping and scratching her and pulling on her sandy blond hair. Her terror thoughts made her run faster. Her breathing was becoming labored, but she didn't even notice, and she didn't care. She only knew that she had to run, be free of whatever it was that had tried to attack her.

She continued running.

She had been face-to-face with one of the Enemy! It had tried to kill her. It had been in *her* woods! It was the most evil-looking thing she'd ever seen, a thousand times worse than seeing a picture of it. It was so mind-shatteringly repulsive and abominable in real life. As she ran, her body automatically, but unsuccessfully, attempted to wretch. The creature was so incredibly repugnant and awful.

She continued running.

Slowly Sarah tried to clear her mind. She tried to let the whipping of the surrounding plants against her body give her mental clarity. She was just about to the point of regaining a modicum of control when she heard a far-away noise. *Could it be another one of those monsters, like I heard before?* She paused for a moment to listen and to catch her breath. Then she heard it again.

"Sarah!"

She immediately resumed her impromptu bushwhacking, but faster. What kind of a creature would know her name <u>and</u> be able to articulate it vocally? It was worse than every nightmare come true.

And so she continued to run.

Finally, she was simply too exhausted to continue. As soon as she spotted a good place to hide at the base of a large pine tree, she ducked into its concealment, panting heavily. She knew she should try to breathe quietly, but she was too hysterical to control her breathing. Gradually, her breathing slowed and she was able to more easily listen to the sounds of the forest. She was listening for sounds of pursuit or danger, but all she heard were the soothing sounds of the nighttime woodlands.

Then she heard it again. "Sarah!"

She felt like running again, but she'd calmed down a bit and with that calm came a clearer head. So she waited and listened to find out what she could before she revealed herself from her place of relative safety.

"Sarah! It's Major Pete Garrison! Where are you?"

Sarah felt a flood of relief such as she had never known before. She had never personally subscribed to the "white knight on a horse, rescuing a damsel in distress" cliché, but she was gratefully ready to run to this man who represented safety.

She wriggled out from under the concealing branches and stood up. "I'm over here," she said.

He quickly ran to her, his piercing gray eyes standing out in the dark. Seeing her covered in gore, he began to fear the worst.

Looking aghast, he asked, "Are you all right?"

Looking down at herself and feeling for injuries she replied, "I think so," came her quick, but trembling, reply.

More slowly, Garrison inquired, "But you're covered in...?"

Sarah looked down at herself and, for the first time, really saw the body fluids and entrails from the Enemy creature that had been killed. Her mind still somewhat numb from the experience, she didn't miss a beat. "It's okay. It's not mine."

Looking genuinely relieved, Garrison lead her back toward the road. After a few moments he said, "I'm glad you're safe."

"How did you find me?"

"I think it would be better if we left explanations for later. Let's move," and then he added in a whisper, "quietly."

Sarah then noticed the other men and women who had come with Garrison. She also noticed that, even though they'd found her, they couldn't possibly have relaxed one iota. They were obviously very alert and not only ready for an attack, but expecting one, as well. She didn't know what was going on but she figured it was probably good to stay quiet and ask questions later.

They stealthily snaked their way back to her jeep, the way they had come. They used the trail Sarah had just blazed since it was relatively easy to follow, even in the dark.

When they got back to the road, they passed by Sarah's jeep and hiked another quarter mile, only occasionally hearing various forest sounds. They got back to their jeep and everyone climbed on board, like an old car from the Great Depression, carrying everything the owners owned and heading out to an uncertain future. That's when Sarah saw the body. One of Garrison's men had died a few minutes before and his body was already loaded on board. It was awful. A jagged slash from shoulder to opposite hip and two well-defined puncture marks at the floating ribs. Sarah could only stare in horror. Who was he, or rather, who had he been?

When they got back to camp, it was nearly 4:00 in the morning.

Everyone was tired and so Major Garrison assigned Sarah a tent, postponing any explanations until later.

Sarah's nightmares were certainly creative, to say the least. The first one involved a multitude of spiders of various sizes that pursued her everywhere she went. The second dream was of her running through a forest with Major Garrison, running away from some unseen enemy that howled and shrieked at them. Just when they thought they were safely away, Major Garrison morphed into a spider-like creature with fangs that dragged in the dirt and were dripping with venom. The dreams got worse from there.

In the morning, Sarah awoke late and felt like she'd spent the night wrestling a bear. Her whole body ached and the scratches she'd received during her late night mad-dash in the woods all felt like they were on fire. She sat up anyway, certain that when she looked in a mirror, her body would more accurately resemble a corpse rather than a young woman full of life.

Since she didn't really have a chance the night before, she took her first look around at the spartan furnishings of the tent. A cot, a three-legged stool that was perilously close to tipping over if someone were to actually sit on it, and something that looked like a TV dinner tray. On the tray was a cup of water, a mirror, and a comb.

She sort of hunched down so her head didn't hit the top of the tent and took the one step required to cross the tent, proceeding to comb some of the knots out of her hair, as well as some of the leaves and twigs. I must look a sight, she thought to herself, and that's when she looked down at herself. She was still wearing the same clothing from last night, including that...THING'S blood and other bodily fluids.

She shuddered as she remembered what happened, why and how she had ended up back here today. She had thought that with the light of day and a night of sleep between her and last night's events, she would feel better. Perhaps she did, but if this was better, then she must've really been in bad shape last night.

Through the soreness she felt, and the emotional distress that she was trying to push aside, she knew that her first order of business for the day was to get something to eat. Despite the loud grumblings of her stomach, however, all she really wanted was to get cleaned up.

As she exited the tent, the previously muffled sounds of camp came streaming into her ears. She immediately became aware of the hustle and bustle of the camp and that these people must've been up and working a whole lot earlier than her. She saw people preparing weapons and ammunition. She saw others walking the perimeter. Of course, some of the soldiers were quietly discussing things and pouring over maps, but what struck her most of all was that a fair number of the men and women were obviously working at fortifying the camp's perimeter. "What's going on?" Sarah asked.

Apparently, she spoke this last thought out loud because a passing sentry piped up, "We're at OpCon Delta, Ma'am." When she asked what he meant, he replied, "It's like DefCon 1."

She looked around for the brown-haired Major Garrison, but didn't find him, so she went looking for someone who might be able to point her in the direction of a shower. Instead of a shower, she soon had a washcloth and a jug of water for bathing herself. As she cleaned herself up, she looked around and thought, *What a rough job these people have.*

She continued getting cleaned up and then afterwards decided to stroll around the camp. *Time to get home*, she silently mused. As she walked around the camp, trying to stay out of the way, she searched for her jeep. When she had looked everywhere with no luck, she figured that it hadn't yet been towed up to the camp. She asked another soldier for directions, "Excuse me, Sergeant?"

"Corporal, Ma'am."

"Oh, sorry."

"Quite all right, Ma'am. I don't mind a field promotion."

It took Sarah just a second to catch the joke and, when she did, she realized that she liked this guy.

He continued, "Corporal Stevens."

"Pardon me?"

"My name is Corporal Stevens. What can I do for you?"

"Have you seen Major Garrison today?"

"Yes, Ma'am. He took a squad with him to recon the north side of this mountain."

"Any idea when he'll return?"

"No, Ma'am."

She thought for a moment and then asked, "Stevens, how do I get my jeep back and—why is the camp at OpCon Delta?"

"I wasn't part of the rescue party last night, but I think we just haven't had time or resources to safely bring your jeep in. As far as the camp status, well...".

Just then, from across the compound, a voice called for Corporal Stevens. "Sorry, Ma'am. I need to get back to work."

Sarah watched him trail off to other tasks and again donned her feelings of abject loneliness. What was she doing here in this military camp? Why hadn't anyone given her more than just a passing glance? And what exactly happened last night.

The pangs of hunger in her belly stirred her from her reverie. She knew she needed to eat soon. She didn't care if everyone was too busy to speak to her. With a sudden sense of frustration born out of the culmination of recent events, she walked right up to someone and said, "Private, I need some food. Where do I get some?"

The bulky, mountain of a man slowly turned toward her and, before she saw his captain's bars, she knew he was no private. He slowly grated, "Excuse me?" His bearing was incredibly reminiscent of a dump truck barreling down a highway.

With a splash of humility she replied, "I was part of that...attack last night. I'm hungry. I just need some food. Where would I find some?"

He pointed stiffly toward a larger tent, visibly restraining himself from providing any further response.

She immediately began walking in the direction he had indicated, glad to get away from him. When she arrived at what passed for a mess hall in the makeshift camp she went and found some food in the stores. It wasn't exactly five-star dining, but she hadn't expected much. What she settled on were a few slices of bread that were only a little stale, a cup of water, and some kind of fruit spread.

She moved away from the mess hall and found a place to eat. As she sat eating, she began to notice what the hustle and bustle of the camp was mainly about. It appeared that nearly everyone was working at fortifying the perimeter of the camp. They were primarily erecting a barbed wire fence. *That fence has nothing to do with cattle,* she thought to herself. Those lines of wire were much too close together for that. There must've been a line of wire every six inches. *What was going on? Surely the Enemy wouldn't attack here!* she desperately thought. *The Enemy couldn't possibly get in here. This is shaping up to be the safest place in the world.* Even as she thought it, however, she knew she was just trying to convince herself of the security and protection of the camp.

Dispelling her more serious thoughts, she continued taking note of what was going on around her. She noticed the battlements that they were setting up out of downed trees. It appeared that they were building some kind of elevated enclosures wherein two or three men could be protected and see anything coming their way. Whatever was going on, it sure didn't seem to be particularly calm or benign. As she sat watching the individual people, as well as what they were doing, what "Stocky" had said became much more poignant to her. This camp was definitely at OpCon Delta.

She waited patiently throughout the day for her jeep to arrive. When dinner arrived and her jeep hadn't, she finally began to let herself feel worried. Just as she was getting ready to take matters into her own hands (what she would've done, she had no idea), she heard a cry from the front of the camp. An order was given and the gate was opened up, allowing a jeep to come through. Her heart sank. It wasn't her jeep. It was just another military vehicle. But then she saw Major Garrison and she grew excited again. *Maybe now I'll be able to get home.*

She held back where she was sitting, feeling uncomfortable about speaking to him right away. After all, she didn't know him and he didn't owe her anything. Besides, these were his men, and he'd been out all day with little or no sleep the night before. Notwithstanding her angry feelings before, Sarah had to admit that this well-built man was impressive.

She had also gleaned that he was the kind of leader who actually led. He didn't shirk from a tough assignment and he only asked his men to do what he himself was willing to do. And he knew how to push himself hard without making big mistakes. That part was clear since he had just returned to camp with no casualties, and not even an injury. Whatever he may be, Sarah was intrigued by him.

Sarah watched Garrison head toward the mess hall for some much needed food and water. He patiently and carefully listened to reports while he ate. He occasionally nodded, but mainly just listened and took it all in.

When everyone around him ran out of reports, he began giving orders—orders for modifying the night watch, orders for running an electric current through the wire fence, and orders for additional bulwarks and the like to begin being built immediately.

When he was finished, his gaze immediately shifted to Sarah, sitting quietly and forlornly nearby. She was surprised that he had even noticed her. He picked up the last of his plate of beans and sauntered over to where she sat.

"May I join you?" he asked her.

For some reason, her breath caught. She covered it up with a hastily expressed, "Sure."

He sat down and just looked at the preparations that his men had so far achieved on the fence. Or perhaps he was looking at the forest and what might be hiding and lurking in it. At last he seemed to break away from his reverie, but Sarah suspected that his attention had never truly wandered as far as all that. "How are you doing?" he asked her.

"Well, I was given food and a place to sleep, but I'm still waiting for my jeep," Sarah replied. As soon as she'd said it, she wished she could take those words back. After all that he'd been through, not just with saving her life the night before, but also roaming the countryside in a state of near exhaustion, her words sounded petty and selfish to her. Instead of apologizing she blurted, "I know you've had a rough twenty-four hours. The jeep can wait 'til tomorrow."

Major Garrison just smiled that smile that somehow looked so incongruous on the face of a man in command, a man who was skilled at commanding others. Perhaps it was the look of boyhood innocence that emanated from that smile.

Finally, he said, "I know you want to get home, but right now, it's too dangerous to go after your jeep. If I send men into that vicinity again, someone else might very well get killed."

Sarah knew that Garrison wasn't trying to sting her with the barb of losing a man who had been part of her rescue. He was just telling her the facts. Nevertheless, it burned a hole in her gut that she had been the cause of that man's death the night before. She felt like trash.

"Can I ask you a question?" Sarah asked.

"I think you just did," Major Garrison replied wistfully, again seeming to lose all focus on his immediate surroundings and looking elsewhere.

"What was his name? The man who died for me last night?"

Outwardly, Major Garrison showed no signs of emotions—he didn't even swallow—but Sarah knew that the loss of this man was eating him up inside.

"Captain Marshall. Captain Blake Marshall. I called him Blake." He paused and looked up at the stars, perhaps wishing that the lights of the camp could be extinguished for a few moments so that he could see the glittering blaze of the Milky Way in all its glory. With a sudden eruption of emotion, he added, "I know I don't have to tell you. In this War, there's been just so much death and destruction already." He looked around, as if for answers, and concluded, "I suppose the death toll across the world must be at least five hundred million, maybe more." Then, under his breath, he added, "Maybe a lot more."

When he resumed, Sarah saw one small tear in his eye. He didn't bother to wipe it away. He was who he was and he was comfortable with himself. In a flat voice he returned to her question, saying, "He was my second in command. He was my friend."

He suddenly realized how she might be feeling about all this and so he quickly interjected, "I don't want you to feel responsible. It's not your fault. It's just the casualties of war. Nobody blames you for what happened."

Sarah looked up and met his eyes. "I'm not so sure about that. After how this day and the previous night have gone, I'm pretty sure I don't have a friend in the camp."

"Well...you have me," and then he hurriedly, yet awkwardly, added, "as a friend."

Sarah smiled inwardly. It felt good to feel some of her tension ease just a bit, due to his kind words. She suddenly realized that although this day had been rough on Major Garrison and his men, it most assuredly had been no picnic for her, either. For some reason, she took comfort in that. Maybe she had more in common with these men and women than she had thought.

They both sat there, listening to the sounds of the camp and the surrounding forest, looking up at the clouds, both wondering just a little what the other was thinking about.

Sarah suddenly realized that Major Garrison must be a very busy person and wouldn't have much more time to talk to her. She knew that if she had any more questions that needed answering, it would be best if she could ask them now.

Though she didn't really want to talk about last night, she couldn't help but ask about it. "I've seen pictures. That was one of the Enemy I saw last night, wasn't it."

"Yes," came the soothing reply.

"Was it alone?"

"Probably. I figure it was a scout."

Sarah tried to think up another question. Thinking analytically felt good. It detached her from her emotions.

"So, was that a typical size for the Enemy?"

Garrison looked at her for a moment, confused, but before she could add more, a look of understanding came into his eyes. "Yes, that one was about the same size as all the others, about three feet tall."

Shuddering at the memory of the creature, she asked, "Are they really as strong as people say? Three feet isn't very big." She forced a small laugh and Garrison joined her with a sincere one.

Pete took another bite of beans. He chewed it for a few moments and swallowed. Then he washed it down with some lukewarm water that had a slightly bitter taste to it. "Oh,   yes. Despite their size, they're quite strong." He saw the fear begin to come back into her eyes, so he added, "It wouldn't be like wrestling a bear or a gorilla, but they're tough."

Sarah blurted out her next question. "Where do they come from? Nobody I talk to in town or anywhere else seems to know."

"I don't know either. Certainly not from around here."

Sarah was pleased that she understood his jargon, that "around here" meant Earth.

She sat quietly, musing. She was thinking about the appearance of the Enemy creature. At last she said, "Something doesn't add up." He turned to look at her with curiosity in his eyes. "I know that creature looked kind of like a giant spider, but there was something non-spider-like about it, but I can't put my finger on it."

"I think I know what you mean. They don't have eight legs. They have nine."

Despite the seriousness of the discussion and the situation, Sarah could only reply, "That's weird."

Garrison smiled and replied in kind, "No argument here."

Unfortunately, thinking about the legs of the extraterrestrial abomination got her to thinking about everything else. Her mind reeled as she again tried to take it all in. That repulsive killing machine that she had seen last night was one of the Enemy. Its entire body seemed especially designed for mutilating and killing. Those fangs, those claws, that sound, and that speed. It had covered so much ground so quickly! *No wonder our soldiers are having so much difficulty. No wonder so many have died,* Sarah thought to herself.

When Sarah could finally speak, it first came out as a croak. She cleared her throat as best she could, trying not to breathe too fast or heavily, and said, "I'm scared." She was pleased with herself that she didn't burst into tears. "This...Enemy...is so awful and terrible. Are we going to win? What I mean is, do we have a chance to beat back these monsters?"

"I don't know. I think so. I hope so, but right now, humanity is kind of up against the ropes and... I just don't know." Again, he paused and then said, "We'll just do the best we can. No point in crying over spilled milk." He managed a slight grin.

She responded in kind and asked, "Spilled milk? I think it's a little more serious than that. More like a broken and bleeding dam."

They sat quietly for a few more moments, enjoying the mild lightening of the mood. She knew she needed to let him get to his tent. He must have been completely exhausted. Then she said, "Okay, one more question and then I'll let you get some sleep."

The look of elation on his face betrayed his desire for much needed rest.

"Why do they make those crazy, high-pitched shrieking sounds?"

Sarah could see that, at first, he was trying to figure out what she was talking about. Then it seemed that he understood, and his mood became grave. "I don't know, but whatever makes that sound, it's not the Enemy. It's something else altogether."

CHAPTER 6
News From Above

Early the next morning, Garrison stopped by to visit Sarah. He'd obviously been up for a while and didn't look tired at all. He had a job to do. She realized that she really appreciated him.

He came right over and didn't even say anything about her sleeping in till the relatively late hour of 6:45 am. He just sat down and started talking to her.

"Ms. Scott. We expect an attack from the Enemy to come at any time. We're going to continue to work at strengthening our defenses. I don't know that you'll be able to help but I do have a job for you. Needless to say, I'm not going to be able to get you home just yet. I will when I can but right now it would be a completely unwarranted gamble." He paused and then continued, "I need you to practice with a rifle. If an attack does come, and I pray that it doesn't, it could very well be that we'll need everyone we can get. So..." he paused and looked around, seemingly uncertain of what he was asking. "...will you help us out?"

For a brief moment, the freckle-cheeked Sarah had a slight understanding of the pride that veterans always spoke of. The pride that they had in their service and in the men and women with whom they served so valiantly. For the first time in days—no, in her whole life—she felt she was beginning to understand the men and women in uniform. She began to feel a sense of appreciation for them and their service that she had never felt before. She knew that didn't mean she'd get along with all of them, but Sarah knew that the way she looked at military men and women would never be the same.

Instead of replying with a 'sure' or 'why not', she gave a strong affirmative. "Yes. I'm ready. When can I start?"

Major Garrison looked surprised and then a warm smile took his strong features.

"Right now. Go report to Corporal Frank. He should be somewhere over there," he said as he pointed toward the ammo supply tent.

Sarah turned and headed over. As she got closer to the indicated place she began asking men and women regarding the whereabouts of Corporal Frank. Upon asking several people, she noticed that her new feelings about the military from moments before were continuing to blossom. She felt, in a small way, that she was one of them.

When she finally found the corporal, she let him know that she was there under Major Garrison's orders. Upon hearing that, from a civilian, he did a double-take and then left her for a few moments to confirm those orders. When he returned he asked her about her firearm experience.

"When I was about thirteen years old, my dad took me shooting. I think we used a shotgun."

"How did you do?" Frank inquired.

"All I really remember is that I thought I'd broken my shoulder and I couldn't hit anything that I aimed at."

"With a shotgun? Well, let's hope your aim has improved since then," he said as he cocked a cautious eyebrow at her.

He opened up a case and pulled out an M16. Though totally unfamiliar with the weapon, she took it, determined to learn.

"Whoa. Let's take it slow. First, never aim it at anything you don't want to kill. Second, since you've never used an automatic firearm, there are a couple things we're going to need to cover before you actually use it."

Corporal Frank proceeded to explain the various mechanisms of the weapon and how to use it safely. At first he was almost offended that he would have to "babysit" a civilian, but he could see the sincerity in Sarah's eyes and her willingness to learn. It also reminded him of when he was a boy. His dad would take him hunting and occasionally shake his head when he would see his son miss a deer or elk due to his inexperience. Frank shook his head to clear it and paid attention to the task at hand. Soon he was surprised to find that he was enjoying himself.

The corporal escorted her to just outside the wire and said, "All right. Let's start you out with a 30-round mag, and let's have you try shooting at a stationary target. Pick a tree just over there and have at it."

Doing as she had been told she pulled the stock into her shoulder, sighted along the barrel, held her breath in anticipation of a sore shoulder, and then pulled the trigger. To say that she was astonished by the raw power of the weapon would not do justice to the situation. Though the recoil was less than that of her childhood shotgun, she felt the recoil in her shoulder. Her ears were immediately ringing and she wondered how people in a prolonged firefight could endure the sonic pounding. Notwithstanding the initial blast of sensation, she was pleased with herself that she held onto the weapon. She was pretty sure that she had kept her sights on the tree she'd selected.

When the initial shock of such a powerful firearm had subsided slightly, she looked over at Corporal Frank with a smile. He returned her smile with a profound look of disappointment. "Which of those four trees that you hit were you aiming at?"

Sarah felt that her impromptu training never really did get much better, but she had to admit that though she was rarely hitting what she aimed at, she was getting better at confining her shots to fewer trees.

Around lunchtime Sarah took a break. As she leisurely ate a MRE (Meals Ready to Eat), she noticed for the first time just how in earnest the perimeter was being fortified and built up. There were men still putting up additional barbed wire. There were people digging a trench around the exterior of the fence. It looked to Sarah like a waterless moat for a ramshackle castle. She also saw soldiers running wires around the camp and connecting them at one end to various parts of the fence, and at the other end to a backup generator. Of course, she couldn't help but notice the men and women working on the machine gun nests up high in quickly erected structures. There didn't seem to be one person at Oscar-Romeo-17 who wasn't actively helping. Sarah was glad that she could be one of them. Though she realized her small efforts probably wouldn't make a difference in the upcoming battle, she was grateful for Garrison giving her something to do.

That night she had many dreams, but when she awoke she felt rested and peaceful. She was ready for the day, come what may.

She quickly took her tent's basin to fill it with water and, upon returning to her tent, she washed her face and hands. She proceeded to brush the tangles out of her sandy blond hair and was more than a little grateful that she didn't have access to a mirror at that moment.

After getting cleaned up, she went to the supply tent where she knew she would be able to get a bite to eat. She thought to herself, *These MRE's are better than I thought. I figured they'd taste like cardboard.*

After breakfast Sarah continued her rapid training, designed to make her someone who could help out if an attack came, rather than hinder or harm the people around her. Throughout that day she also learned how to feed belts into the various high caliber machine guns. Her instructor for the day was Sergeant Jameson. He was still stiff and formal with her, just like the day he had brought her to camp Oscar-Romeo-17 a few days prior, but she'd been observant and had noticed that he had that same attitude with everyone. Since that first moment she'd come to this camp she had seen that he had opened up to her, a little.

After lunch, Sergeant Jameson handed Sarah off to Corporal Cornwall. He was a young man; he couldn't have been more than twenty years old. He had short-cropped blond hair and was just shy of six feet tall. Sarah also noticed how deep blue his eyes were. *Except for his hairstyle, he looks like he should be surfing,* she thought silently. Like everyone else in the camp, he knew his job, he did it well and he believed in what he was doing. As he taught Sarah about how to effectively serve as a gopher and bring fighting men supplies they might need, she noticed something about him. At first she wasn't sure what it was. Then she realized it was a funny gleam in his eye that could only be described as *mischievous.* It made her want to laugh. He joked around a little but that look in his eye spoke volumes about the kind of kid he'd been before he joined the military.

Shortly after dinner, Sarah was sitting on a tree stump, her sky blue eyes shining. She was looking around, thinking of the imminent danger in which they might all find themselves at any moment, and yet she was content. In a very small way, she was helping to fight these other-worldly monsters that had attacked her people, the citizens of the earth.

Suddenly her reverie was cut short. It began simply with a sound that was familiar yet no longer common. It was an air plane high up in the sky. Along with most everyone around her, Sarah held a hand to her forehead to shield her eyes from the sun as she peered up at the source of the noise. It came closer and closer from the east until it was nearly directly above them. At that moment, some small point in the sky broke away from the plane. It didn't appear to be a piece of the plane but rather an object being discharged from the craft. It fell very quickly and the people around Sarah began to mutter at the strangeness of this. If it was a person, then he should've opened his parachute by now. If it was something else, then the chute should have opened immediately upon exiting the plane.

As everyone watched with rapt fascination, the object appeared to be... No, it couldn't be. It looked like a person and he wasn't flailing about in terror at the lack of an opened parachute! Still, he was falling so fast. What could he be thinking? He needed to open his parachute a few seconds earlier to ensure a safe landing. If he ever opened his chute he no longer had any kind of guarantee of a safe landing, what with all the trees around.

The man was falling nearly directly above them. A few precious seconds of life ticked by as the parachutist continued to descend so very rapidly. Someone called out for a medic to stand by. *At this point the falling man couldn't possibly survive,* Sarah thought to herself. She didn't want to watch but something horrible inside her, inside of everyone there kept their attention fixed on this ghastly sight that was unfolding right before them.

Suddenly the chute opened and, when the man was only 500 feet above the ground, the parachute was fully deployed. The certain death, wrapped in a horribly gory finish, was gratefully stymied. Several people exhaled a collective sigh of relief. Sarah noticed that she was among them.

The lean man descended gently as he expertly maneuvered himself through the last remaining bits of sky before he crested the tree tops. It was obvious he'd made hundreds, perhaps thousands, of jumps in the past. This guy *really* knew what he was doing.

As he descended into the midst of the trees, careful to make sure his parachute didn't snag on anything, everyone could see that the figure wore a helmet, obscuring his features. Sarah could also tell that everyone around her knew just as much about what was going on as she did—including Major Garrison. That surprised her. She peered at him out of the corner of her eye and saw a quizzical look stretch across his face. It certainly wasn't fear that she saw. Not even concern. Just a strong case of curiosity, an unexpected puzzle that needed solving.

The person finally alighted gently to the earth in the middle of the compound. He detached his parachute and looked around through his helmet that obscured his face When he spotted the brown-haired Major Garrison, he strode toward him. Immediately several people became tense, unsure if this was a threat to their commanding officer. Garrison continued to look like he was working out a puzzle, or perhaps a riddle.

The figure stopped about ten feet away from the major and then proceeded to unfasten the safety clasps on the helmet. The helmet came off and a shock of gorgeous, long, fiery-red hair spilled out.

"Captain Sonya Smith, reporting for duty, Sir!" she barked at Major Garrison. She pulled out some papers, handed them to the major and stiffly announced, "I'm your new second in command."

CHAPTER 7
Up the Ante

The woman was about five foot, eight inches tall. She was definitely not fat but was not supermodel thin either. She was muscular but not in a steroidal way. As Sarah looked at her she couldn't help thinking that this was what a lot of female firefighters probably looked like—or *wanted* to look like. The mysterious woman didn't seem to know anyone there but didn't seem to care. She walked through the mass of soldiers with aloofness. There was certainly an aura of mystery and confidence surrounding her.

Further examination revealed that Captain Smith had some kind of firearm on a strap across her chest. Sarah would later find out it was an SAR-21 with the M203 grenade launcher attachment. She could see multiple spare clips as well as grenades that could also be loaded into the weapon. On her right thigh, hanging from her belt, a large bowie knife was visible. She was also wearing some type of bullet-proof vest, probably kevlar. Sarah mused, *Who is this? Rambo? She looks like she's ready to single-handedly take on the Enemy.*

Major Garrison took the proffered papers without showing any of the surprise that he was feeling. He knew that everyone was watching Captain Smith, and him. So he calmly hollered, "As you were," to everyone around. For good measure he added, "Let's pick up the pace. You know what we're preparing for. I want this place ready for anything, and I do mean *anything*." With that, he escorted Captain Smith, who was looking anything but impressed, to his tent where they would be able to speak more privately.

Major Garrison didn't say anything as they walked and Smith didn't seem very prone to making polite conversation anyway. Garrison was grateful for the brief respite of speech to gather his thoughts and try to figure out what was going on.

After they entered the tent, which was large only compared to the tents of the other troops in the unit, he gave her a small 3-legged stool. It wasn't much and you had to sit on it just right or it would collapse on you, but it was all he had. Garrison sat on his cot. He spoke first.

"Are you aware that I was completely in the dark about all this...hoopla?"

"Sir?"

"I mean, the show you put on out there. I had no idea anyone was coming. Nor that someone would be coming by plane. Nor that I was being sent a new second-in-command. Any light you can shed on why this all took place *and* why I wasn't kept in the loop would be helpful."

Captain Smith's reply was simply, "I was told you wouldn't need to know until my arrival."

Major Garrison just stared at her and began to size her up. The fact that she was completely unintimidated was obvious, but he also noticed that she appeared to be incredibly confident, even more than most generals that he knew. She even made that ridiculous stool she was perched on look like a throne. Or maybe the driver's hatch in a tank. If he didn't know any better he could've sworn that she was merely tolerating him.

"Well, let's make the best of this." Not sure about her, he said, "We're short on bunks. You can share a tent with Ms. Scott. She's a visitor from one of the nearby towns. I'm sure you two will get along just fine." More amazing than Captain Smith not showing how she really felt about bunking with a civilian was Pete's ability to make that last statement without any audible sarcasm. He was pleased with himself. *Maybe I should take up acting after the War,* he considered silently.

"That will be...just fine," Smith replied. "For now, what are your orders?"

"I'll consider it tonight and let you know in the morning. Let's meet together at 0800. That will be all."

For one very brief moment the cool, hard shell that was her walled exterior cracked as Smith realized she was being dismissed like a common school girl, but only for a moment. She slowly arose from the stool and by the time she was standing, she was once again a monolith of willpower and self-assurance. She saluted smartly and then briskly left the tent.

Once she was gone, Pete released a breath he didn't know he was holding. He wasn't sure what he was going to do with this one. Of course, he'd heard of people like this being assigned to other men's units but it had never happened to him. He ran his hand through his thick brown hair and thought, *Good grief.*

How would he deal with this new and unnecessary fly in his ointment? One thing that he knew he would do is keep her as his *official* second-in-command but give most of the duties of that position to another. *No point shaking things up right now with the Enemy likely to attack at any minute.*

Right after Captain Smith arrived by air, Sarah watched her and Major Garrison head over to his tent to talk. She wondered if she would ever get used to what she was calling the 'military mentality' with all its hierarchy, orders, getting up before the sun and everything.

By the time Sarah reached her tent, she knew everything that everyone else knew about Smith, which wasn't much. She didn't have any family connections to the top brass, at least not that anyone in the camp knew of. Based on her attire, she was probably pretty good in any kind of a fight, and of course she was obviously an ace paratrooper.

Someone explained to Sarah the maneuver Captain Smith had executed on the way down from the plane. She'd waited till the last possible moment to open her chute so that, in the event an enemy was attempting to target her, that enemy would have much more difficulty. In fact, it would be nearly impossible to hit her. Also, there was her expert navigation through the trees—no mean feat.

After Sarah slowly meandered through camp and opened her tent she was surprised to see Captain Smith lying on her cot in just about the only space left over from her own cot. It was almost comical since the two cots nearly formed a "queen-size cot." Of course, neither woman was laughing. Neither woman spoke to the other. As Sarah brushed her hair and her teeth for the night, she couldn't help wondering why the two of them probably weren't going to become friends any time soon.

After a few minutes, Sarah looked at Smith out of the corner of her eye. Now that her roommate was not wearing a uniform or any weapons she could see that she had a jagged scar on her upper left arm. It looked like it had been treated in the field without proper medical conditions. She shuddered at what might have caused that. She also had something that looked like a cross between a scar and a rash just above her right ankle. Sarah didn't want to try to imagine what that was or how it was obtained.

She could also see that Captain Smith wasn't just ignoring her. It appeared that Smith had forgotten about her. This didn't seem like the kind of woman who forgets anything. Sarah figured the other woman merely acknowledged that Sarah was not a threat, or an asset, and then disregarded her. That seemed eerily like some kind of future robot. With that thought, Sarah was certain she was getting paranoid. Out of habit she said, "Good night." She was rewarded with a quiet grunt.

The next morning, Sarah awoke and was not at all surprised to find herself alone in the tent. In the light of day she thought, *I don't know how long we're going to be sharing this tent so I'd better make this work.* So, after getting cleaned up and eating a small breakfast of oatmeal with raisins and a glass of Tang to wash it down, she went looking for her new roommate.

Since the camp wasn't particularly large as military installations go, it didn't take long to find her. Captain Smith was outside one of the very few prefab buildings discussing some reports with some enlisted men. She didn't look happy. She wasn't exactly yelling at them but her mood was like a mild thunderhead. Sarah figured this wasn't the best time to extend the olive branch. As she moved away she noticed something. As Captain Smith was discussing the written reports with her underlings, she wouldn't let them see the actual reports. It wasn't obvious the way she shielded them but she certainly made sure that no one else saw them. That struck Sarah as odd. She also observed that Captain Smith seemed to be purposefully avoiding looking at Sarah. Sarah told herself that she was being paranoid again. Or was she?

She meandered away and couldn't help looking at the surrounding woods—*her* woods, *her* forest—and now it seemed to be only a matter of time before they would be the next scene of so much death and destruction. *Just like D.C. and many other sites around the world.* She paused in that thought. *Why would they be here? They've pretty much hit only big cities. Why the forest? Why now?* But maybe it wouldn't come to that. Garrison had said that all the precautions that they were making were for the *possibility* that the aliens came and attacked them in force in this small part of the state of Oregon. *Maybe there was no regiment of Enemy foot soldiers making their way through the forest,* she thought. *After all, what would be the point? There's nothing in the area but a podunk town in the middle of nowhere.*

Thinking about the aliens brought it all back to her again. Trying to push the memories of that repulsive creature out of her conscious thoughts was like trying to close one's eyes to the burning light of the sun. She remembered with horror the grotesque, spider-like bodies of those creatures. Unbidden, her mind conjured up the images of those vicious, dripping fangs that they brandished. It was hard to believe that creature actually *wanted* to kill her. It wasn't some instinct on its part. It was sentient. It knew what it was doing. It wanted to kill her even though it knew nothing about her as an individual.

As the terror of war settled in on her mind, she felt like she was being beaten down by a suffocating, torrential downpour of emotion. She was grateful that no one saw her in that condition. It was hard enough just to keep her feet beneath her, and that's when she realized something—something important. If necessary, part of her was willing to let go of her forest if that's what it took to get rid of those abominations. It was a powerful realization, primarily because of how dear her forest was to her, but in that one, brief moment she understood the sense of community that so few people ever truly feel or comprehend.

Garrison walked over to the communications tent. It wasn't much. It was a small, canvas structure that housed a single short-wave radio and headset. He stood next to the radioman and requested that he contact Command. A minute or two later the young man working the radio handed the headset to Pete. "They're ready for you, Sir."

"This is Major Pete Garrison, leader of camp Oscar-Romeo-17. With whom am I speaking?"

"This is Lieutenant Cason," a young man replied. "What do you need Major?"

Pete wiped his forehead with the back of one hand. "I just received a replacement for my recently deceased first officer. The new one is Captain Sonya Smith. I was wondering what you could tell me about her."

"One moment please."

The "one moment" soon stretched to several minutes. Pete began to wonder if the computers were no longer functioning at Command headquarters. Finally, the young lieutenant on the other end said, "Sir, I'm not sure what to tell you. I do show that a Sonya Smith was sent to your camp, but..."

"But what?" Garrison inquired.

"Well, Sir. I've never seen a file quite like this one. Apparently her file is sealed. I have a pretty high level of clearance for these types of things but I'd probably have to be the Secretary of Defense to access this file. I'm sorry, Sir."

"No problem," Garrison replied quietly. "Thank you."

A few minutes later, Garrison was back in his own tent. After several minutes of unsuccessfully wrestling with what he was beginning to think of as the "Smith Issue," he sent someone to find Sarah. As Sarah came into his tent, Major Garrison quickly stood and shook her hand. "Well, how are you getting on during your stay with us?"

Surprised by the question she responded a little hesitantly, "Just fine. Most everyone I've met has been friendly enough."

"Excellent. I'm glad." He stopped speaking and seemed to be, of all things, fidgeting. It was as if he was nervous about whatever it was he had to say.

"Ms. Scott, I had hoped to have the resources to move you back into town by now, but as you could see from Captain Smith's entrance to the camp, moving around these woods is very dangerous right now. The only way I'm going to be able to get you anywhere near town right soon is to use a chopper. As you've undoubtedly noticed, this camp doesn't have one." He waved his arms out in the air to accentuate the point. "And although we have communications with our regional commanders, that isn't going to help us any time soon. I mean," he ran a hand through his hair, like a comb, and in apparent exasperation said, "there's only so much materiel to go around and one little outpost camp in Oregon isn't exactly high on the priority list to receive a luxury item like a helicopter."

Sarah nodded in understanding. In her job before the War, she had been all too familiar with supplies running out. Working with her War-time tribe back in Drain, supplies were always atrociously low, but at this camp it could mean the difference between life and a quick death for every man and woman. *Things must really be going bad in the War*, she thought morosely. Then she thought to ask a question that had been gnawing at the back of her mind for days but she just hadn't wanted to ask. "Major", she began. She was nervous. She didn't want to ask but she knew she had to. "Shortly before I came here I heard a rumor that Washington, D.C. had been totally destroyed." She took a deep breath and finished. "Is that true?"

Garrison looked up at her and said, "No." Before a wave of relief finished washing over Sarah's mind and heart, he continued. "D.C. got hit—it got hit hard—but it's not totally destroyed. I don't know exactly how it turned out but I'd estimate that around two-thirds of the city was wiped out." He paused to let it sink in. With her mind wandering and stomach churning he added, "I expect most of the survivors are living like animals, trying to eke out some sort of existence in the tunnels and rubble."

Through her shock she barely managed to get the words out, "I...I wonder if you could tell me. Do we still have a president? A functioning government?"

He quickly replied, "We certainly do have a functioning government. I expect the president is still Mark S. Wagner. But," then he looked away for a moment, "I don't know." His words sounded hollow and far away. Then, wanting to change the subject he said, "Anyway, I'm sorry if you've been inconvenienced."

Again he paused and Sarah took the opportunity to try to shatter the thin shell of shock that was causing her mind to feel numb. With only a slight choke in her voice she said, "That's okay. I've been having a good time here." He raised an eyebrow in surprise. "Really. I've definitely learned a few things."

She sensed his uneasiness about something. Strange as it was it didn't seem to be related to D.C.

"Ms. Scott, part of what we've learned about the Enemy since the War began is that they tend to spread out around their targets."

"You mean like a siege," Sarah offered.

Major Garrison paused and looked at her freckled face with the hint of a smile in his eyes. "Yes. That's exactly it." After another brief pause he continued. "We've been seeing evidence of what might suggest this type of siege activity going on in this area."

"So, that's why you've been trying to turn this camp into a fort and get it more prepared." It wasn't a question.

"That's right. Anyway, if we can't get you out of here before something happens...IF something happens," again he paused, as if resisting what he knew he must say. "If things get dicey, I want you to stay near the middle of the camp."

"But I can help," Sarah insisted.

"I know. Do you have any experience at triage?"

"I only know normal first aid and CPR."

Major Garrison smiled again. "That could really come in handy." His expression turned grim. "Experience has taught all of us that the Enemy moves so fast and is so savage that we invariably end up having need of a lot of...first aid and CPR."

Sarah felt something inside her turn very *cold.* She once again began to feel true fear. She did her best to suppress it and turned her attention back to her task at hand. "Do you have any idea when—"

Just at that moment, a sentry fired a flare up into the late twilight sky. Major Garrison looked up and with a hollow yet controlled voice said, "They're here. The Enemy is about to attack."

CHAPTER 8
New Strategies

"... that I will faithfully execute the Office of President of the United States, and will to the best of my ability, preserve, protect and defend the Constitution of the United States."

Standing in a white pants suit, former Secretary of the Interior, Gwyneth Griffith, exhaled sharply after completing the oath of office. With the death of President Wagner and the nearly simultaneous deaths of the next six people in the line of succession for president of the United States of America, it fell to Secretary Griffith to serve as the next president.

Since she had not been the vice president or even the speaker of the house, she was definitely a bit of an unknown quantity. This was especially true in light of the fact that, since the War had begun, her Department of the Interior had largely gone unused and unnoticed. Nearly the only activity she'd seen since the advent of the War had been to work with Homeland Security and especially the military to preserve and protect American citizens domestically. That specific assignment was over now, for her, and she needed to focus on the bigger picture. She didn't think she would find a replacement for the position she'd just vacated. It had only been unnecessary redundancy. Be that as it may, she knew she needed to focus on the herculean tasks at hand—and allow people to get to know their new president.

One of the first things that people noticed about the new President was her savage eyes that spoke of dauntless determination.

She was in an underground bunker in Iowa. The facility was called Camp Dodge. Unbeknownst to the public, it had previously been retrofit to withstand all kinds of weapons, including bunker-buster bombs. It was fairly large and there was concrete everywhere you looked. In fact, due to repairs and current modifications, there seemed to be a perpetual taste of cement in the air.

President Griffith realized that since this place might end up serving as the White House for a while, some changes and additions would need to be made. She just wished that she could get away from the flavor of concrete without having to drink a cup of coffee. With that thought in her head she peered over at the table in the corner of the room. Just about the only thing on it was an old Mr. Coffee. It made a halfway decent cup of joe but the only thing that was emanating from it right then was the pungent scent of stale grounds.

President Griffith—she was quickly taking a liking to how that sounded—returned her attention to the meeting at hand. The country's leading military officer, Chairman of the Joint Chiefs of Staff (CJCS) General Thomas Q. Martin, was briefing her on where the country was militarily and logistically. "...and so, our forces are spread out fairly thin. We still have approximately 20% of our forces outside the U.S. and our total forces are down 35% from where they were six months ago before the War began. Regarding our forces, the good news is they are not likely to further suffer such significant and rapid casualties any time soon." He paused for a moment, uncertain whether what he was saying should be a feather in his cap or a blemish on his record. "When the Enemy first arrived, we were caught without our lines in the water. That won't happen again!" Sometimes his grandfatherly smile was his defining characteristic. This time it was his intelligent eyes, and his angling metaphor.

The president tried not to sigh. She wasn't really upset with General Martin. She was just tired of everything that was going on and how futile their efforts seemed. It constantly felt like she was supposed to gather up as much oil as she could with her bare hands. It was incredibly frustrating and not the best way to start a new job. "What can you tell me about the cities we've lost?"

General Martin scratched his chin full of stubble. Griffith was certain that this was the first time in a long time that the General had not been able to keep his face as smooth as a baby's bottom. "That's where it gets more interesting. Our intel suggests that we maybe have some good news amidst all the bad." He stood up and walked over to a large wall map of the country. His muscular build was obvious despite the uniform and his age. "Of course, D.C. was hit pretty hard. We lost most of it, but enough of it is still intact that it can still be called a city. We also lost parts of L.A. Probably about 50%, give or take. We also lost the majority of Houston, Miami, Seattle, and Chicago."

"I already know all of this," the president replied impatiently. "I hope you're not going to try to tell me that all this destruction is good news."

"No, Ma'am. But the first good thing to report is that, unlike humans, when the Enemy attacks a city, it apparently has no intention of occupying it." He paused for a moment before continuing. "So they're not digging in. Of course, that means that they're harder to find—when they're not in orbit in those confounded starships that brought them here." He nearly spat in disgust before remembering where he was and with whom he was speaking. "The second item of good news is this. As you know, we've been engaged in this war for nearly six months and we've been able to do very little to stop the planetary bombardments when they come. Shoot, no one else from any other country has any idea how to even slow them down <u>when</u> they bother to try to counter-attack." Martin said that last part with a mild twinkle in his eye that belied his disdain for some of his foreign counterparts.

"What are you saying?" the Secretary of Commerce, seated on his right, asked with more than a hint of interest. Phil Johnson had not been on the cabinet very long. In fact, he was the newest member. He had a nervous habit of tugging on his right ear when he spoke in meetings like this, meetings where tensions are high and nerves are frayed.

Tough as nails, the general looked like the kind of soldier who couldn't remember the last time he slept past 0500, or wasn't ready for action at that time. Rumor had it that whenever he visited a training facility, he would compete with the young soldiers whether they were doing target practice, obstacle courses or even sparring, just to stay in shape—and he usually won. Mr. Johnson resumed, "My question is, since we've been able to do next to nothing to affect or change the outcome, or just plain slow down those orbital bombardments from their ships, why haven't they completely wiped us out?" He paused for several moments to let the all-important question settle into their minds. Like everyone else in the room, the general's attention was instantly piqued. It reminded him of why he liked to surround himself with people he referred to as "smarter than me."

The only sounds that were heard were a low whistle from someone who was just beginning to understand the full import of the question and the constant low humming of electricity.

The Sudanese ambassador, who had been in D.C. during the evacuation and had been swept up with the rest of the people in the room asked in his fairly Americanized accent, "You're saying that the Enemy has some sort of...exploitable weakness?"

"Exactly," General Martin said to everyone in the room. "I don't yet know what this weakness is, but I've no doubt that one exists which might very well prove the key to defeating them."

"If you're right," the President of Brazil interjected in his broken English, "and I not entirely convinced that you are, we would need devote our many resources to discovering this Achille's heal as fastly as possible—while there's still something to save!" He too had been near D.C. when the sacking of the capital took place. He had been staying in the same hotel as the ambassador from Sudan. Somehow, he had gotten on one of the transports with the other government leaders. He was still hoping to get back to his native land as soon as he could but willing to do what he could now to help battle the Enemy.

President Griffith spoke up, "Well then, I guess we have a mandate. Determine the cause of the Enemy's slowed destruction of the human race, because General Martin's right," she winced involuntarily, hating to admit it. "We've been able to do next to nothing when it comes to slowing down their orbital bombardments." She paused and then looked around at the couple dozen or so people in attendance. "Any ideas?"

After several moments John Dillon, Secretary of Veterans Affairs, spoke in a measured cadence, "It seems to me that the Enemy is waiting for something." Dillon sat with perfect composure in his seat. His suit looked a little out-of-date, but somehow it seemed to work well on him.

Upon hearing that, General Martin noticed that most people around the room were squinting their eyes, thinking about what he said.

A few moments later the president spoke again in a slow and careful tone. "I'd be very surprised to find that you were wrong, Mr. Dillon." She smiled slightly but it was a cold gesture, one that promised vengeance on the Enemy. "Let's take a break for lunch and continue this discussion afterwards."

During the noon hour General Martin walked over to where Mr. Dillon was eating some lunch and reading a recently received memo. He noticed that Mr. Dillon appeared to be very well-groomed without being pretentious. Dillon wore an outdated suit that was in good repair. It was one of those choices that is bold and never goes out of style. Martin saw a man who liked the fine things in life but didn't place his heart upon them. He also appeared a bit shaken.

"Mr. Dillon, are you all right?" the general asked. "If I may be so bold, you appear to be a little...um...out of sorts."

Trying to hide his emotions he merely quipped, "It is nothing. I was just thinking of someone I knew."

Despite wanting to discuss the question that Mr. Dillon posed during the meeting, Martin allowed himself to be distracted from his venture, if only for a moment. "Are you sure? You really do seem rather distraught."

John Dillon looked around the room at the unfamiliar surroundings. He saw the one lone vestige of decoration, a vase with nothing in it. He thought about how like that empty vase his heart was feeling. Finally he said, in a measured tone, "I'd never even been to Iowa before. This isn't a place I know." He paused and took a deep breath before continuing. He didn't want to say more, not then, but he knew he should. "There aren't any people here I know. I'll do my duty to help this great nation and her soldiers, but...everything feels so foreign to me."

He took a drink of whatever he had in his cup and looked away for a moment, trying to keep his emotions from showing. Again he resumed, "Like most everyone else here, I was maneuvered out of Washington D.C. just before it was too late." His face took on an ashen pallor. He had the look of death inscribed upon his features. "Until a few days ago, my permanent residence was in D.C."

Dillon nearly choked on those last few words. General Martin didn't need to hear more to know that Mr. Dillon was pretty sure that his family was now dead. Of course, all he could say is, "I'm sorry."

They stood there together, quietly, for a few minutes. Finally, Mr. Dillon spoke up. "Well, I doubt you came over here to hear about me." He sniffed only once. "What's on your mind?"

Feeling a little callous for proceeding but knowing it would get Dillon's mind off his troubles he said, "Actually it was that last question you posed. I don't know why my people never considered it, but it seemed to hit the nail on the head." General Martin had a gleam in his eye now. It spoke of admiration. "How did you come to that conclusion, that the Enemy is waiting for something during this recent reprieve from hostilities?"

"Actually, it just seemed like the most reasonable possibility."

"Well, after this is all over, if you ever want to serve on my staff as an analyst, I'd be obliged to have you."

They shook hands and the general retreated back to his aides.

Shortly after that conversation, General Martin was making his way through the labyrinth of corridors and passageways. He wanted to get a quick snack from his room, the kind the cafeteria certainly would not provide. On his way there, he passed a small utility room and noticed that the door was slightly ajar. As he passed it, he heard a very low sound and wondered what it might be. He didn't think much of it until he was past it. After he passed the room he realized that he had heard voices speaking very quietly. He forgot about it almost immediately.

In his room he found it. One of his few remaining 'contraband' granola bars that he had hidden away. He opened one and began to savor it. He slowly enjoyed it for a while. Finally, he looked down at his watch and exclaimed, "I guess I'd better get back."

He left his quarters and silently thought, *I'm glad the Enemy didn't invade until I was a general. In a situation like this, it sure is nice to have my own room.* As he walked back up to the conference room he slowed down and listened as he quietly approached the same utility closet. As he listened carefully he could just make out two different voices, but they were speaking so quietly he had no idea who they were.

One of them said, "Good, I'm glad that's sorted out. Because you do realize that, for the good of the world, America has to step up to the plate and be the leader?"

The other voice replied, "I already told you I agreed, or that I was at least willing to go along with this crazy long-shot! You just make sure you keep up your end of the bargain when the time comes—and don't take me for a fool. I recognize this idea of yours isn't going to be entirely popular with everybody. I also realize that you probably see me as expendable." The voice began to take on more confidence, and volume. "Rest assured that I have taken steps to ensure that, should I have an...untimely accident...my role in this plan will not go...unnoticed."

General Martin wondered, *Is that a man and a woman?*

The other spoke again. "Sshhh. Keep your voice down. So when the time comes, I will be counting on your support."

General Martin noticed that this last statement didn't sound like a question, or even a suggestion. It sounded more like coercion, or even a threat. With that, he quietly made his way up the hall and back to the conference room. On the way back he felt like he was walking in a fog. His intelligent eyes went to work. Who had been speaking? What plans were they talking about? They must've been shady to be talking in such a place. With the government and the rest of the world in a shambles and in disarray, those two could've been anyone talking about anything.

As he entered the room General Martin scolded himself for being polite and not taking the initiative immediately and finding out who those people were. Sitting in the conference room and waiting for the meeting to resume, he found himself peering at each person with suspicion as they entered the large chamber. Who could those people be? And what were they talking about? It sounded like some sort of political power play but it could just as easily have been something much less sinister.

General Martin watched Cheryl Rodriguez enter the room. The representative of the C.I.A. would certainly be someone crafty enough to come up with some sort of bold plan. Perhaps it had been her. She looked around shiftily, perhaps looking paranoid or nervous. *But then,* Martin thought, *she always looked like that.* He didn't know much about her, but he knew that a lot of those people in the C.I.A. were clever and adroit, or at least *they* thought so.

Eventually the waiting was over and President Griffith returned. She immediately took command and resumed the meeting where she'd left off. "Let's continue. Mr. Dillon, you had said that the Enemy is waiting for something. Well, you've all had a few minutes to think about it. What do you think? What are they waiting for?" Her briskness was mildly surprising. She seemed impatient. Who didn't? There was so much lost ground to regain. So many individual pockets of the earth had been laid waste by those terrible orbital bombardments!

Lieutenant Grace Malistair, one of General Martin's aides, looking a little impatient herself for some reason, spoke up. "Perhaps it's a logistical issue." She had a long dark braid that gave her a look of added youth. She was pretty but seemed oblivious to that fact.

Everyone tried to look like they *weren't* on the edges of their seats. After a few moments of nervous pause at being the speaker in such a venue, a not-so-polite cough from somewhere in the room got her talking again. "It could be that the force that we've encountered thus far is the forward assault group. The...shock troops, you might say." The lieutenant continued. "That would explain why they've attacked *where* they have as well as *why* they've ceased. Presumably temporarily."

Around the room there were furrowed brows. Everyone was processing information, running scenarios through their minds and creating projections of motives and likely outcomes. Even the people assigned to bring coffee were beginning to take notice. They too were anxious and hoping against hope that the lieutenant was on to something.

General Martin tried to help her out with her explanation without seeming to take her under his wing. "So, you're saying there are more fish in the pond? If these are shock troops then we can assume that what we've faced so far is a fraction of what's coming." The groans that echoed around the room were audible enough for the president to peer around and silence everyone with a vicious look of pure annoyance and impatience. She took a moment to make sure everyone knew she wasn't president *just* by default but that the mantle of authority really was hers. She looked each person in the eye individually until her stern gaze finally rested on Lieutenant Malistair.

At last she bade the Lieutenant, "Continue."

"General Martin is most likely right. If these..."

A semi-sarcastic voice cut her off. "Not to downplay the painful possibility that what we've already faced, what's already stretched us quite thin, is just an advance force, but..." the oily Secretary of State Carmine Michaels paused for a moment. He had a full head of dark hair and was impeccably dressed despite the living conditions, and he seemed to know it. With the demise of the previous Secretary of State, he had been a logical—if not pleasant—choice for the replacement. Michaels continued. "But you said that General Martin is "most likely right." I am, of course, familiar with warfare and shock troops. If your hypothesis is correct, how could General Martin be wrong?"

General Martin, never one to back down from a fight, and having very little respect for this particular Secretary of State, casually and lightly touched the lieutenant's hand to let her know he would be fielding this question. Before he spoke the general took half a second to organize his thoughts and prepared to spar with his opponent. He knew there would be no love lost between Michaels and himself. Unable to do much at the moment to the Enemy, he allowed himself a childish satisfaction at verbally skewering the Secretary of State.

"Mr. Secretary, I would call your mind back to the past–a mere six months ago." Martin noticed that Michaels was beginning to give that outwardly bored expression that he sometimes used for distracting others or to show disdain in a semi-polite way. *Good*, the general thought. *We're both behaving like children.* "When that took place, we were slow to move as a military body." Secretary Michaels' bored expression took on a hint of superiority, and caution. "We were also slow to move politically." Michael's look of superiority changed to aggression. "And in just about every other way, it seemed we hit the ground rather flat-footed." Martin began to address everyone at that point. "And do you know why?"

Michaels immediately spoke up, having resumed his bored expression, "Among other things, we were outmatched technologically and especially militarily."

Though he was a military man, General Martin hadn't been appointed to the post of the CJCS only for his military prowess but also for his acumen as a negotiator and a diplomat. With Michaels' last response Martin thought to himself, *Touché.* He continued. "One of the primary...'other things' was our total lack of experience with extraterrestrial life. Up till a few months ago we didn't even know there was extraterrestrial life. That complete lack of experience made us ripe for invasion. At least up front."

Michaels interrupted in his politically, oily way, "General, I'm sure we're all grateful for this history lesson, albeit recent history, but we have important matters to discuss." Michaels' manner became smug.

"Exactly! We were discussing the possibility that what we've seen so far is something akin to shock troops. The lieutenant astutely pointed out that I was 'most likely' correct. Remember, just as we were slow to react and to react properly when the War began, due to lack of information and experience, so too it may be that the Enemy doesn't respond the way we do. These may be shock troops and they may not. Just because *we* would employ certain tactics as humans does not mean that the Enemy would do the same. For all we know the Enemy might have a ceremonial ritual of throwing away their first troops like cannon fodder. There's just so much we still don't know."

Michaels' smug expression appeared to be failing him in favor of disdain again.

President Griffith, ever a good organizer, attempted to summarize, "So, based on what we've heard so far, what do you think?" She was addressing everyone. "Is it likely that what we've faced so far is some sort of advance army?"

Dillon in his antique suit began speaking again. "I don't think so. I know we don't know how the Enemy thinks or how they operate. We don't even know what they're called, but I think we have to assume that certain characteristics are inherent to all sentient species. Like the desire to stay alive or the decision to finish off your enemy when you've previously shown no compassion nor experienced much effective resistance. I just don't think that voluntarily pulling back while they have us up against the ropes is particularly likely. It must be something else."

"I agree with Mr. Dillon." That was President Jose Marquez, the leader of Brazil. His accent was found to be oddly calming by several of the people present.

The president continued, "I too agree. What else do we have?"

During the next two hours, other ideas were presented and shot down. Some seemed reasonable on the surface but only just. Others were more obviously riddled with holes of erroneous thinking. Tempers were getting hotter. Some in the room began to wonder if they would ever figure out this mystery of ceased hostilities. Some wondered if it could really make a difference, or if they would ever figure out how to beat the Enemy.

Midway through the various discussions a young aide to someone spoke up and actually suggested that the reason was probably something similar to what stopped the aliens in the story *War of the Worlds*. A few people listened but most discarded that idea on the top of the midden heap of lousy ideas already championed that day.

Toward the end of the day, another aide said, "I don't know. Maybe they're just...taking time to position themselves more strategically. For how long or to what exact purposes, I don't know." As he paused for a moment, some of the people around the room still jeered but several people stopped laughing or arguing just a bit and began to chew on what the young aide had said. He continued, "After all, has anyone even determined where they're at, where they're digging in, and seeing if those locations have anything in common?"

Now the joviality and flippancy that had been the mood off and on was replaced by a renewed sense of earnestness—and hope. Despite the hour, no one was talking any longer about what they would or wouldn't have for dinner. All eyes were on the aide, Phil Morrison. For a moment, you could've heard a pin drop as everyone began again to think, calculate, and determine the likelihood of the accuracy of Mr. Morrison's conjectures.

At last, Mr. Dillon in his old suit spoke up. He spoke slowly and calculatedly, as if he hadn't yet finished formulating what he was going to say. "In college I was not exactly the most popular young man around. This was perhaps best evidenced by my being captain of the Chess Club." He looked around to see if anyone was paying attention. All eyes were on him. Some showed extreme interest, hanging on his every word. Others showed confusion, wondering if what he was saying would end up being germane to the subject at hand. Of course, there was the oily Carmine Michaels. His eyes suggesting that John Dillon was a complete moron.

"One of the first things we learned when playing chess was that there are three primary issues with which to be concerned. Position, timing, and strength." He looked around the room without arrogance, just a certainty in his eyes that said he was sure he was on to something. In his pinstripe suit that was surprisingly clean, he somehow radiated confidence in a way that should've made the new president jealous. "It seems that the Enemy is, as the aide said, acquiring a more optimal position, but I don't think that's the only thing going on." He paused to take a sip of coffee and winced at the flavor. One or two involuntary smiles crept on to faces around the room. They felt the same way about the stale brew. Secretary Dillon continued, "I suppose part of the break in the attacks has to do with timing, but we've already discussed that and it just doesn't seem to wash."

Now General Martin spoke again with a smile in his intelligent eyes. "I guess that just leaves one thing. Strength."

"Precisely," Dillon replied. "They must be building up their strength."

"And if they're pausing to build up their strength," Martin continued, "then it must be that they *need* to be building up their strength."

The young aide, Mr. Morrison, interrupted adding, "You mean to say that they're not attacking now because they're not able to?"

At the same moment, Dillon and Martin blurted, "Exactly!"

They looked at each other, slightly abashed, and then the general leaned back in his chair and smiled as he said, "It's the only thing that makes sense. It fits perfectly." He felt like he'd already won the War.

The president, in her white pants suit, took control again, "So I guess the only thing to do now is to figure out how it is that they're building up their strength." Everyone in the room nodded, no one doubting that that was the correct course of action to pursue. For the first time in dozens of weeks there was an electricity and an excitement in the leaders of the United States of America. It was infectious and it showed on the faces of all present. Even General Thomas Martin had temporarily forgotten the surreptitious conversation he had overheard earlier.

"Excellent! We have a direction to pursue," President Griffith summarized. She turned to Martin and said, "General, deploy recon teams to determine why the Enemy has halted attacks and in what way they are building up strength for a renewed assault."

"Yes, Ma'am," Martin said smiling. He was not flashing his grandfatherly smile. It was the grim smile of a soldier who knew in his heart he would soon be dealing out a just retribution on his enemies. "I'll see to it personally. If you like, I'll have plans drawn up and on your desk first thing in the morning."

"Thank you. I would appreciate that," President Griffith replied. She did not smile.

The room was obviously about to degrade into a sort of organized chaos of glad-handing and exiting when the president cut things short. She stood up and motioned everyone to sit down. There were some looks of confusion and surprise but everyone took their seats. She stood there, waiting for silence to reign before speaking. Soon all that could be heard was the Mr. Coffee and some sort of conversations going on outside the room in the hallway.

Despite the improving mood that everyone was enjoying, some around the table began to feel something uncomfortable as they sat back down, watching the president. And the more they looked, the more they could feel some type of surprisingly icy hand clutching their hearts. No one understood it so each ignored the feeling the best they could, certain it was just their imaginations.

"I know you're all hungry and tired but there is one more item of business that needs to be discussed before we adjourn today." She paused and looked rather wistful, as if she weren't sure she should continue. She adjusted her suit jacket and looked at the American flag in the corner. "We've made some good progress today. We have a course of action. What we've discussed today could possibly be the seeds of our victory, but I suspect that, even should today's discussions prove fruitful, victory will still be a long and lengthy process. And so, effective immediately, there will be another policy shift to help deal with the War. After all, if we don't win...what's the point."

Everyone in the room began to look askance at the president, but in a very sober way. It was almost like when people are watching a terrible event unfold and are somehow paralyzed to do anything but watch.

She continued, "I know that my predecessor, President Wagner, already temporarily rescinded the third amendment to the Constitution. Of course," the president seemed to look at something far away, just out of focus, "a lot of people, a lot of us here, had a tough time stomaching that—the idea of soldiers being able to go into anyone's home whenever they needed to. I know we all thought the same thing," she sighed deeply. "We thought if property rights are gone to this extent, then what's next? Will there be anything worth fighting for when this is all over?" She paused and looked at several people with a hard stare. "But we were told, as soon as the War is over, the third amendment will certainly go back into effect." Around the room there were mixed reactions. Some people nodded in agreement and relief. Others looked less certain of how freedoms would be restored.

"And so, in order to help us take the fight to the Enemy and protect our people, I believe we need to temporarily suspend the fourth amendment as well." There was a collective gasp that quickly made its way around the room. "I know this rubs everyone the wrong way, myself most of all, but if we maintain the need for 'search and seizure'...we could very possibly be limiting our ability to find and destroy the Enemy. I believe that we will find ourselves in situations wherein we will need to immediately conduct searches of any structure to help us with the War, especially when street fighting becomes more commonplace."

The room was deafeningly quiet. Everyone scarcely breathed. Some looked like they were choking on something. Others looked defiant. A couple of people looked crestfallen. Of all people, Carmine Michaels looked...aggressive. General Martin looked around the room and his eyes met those of John Dillon. They looked at each other for a long moment, somehow communicating to each other their distaste for this shift in policy. Their eyes seemed to ask each other, *Is this a power grab or is it an attempt to address a legitimate concern? Either way, would it matter? Would it make a difference?*

After a few moments of a vast network of quiet looks being exchanged around the room, the questions came loudly and forcefully.

"Have you told anyone about this before?"

"You might as well burn the Constitution right now!"

"What kind of insanity is this?"

"It's about time."

"This can't be happening!"

"This is a heck of a first day for being president!"

"I won't stand for this!"

"What's next, a presidential Gestapo to match?!?"

After a few moments of 'discussion', President Griffith called a cessation to the noise. "I know that you have strong feelings about this. We *all* do. I don't like it any more than you do, but if we're going to root out the Enemy, once and for all, we're going to have to have the tools we need, already in place, to enable us to not only eliminate them where we find them, but to find them in the first place." She paused again and took off her glasses. She rubbed her eyes, looking tired. "I don't make this decision lightly, but I feel it is the best course of action that we can make at this time."

For a long moment, no one said anything. Then Mr. Dillon cleared his throat as if he were about to speak. Before he could, Roger Tremayne, the Secretary of the Treasury, spoke up. He was dark-skinned and always wore expensive Italian clothes. Apparently he'd worked hard to take care of them after the War began. In his sonorous African accent he said, "I don't like this any more than anyone else, but I can see how the President may have come to this decision. After all, if we don't do what it takes to destroy the Enemy, then any freedoms or privileges we may have enjoyed won't be worth the paper they were printed on." He paused for a moment before adding, "Because we'll be dead." The tone of finality in his statement wasn't lost on anyone present. It seemed to bring a sense of clarity and perspective back to everyone's thinking. Tremayne took a calming breath and continued, "I can support this, but I've got to have it in writing that when the *congress* decides to end this policy, the policy ends in its entirety. Period."

After that, it didn't take too long for enough people in the room to get on board with Secretary Tremayne's provision.

At last the meeting ended with most everyone present feeling that they had somehow made a deal with the devil.

CHAPTER 9
Last Woman Standing

As Sarah heard Garrison tell her that the Enemy was attacking, it occurred to her just how unprepared for this she truly was. She knew that the small amount of helping around and target practice that she'd done over the last few days would help, but it was most certainly too little too late. It seemed like it might, at best, prolong her life an extra few seconds. What might she do with those precious seconds?

She looked at the organized chaos that was beginning to develop around her and she remembered what someone in camp had told her. "When things get hairy, you're gonna find that the best battle plan gets tossed out the window almost as soon as the fight starts."

Sarah could hear Major Garrison barking orders in a voice that she'd never heard from him before. She could see the afterglow of the signal flare that had been shot high into the sky to make sure everyone in camp knew the Enemy was coming. She smelled the pungent odor of sweat rather than fear as every last person got into position. For just a moment time was frozen and she became keenly aware of her surroundings like never before in her life. It wasn't shock that she was experiencing, but some other species of sensation that could only be described as "semi-detached." It lasted only for a moment, and then it seemed the world came crashing down all around her.

The next thing she was aware of was the soldiers around her running to various destinations throughout the camp. They all seemed to know where they were heading. There was a fair amount of noise, but nothing like what she was certain she would hear soon enough—when the shooting would begin in earnest. She was already beginning to smell the scent of spent gunpowder. Some of the soldiers were firing into the surrounding forest from behind the comparative safety of their bulwarks. It didn't appear that they were hitting anything but trees and bushes. Sarah couldn't even see the Enemy yet.

Sarah took cover behind a felled tree along the fence-line. There were only two or three soldiers guarding this small stretch of the perimeter. She didn't recognize them. As she lay there she slowly peered over the log and through its branches that were now standing straight up. She was grateful for the added protection. She looked out through the night forest and, for once, didn't see it as being so lovely. This time it looked like some kind of giant death-trap, like a tortuous sewer pipe in which a million rats would soon come from everywhere and attack. It reminded her of General Custer's last stand. She tried not to think of how that turned out.

Through the logs she could see slashes of forest, darkened by the quickly waning twilight. She was grateful for the electric lights the camp provided. Though she didn't know why, she somehow got the feeling that if everything went dark the Spiders would have a distinct advantage.

As she looked through the logs she thought she saw flitterings of...something quietly and quickly ghosting through the trees. At first she thought it was a trick of the night. Then, as they appeared to get closer, they began to be, almost imperceptibly, accompanied by some kind of creepy, whispering sound. She'd heard that sound once before, the night she was nearly killed by one of the Enemy—the night Major Garrison had saved her life.

It was then she began to ask herself questions. *What was the point? If she was only going to die at the 'hands' of the Enemy, did it really matter that she had been rescued? Were they all doomed to die right here on this very night?*

As she cast her glance across the soldiers and the camp she couldn't help but notice Major Garrison, his fine brown hair adorning his head like it was part of his uniform. He stood in his position like a statue, giving orders and checking on things that needed doing. It was almost like all the strength the men and women in the camp had emanated from him. All except Captain Smith. She too did her part directing traffic and making sure holes in the line were plugged, soldiers had the ammo and other supplies they needed, and backup systems were ready at a moment's notice. Sarah had to admit, though she didn't care a wink for Smith, that woman knew her job and did it well.

The once lush grass of the camp was long since trampled by the personnel and their errands, but because of the setting of the sun, it was barely visible. *Just as the people of this camp are scarcely in the minds of anyone anywhere,* Sarah mused.

"You all right?" the soldier next to Sarah asked. She didn't know him but his face was vaguely familiar.

"Fine. I'm just ready to defend home," she replied reflexively.

The soldier looked back at her, only a little puzzled. The brief exchange ended with a strange sound that came from without the camp. It was slowly increasing in volume. Sarah and the corporal looked at each other and he uttered, "You know what that sound is?" It was a sly, soft mewling sound. It was almost like there were thousands of people in the nearby forest who were whispering loudly. Or like a multitude of young children whimpering in the night. It was, at first, only a little unnerving, but when the man answered his own question, she began to be genuinely scared. "It's the sound the Enemy makes when they're together. It's probably them talking to each other."

"What?" the sandy blond-haired woman found herself asking. "I guess I just assumed that, looking so horrid they would have some sort of creepy sound to match like...a scraping or clicking sound."

The corporal spared her a quick smile. "We're going to be fine. Just do your best when the fighting starts, and remember, these guys are *fast*. So you *really* have to lead your targets."

Sarah quickly digested what he said. She again had to swallow the fear that was threatening to bubble up like an over-ripe case of heart burn. She looked through the bulwarks out at the forest, straining her eyes to pick out an Enemy she might kill.

As she peered around, the camp began to get eerily quiet. It seemed to her like the calm before a storm. She strained her eyes and her ears as much as she could to get some kind of fix on where any of them were. *From which direction would they attack? Would they come in waves? How many were out there? If it came to it, would they take prisoners?* She realized there was very little that she knew about the Spiders.

The corporal suddenly whispered, "They're getting close. Keep your eyes open because things are probably about to really—".

Right at that moment a large globule of some kind of green sludge hit the corporal full on in the face. The stuff that hit him was nearly as firm as jello. It came from outside the camp. An instant before it made contact a report was heard from some sort of projectile weapon. It made a deep *wump* sound. The green slag immediately began to eat away at everything it touched. It appeared to burn like some sort of high-powered acid. *Those weapons are terrible!* she silently wailed.

It didn't take long before the corporal stopped moving. He was dead. Between the severe shock to his system and the acidic green globules continuing to burn away right through him, there was no way he could've lived long. When it was over, Sarah knelt down behind the felled tree that had not protected her comrade very well and wretched. She couldn't help but remember the old cliché-*war is hell*. She realized she was beginning to understand that axiom in a much more personal way than she ever had before.

Soon, she began to again hear that surprisingly mellow sound of the Enemy. It was getting louder much more quickly than Sarah had anticipated. She got back up to her position, trying not to look at the young man she'd been befriending. She tried not to think about the fact that she had already been starting to look at him kind of like an older brother. As she looked out at the forest and saw the silhouetted, shadowy movements out there, she realized that she never even knew the young man's name. He had died with her at his side, in anonymity. Anonymous perhaps, but Sarah silently vowed that his death would not be in vain. She would see to that.

She knew that she'd have to place all of her attention on what was in front of her—the battle—if she was going to live through this night. She knew the odds were woefully against her but she was determined to survive. For an instant, she thought maybe she understood Captain Smith a little bit. Maybe.

As the dark movements among the pines and evergreens around the camp began to get close, soldiers began firing. Soon, there was firing coming from all around the perimeter of the camp. Despite her brief training she was still surprised to find just how loud those guns were, especially when so many were firing at the same time.

And that's when she realized something else. The Enemy was attacking from *every* direction! There must have been an awful lot of them around for this battle!

Soon the air was a mass of chaos and destruction. She saw more green material being fired into the camp. Often it would miss, but not often enough. Several people had already been hit. Sarah noticed that, as men and women moved around the camp, they were careful not to step in those little piles of green acid that burned themselves out by melting away anything they touched. It reminded Sarah of when she'd been a kid and gone to her grandfather's cattle ranch. You had to be careful where you stepped. Only here, the results were much worse.

She tried to fire at the various Enemy combatants and was pretty sure that she missed them all. That corporal had been right. They really were *fast*. Occasionally she would see one crumple to the ground, bleeding some kind of liquid whose color she couldn't have named.

She tried to conserve her ammunition but found that that made it even less likely that she would hit anything. She concentrated on one, tried to lead him and then fired. She was pleased that she missed by only four feet. After all, she noticed that some of the soldiers were doing just as well.

Amidst the noise and confusion, she looked around and noticed Corporal Cornwall nailed one of them. He was nestled safely behind a half-track and firing fairly judiciously. When she saw him hit another she noticed that mischievous grin come into his eyes. Sarah took heart and fired again. She missed but at least the creature she'd fired at had noticed the shot and changed direction.

At first all seemed to be going as well as they could hope, but from what Sarah had been told she knew that this was most likely just the beginning. Sure enough, after just a few minutes of fighting, a couple of the Enemy combatants made it through the bulwarks. They had used their weapons to burn through the barricade. It was a small hole but she knew they would soon begin to poor through. In a straight line they were about fifty meters from Sarah's position. When she saw them within the camp she was horrified and felt herself begin to lose what little nerve she had. One of the repulsive looking Enemy soldiers was quickly eliminated but the other moved about so evasively that it was able to dance out of the line of fire and take cover behind a jeep.

Sarah was aghast, watching it move along, half slithering, half clambering about so gracefully on its nine grotesque, spider-like legs. Its fluid movements were a sharp counterpoint to its malignant appearance and nature. If not for the commotion going on around her and driving her to focus on survival, Sarah was certain she would've emptied her stomach yet again.

A door to an outbuilding opened just behind the creature. It spun in almost a perfect spider-style pirouette and launched itself at the man exiting the building. The man quickly died as the creatures' two large fangs struck. He cried out for only a moment and was gone.

Too horrified to scream, Sarah was even more surprised when a second man came out the same door. It was Captain Murphy. That mountain of a man immediately sized up the situation and drew his pistol. As he fired an alien leg whipped out and knocked the gun away. Murphy grabbed the abomination by its body and slammed it down. He took a nasty cut across his arm for his troubles, but the creature was momentarily stunned. Captain Murphy didn't waste any time. He grabbed the only thing at hand–a replacement muffler. He swung it down but the creature's dizziness was quickly wearing off and it barely dodged out of the way, immediately lunging for the captain with its fangs. Murphy brought the muffler up, angling it into the alien's mouth and used it to hold off his enemy. The fangs were gnashing and trying to reach the man's soft flesh only millimeters away. With a burst of herculean-like strength he trudged forward, pushing the alien, until it suddenly ceased fighting. Captain Murphy noticed a pool of rancid smelling liquid forming beneath the monster. Then he saw the reason. He had inadvertently impaled it on a metal AC hose that had been waiting in a vice for its repair. Aloud he gasped, "There is a God."

Realizing that both of the creatures that had slipped inside the compound were now dead, Sarah breathed a sigh of relief. Then the thick sounds of machine gun fire around her brought her back to the moment. She turned and faced the exterior of the camp. The amount of motion taking place at or near the tree-line surrounding the camp was increasing. To Sarah's left, the dead corporal was still there. She didn't look at him. A pang struck inside her when she again thought that she never even knew his name. She'd never get the chance to thank him for his words just a few minutes ago, words that had helped her to be brave.

Sarah looked to her right. She saw another soldier firing away at anything that moved and staying calm–barely. She could see it in his young, brown eyes. During a brief lull in his shooting, she called out to him. "Hey!"

He looked at her and nodded.

"Take it easy," she said, drawing upon some inner strength she did not know she possessed. "You're gonna be fine."

He never did say anything to her but the look he gave her was one of gratitude and determination. She was pleased that she could help his morale improve. He went back to his task at hand. She noticed the slight growth of beard that he had. She felt sorry that he probably hadn't slept much in a few days.

Sarah once again turned her attention to the savage, feral Enemy soldiers outside the camp. They were getting more brazen, taking more chances, coming closer. True, there were consequently more of their dead littering the ground like so much rubbish, but not that much. It wasn't at all like when she watched the movie *Gallipoli*. In that movie she had seen an army rush an opposing force that was entrenched. The oncoming force had been cut to pieces losing a huge percentage of their troops. In this case, the Enemy was losing a few but...that was about it. They really were as fast and evasive as she'd been lead to believe.

She saw one coming straight at her position. She raised the barrel of her gun and fired. It dodged, almost in time, and was winged, but it kept on coming. She fired again and missed. She could see those tell-tale fangs coming right for her. She stayed calm but couldn't help imagining this particular monster finishing the job its comrade had begun that first night she came to camp Oscar-Romeo-17. Fortunately, she was mistaken. It wasn't coming after her to tear out her individual throat. When it was close enough to the perimeter of the camp, it fired a weapon directly at her section of bulwarks.

For just an instant she saw some sort of red material erupt toward her from the weapon. During that instant she could tell that it was more viscous (though not truly solid) than the green stuff she'd already seen. During that realization, she heard the man to her right yell, "Incoming!"

And that's when it hit the protective wall. Instead of burning in an acidic way, it exploded on contact with the bulwark. Pieces of wood, dirt and anything else with which it made contact were sent everywhere. Sarah felt herself launched several feet. The soldier to her right wasn't so lucky.

When she hit the ground, the wind was knocked out of her. She hoped that was all. She couldn't imagine that she'd gotten off that easily. She tried to push herself up to her knees. She failed miserably. Dizziness from the blast and a disturbing ringing in her ears gave her pause. With her face in the dirt, she opened one sky blue eye and saw red soil around her. For a moment she wondered at that. She knew soil wasn't red. Then her senses began to come back to her, along with a lot of pain. That was blood. Her blood. As quickly as she could, she pushed herself up to her knees and then slowly up to her feet.

She could feel a knot forming on the side of her head. She noticed a bruise was already beginning to form on her left collarbone. She felt like her face had been through a meat grinder. Tentatively she picked at one spot and her fingers came away with a large splinter that had come from the tree that had been her protection.

She continued to come to her senses more fully, grabbed her rifle and looked around. The place where she'd been hunkered down was now a large gap in the perimeter. Several Enemy soldiers had poured through the hole in the wall that stood there like a gaping wound. Still standing in her blood-sodden dirt, she fired at the nearest Enemy combatant and she dropped it. *Apparently*, she thought with grim satisfaction, *they don't have eyes in the backs of their heads.*

Sarah looked around for some place, any place nearby, to take cover. She spied a greasy looking jeep. She was mildly surprised to find that, amidst all the destruction going on around her, it was relatively unscathed. She knew that wasn't likely to last but she immediately took refuge alongside it.

Sarah dove for the jeep and as she did, she felt a tiny part of her leg begin to burn. Her first thought was, *I can't believe it! I've been shot. I've never been shot in my life. Am I going to die?!?* But she found that she was still able to scramble without difficulty over to the military-green jeep. Relatively safe for the moment she looked down to assess the damage. She found that some green goop had splashed onto her leg from somewhere. Fortunately, only a drop or two had found its way onto her pants and most of it had used itself up burning a small hole through her jeans. She quickly grabbed a handful of grass and rubbed the wound, attempting to scoop off as much of the stuff as she could. She was totally unprepared for the pain that resulted. Later she would wonder why she had been surprised that this third-degree burn would hurt when rubbed. With less of the green stuff on her leg she found that the burning soon subsided. A little. The burn, she knew, would continue to hurt for quite a while. She couldn't wait to dip her leg in some cool water!

Though the pain in her leg was intense, she took only a moment to engage in additional first aid on herself. She was grateful that the wound, the third-degree chemical burn, was confined to an area on her leg about the size of a dime. As soon as she was done treating herself she gritted her teeth against the pain and gripped her rifle and surveyed what was going on around her. The Enemy was still pouring through the breach in the camp defenses.

People and Spiders were dying everywhere. More people than Spiders. It was horrific. She could hear bullets flying and ricocheting around the area. She frequently heard the deep *wump* sound that the Enemy guns made when they launched their green and red globules. The various stenches that surrounded her were nearly overpowering.

As she looked around again, she noticed that things were happening so fast that she could barely tell who anyone was. Nearly all she saw were uniforms and disgustingly long, spindly legs. It was psychologically over-whelming for Sarah. She realized that she was sliding into something worse than shock. It was more like paralysis. She had to resist. She had to do something! As the Enemy was no longer pouring in through the breach, she prepared to run straight for that point in the perimeter. *All right,* she told herself. *On the count of three. One! Two! Thr—.* At that very moment a spray of green muck slathered much of the surface of the jeep Sarah was using for cover. Thrust through the throws of terror once again, she immediately bolted into her plan. After she'd take only a few steps the ground nearby her erupted as a batch of the Enemy's red sludge material threw dirt, branches and rocks in all directions. She fell to the ground, her freckled cheeks covered in dirt. She was grateful that this time the wind was not knocked out of her. She didn't know how much more she could take. Rolling away from the epicenter of the explosion and then climbing back onto her feet, Sarah tried to ignore the new bruises all over her body.

After only a few more steps, she was at the breach. As she was going out, an Enemy combatant was coming through. They both paused for just an instant. In that one brief moment Sarah could've sworn that her Enemy was actually surprised. Just as it shook off its hesitation it collapsed in a burst of gunfire. *Thank you God for whoever took this one out for me,* she prayed.

As she left the camp, she began to develop second thoughts about her course of action. *This is madness,* she told herself. *Now I'm right in the middle of where these monsters came from! And they'll be hidden in the trees! I'll be lucky if I last one whole minute!*

She stared out into the surrounding nighttime forest. She found herself making quick, jerky movements trying to watch every direction at once. Sarah tried to abstain from letting her hands shake out of sheer fright. She took an instant to see how she was doing. She was only marginally pleased with her composure. As she continued trying to see and hear everything around her a random thought crossed her mind. *Can they climb trees?* She immediately peered up into the air as she desperately searched the canopy above, certain it was another death-trap designed just for her. A sense of paranoia was threatening to overtake her. It was then that she realized she had dropped her rifle some time after she had made her quick exit from the camp. Silently berating herself she forcefully caused her thoughts to move on to something that she could affect. Refusing to allow herself to be frozen in place, she rapidly moved on.

As she ran away from the camp, away from the sounds of fighting, death and destruction, she found that her minute came and went—and she still lived. She stopped to get her breath. All she could hear were the distant sounds of weapons...and her own heartbeat. It sounded surprisingly loud in her ears.

She knew she needed to plan, but first, she would need to get under cover while she finished catching her breath as well as deciding what to do next. *At least the darkness will help me to hide,* she thought through a decreasingly numb and foggy mind.

She ducked under some nearby ferns that were effectively covering the ground. She lay there and, out of a need to protect herself, her mind reflexively wandered. She thought about how beautiful she'd always found various ferns to be. The intricate structure of each leaf in the moonlight impressed her. She felt that she could look at these plants, that were doing their best to protect her, forever.

I've got to focus. I need a plan.

As Sarah lay in the cool, night-time embrace of those safe ferns, she forced herself to relax. She made herself breath slower. She especially tried not to think about the terrible scene she had just witnessed. She was still amazed that she hadn't been killed. She feared what all damage she may have sustained. So she rested her head on the soft mossy undergrowth. She would've laid there much longer but the pain in her leg was beginning to throb. She knew that the adrenalin rush she'd experienced before had numbed the pain in her leg to a certain extent, and the various other pains, until now. Now she needed to do what she could to care for her injuries.

Forcing herself to think logically she thought to herself, *What should I do?* She promptly answered. *Get somewhere where I can take care of myself, at least temporarily.*

She continued the dialogue with herself. *What do I need?*

Water for drinking and cleaning my wounds.

I don't have any water with me. I don't see any. Where am I going to find some?

Downhill. I need to travel downhill and maybe find a stream in one of the draws.

Curse myself for never looking at the maps while in camp. Water will be good. What else?

I'll need food. I know which plants I can eat. Dandelions, clover, fireweed. They taste lousy but they'll keep me going. What else?

I'll need shelter. A place to hide from the Enemy and protect me from the weather. Where will I find such a place?

I don't know. I'll figure that out after I have water. I can eat plants on the way till I find some. But I don't know how long I can go without medical treatment. I'm sore all over and I have that small burn on my leg. That wound might get infected.

I can find peppermint along the way and use that until I can find something better.

I knew those days of Dad pushing me to learn how to live in the forest would pay off!

With a plan in mind, Sarah determined that she was ready to move again. She lay extra still, listening carefully for any tell-tale sounds of danger. She waited several minutes before she was satisfied. Finally, Sarah stood up and began to move downhill. She tried to move as soundlessly as she could. It made her think of the stories she read as a child about the Native Americans. What she wouldn't have done right then for a pair of quiet, soft-leather moccasins!

Sarah carefully walked along, jumping or pausing every time she snapped a twig or heard a sound that she had not caused. She realized she was pretty jumpy and nervous, knew that she needed to relax and keep her emotions in check. She physically forced herself to calm down. When she had acquired some control, she began thinking about the broken tree branches she'd seen before this all started. *What were they? What made them? Was it an animal or something else that had caused them?*

As Sarah quietly considered these thoughts, she slowly became aware of something—a sound that she could hear in the distance. Because it came on so slowly, she hadn't noticed it at first. Finally, as she drew nearer to it, she paused where she was, next to a giant evergreen and listened intently. Was she imagining it? No, that was the sound of running water! She waited patiently until she was pretty sure of which direction to travel to get to it.

As soon as she was certain, she carefully headed out. With the sound of water in her ears she felt a renewed vigor in her step, a greater strength that she had not known since before the attack had begun. She moved with purpose, paying less attention to making noise as she stepped across the rich soil of the forest floor. She was getting closer. She could hear the gentle burbling of the stream growing louder. That life-giving liquid would soon be hers. She hadn't had a drink in many hours. She was so thirsty. She'd soon be able to treat her wounds and drink her fill.

As she moved she automatically picked some fireweed to eat. Feeling nutrition rushing back into her, she continued moving toward the sounds of the stream. She felt a tinge of exhilaration that temporarily washed away her fatigue and her fear. Sarah felt like she could almost taste the water in the air, like some sort of sea of life and health was nearby, beckoning her onward.

Before reaching the water however, she came up short when a realization occurred to her. The Enemy must know how valuable water is to humans. What if they're patrolling the streams?

Sarah stood there in the middle of a clearing, out in the open, processing this thought. *What should I do?*

I don't want to die.

I need water. It doesn't matter if they're there or not. I can't survive very long without water.

She headed on toward the water, taking greater care to be more quiet than before. She found herself dashing from tree to tree, doing her best to be one with the shade the moon was casting. As she approached each tree, she felt herself almost trying to merge with the mighty forest guardians so as to avoid detection.

As she was getting very near the stream, she paused once to listen to a sound she'd heard. She waited and listened for several minutes. At last a chipmunk scampered across her path a few yards ahead of her. She let out a sigh of relief and smiled.

Continuing on, she was careful to be quiet and, knowing that although the stream would help mask her sounds, it would do the same for anything else within its proximity—including the Spiders.

At last, she came through some brush and saw it. The stream was before her. She crouched down amidst the bulrushes and absently noted that if she was going to have to stay here for an extended period of time, she would want to grind up their roots and make flour out of them to eat.

She slowly crawled to the bank of the stream, not worrying about dirtying her entirely filthy attire or her matted sandy blond hair. When she finally reached the water she lay down on her belly and scooped up a handful of the heavenly liquid and took a drink.

She would always remember how good that first sip tasted.

Sarah drank her fill and felt truly refreshed, rejuvenated. She then proceeded to dip her leg that had received the small burn during the battle. She didn't think anything could've felt better than that first drink of water she'd just had, but the coolness of the water on her burnt flesh was exquisite. With her leg still in the blessedly cool water, she rested for a few minutes and then began to think about her next move. She looked up and saw that the moon was in the west. It had been a long night. The sun would be coming up soon and with it would be greater danger of being seen. She was so tired from a long night of hiking, foraging and anxiety. She knew she needed rest. Sarah wanted so badly to just lay down and sleep where she was. Yet the thought of sleeping somewhere safe kept penetrating through her increasingly exhausted and sluggish mind.

She looked around and, after moving downstream for a few minutes, found a small indenture in the side of the stream bank. It had bulrushes growing in front of it, obscuring its view from prying eyes. She took one more draught of water and then eagerly climbed into her blind. Despite the cool of the early morning, she succumbed to sleep immediately.

CHAPTER 10
Unexpected Meetings

Sarah awoke in the mid-afternoon. She had slept for several hours. Between sleeping on an uncomfortable patch of ground and the night's activities, she slept hard and awoke with her muscles sore and tight. She slowly opened her sky blue eyes and found that her tiny 'cave', if it could be called that, was facing west. The powerful rays of the afternoon sun blasted into her eyes as she carefully opened them. She immediately wished she hadn't.

The first sensation she experienced upon waking, after noticing her sore muscles and the blinding light of the sun, was just how hungry she was.

Before seeking food, Sarah took a moment to notice that the small hole in the side of the riverbank was pleasantly grassy. She stretched and tried to enjoy its coziness. After a few moments she was disturbed by loud grumblings coming from her stomach. She looked down at her belly and was surprised at how thin it looked. She figured it must be her imagination trying to convince her that she was starving. As she looked down at herself she also noticed just how filthy her clothes were. Her jeans were torn in several places and her once white shirt now looked like the perfect forest camouflage.

Carefully she slithered out of her protection, ever vigilant of any tell-tale sound, sight or smell that might suggest danger. As she emerged she noticed that, as far as she was able to discern, everything was right with the world. Except for her memories of the previous night and her disheveled appearance, it was as if no attack had taken place, like the Enemy had never come to Earth. However, she couldn't help but remember those feral, wrenching images she'd experienced in the battle so recently. *So many died. Some of them I knew, people who were becoming my friends. Why didn't I die? I'm not trained like the rest of them.* She paused in her movements for a moment. *I'm just lucky,* she thought guiltily and with a measure of self-loathing.

Feeling guilty for surviving she added, *I'll miss you Major Garrison.* A handful of tears slowly made their way down her dirty face, leaving some streaks. *You were a much better friend to me than I deserved.*

Knowing that focusing on the battle was only going to distract her and get her killed, she once again directed her thoughts toward the all-important issue of survival.

She used her hand to scoop up some water out of the stream and drank as much water as she could. Then she knew she had to eat. *I'm so hungry!*

She returned her attention to the surrounding bulrushes. Knowing just how terrible the taste would be she picked a few young, green cattails and then sat down by the stream, ready to wash out the flavor with some clean water. She ate a few of them and thought, *I suppose I could do this indefinitely.* She paused for a drink to wash down a particularly nasty bite. *I'd really rather find civilization instead!*

She finished eating some cattails and then, still being terribly famished, looked around for something different. She saw a beautiful patch of clovers just across the stream. The meandering vein of water was pretty deep right there so she walked downstream a little, looking for a place to fjord.

After about a hundred yards she spied a spot in the stream where it got wide and slowed down considerably. She found some rocks in the middle of the water's path and scurried over them, getting wetter than she'd hoped. While she was making her crossing, she used the surrounding water to get cleaned up a bit. Crossing made her think of the Bering Straits.

Once across, movement was easy through the lush grasses. *It's so beautiful here, being a part of my mountains like never before.* She quickly moved through the pristine forest until she arrived at the small glen of clovers that she'd seen from across the stream. Immediately she began to gather them up. Every time she had several in her hand she would plop them into her mouth and eat. Though not as tasty as a grilled ham and cheese sandwich, they were nevertheless much less bitter than most of the plants available to eat. She just hoped that she didn't have to resort to eating too many dandelions. *What I wouldn't do right now for some wild strawberries.*

She sat under a tree, slowly munching on her meal, trying not to think that she would eventually need something more than just plants and roots. *If this foraging lasts very long, I'm going to need to eat something with some fat in it.*

The sunlight cascading down through the openings in the forest felt so pleasant and warm. She noticed just how peaceful it really was right there at that particular moment, and it made her think how little she really knew *her* woods.

Sarah luxuriated in the warming of her feet, made wet from her recent crossing of the stream. She continually made an effort to not think about the night before. With a slight chuckle she thought, *I should be able to make my way by foot all the way to a town.* She looked around at the vastness of the forest. *Thank goodness it doesn't snow much around here.*

As she was finishing her scarcely adequate meal she thought, *I suppose I'd better figure out what I'm going to do next.* Sarah stared at the last bit of unappetizing food and began to think. *I need to know which way is north.* She looked around at the sun and then turned right a quarter turn. *All right. I can't count on anyone from camp surviving.* She shuddered at that thought. *Even if they did, the odds of me ever bumping into any of them ever again would be like finding a cow on a super-model runway.* She looked around and sighed. *So, it's just me. Well, I was northeast of civilization back at camp. Probably no more than about 100 miles. If I push hard I can be back there within a week.*

She looked up and shaded her eyes from the intense glare of the sun. *I'll need to stay by the water, and I'm going to need a weapon.* She checked her pockets looking for something, anything that she might use as a weapon. She didn't have much but she was happy she had had the foresight to keep her large hunting knife on her. That would make a good weapon and all around tool! *And I can use it to sharpen the end of a large walking stick in case I need something like a spear.*

Sarah immediately set to work and soon had a good walking stick with a wickedly sharp end.

She carefully looked at the stream and surrounding mountains and determined that to get home, she should probably head downstream. She headed out, picking up plants along the way to munch on. She was already beginning to feel the effects of such a drastic change in her diet, but the thing that was more prominent in her mind was the fact that, despite constantly eating, she was still fairly hungry. So as she walked, she looked for anything she might use to make a snare. *It won't be long and I'm going to be severely lacking protein and fat. Maybe I can snare a rabbit or a squirrel.*

Sarah had to admit that, although she'd made snares before, she wasn't the best at it. She simply hadn't ever gotten around to practicing very much. As a result, she knew she'd have to work at it for a while before she was likely to catch anything. However, she figured that since she was now faced with proper motivation, she would quickly figure it out and improve her skills. She knew that until she caught something, she would need to do the one thing her dad had taught her that she resisted more than anything else-eating bugs.

It would help sustain her and keep her strength up. She knew this. In the western Oregon soil-rich environment such as this, finding them would be easy. All you had to do was dig a bit and then eat what you found. But as she had told her father when she was a young girl, *That just grosses me out!*

As she walked along the stream's bank, she repeatedly found herself reverting to habits she frequently exhibited before the War, like simply hiking and enjoying the beauties around her. *But I can't do that now. I have to pay attention. If I don't, I'll likely bump into the Enemy, and I'm pretty sure this spear isn't going to be enough to protect me. Even if it is, I sure don't want to get close enough to one of them to use it.*

She continued to focus on the sounds of the forest, straining her ears for any sound that might indicate danger. Occasionally she would hear something. When that happened, she'd stop and drop to the ground. She would quietly wait, listening for all she was worth. So far, each time she'd heard a suspicious noise it had ambled away or not repeated itself. *How many of these times has true danger been near? Have I heard the Enemy moving around and didn't know it?* That sent a shiver down to her bones.

She moved carefully on.

After hiking for a few hours, the sun was setting and Sarah knew she should hurry and find a place to rest for the night, and hide. She walked another quarter mile before she found a stand of deciduous and evergreen trees growing very close together. She judged they would provide her shelter from wind, rain and, most especially, unfriendly eyes. They yielded her a space to lay down that was only a little larger than what she needed. Despite the chill in the air coming on with the night, it felt cozy and safe. As she prepared to bed down for the evening she thought, *I sure wish I could make a fire, but I suppose not having a fire is a small price to pay to avoid those monsters.*

She quietly walked up to her place of refuge to sleep for the night and then laid down to rest.

Sometime in the middle of the night, Sarah awoke. At first she was a little frightened, unsure of where she was and how she got there. The dark shadows within shadows cast by the surrounding trees made her feel like she was seven years old again and afraid of the dark. She soon remembered the preceding day and how she'd arrived at her primitive bed-chamber.

She rolled over, trying to get comfortable. *I should've picked a different place to sleep. That blasted root in my back is driving me crazy!* she thought. As she finished selecting a position that she would define as 'least uncomfortable' she heard something.

Probably my imagination, she reasoned.

She heard it again.

That must be an animal passing through.

This time the sound was more distinct. It sounded to Sarah like a twig snapping.

Animals don't usually make that much noise when they're walking around.

Suddenly the root in her back became completely unimportant to her. She immediately became profoundly grateful for the protection of the trees around her. She knew it would be very difficult for anything to see her.

Sarah slowly moved her hand over to her spear, her sandy blond hair falling around her shoulders. She gripped it tightly and used it to lever herself up to a sitting position so that she could see out through the dense copse of trees surrounding her. The sounds were getting closer—quiet, rhythmic sounds of rustling grasses and the gentle shuffling of feet through dirt. She sat up and leaned on one of the trees that formed her nighttime fort. As she did so, a loose piece of bark broke off and landed on the ground. Anywhere else, that would've barely been audible, but in those circumstances, it sounded in her ears like a gun discharging.

She froze in place, deathly afraid to move, almost too nervous to look about. After a pair of heartbeats, she noticed that the sounds of movement she had been tracking had also ceased. She was too afraid to move about any further to look around and see what was out there. Was it a person, the Enemy, or something else? Any living creature wandering around at night would have stopped moving upon hearing her.

As Sarah stood up, trying to will her ears to hear more than they were made for, she became more still than she ever had before. A fleeting thought gently passed through her mind, *If only my 8th grade teachers could see me now. They'd never believe I could be so quiet and still!*

After several moments of silence throughout the forest, she mustered the courage to ever so slowly move a branch that was obscuring her view of the movement she'd heard. At first she couldn't see anything but more ferns, trees and other forms of forest fauna. Then she saw it. It was too far away to see clearly at all, probably about fifty yards away and through plenty of underbrush. Finally, she saw a slight bit of movement. There it was, whatever it was. As it moved, she became gradually aware that there was more than one of them out there. She could see them moving together.

Sarah took a moment to again suppress the overwhelming terror that was threatening to swallow her. She continued to watch and try to figure out what was out there. They kept moving. It appeared that they would pass by within about twenty-five yards of her place of refuge. Maybe closer. *Why did I have to lose that rifle? Where did I drop it?*

Whatever the creatures were that Sarah was tracking, they were getting closer. They moved quietly like wraiths ghosting along their path. As they passed through the trees, she got a better view and breathed an almost audible sigh of relief. They were definitely <u>not</u> the Enemy. They were too tall. *If only the moon was doing its job. I can barely see a thing out there!*

At last they were close enough that she could hear the faint sounds that they made. They were like whispers that the surrounding foliage tried to absorb.

They were closer. The sounds sounded more and more like language. English! It was some of the soldiers from Oscar-Romeo-17! Forgetting everything else and relieved to see other people again, she forgot about her caution and rushed out of her trees. She expected a warm reception. Instead she found herself staring down the barrels of three separate rifles.

"Scott? Is that you? Are you an idiot? You were this close to getting your head blown off!" Captain Smith said, holding her thumb and forefinger together.

Recognizing Captain Smith, Sarah involuntarily exclaimed, "My cow!"

Wondering at her response, Smith asked, "Are you sick? Which plants did you eat?"

Sarah couldn't help the tears of hope and happiness from trickling down her cheeks. Instead she replied, "I'm fine. It's just...something I was thinking about before." She giggled and then turned to Smith's two companions, Sergeant Jameson and Private Stansbury. She eagerly gave them a hug and they returned the gesture, while looking sheepish and surprised. She knew Jameson from camp but hadn't gotten to know Stansbury as well. The young man seemed to Sarah to be quiet and thoughtful, and hopeful too. He appeared to be private but without being at all suspicious. His mane of brown hair that was devoid of a part hung simply down to his ears.

Captain Smith merely glared at her. "Let's go," she said with a surprising amount of venom.

After her three companions took a few steps, Sarah exclaimed, "Wait a second! It's the middle of the night. Those...things blend in with the darkness pretty well. Shouldn't we be hunkering down or something until daylight?"

Captain Sonya Smith rounded on her immediately. "First of all," she hissed in a loud whisper, "if you want to avoid the Enemy, shut up! You're loud enough to be heard for a quarter mile! Second, I don't know if you noticed the night-vision goggles I'm wearing but they'll allow us to see the Enemy in the dark a lot more easily than regular sight during the day time." She paused only briefly to let her diatribe sink it. "You got it?!"

Sarah felt like belting her right then and there. Except that she was pretty sure she'd end up on the ground in the span of a couple of seconds. Maybe less. *What an arrogant, self-righteous jerk!* But as they moved out, Sarah began to calm down, slowly. As she did, she could see that Smith was right, about everything, and that made her start getting angry all over again.

After about an hour of walking, with Smith wearing the goggles at point, Sarah chanced to speak a little. She moved so that she was walking along beside Sergeant Jameson and whispered, "Hey, Jameson. How long are we going to walk?"

In his stiffly formal way that he had with everyone, he replied, "We'll hike until around dawn. Then, we'll find a place to sleep until an hour or two before dusk."

Sarah walked for a few moments, thinking about that. She had so many questions to ask, mainly about what happened at the camp. How many people were still alive? What happened to the camp? Did their leader, Pete Garrison, still live? Where were they headed? What happened to the Enemy force that hit them? She asked, "So, what happened back there?"

His eyes took on a haunting look, gray and ghostly. "Later." She took the hint and got back into line, walking as quietly as she could.

Abruptly, Sarah saw something and stopped. Her three companions immediately followed suit, kneeling down and taking up defensive positions, forming a triangle. They looked positively deadly. Sarah was standing by a tree and examining it. "What is it?" Captain Smith hissed at her.

"It's another broken tree limb. I've seen them before, but they don't match up with the behavior of any animal that I'm aware of." She continued to study it, intrigued.

"What?!" was all Captain Smith could quietly, but viciously, rasp. She took half a second to gain control of her somewhat frayed nerves. "We're trying to escape a lost battle. We could bump into overwhelming odds at any moment and you—" She paused again. Through grated teeth she continued, "—you're stopping to look at some marks on a tree?! Marks that have nothing to do with our circumstances?"

For a moment, Sarah was certain the situation was going to come to blows. Despite her certainty that she would lose, she half hoped it would turn ugly. At perhaps the last possible moment of self-control, Captain Smith turned around and headed out again, resuming her position at point.

They walked the remainder of the night with no other incidents. After a while, Sarah calmed down enough to be able to appreciate that. For some reason, she didn't feel any hostility or disdain for not having been offered to take the lead position–and the goggles. About half an hour before sunrise, Smith called a halt to their forced march. She led them to a rocky area on an incline along the stream. "This is about as defensible a position as we're going to find. I'll take the first watch while you three sleep."

Sarah had to admit that the captain was awfully strong-willed. After a night like that, Sarah was ready to collapse and sleep the day away. As soon as her head hit the ground, she was out. She woke up in mid-afternoon, wondering why she hadn't been woken for her turn to take watch. Then she remembered her unforgettable relationship with their leader. *Oh, well,* she thought. *At least I'm rested and I have some food in me with a whole lot more carbs than those plants had to offer. I never thought I'd appreciate military rations this much!*

She went down to the stream to wash the sleep out of her eyes. While bending over to get slightly cleaned up she spied Private Stansbury sitting a few yards down the stream. She noticed that he was sitting against a tree, staring off at a purple mountain in the distant east. He was leaning against a pine tree whose base was probably submerged whenever the stream flooded. He hummed a gentle tune that she didn't recognize. He seemed likeable enough.

She queried, "It's pretty. What's the tune?"

He turned his head toward her, not overly quickly, and replied, "It's just a song I heard growing up." Though his words were somewhat curt, his eyes said that he simply didn't have a lot to say at the moment. Perhaps the pain of the battle was still too recent. They sat in silence a few moments longer.

The moment of peace and tranquility was shattered by Captain Smith's bark, "Let's go. It'll be sundown soon. Time to move out!" Smith continued, "Jameson, you'll start at point."

"Yes, Ma'am," was the crisp, hasty reply.

A few minute later, they were on the trail again. As Sarah had been told earlier, they were making their way toward another military camp, similar to Oscar-Romeo-17. This one was called Oscar-Romeo-6. It was supposed to be only about a three-day march from 17. If they were lucky, they'd find food and shelter when they arrived. If they arrived. They also needed to give their comrades any information about the Enemy they could.

They quietly walked along streams and rivers, pausing occasionally to check the map to make sure they were going the right way. Every hour Captain Smith would rotate a new person to the point position with the night goggles, not including Sarah. Though Sarah was a little upset by this at first, she thought back to all those military movies she'd seen where a patrol of soldiers is moving through unfriendly territory. She also remembered that the man in front always seemed to be in the most danger. So, she consoled herself with that knowledge.

At one point in the night they took a break near a small river. Sarah couldn't be sure but she thought it was the McKenzie River. She listened to the musical notes the life-giving water played on the rocks as it rushed by. If it hadn't been so cold, she'd have been tempted to take her shoes off and soak her tired feet for a minute or two. *I wonder if anyone else is thinking the same thing*, she thought.

While sitting there, Captain Smith walked over to Sarah, sat down and then hailed Stansbury and Jameson. When they had joined her and sat down close, Smith opened up her map and began to quietly speak to them. "We're about here," she said pointing at a particular spot on the map. "As you can see, we're getting close to 6. I expect it should be on that mountain." She looked up at the surrounding topography and then pointed at a distant hill. "About there. I expect we'll be there sometime tomorrow night." She paused for a moment. "We now have an approximate line-of-sight with 6." She looked up again at where she had pointed and then looked into the eyes of her three companions. "I expected that we'd be able to see at least some light coming from the camp-even at this distance. As you can see, there's nothing. Oscar-Romeo-6 may have been overrun as well. We need to be prepared for that possibility." She began to put away her map and then casually said, "Of course, it may just be that we're off course a little or they're operating under a blackout policy." She took the goggles from Jameson and concluded her quiet barking, "Let's move."

As they trudged on, Sarah thought about what Smith had said. *Was Oscar-Romeo-6 overrun? Are we lost? How many of those...abominations are out there in these woods right now?*

They marched on.

A few minutes before dawn they called a halt to their march for the night. They had marched well that night. Sarah was proud of herself that she had not slowed them down, or had an altercation with Smith. *It's easier to go with the flow than fight the whole way.*

After they'd had a brief meal, Sarah looked around for a place to rest for the day. She found a place that would afford her some shade when the sun would rise and heat up the forest floor. She finished gathering some soft grasses and leaves for a pillow. She was exhausted, but she was beginning to feel her body get stronger and develop more stamina.

When she awoke, the sun was half way down to its horizon. She figured it must be around 4:00 in the afternoon. It felt so liberating to neither know what time it was nor need to know. It was one piece of the life she'd always dreamed of living. Of course, being hunted never was part of that dream.

She stood up and ate a little of their meager rations. The bread was only a little stale and the granola bars were tasty. Two or three hours later, it was time to resume their march. Sarah was excited about getting to a place of relative safety and it showed in her sky blue eyes. *Would Oscar-Romeo-6 still stand? Would it be able to receive them? Will I ever get back to civilization? I can't wait to sleep in a bed again!*

It was shaping up to be a beautiful, Pacific coast sunset. The clouds were already beginning to take on varying hues of pinks and purples, soon to transform into reds, golds and oranges. *Nature always was better at putting on a show than anything Hollywood could make,* she recognized.

With only a couple of hours of light remaining, they headed out. After only an hour they came upon a small waterfall, only ten or twenty feet tall. It surprised Sarah that they came to a halt from a short distance away from it. *Hmmm, maybe I'm rubbing off on them. I never thought we'd stop to admire nature.*

As she looked at the furtive nature and gestures of her companions she realized they weren't enjoying the natural beauties of their surroundings. They had obviously perceived a potential danger of some sort. Peering around her comrades, Sarah tried to see what was drawing their interest. Near the base of the waterfall was a man kneeling down and drinking. With his back to Sarah and the three soldiers, he was cupping his hands together and carefully bringing the cool, clean water to his lips. Sarah wasn't certain why her trio of bodyguards was behaving so cautiously around this person. He sure didn't seem like a threat to her.

Finally, after a couple of minutes of surveying the area, assessing for potential threats, and sitting very still in the bushes, Captain Smith shifted her weight as if to stand up and hail the man. Yet just as she did, the man, who still has his back to them, threw an arm over behind him, gesturing at something. They continued to sit still. After a few moments more of waiting, the man turned and looked directly at them in their blind and hollered, "Well? Come on out. I'm not gonna bite ya." He turned back to his waterfall.

Gun ready, Smith led them down to the strange man. Stansbury and Jameson fanned out so as to provide flanks if necessary. All six of their eyes were constantly darting about, searching for dangers and undiscovered threats.

When they approached, the man didn't wait for them to speak. "Hi. The name's Armstrong. Jack Armstrong." He looked at them and apparently noticed the dirt streaking so much of their clothing. "You soldiers lost?"

"My name is Captain Smith. Why are you here?"

Jack didn't seem taken aback by her hostile attitude and just smiled. He must've been nearly sixty years old. He had the look about him as if he didn't have a care in the world. Sarah was tempted to think that he wasn't playing with a full deck, but as she looked into those eyes she could see knowledge, understanding and wisdom—and plenty of experience. He looked to be about five foot, eleven inches. He had a full head of hair that was shot through with gray. Surprisingly, he didn't have a beard or even any stubble. He was skinny as a rail and looked like he'd blow away if a stiff breeze whipped up. Perhaps the main thing Sarah noticed about him was his smile. It was a pleasant, peaceful smile.

"I was just getting a drink of water. There's plenty for all," he said with a chuckle.

"No thanks," the captain replied in her characteristically clipped tone. "This land has been declared 'off limits' by the federal government. You have no right to be here."

Again he smiled. Sarah thought, *Doesn't anything ruffle this guy's feathers?*

"I've been coming out here since before you were born. I keep to myself and don't bother anyone. Whatever the government has planned for this area, I'm sure I won't be in the way."

"Sir—" Captain Smith said rather forcefully as she grabbed his shoulder. In one fluid movement, the man reached back, grabbed her hand, pulled her over him and had her on her back with a large hunting knife at her throat. If Sarah hadn't seen it, she wouldn't have believed it possible.

Who is this guy?!?, she continued to wonder. *He's as fast as lightning and twice as lethal!*

Armstrong noticed the surprise and carefully masked terror on the face of his captive and seemed to check himself. "Sorry about that ma'am," he said as he got up off of her. As he sheathed his knife he continued on in that oddly musical voice of his. "Old habits die hard. If you want, we can talk, but I don't see any need for you to go about trying to boss everyone around."

He smiled at Smith. She scowled at him as she stood up. Her eyes were like daggers. Something in the back of Sarah's mind told her that Smith was extra angry since Jameson and Stansbury were there to witness what had just happened.

Armstrong stretched out his hand and said, "Pax?"

Smith looked at his hand like it was a venomous snake and, after a moment, took it and in a surprisingly civil tone replied, "Pax."

Immediately, Jack enthusiastically said, "Great! So, what brings you kids out this way?"

Smith's civil tone seemed to slide right off her dagger-eyes. "We're on military assignment."

"I understand," Armstrong replied, looking like he actually did. "Hush-hush and all that. Well, by the looks of you I suppose you've seen some of them spider-creatures hustling about."

It sounded like a question but Sarah knew it wasn't. Captain Smith looked weary, as if she wasn't sure how much to tell this civilian. Sarah was tired of what she considered to be pointless cloak-and-dagger maneuverings so she volunteered, "We've seen them. When and where did you last see them?"

For the first time he looked at Sarah and gave her a short but appraising look. Sarah recognized it as the same look her grandfather used to send her way when he was pleasantly surprised by something she'd done. Armstrong began to talk, seemingly to everyone. "A couple of days back I saw them come through this way. They were heading west. I ain't never seen nothing like that before. A huge procession of the creatures they were, but nearly silent as they paraded past here, except for that weird sound they make," he added, almost as an afterthought.

Jack paused, perhaps waiting for Smith to politely ask him for further information, like what he might have learned. She didn't, so he continued, "I saw them coming a little ways off so I hustled over into the waterfall. I barely had time to hide before they were walking all through this area."

Sarah shivered at the thought that the Enemy had been *right there*, and so recently!

Jack took his knife out again and didn't seem to notice Smith's caution automatically increase. He pulled a half-finished carving out of a back pocket and continued to whittle on it. As he carved, he spoke. "I watched them carefully while they walked by. They glided over that hill there to the west and then were gone as quick as they'd arrived." He looked over at the rapidly setting sun and seemed to take a moment to enjoy the sunset. "When I was sure they'd gone, I came out of the water, and by gum I was glad to be out of there. It was getting right cold in there." Sarah found it odd that he spoke of such a terrifying experience with such a charming and ready laugh. "Funny thing though. They were moving so fast, I never dreamed they'd have a rearguard."

He turned himself around and looked into the east at the moon that was already well on its way to its apex. "Well, that blasted rearguard Spider saw me and I knew what I had to do, but I was amazed how blindingly fast it came at me. All I had on me was my knife." He smirked at Sarah and then said, "That was one tough critter, but they bleed and die like anything else if you stab them deep."

Not waiting for Smith to give her blessing, Sarah blurted, "That's amazing that you survived. We fought them a few days back."

For a handful of heartbeats no one said anything. Jack just stared at her and then each one in turn, looking uncharacteristically grim. Then he was back to his normal, cheerful self. "Well, I'm sorry things didn't turn out better for you kids."

He stood up and seemed to be unaware that he'd put his knife and wood carving away. Finally, he finished with, "So where are you headed?"

With a look of exasperation and entirely no desire to reveal that information (or any other), Smith replied, "We're heading for a military outpost. It should be west of here." Smith waited for the unavoidable gasps and groans from her three companions to run their course. She was all too aware that she wasn't exactly free with the sharing of information. "We're on our way their now. We should be arriving there some time in the middle of the night tonight."

"Well, since I know you won't ask, I suppose I should volunteer to help," Jack said, "seeing how it's the Enemy that you're tangling with." He began to move over to a lean-to that Sarah hadn't noticed before. "Just give me a second and I'll be ready to go. Wouldn't do to have some soldiers get lost or killed."

Though he said it all with a smile and not a shred of arrogance or condescension, Smith looked like she was ready to have an aneurism. *Maybe she really is,* Sarah thought hopefully.

"You're not coming. I'm barely willing to tolerate having her along," the captain said rather authoritatively while pointing at Sarah. Upon pointing at her, Jack gave her a warm smile. Smith continued, "I'm the leader of this expedition and I'm fully qualified to get the job done. So, you can just stick around here, Grizzly Adams."

Again, her cold disdain just slid right off Armstrong as if he hadn't even heard her. He finished pulling together his meager belongings, put his pack on and then said, "Well, I'm ready to go. I know just where this military camp of yours is. Follow me."

He headed out and Sarah immediately followed, finding him to be very pleasant and charming. She also felt very safe with him. Sergeant Jameson and Private Stansbury looked at each other and then followed. Captain Smith stood there, staring at the four people walking away. She couldn't believe it. She felt like yelling out some orders, getting angry and threatening them with court-marshals, or something else, but nothing came out. She quickly thought and realized that, for the moment, there was nothing she could really do except follow along with everyone else.

One thing Sarah noticed was the way Armstrong moved through the forest. He seemed to slide along their path in his easy going manner, looking for all the world like he wasn't in a potentially dangerous situation—and he was quiet, really quiet. He scarcely made a sound unless he was speaking. Sarah couldn't tell for sure but he seemed to see almost as well as someone with the goggles. No, it wasn't what he could <u>see</u> exactly. He just seemed to be able to...<u>perceive</u> what was out there, all of his senses continuously alert.

Just after midnight the moon broke out upon them from behind the trees. It was a relief to again have more light than the intermittent glow of slivered moonlight and shadow. Sarah could again make out the occasional opening to a rabbit warren and the individual leaves on the white firs and sugar pines that they passed. She noted to herself, *It's like walking in a dream.*

A twig snapped and she instantly came out of her reverie, silently chiding herself for her lax attention to the potential dangers around them. They all stopped and Private Jameson looked sheepishly at each of them and mouthed, "Sorry."

They proceeded along the path that Armstrong had selected. Sarah was certain that Smith was mentally reviewing their map at every bend in the stream to make certain they were still heading the right way. Apparently they were since she wasn't saying anything to change their heading or call a halt to their progress.

Sarah noted with amazement how sure-footed and *aware* Jack seemed to be. Without a map he moved like he was part of the forest. He might have been a raccoon passing through the night, stealthily creeping along a trail, following it by instinct. *No,* Sarah thought. *He's not a raccoon. He's a wolf.* She found herself watching him from behind, noting the sure gait that was clearly not an act. She thought back to a few hours earlier when he had quickly and easily bested Smith, a very capable and fierce combatant in her own right, and not much more than half his age. *Who is this guy?* she repeated to herself throughout the night, *and what's his story?*

An hour or three after midnight, Armstrong called a halt and hustled everyone into a stand of western larch. "The camp you're looking for is just around this bend," he whispered. "Maybe another half mile." He let his glance smoothly move across each of them. He ended with Captain Smith and held her gaze. Despite her scowl, his country smile never faltered. "If you want to follow this path, we can do that. Or we can come in through the bush. What do you want to do?"

Smith glared at him and Sarah couldn't help thinking, *Oh, grow up!* Finally the captain said, "If everything's okay there, we could get shot coming out of the woods." She paused and let her scowl slide off her face only for a moment. She continued, "But if the Enemy has already assaulted this place there won't be anyone to shoot at us. Not from our side anyway." Sarah could tell she was just about to give the order, probably to leave the path when she looked up. "I think the camp is wiped out and, on the path, the Enemy will have to come out of hiding a little bit more to attack us...."

Unless they use their guns that shoot that green and red stuff, Sarah quietly finished the sentence. As she looked at the ground she thought she saw small, circular indentations peppered here and there. She thought those might be the footprints the Spiders left behind.

"We take the path," Smith said firmly.

Armstrong looked at her with his calm smile and his eyes seemed to salute her. Perhaps this was due to her assessment of the situation. *Had he been testing her? Maybe curious about what she would decide?* Sarah suspected that, should they be ambushed, Armstrong was even more likely to survive than Smith.

They moved off and headed down the path, every sense at a higher state of alertness than they'd been all night. Moving slowly, they searched the surrounding bushes, trees and dips in the topography for any sign of danger. The three soldiers seemed to look all directions at once, rifles held at the ready. Sarah unconsciously slid her hand across the sheath that held her large knife, making sure the strap that held it in place was secure, her other hand silently adjusting the homemade spear, rolling it along her fingers until it felt "just right." Armstrong was the only one whose level of preparedness did not seem to have changed at all. Sarah got the feeling that this was a guy who had "been everywhere and done everything." Twice.

After a ten-minute eternity of walking along the well-used path, they came around a large copse of noble firs and there it was, Oscar-Romeo-6. Even from that distance, Sarah could tell it had been destroyed. The mood suddenly turned from cautious and alert to deathly somber. All five of them stood there quietly and crestfallen for several seconds.

Surprisingly, the main gate was still sound. Jameson slowly moved it out of their way. They stayed fairly close together as they moved through the camp, checking for survivors, careful to make as little noise as possible. It took about an hour and, when they were done, they'd found nothing living. As in Oscar-Romeo-17, there were painfully more dead people than there were dead Spiders.

When their search was obviously winding down, Smith signaled everyone to come join her. They huddled together in the shelter of the only building left standing. It looked like it had belonged to the commanding officer. The inside was scored with residue of the green slag. It appeared the stuff had been splattered around the room. Everything that it had touched had disintegrated in varying amounts.

They knelt down together in a tight circle so that they could speak to each other without having to do more than whisper. Skipping the obvious, like stating that everyone in the camp was dead, Smith spoke. "All right. We have to assume that Command doesn't know about this camp or our own. We need to get that information to them. Maybe we can advise them before more camps are lost. Like our own, the radio equipment here has been destroyed. So, we head for the nearest city."

As she began to pull out her map, Jack volunteered, "If I may?"

Smith stopped what she was doing to glare poison-tipped daggers at him. After a moment she tiredly and unhappily said, "Go ahead."

"Thanks," he replied with a genuine smile. "The nearest town is Point Terrace. We should be able to get there in...oh, I'd say four days if we keep up a good pace."

"Point Terrace?" Sarah queried. "I know every nook and cranny around here and I've never heard of that."

He smiled inwardly to himself. "There's not much there. I guess you probably wouldn't even call it a village," he chuckled. "More like a...settlement, I suppose. But it's the closest thing we'll find." Jack looked up and with a twinkle in his eye said, "And they have a shortwave radio."

Sarah interrupted. "By the way," she said as all eyes turned to her. "What the heck are those weapons the Spiders use?"

Offended by her supposed impertinence, the fiery red-haired women replied, "What are you talking about?"

Trying not to look incompetent, Sarah plodded on. "Those guns they use that fire the green and red stuff. What are they? What is that stuff?"

Rolling her eyes in annoyance as she would with a child, Smith replied, "We call them SPAWNs. It stands for Semisolid Projectile Annihilative WeapoN. As you saw, they're nasty things. The green stuff they shoot burns like acid and the red stuff explodes on contact with any solid object."

Satisfied with the answer, Sarah merely nodded in acknowledgement.

Since it was still a few hours till dawn, they decided to finish looking around and see what they could salvage. At first they only found a few odds and ends that might prove useful. A handful of bullets here, an extra blanket there. When Jameson found an extra rifle and ammunition he proffered it to Sarah. She was mildly surprised to find that she didn't want it. She didn't feel an adverse reaction to the firearm like she had her first day in Oscar-Romeo-17. It was just that she was feeling sort of apathetic about fighting and battle.

"Please take it," Jameson insisted. "Later on, you'll probably need it."

Woodenly, suddenly feeling more tired than she had in days, Sarah took the gifts only so that she wouldn't have to go through the effort of discussion.

Soon, they explored an out-building that was partially destroyed. It took some time but they excavated the contents. After a short while of speechless searching and toil, everyone was startled to hear Jack exclaim, "Bingo! Look what we have here."

He had found the camp's food stores. He immediately began to haul out beans, tinned meats, some fresh fruits, vegetables and more. They couldn't believe it. It looked like a meal fit for a king and it tasted as good as it looked. They all sat together, enjoying their "evening" meal as dawn approached. For just a few minutes, they didn't feel like they were being hunted. They didn't feel like their world was about to be overrun or that an alien force was attempting to effect a genocide upon them and their species. It just felt...peaceful.

Since the Enemy had already destroyed Oscar-Romeo-6, they all figured it was a good bet they wouldn't be back. They found another outbuilding that was only partially destroyed and decided to bed down within it for the "night." It was, at best, a ramshackle prefab shed but it would certainly provide some protection from the elements and the Enemy. Not to mention, it removed them from most lines-of-sight.

Before Smith had a chance to voice an opinion, Jack said, "Sarah. How about you take the first watch." Captain Smith opened her mouth to give voice to her most decidedly negative attitude about this choice, but before she could speak Jack continued, "Wake me in a couple of hours and I'll take over."

For just a moment, Sarah thought he was unaware of how he seemed to be undermining Smith, or at least annoying her in a grand way, but when he finished speaking to her, he turned toward Smith and gave her a smile and a wink. He then lay down and was soon asleep.

Not sure what else to do, Sarah picked up her newly acquired weapon, the Tromix Jameson had given her a few hours earlier.

She made sure she had a full magazine loaded, just like she'd been taught by Sergeant Jameson back at Oscar-Romeo-17. She caught a satisfied nod from him as she finished preparing her weapon and took up her station by the shed's busted doorway.

After a pair of thoroughly uneventful hours, she gratefully woke Jack. She whispered, "Jack, your turn."

His eyes immediately snapped open, almost like he hadn't been sleeping at all. Though it was characteristically him, it was still weird to see someone get a smile on his face so quickly after being woken up after only two hours of sleep.

"Thanks. Get yourself some sleep, Kid."

She was asleep as soon as her head touched the piece of wood she was using for a pillow. It might as well have been goose down, it felt so good to rest.

After several hours, she woke up. The sun was well on its way down and everyone else was already awake.

They quickly finished gathering what supplies they thought they'd need and be able to carry.

Quietly, they moved out, lead again by Jack who seemed to be the only one who knew the way to Point Terrace. Sarah noted that they were indeed heading approximately north so perhaps he knew where he was going.

They silently trekked across the landscape, passing a myriad of plant life species. The gnarled, twisted pacific madrones had always interested Sarah. Their pealing bark, like paper, coming off in sheets made them especially interesting trees.

As the night wore on, the moon set early and made travel increasingly slow. Ears ever alert for a stray sound, Sarah felt like they were five radar stations working in concert.

As the last few shreds of moonlight permeated their way down through the canopy of trees, Jack pulled up short. At first he only stopped, immovable as a statue carved from strong and steady rock. Then his head turned very slowly, this way and that. Sarah noticed that despite the cold she was beginning to sweat. After a few silent moments, he knelt down, close to a nearby hairy manzanita tree. Stansbury and Jameson didn't seem to know what he was sensing but they immediately turned, facing the surrounding forest, forming a circle with Armstrong. Even Smith wasn't detecting anything with the night vision goggles. Sarah took up station between Jameson and Stansbury.

After several tense seconds, Jack slowly whispered in his measured voice, "There's something up ahead." Though a whisper, it seemed to shatter the stillness of the night like the crack of a whip. There was scarcely a breeze to rustle through the trees and mask his voice.

He slowly stood up again and, ever so cautiously, proceeded forward. They all followed, each one striving to be as aware of any impending danger as a mouse in a snake pit. It was unnerving and Sarah wanted to ask something. Anything! *What's he sensing? Is he really sensing anything?*

Sarah began to notice a strange smell—an unusual smell. Soon they crept around a thicket in their path and—

There it stood. Some kind of large, powerful, ape-like animal with a hoary glow of waning moonlight surrounding it.

CHAPTER 11
The Message and the Messenger

"They're here!" an aide exclaimed to President Griffith as he hurriedly entered the room. He was a beady-eyed, young man in his early thirties.

Dressed in a navy blue pants suit, she looked up at him with her perpetually angry eyes and squinted. Her eyes were tired from all the reading she'd been doing. She felt like she was trying to keep up with a country that seemed to be quickly unraveling like a tapestry where someone is pulling on the main thread. Except the tapestry of America seemed to have many different people, problems and aliens pulling on random threads all over the place. How she was supposed to hold it all together seemed beyond her, *But hold on to it I will*, she thought with unparalleled passion and resolve.

"Who's here?" she asked curtly.

"The spies you sent out to do recon. The SEALs. They're back."

"Excellent." She looked around at her makeshift office. She regretted that it was rectangular, not oval. Her desk was expensive mahogany, dyed a deep blood red. She liked it. The chairs around the office for guests were all made of oak. There was a bookcase off to the side and she had to admit that the literature it contained was, so far, just there for show. The ensemble was completed by a vase of artificial flowers. *How appropriate*, she thought. *There are probably plenty of people who believe my abilities and leadership are as fake as those flowers. Well, I'll show them. They'll see that I'm made of sterner stuff.*

"All right," she continued. "Alert the cabinet and all the other usual suspects. We'll be meeting in the main audience hall in fifteen minutes."

The young aide was gone in a flash. President Griffith stood and moved away from her desk. She afforded herself the luxury of rubbing her eyes one more time.

As she moved into the hallway she glanced at a wall clock and remarked the time–10:15 pm. A little late for a meeting but she knew everyone who would be in attendance was probably still awake. Besides, with the condition that things were in, they needed to endure some inconveniences if they were going to restore

America to her greatness, to say nothing of simply surviving as a species.

As the president walked down the hall, aides here and there were found to still be at work. She mentally noted who they were. She would need to be surrounded by good, solid people in the harder days to come. As she walked slowly, but with a purposeful stride designed to instill confidence, she returned polite greetings that were proffered her.

She turned a corner on her way to her destination and she silently mused, *As a new president there are so many things to do, especially under the conditions of this War. So many responsibilities. So many people to take care of. I'm the president of these United States of America.* She sighed. *So few people to trust. Which people do I trust with which secrets.*

As she entered the main audience hall she thought, *Plots within plots within... Secrets about everything—and I certainly have my own.*

A few minutes later, everyone had filed into the audience hall. There was Phil Johnson, the new secretary of commerce. Upon entering the room, President Griffith was not surprised to see him tugging on his ear. The man knew something was up and that type of thing always made him nervous.

Abe Smith was also present. The moment the secretary of agriculture walked into the room, Griffith realized the only reason she hadn't gotten rid of him was because she saw him as a useful idiot. He entered the room with John Dillon, the shrewd secretary of veterans affairs. *Why would they come at the same time? Are they working together in some sort of an alliance?* President Griffith made a mental note to keep an eye on their relationship.

A moment later, General Martin and Secretary of State Carmine Michaels entered the room at the same time. The president didn't spare a thought for the possibility of those two being in cahoots in any way. *Who knows. Perhaps their mutual animosity is a charade; I've heard of such things before,* the president considered. *But I wouldn't bet a plug nickel they were anything but enemies.*

Several other people arrived, primarily cabinet members. When it appeared that no one else would be arriving, President Griffith stood and immediately began addressing everyone. Looking at the guard at the back of the room she hailed, "Bring them in."

The guard saluted his commander-in-chief smartly and then ushered in the SEAL commander that had just arrived from his recon assignment. He walked past everyone and was very respectful. However, it was impossible not to note the deadly efficiency with which he held himself and moved toward the front of the room. The graceful way he walked suggested that he was equally effective at his job whether he had his weapons with him or, as was the case at this time, he was devoid of such armaments. His eyes moved continuously, seeking potential threats and plotting possible escape routes. Clearly this man knew his job and was awfully good at it.

When he had moved to the front of the room, the president again addressed everyone present. "This brave man and his team have just returned from a reconnaissance assignment. They were sent to collect as much information about the Enemy as they could get. Their focus was information associated with large groups of Enemy ground units." She turned and looked at the leader of the group and said, "Captain Nishomoto. You may share your findings."

The captain took a half-step forward and then resumed his stiffly, formal at-ease stance. His Japanese facial features and black hair were certainly not his most poignant characteristics. It was his eyes. They were bright and alert in a very healthy way. Everyone in the room, with the exception of General Martin, noted his impressive physique as something they would never experience personally.

The captain began, "Madame President, members of the cabinet, honored guests. My team was sent to what initially appeared to be a typical Enemy stronghold. We were transported by Humvee to a location sixteen kilometers out from the target site, the El Limón mine near Managua Lake in Nicaragua." Not being a diplomat or a politician, Captain Nishomoto did not pause for dramatic effect or for the information to sink in. No one was particularly surprised at the report of their incursion into a foreign country. What with the War, everyone knew it was incredibly challenging to maintain borders. "From there we proceeded on foot to the target. From approximately 1.5 kilometers out we began our surveillance."

President Griffith remembered reading this man's dossier and finding him to be a very precise, accurate, by-the-book soldier. He continued, "Of course, we knew this would not ultimately prove to be a useful location for surveillance since the information we would be able to acquire from there would likely be the same information our satellites already had. We assessed the best way to get closer to the mine and when night came we moved in, wearing night-vision goggles." As if on cue, all eyes in the audience made their way down the captain's uniform until settling on the goggles still hanging from his neck.

"Armed with ultrasonic, phase-cancellation silencers, we were able to eliminate any Enemy combatants as the need arose without alerting the rest of the base to our presence." That being said, several of the captain's listeners began to get an eager look in their eyes. Knowing the unspoken question regarding using the high-tech silencers to move in and wipe out a colony of Enemies would now be on the lips of his listeners, Captain Nishomoto decided to address the issue immediately. "Moving in to their strongholds and attempting to dispatch the Enemy one by one in this way would ultimately prove ineffective. We recognized that we would not have been able to eliminate very many of them before they were missed by their companions. We had to keep their casualties down to a minimum. I believe we only killed three of them."

Several of the pairs of watching eyes resumed their despondent caste. "As per our first objective, we attempted to gain access to the DEWs, and determine the feasibility of destroying them. Upon—."

President Jose Marquez of Brazil still hadn't found a way to get back to his country. With his thick Brazilian accent he interrupted, "Wait a moment. You say 'DEWs'. What is 'DEWs'?"

"Directed energy weapons," was the immediately reply.

President Marquez stared blankly at Captain Nishomoto, waiting for some elaboration. When it didn't come he queried further, "My English is not so good. What does 'directed energy weapon' means?"

Without skipping a beat Nishomoto explained, "Directed energy weapons are weapons that emit energy at a specific target. The energy is not transported via projectile. Rather it is like firing a wave of sonic energy, or electromagnetic interference or, as is the case with some of the Enemy DEWs, a HERF, a high-energy radio-frequency weapon. Essentially, their HERFs have been designed to disrupt the electronics of virtually anything we throw at them. Of course, we have our own HERFs but they're barely past the experimental stage. The main difference between the Enemy HERF and experimental models that we've devised is that their devices are tremendously more powerful and have a much higher range. That's why whenever we've attempted to send in any kind of a missile with an explosive payload, it's been shot down and detonated by the Enemies DEWs long before the missiles could hit their facilities."

He finally paused, presumably to allow those present to ask questions. The oily secretary of state, Carmine Michaels beat everyone else to the punch. "How deep into the facility did you and your men penetrate?"

In his no-nonsense way, Captain Nishomoto replied, "We managed to get approximately three hundred feet below the surface."

Michaels continued, "How did you manage to get that deep and only have to kill three of the Spiders? It seems like you would've run into more of them as you made your way through the tunnels."

The captain didn't look at all flustered. He'd faced terribly deadly enemies for many years. This was a time to relax, but he looked anything but relaxed. Wiping at a spot of blood on his uniform Nishomoto said, "We had access to the mine's blueprints and schematics. We used that information to enter the tunnels through a little used entry point nearly a kilometer from the main portal." He paused only a moment to look around. "From there we were able to move sufficiently deep into the mine to gather information regarding what the Enemy is up to."

The mood in the room increased in intensity. Had these men found the information that would prove to be a golden goose? Would the information they brought be useful? If so, would they be able to put it in to action in sufficiently short order, before the Enemy finished their genocide?

John Dillon, the intelligent secretary of veterans affairs who had previously shown the way to getting this recon mission under way asked, "Like everyone else here, I am understandably curious as to what you and your brave men have found. Please, do tell."

Unlike some soldiers in President Griffith's experience, this one didn't seem bothered by going through a Q&A with civilians. Though as a rule she wasn't particularly impressed with soldiers, she found this one to be tolerable.

The captain looked at Mr. Dillon and replied, "Not being geologists, we were not able to make any determinations visually. Therefore, we had to acquire specimens of the materials being mined so that we might have a better idea what they were up to." He paused and gave the slightest smile, "That's where our three zombies...er...dead Enemies come in."

The president noticed a mild amount of token laughter at the captain's quip. *For his sake, I hope he never takes up stand-up comedy,* the president thought.

Nishomoto continued, "We took our samples with us and quickly made our way to the evac chopper so that we could get the ore samples analyzed for the purpose of determining what the Enemy is pursuing in mines around the world. We had a pair of geologists standing by in the chopper so we could have the minerals identified as quickly as possible."

With that he simply stepped back and resumed a statue-like stance. Immediately another man who'd entered the room at the onset of the meeting stood up, carrying a fairly large box to the front of the chamber, and began placing various minerals and ores on the podium. Most people in the room quickly surmised that this must have been the more senior of the two geologists. The man didn't say a word while he removed the samples from the box. In fact, he looked surprisingly calm, as if he were relishing the surprise he was about to spring.

When he finished unloading his box, he turned and faced his audience. He had a long, white, heavy beard. Little of his face was visible behind that castaway beard. As some of the people in the room looked at him, they noticed something was niggling at the back of their minds, like a dull scratching. Something of recognition, but they couldn't put their fingers on what it was. Some were surprised to find their skin become involuntarily clammy. The president looked at Secretary of State Carmine Michaels and noticed even he seemed to be having a similar reaction.

"Hello," the man began in a Russian accent as thick as his ample beard. "These are the samples that were retrieved from the mine. From what these men have told me there was a substantial amount of each of these minerals being mined." Though his accent was thick, he spoke English fluently and was understood with little difficulty. He paused to cock his head in salute to the SEAL, but the president thought it looked like he saw the soldier as being beneath him, or maybe a tool to use and then discard.

"This first one," he resumed, "is altaite. This mineral is known to have little or no use. As you can see, it primarily makes a beautiful paper-weight." Unlike Captain Nishomoto's joke, this one got a little bit of genuine laughter. *This guy is better at working a crowd*, the president thought. He continued, "This next one is chalcopyrite. Its primary use is in making copper. This last one is acanthite. Similar to chalcopyrite, nature uses acanthite to make silver."

The man stood looking...smug? What was he waiting for? Mr. Dillon didn't wait. "What can you deduce from this combination of elements?"

The bearded stranger replied, "There is no known single substance that these *minerals* make when combined."

As the man paused for a moment, the president happened to look over at General Martin. He seemed to be, of all things, squirming in his chair. It was ever so slight, but apparently something was tugging at the back of his mind as well, and she could tell it had everything to do with the newcomer.

President Griffith decided it was time to speak up. "Though we don't yet know why this material is being mined, I think it's safe to say that it's most likely being excavated for some military purpose. Wouldn't you agree General?"

Griffith knew she was right and didn't require the general's consent on the matter. She just wanted to catch him off guard. She was only mildly pleased with the results. *That man is almost as unflappable as Dillon.*

"Yes, Ma'am," Martin quickly agreed. "So, the question that leaves us with is 'what do you get when you mix these three minerals?'" He looked directly at the geologist as he stated the query.

Smiling a well-hidden, disdainful smile, the geologist replied in his cock-sure way. "It's not as easy as that. There is no magic blender that will combine these substances and tell us what the result is. Unfortunately, it could take months, perhaps years to figure this out." He paused to...enjoy?...the hopeless looks on the faces of his audience. At last he continued, ticking off a finger with each statement, "There are the different amounts of each mineral to combine that needs to be considered. There's also the temperature at which they're combined." The man was really in his element now, lecturing people-of-power. "And don't forget the order in which the minerals are combined. Of course, there's the different means of combining: pressure, temperature—"

"We get the point," President Griffith cut him off. "We will of course devote as many resources as we can to you and a team discovering the secret of this mystery."

General Martin was still wiggling around in his seat, obviously thinking furiously. Then, as suddenly as he had begun fidgeting, he stopped and turned to his aide, Lieutenant Malistair. He whispered something to her and she immediately arose and departed the room. The president figured it wasn't important. The man had probably forgotten to take some kind of medication. With his main aide on his errand, he sat down.

The president returned her attention to the ensuing discussion. Ideas were being bandied about regarding how these minerals might be used to make anything from weapons to structures to hydroponics facilities. Nothing seemed to make sense. At last, the president cut into the discussion and asked the geologist, "Sir, you mentioned various ways to combine these minerals. Now, I recognize that there are likely many factors involved regarding the process the Enemy is using to make...whatever they're making. How else might they be combined?"

The geologist looked apathetic and replied, "I'm not exactly certain. That's not my specialty. I think your question might be better answered by a chemist or perhaps a physicist."

All eyes turned towards him and more than one person wondered at his flippant attitude. There were several people in the room who thought to themselves, *Prima donnas!*

While this was taking place, Martin's aide returned. The lieutenant looked slightly flushed. She must've hurried to do whatever task she'd been given. Griffith noticed out of the corner of her eye that the aide resumed her seat and then handed some papers to the general. He immediately began leafing through them. After several moments he cut into the discussion.

General Martin said, "Madame President, as this geologist was making his report, I couldn't help but remember something." For some reason, the geologist took on a look of mild concern but it was gone as quick as it had come. Martin resumed, "A few months back I vaguely remembered looking through a report on the destruction of L.A." He paused and couldn't help the catch in his throat. Most people in the room were just as sympathetic. Even Martin's nemesis, Secretary of State Michaels, did not take the opportunity to prod him. He too had lost loved ones in that battle. He too still hurt.

The general quickly got himself under control and continued. "I remembered something in the report that, at the time, seemed pointless and almost certainly inconsequential." He rubbed his eyes, looking tired. "It was a chemical analysis of various affected objects from the attack. More specifically, it was an analysis of anything that had contact with the materials from the Enemy's orbital bombardments." Now he stopped looking emotional and sad and began to take on his characteristic look of initiative and confidence. "Now, I haven't verified that similar reports summarizing other battles will tell the same story, but this one," he tossed the hardcopy of the L.A. report onto the middle of the massive table, "shows that there are detectible amounts of altaite, chalcopyrite, and acanthite." Suddenly all noises in the room ceased. Someone immediately grabbed the report General Martin had tossed down and began leafing through it until he found the information he sought. It was indeed as the general had stated!

"Therefore," Phil Johnson, the secretary of commerce, took up the dialogue, "that must mean that the Enemy is using these ores in their attacks! Probably as ammunition!" He was so excited he had forgotten to nervously tug on his ear.

"I think that's safe to say," the geologist chimed in, "but explain to me how these minerals are being combined or what use they could possibly have as some sort of weapon, other than a blunt object."

That raised a few eyebrows, and not just because no one knew the answer to his question. Nearly everyone in the room experienced at least some measure of surprise at the newcomer's almost egotistical attitude regarding the discussion.

The pause in the discussion didn't last long. It was broken by Carmine Michaels. "Who cares how they combine it! We can figure that out later. What matters now is that these materials are apparently part, or all, of what the Enemy uses in its orbital attacks. Like the one on L.A."

President Griffith found it interesting to note that, as Michaels progressed through his brief soliloquy, the geologist became more and more red-faced and upset while General Martin's grin grew in size. When Michaels finished, he looked over at Martin and, for just a moment, they shared a look that held no aggression or animosity. That shared look was not lost on the president. *Perhaps I may have to keep those two at odds,* she thought. *They could be a very powerful alliance if they end up getting along.*

After Secretary of State Michaels made his pronouncement, the room erupted into a minor form of celebration. A few minutes of glad-handing and back-slapping later, the president called for order. "I'm proud of what we've been able to accomplish tonight. I think we have a pretty good idea which way we need to head. With this information, we just might be able to stop the crippling orbital bombardments from resuming. I'm sure we'll soon have a counter-attack put in place." Again there was an impromptu celebration of clapping. "And we owe a lot of it to General Martin and this good man," President Griffith proclaimed while pointing at the general and the geologist. Then, looking only at the latter, she said, "I admit, I should've asked sooner. What is your name?"

The geologist seemed to positively glow with something akin to triumph, or at least elation. He stood up and, basking in his moment of revelation, he pronounced, "Though you may doubt it, my name is Dr. Nicolai Reznikov." The shocked response that he'd hoped for certainly left nothing to be desired. It climaxed when he heard a hushed whisper from somewhere in the room...

"The Butcher of Bryanskaya!"

CHAPTER 12
From Forest to Jungle

No, not large, Sarah thought with wild fascination. *It's huge! Like a grizzly bear.* Only it wasn't like any kind of bear she'd ever seen before. It roughly had the form of a large gorilla, but with a somewhat more human-looking face.

Her first sensation was gratitude there were plenty of automatic weapons around her. That thing looked like it could tear someone's arm off–literally! It was covered in smoky gray hair mottled with some darker color that was almost black. Its coat had a beautiful sheen and its apparent softness belied the obvious power so poorly hidden underneath. The creature stood seven or eight feet tall. *It's like looking up into the face of a mountain. Or a tempest.*

Sarah spared a brief, peripheral glance at her companions. They all looked as thunderstruck as she felt. Sergeant Jameson and Private Stansbury both appeared to be doing their best to hold on to their courage. Captain Smith was tenaciously keeping her fear in check by holding her firearm in a white-knuckle grip. Sarah wasn't entirely certain how Jack was holding out since he was still in the point position and had his back to the rest of the group. From behind, he definitely did *not* look relaxed. However, he didn't appear to be petrified with fear. His posture seemed to suggest that he recognized an unusually large potential threat but that he could handle the situation.

Sarah was surprised that she noticed the sounds of crickets chirping. In fact, they hadn't ever broken their rhythm. The presence of this mountain of a creature had not caused a stir in nature's nighttime alarm system. *What is this thing?* Sarah continued to marvel. Thoughts furiously flashed through her mind. *Is it one of the Enemy? If it is, it sure doesn't look anything like the others I've seen. This one appears to be somewhat humanoid in form. Maybe it's one of their slaves or thralls. Maybe it's one of their ruling class. It couldn't be some undiscovered indigenous species. Humans would have found it by now, what with its size!*

She was surprised how quiet the creature was, standing before her and staring at them all through calm, unblinking eyes. Its eyes didn't look very savage and the loud, heavy breathing she would've expected was oddly absent. It merely breathed quietly, like a human.

Though it felt to Sarah like all of her observations must've taken several minutes to digest, she knew it couldn't have been more than a bare handful of heartbeats that had transpired.

She noticed the barrel of Smith's gun being raised to train itself on the creature. Before Sarah could hinder or encourage Smith's violent reaction she heard the most unbelievable thing of all.

"May your jungle ever run free. My name are sp'atung."

Sarah slowly turned her head back toward the creature. She heard Private Stansbury incredulously ask the creature, "Did you just speak?"

For the moment, all eyes were on the creature but with less threat-sense and more awe and curiosity. The creature seemed to smile but Sarah couldn't be sure. She'd never experienced anything like this before.

"Yes. I spoked," sp'atung replied. "What you doing here? Look like lost wolf pups." It sounded like the creature was chewing on its words, or like it had marbles in its mouth.

Without missing a beat, Jack spoke up. "We're heading to one of our villages." He paused and then returned the question, "What are you doing here?"

For some reason, Sarah found it to be ridiculous and almost comical that Jack had asked this creature a question, but why not? Everything else that had happened to her seemed impossible as well. Hanging out with the Army, aliens attacking the Earth, her killing an alien with a machine gun, and now a walking, talking gorilla that speaks and understands English. Why not?

Sp'atung replied, "I looking for to you." Somehow, sp'atung managed to look a little sheepish. The face it made seemed very incongruous with its naturally ferocious mien. If not for the gravity of the situation, Sarah might've laughed.

"You were looking for us?" Smith nearly sputtered, not lowering her weapon. From behind Sarah, she sounded incredulous and as ferocious as sp'atung looked. Smith quickly continued in her typically clipped tone, "Why are you looking for us?"

The hairy creature took one step forward toward Jack, placing him closer than anyone wanted to be to it. Every weapon, including Jack's, immediately found itself in a more urgent grip, ready for anything. "I is not looking for all you. I want meet one or two sen'."

Confused, Sarah inquired, "What does sen' mean?"

The creature smiled broadly and, if Sarah wasn't mistaken, earnestly. It spread its arms around as if to encompass them all and repeated, "Sen'."

The humans all seemed to understand it meant them. Then the creature added, "Muchly you." It was pointing at Sarah. Sp'atung looked at each person and seemed to become aware of their attitude. "Oh, I am sorry," it said, backing up a step or two. "Those of my mi'tuhng talk close each other."

Awed at the whole situation, Sarah asked, "You mean, you like to get in people's personal space?"

Smiling broadly, it replied, "Yes! That is it. It like flowers. Must be close to enjoy." Sp'atung stepped forward again.

Sarah could feel the icy grip of fear clutch at her heart again. *What's going on? What is this...thing talking about? Me? There must be some mistake? Maybe it wasn't such a bad idea that Smith keep her gun trained on this...sp'atung.*

Noticing the fear and worry on the faces of its audience, sp'atung announced, "No fear. I not here harm you. I want know with you and your ways." It paused and turned away looking...wistful? "The way of many rounds ago." Sp'atung turned back toward them and his excitement returned. "Come. I want learn from you, but this not good place, not for talk. Let us go over to place more secret-like."

It slowly began walking away through the trees. Dumbfounded and scarcely able to talk, let alone move, the five travelers huddled up. Everyone seemed to speak at once.

"Where is that thing going?"

"Do you think it's dangerous?"

"I've never seen anything like it before in my life, and I've been on Safari a few times."

"What do you think we should do?"

After a brief debate, Smith made a decision, "Let's follow it. This could be...useful." She said it with a mischievous twinkle in her eye. Sarah wondered at that. She figured she wasn't the only one.

As they began walking in the direction they'd seen sp'atung go, in the distance they heard, "Come. Follow me." That garbled voice was like nothing they'd ever heard before, and yet it blended in with the forest surprising well. It seemed to Sarah that sp'atung's voice was as indigenous to the woods as trees and streams.

After a few minutes the group of travelers caught up to the creature. Seeing its massively muscled body, they all kept their distance, weapons at the ready. At first, they walked in silence. Then Jack's curiosity got the better of him.

"Are you from around here?"

"Yes," the walking behemoth casually replied with a smile that said this creature knew nothing of guile. "I have travel this jungle many rounds."

Jack quickly inquired, "What do you mean by 'rounds'?"

The large, hairy creature looked quizzically at Jack, apparently surprised that the smaller individual was unfamiliar with such a basic concept. At last it replied, "It is time it takes land go from hot, to cold, and back hot."

Keeping his eyes on the behemoth, Jack exclaimed, "Years. You mean years."

"Yes, that is word you know."

Jack was beginning to warm up to the creature and continued asking questions. "Are you a male or female?"

Looking mildly surprised, sp'atung replied, "You are curious as me." And then realizing it had made some sort of joke, sp'atung began to laugh uproariously. The sound of its laughter was a powerful, rumbling noise. At first, Sarah and her four companions found the creature's laughter to be a little unsettling, but they quickly discerned that it was founded in genuine mirth and they soon lost some of their temerity.

"I male."

At first, they'd found his speech pattern to be a little difficult to understand, but they quickly became accustomed to his version of English and rocks-in-the-mouth sound when he spoke.

"You said you wanted to meet Sarah. Why?" Jack asked like a protective older brother.

"Sarah?" sp'atung replied, struggling to pronounce the word. "Her?" He was pointing right at her. His powerful hand was unnervingly close to her. She involuntarily stopped in the path and became keenly aware of the heightened sense of alert her companions resumed. Sp'atung continued as if he hadn't noticed. Perhaps he didn't understand what guns were. "She the only human I seen more than once."

That sent a shiver down Sarah's spine. It seemed to transmit a bone-deep cold throughout her body. *I have a stalker, and it's a monster,* she thought numbly. *If I ever get out of this alive, I'm writing off men of all species!*

"I seen her asil or katis times before," sp'atung continued as they walked.

"What is 'asil' and...that other word?" Sarah courageously asked.

Sp'atung stopped and looked at her askance before holding up his fingers, two on one hand and three on the other. When his human companions seemed to understand he continued walking. Between his long legs and the pale, glowing cast of the moon, it almost seemed like he glided along the forest floor. It reminded Sarah of seeing people on moving sidewalks at airports. Speaking to Sarah he resumed, "I first see you naqs round ago." Before they could ask what naqs meant, he held up one finger. "You care about my jungle. I watch you do things. Then you leave."

Sp'atung seemed to think the conversation was over. After a minute, as Jack was about to venture another question, sp'atung began speaking again. "I think I not see you again. That fine. Then I see you again. Not many suns ago. I know not how talk you without break law, so I make marks on trees for you." He brandished his powerful arms for effect. This time, the firearms didn't come up as quickly.

A look of realization and understanding came over Sarah's face. "So it was you all along. That's a relief...I guess." She didn't sound entirely certain. "I was afraid it was the beginning of some weird rash of vandalism."

"Wait a minute," Jack quickly interjected. "You said something about breaking a law. What were you talking about?" Jack appeared to be genuinely interested, but concerned as well.

"My mi'tuhng—", sp'atung began.

"My'tong?" Sarah queried, struggling mildly to pronounce the strange word.

"Tribe," came the simple response.

Like a knife being unsheathed, Smith asked, "How many more of you are there?"

Sp'atung stopped and just stared at them for several moments. "I forgotten how curious and hurry you sen' are." With that, he began walking again. "My mi'tuhng has law sen' no talk with us ever."

He kept walking.

Behind sp'atung, the five hastily exchanged glances and then, as if by mutual consent, came to a halt. Hearing them stop, sp'atung followed suit and sat down. He appeared to be taking a rest. He didn't seem to notice the abruptness of their decision to cease moving forward.

Looking marginally flustered, Smith stepped forward and spoke. "Where are we headed?"

As if his answer were of no matter, he replied, "My cave."

With that, the five humans began to look more worried and less intent on learning more about this mysterious species.

After another minute of swimming in feelings of exasperation, Sergeant Jameson asked, "Didn't you just tell us about your law? Wouldn't you taking us to your me'toong (he struggled over the word) be in violation of that law?"

Their fear and trepidation was quickly getting replaced by frustration. *Maybe we've stumbled upon the only creature from this village that isn't playing with a full deck,* Sarah considered. *Or maybe it's something more nefarious.*

"Yes," was the simple response.

With no further explanation forthcoming, Smith asked, "Then why would you take us there? What's your game, sp'atung?" Her weapon was rock-steady in her well-trained hands.

Finally, the creature elaborated. "I keep you safe at cave. Times is changing. I see what Tarantulas are doing. They not interested in hunt my people—yet. I see way they hunt and eat, like bears when crazy." Then he paused for a minute or two as they began walking again. When he resumed, Sarah thought she was able to recognize a melancholy note in his gravelly voice. "I think they not just want destroy sen'. They will come for my mi'tuhng."

After several moments, sp'atung spoke again. "We be at cave in few breaths. Stay close me. My mi'tuhng not know how react to me bring you to cave." His calm, relaxed voice seemed at odds with the severity of the situation. Nevertheless, he continually exuded optimism.

They continued walking but they were as wary as they had been during the attack on Oscar-Romeo-17.

What are we doing? This is insane! Sarah could hear the screams of her own thoughts echoing through her mind. *I hate being scared. I've had enough of it!*

Suddenly they heard a slight rustling in the trees above them. "We there almost. That sound in trees is my people going back to cave to make Lat' know we come."

Sp'atung stopped suddenly. He just stood there in the middle of the path. He didn't move for an entire minute. Just as one of them was about to ask him if he'd had a stroke or something like that, he began walking again. "I want give my people time to be ready for us."

They came around a bend in the path and they saw a cave. Sp'atung motioned to them that this was the way to go. From the outside it didn't look inhabited. It didn't even look like there'd been foot-traffic around it.

Without stopping sp'atung lead them straight in. At first the cave was like any other–dark and foreboding. Then the group soon saw a faint, distant light deep within the recesses of the unending maw. More than one of the newcomers wondered silently how big the cave was and if it was naturally formed or made by these creatures. *What have we gotten ourselves into?* Sarah thought with more than a little trepidation.

They continued walking and it seemed like an eternity before they reached a source of light within, a bend in the cave that lead to a surprisingly large chamber. The room was huge! It could've held hundreds of people. It was well lit and full of torches lining the walls on curiously crafted stone mountings built into the hard rock. The ceiling was fairly high as well. It must've reached up twenty-five feet in the middle of the room. Peppered around the room were found examples of cave art, but not like anything Sarah had ever seen before. Several of the pictures were savage and barbaric, with slashes of reds and blacks cutting across the indistinct images behind. Other wall paintings seemed to purposely form a clear counterpoint. There were pictures of four-legged animals dancing on their hind legs. There were others in which the animals were walking on their forelegs. Sarah would've loved to have spent more time right then enjoying and marveling at the plethora of raw beauty around her.

Except the room wasn't empty.

The massive chamber of art and light was full of creatures that looked like sp'atung. *This must be his village or tribe.* There were dozens and dozens of them. Upon looking at so many of them, she thought she could maybe tell the difference between the males and the females. She most certainly took note of the ones that appeared to be more ferocious and the ones that seemed to be a little more docile. Again she marveled, *What have we gotten ourselves into?* She was surprised to hear the words with her ears. She looked over and saw that Stansbury had said what she'd been thinking.

They kept walking as a small group until they neared the middle of the large chamber. Sarah definitely did not like that position. She figured Captain Smith was liking it even less and was mentally setting up multiple contingency plans, strike, and counter-strike options. Sarah turned and noticed that the way they'd come had subtly, but quickly, become cut off by some of the creatures. They were now completely surrounded and most certainly out of their element.

As Sarah futilely attempted to assess the situation, one of the creature's children scampered out past the large ring of adults. It was chasing what appeared to be a pet badger. The badger was making its characteristic clicking sound, apparently oblivious to the tense situation surrounding it. The pet snapped his strong jaws at the child but the youngling moved its arm away from the badger's teeth and smacked it on the nose. Just as the child caught its pet, one of the adults scooped them both up and moved them out of the ring of adults.

The stand-off continued.

But only for a moment. Sp'atung finally spoke. "My friends, qualut. I know bring sen' here bad. Please wait. I bring them here for good choice." The other creatures didn't seem impressed. Sarah was surprised that she felt less fearful than she had at the battle of Oscar-Romeo-17, if only a little. For some reason she felt like she should say something but had no idea what it should be.

Sp'atung continued. "I find these sen' like water moving through jungle, they no find me. So if punishment be give, it mine, no them."

Sarah noticed that sp'atung seemed to be focusing his speech on three of his fellows at one end of the chamber. *I wonder if they're the ones who do the punishing?*

Sp'atung then said, "We not hasty people, not like these sen'. Listen me before you make decide about this."

Sarah's mind was whirling. This seemed to be going from worse to worst, but she noticed those same three creatures trace circles in the air, which Sarah took to mean that they agreed. They didn't look particularly friendly or cheerful, but at least it appeared that they wouldn't be attacked immediately.

"Speak your words, sp'atung," one of the three said. Like sp'atung, that one also sounded like she was speaking with marbles in her mouth.

Sp'atung bowed and proceeded. "Thank you Lat' tuhngiqr. You know the Tarantulas that have come to our jungle, on xexnut (9) legs and hunt kill all animals. They kill naqs of us. The Tarantulas. In my stridings through jungle I learn what they are." At this point, Sarah noticed many of the creatures began to look marginally less hostile and give nearly all their focus to sp'atung. *They're interested in what he's saying. They must not yet know what the Spiders are or where they come from.*

"They not from our jungle. They come from far away. From sky."

Immediately, one of the creatures spoke up, "Sp'atung, you crazy. He break the law of this mi'tuhng. What foolishness—"

He was cut off by tuhngiqr. "You be silent til it your place to speak." Sarah noticed that the narrow faced tuhngiqr had a clean white pelt with streaks of dark green running from head to toe. The visual effect was dazzling.

Without waiting for further discussion, sp'atung resumed. "I know it seem crazy, think what we seem to these dumb sen'." Jack gave a snort, thinking it to be a funny joke. Stansbury looked fearful. Jameson appeared to be ready to lose his lunch. Smith just scowled. "These sen' and all sen' not know other thinkers live other than them—until Tarantulas come. They like ants that live own hole, see no more." He paused and then said, "The sen' fight the Tarantulas for many suns. They fight alone."

"What you are saying?" tuhngiqr inquired warily, a steel blade in a velvet sheath.

"We help the sen'. I know it been many rounds since we talk to them. The time is good to do again."

One of the individuals standing next to tuhngiqr said, "It their fight. The Tarantulas only bother us naqs (1) time! We no like humans, we no hunt each other and all other things."

Sarah noticed that the anger in that one's words appeared to be a fairly wide-felt sentiment.

Sp'atung replied, "You no seen the killing the Tarantulas have done on our food, the animals of our jungle. When it stop? It only moons of time before Tarantulas know of us and hunt us. What then? I not think they let us live, not when Tarantulas know we can hunt them..."

His words hung in the air like a cloud that could blow in any direction with the slightest breeze. After several moments of no one speaking, another in the ring of adults exclaimed, "The sen' not found us. Tarantulas will not either." The slur against humans was not lost on Sarah. Still, she knew that humans did have a tendency to allow their inquisitiveness to drive them to acts of horror. She couldn't blame the creature that had spoken.

Sp'atung replied again, "The sen' not try kill a whole mi'tuhng. They have their hunts and some those hunts are terrible. From what I seen and learn, the Tarantulas not interested in control like the sen', but kill all and hunt all who might fight. As you say, the Tarantulas even kill many dumb beasts of jungle."

Again a long pause stole over the room. Sarah thought, *Sp'atung isn't a few fries short of a happy meal. He's actually quite intelligent and a skilled orator. These long pauses in the middle of a conversation must be something native to their culture.*

After one or two minutes of complete silence tuhngiqr proclaimed, "We will take break to think what we heard." That seemed to be a common expression in situations similar to this one and everyone immediately broke up and moved freely around the room. Some departed by various adjoining corridors. Most stayed put and talked with others.

Sarah was amazed at the sound of all the voices around her that sounded like people talking with their mouths full of food. She wasn't sure if she should call it a symphony or a cacophony of sound. She heard some creatures supporting their cause in the debate and many speaking against helping them. Still there were many who seemed to be fairly open-minded as they discussed their indecision with their comrades. She heard several speaking in another language. She assumed it was their native tongue.

Sarah and her companions continued to stand in a tight circle near the middle of the chamber. It almost seemed comical to her to see the five of them trying to watch all directions at once and be ready for an assault while, all around them, those massive, hairy creatures talked amongst themselves–ignoring them.

After several minutes of this, one of the creatures approached Sarah. She had a beautiful forest green pelt with only the occasional mottling of black. She was as tall and muscular as the rest of them but seemed to have somewhat of a more mild demeanor. "Sen', I just speak to my husband. He say you good. What you think all this?"

Sarah took a moment to try to process what the woman had asked her. "I'm sorry, your husband is who?"

"Sp'atung. My name is thi'thuhl. Though you maybe in danger, please no be frightened. I know others how spoke earlier but we not had talks with sen' for many rounds." She looked nervous. "And it against law to talk with them...er you."

Sarah finally allowed her frustration to come out. "Thi'thuhl, I'm grateful for your words but I've got to tell you something. Your husband didn't tell us anything. We have a thousand questions and instead of getting answers, we get more questions and the promise that we'll probably be punished just for being here—and it wasn't even our idea in the first place!"

Thi'thuhl listened patiently and, after Sarah ended her tirade, she put a massive paw on Sarah's shoulder. Sarah would never forget the first time one of the creatures touched her and how foreign, yet safe, it felt. She looked deep into Sarah's sky blue eyes and said, "Qualut. I sorry. This be scary for you. I answer questions I can for you."

Feeling some of her angst slide off her mind, Sarah replied, "Thank you. First, you call me Sarah, not 'sen'?"

Thi'thuhl smiled back with warmth. "Sp'atung say your name is Sarah but it hard pronounce so I call you sen'. And since you first humans I meet many rounds I call you sen', our word for human."

Thi'thuhl was smiling and, despite having someone change her name without her permission, Sarah couldn't help smiling back. She could tell she would get along well with this woman. *If I live through the day.*

The conversations regarding them continued all around them.

"What else can I tell you?"

"How do you guys know English? I must admit, we're all absolutely amazed that you not only speak English but that we've never discovered your species before!"

Thi'thuhl cocked her head to one side. It appeared to be a grandmotherly expression of mild amusement. "As you hear before, we not had talk with sen' for many rounds. I was very young, but then I now only one-hundred-fifty-three. We talk the white man a little when he first come. He talk the English so, to trade better we learn the English." She looked around the room, presumably to gauge the mood of the surrounding creatures. "We decide to still talk using it so we know things moving in world."

Sarah found herself standing there silently, as if she were one of the gorilla-like creatures. She was stunned. *How could all of this have remained hidden?* It was amazing.

Before Sarah said anything else, thi'thuhl added, "We talked with sen' before the whites. You call them Indians, I think. They call selves the Salish tribe. Though we not talk their language as much as before, we talk it still." She looked at Sarah conspiratorially and added, "For special things." Then thi'thuhl winked.

It was still amazing to Sarah. To hear the subtlety and inflection of voice in these creatures and to see them use some of the same mannerisms and language as herself left her utterly dumbfounded.

"Sen', what else tell I you?"

Smith bullied into the conversation before Sarah could ask another question, "How is it that your kind have lived here for so long but we've never seen you?" The captain's expression reeked with cynicism and distrust.

Thi'thuhl didn't seem to notice Smith's attitude but Sarah was pretty sure she understood. *Captain Smith's behavior probably coincides with what most of these creatures figure we're all like.*

"Each of us is born with—"

A signal from across the chamber brought all conversations to a halt. Without stepping up on a platform, or even stepping away from those surrounding her, tuhngiqr began speaking, "We have talked and we thinked. I talked with the other two Lat' of the Xruhnituhm Siem. We think we must talk more. This big matter. Biggest in over a hundred rounds. We must be sure what we do." She looked around the room and then proclaimed, "We meet again to talk this when sun setting next."

With that, everyone began to disperse. Many a curious look was aimed at the five humans, and of course some still looked more than a little hostile.

"Follow me," sp'atung told them, materializing from somewhere. "I show you where you sleep while you wait."

As they walked, trailing sp'atung, Sarah noticed that they were being closely followed by two of the biggest behemoths she'd yet seen. *They must be our guards.*

On their way to their quarters Jack made sure he was walking alongside Sarah before he loudly announced, "Well, Kid. I've got to admit. After meeting and tussling with one of the Enemy, I thought I'd been everywhere and done everything, but hanging out with you keeps proving I was wrong." He had a firm element of mirth in his voice and he reminded more than one of his companions of those good-natured pirates in children's books.

After walking through a labyrinth of corridors, they arrived at a small hole in the wall of the walkway. It looked to be big enough for all five of them to lie down comfortably—but only just.

"I find food for you," sp'atung told them. "Stay here and everything be fine."

Sarah wasn't the only one who wasn't so sure about "everything be fine," and even if things were okay, the War was still going on "out there," throughout the world, where people were dying. She figured if she tried to escape she would get herself hopelessly lost. Again she asked herself, *What have we gotten ourselves into?*

Just as sp'atung was preparing to leave them, he said, "Not worry. I take care of you. I be back and then we talk more. Please wait good and not worry. We sasquatch very kind."

CHAPTER 13
Audible Revelations

I suspect we're safe-for the moment, Captain Smith thought, her fiery red hair now tangled. She sat in the small earthen room given to her and her companions. She peered around their temporary domicile with the experienced eye of a soldier. She was pretty sure she could remember the way out. She'd paid close attention to the tortuous twistings and turnings they'd followed to arrive at their current location.

The two sasquatch that followed them there were still outside the room. *Amateurs!* she silently scoffed. *They didn't even take our weapons.* Then she let that idea roll around her mind a moment longer. *They seem to be educated just fine. They must know about firearms. So why didn't they confiscate our weapons?*

Smith continued her analysis of the natural cave room. She noticed that there appeared to be more sounds coming from the way they had come than the way they'd been heading. *If we need to play hide-and-seek with these...things, we'll probably need to head deeper into the cave. Less people and that's where they won't expect us to go.*

She sat with her back against the wall facing the only source of egress. Her mind was sharp and she knew it. She'd been trained to handle anything, even going head to head with the Enemy. Surely she could handle these beasts. She was, however, still completely surprised that there really were sasquatch. *They really exist! I didn't see that coming. That's one for the record books. I'll need to report all of this back to my superiors A.S.A.P. There might even be some way to use them against the Enemy.*

Since there wasn't any food yet, and none of her companions were worth her time, she figured she'd just mentally recall everything she'd seen and heard and put the pieces together.

I heard them mention the Lat' more than once. That sounded like a title of sorts. She adjusted her position, trying in vain to find a comfortable sitting position on the floor. *I'll bet it makes reference to some sort of position of authority. That would make sense based on how tuhngiqr was addressed and treated.* Smith felt a large drop of water hit her in the top of the head. She looked up at the ceiling and noticed a small hole in the earthen canopy yielding a slow drip. Ignoring it, she returned to her musings.

These sasquatch speak English surprisingly well. Therefore, they most likely have the mental capacity to understand abstract concepts like politics, religion, and...alliance. She allowed a grin to slide across her face as the potential of her thoughts began to sink in.

Smith then changed her thoughts to their guide, thi'thuhl. *She said she's only one-hundred-fifty-three. Perhaps they reckon time differently than we do, but I doubt it. If they all live such long lives, then I'd expect there to be millions or billions of these...sasquatch. And if there are, how come we humans have scarcely seen them? There just can't be that many, can there?* She looked up again just as a particularly large drop of water hit her in the eye. She ignored it. *So why aren't there more? Inter-tribal wars? No, there'd be evidence. Poor immune systems? Not likely. Sacrifices to idol Gods? Doubtful. They'd have to sacrifice an awful lot of their kindred to keep the population so low.*

Smith looked around the room and noticed the other four all huddled together, talking. *Probably trying to make sense of all of this. Well good luck. They're going to need it. The only one of them seems like he just might be bright at all is that Jack.* Smith tried ignoring them but, thinking about Jack got her dander up. *When this is all over...*

She yanked her mind back to focus. *The only thing that makes sense about their population is that they just don't have many babies very often. Or their period of fertility is short. Either way, it probably won't make much of a difference.*

Captain Smith diverted her attention back to her companions. She focused on Sarah and thought, *That smug, little upstart. How dare she get involved with me and the military. That brainless Garrison should've immediately sent her packing when he had the chance.*

She looked away, unwilling to give Sarah any more of her time or attention.

I wish we hadn't been interrupted before thi'thuhl could answer my question. She rubbed the strong muscles in the back of her neck and reflected, *Doesn't matter. I'll get the answers I want eventually—one way or another.*

After nearly two hours, sp'atung returned with a ready smile. Captain Smith felt slight misgivings at not seeing his wife instead. It seemed to be much easier to extract information from her. He carried with him several objects that could best be described as packets. They appeared to contain something inside, though Smith had no idea what it might be. Since there were five of them, she figured there was one for each of them. Never letting go of her rifle, she moved over to take one of the proffered packets.

It seemed to be made out of a multitude of leaves thatched together in some sort of ingenious way. She figured it would be damp to the touch but it was not only dry, it seemed reasonably solid. She found the opening and peered inside, ever wary. She waited just a moment to see what her companions found within, feeling no compunction about using them as guinea pigs. Seeing that it was merely the promised food, she drew her own out and ate heartily.

The food tasted only a little slimy but was obviously very healthy. Ignoring the flavor and texture, she ate.

Sp'atung sat down and watched them eat. After a minute or two, he spoke. "I hope you comfortable so far." He misinterpreted the resultant silence as assent. "I not believe the Tarantulas leave us alone. If they kill sen', I think we next. They worse than food go bad. Now you understand why I bring you here." Smith found that she was beginning to become accustomed to the way the sasquatch spoke, like someone speaking while gnawing on a hunk of meat.

Jack slowly answered, "Well, I don't know that we fully understand why you brought us here, but it's coming." He took another bite and didn't show any of the disgust at the flavor that the others were experiencing. "It seems to me that you want your sasquatch...er... brethren to fight the Spiders in some way. Is that right?"

Beaming with a smile that said he was grateful for Jack's understanding sp'atung replied, "Yes, that is it. We sasquatch need protect our jungle. We fierce warriors—" Smith's head cocked slightly at that, "—and we need stop destroyer that is worse than sen'. We need join The Hunt." The sasquatch with smoky gray hair looked around at his present company and abashedly added, "I am sorry. It is that sen' been bad to us so we say mean things of them. Er, you."

Smith didn't particularly care what they thought of humans. What she knew was that, at the end of the day, she and her species would come out on top—the way they always did. She was also certain that America would still be at the top of the heap when the dust settled. She was also grateful that it was she who had ended up in this situation, and not Major Garrison. She hadn't wished for his death at OR-17, but she firmly believed her abilities and decision-making skills were superior.

Jack then asked, "So, do you have some sort of plan as to how the sasquatch will do their part?"

Surprisingly, sp'atung didn't look ashamed at all when he replied with a simple, "No."

The captain rolled her eyes and saw Jack look a little disappointed. "So, in the off chance that you guys decide to enter the War, what then? Are you thinking of waging your own war or fighting alongside us? Would you stick to your forests or wage the war in multiple locations? What would you use for weapons? How—"

Sp'atung raised a hand to stop him and Jack obliged him. This time he looked a little sheepish when he said, "I see there lot of things to talk about. We not do war for many rounds. We need learn things if we win."

Upon hearing that, Smith carefully tucked away each word as a tool to be used later—or a trap to be sprung.

They sat and ate, talking about all kinds of things for another hour. The humans asked sp'atung questions and he in turn queried them. They talked about the structure of the cave and diets. They conversed about the rudiments of religion and geography. All six of them participated in the discussion, even Captain Smith. It was a pleasant respite from their activities since they'd met the sasqatch.

At last, sp'atung could see that they were getting tired, the night being long since spent. He departed, giving them the opportunity to sleep. They each removed their bedrolls and got as comfortable as they could. Within moments, they were asleep.

All except Smith. When she was certain the others were asleep, she stood and prepared to do a little exploring. She grabbed her rifle and carefully stepped over the sleeping forms of her companions. Without making a sound, she made her way to the doorway. Just before she reached it she heard Jack's casual voice rattle the quiet stillness. "I wouldn't do that if I were you. Just sit tight and get some rest. Whatever your...plans are you'll be able to execute them more effectively on a full night's sleep."

Smith listened to the brief speech. He never did open his eyes. When he was done speaking, Smith could feel the bile in her stomach churn at knowing he was right. *Even if he isn't, how do I know he won't turn me in to these creatures?*

Without a word, she moved back to her bedding and silently cursed the name of Jack Armstrong.

Due to the nocturnal schedule they'd adopted, they awoke late the next day. There were two sasquatch outside their room. It was difficult to tell if they were the same ones 'assisting' them from before they fell asleep. Some of the humans instinctively looked up and over at one of the side walls to see if the sun was up. Of course there was nothing to see but the hard-packed earth that formed their room.

Smith knew she needed to get up and moving, and though she held a certain amount of disdain for her companions, she knew that they were her responsibility. *Well, not Armstrong, but I need to get the others to safety,* she dutifully thought.

She walked over to the two sasquatch hovering just outside the door and they immediately tensed. *So much for putting them at ease. I might as well try the direct approach.* She slowly stepped outside, trying to hold her rifle in a non-threatening, but prepared way. She looked up into their hairy, ferocious faces and casually said, "My people are in need of exercise. We need to get up and move around. We can't stay here all day." She paused to see how they would respond. They both stood dumbly and she wondered if these two were selected to guard them because they were mutes. When they didn't reply Smith pressed on, "I need to speak with someone who's in charge. Where's tuhngiqr? She'll do."

With that brief, yet fearless speech one of the two sasquatch took on a look of ferocity. Smith thought to herself, *I'm not sure how but I just might have pushed them too far.*

As the smoldering volcano of a sasquatch was slowly beginning to erupt, sp'atung came around the corner. "You are awake. Come inside and I food will come."

They passed back inside their apartment and Smith wondered if sp'atung had noticed the altercation that had been on the verge of taking place. Though he seemed oblivious, somehow she knew that he'd been aware. *This one is good at diplomacy,* she thought of her host.

Before the food came, Smith started the conversation. "Listen. We're grateful for your hospitality but we need to get up and move around. Staying cooped up in here is going to drive us crazy. Maybe you could take us on a tour of the cave."

Without missing a beat, sp'atung replied, "Soon. For now, you safer in here." As the food arrived he spoke more quietly to the huddled group of humans. "The Xruhnituhm Siem soon make choice about talk last night. So, I think—"

"What do you mean by soon?" Smith cut in.

"Before another sun comes."

"Fine." The captain squirmed around a little, trying to get comfortable around a bump in the floor. "Listen, your wife was going to tell us something at that meeting last night. She was going to tell us why we've never seen you sasquatch before."

Immediately sp'atung made a shushing motion toward everyone. He looked around nervously and over his shoulder at the two guards standing motionless outside the room. He sat quietly, watching the door for several seconds more before he was certain the guards had not heard. Then he began to speak again, but this time in a hushed tone. Everyone huddled closer to him. In his voice that sounded like he were munching a wedge of rabbit meat, sp'atung said, "This big secret. Compared to sen', we very strong." He kept cocking his head to see if the guards could hear him or were suspicious of his actions.

"Is there a better place we should talk about this?" Sarah asked. "If this makes you uncomfortable or will cause problems for telling us, we understand." She put a hand on sp'atung's knee. "We don't want to get you in trouble."

Between the food they were eating and Sarah's naïve speech, Captain Sonya Smith was surprised she didn't wretch. *Where do these people come from?* she asked herself with not a little vitriol or contempt.

Sp'atung replied to her, "It okay. You need know this thing. I think it somehow help hunt Tarantulas. We need hunt like mountain lion hunt rabbits."

Forgetting Sarah, Smith's interest was peeking to a fever pitch.

Sp'atung resumed, "Sasquatch are born with a...tool." Smith noticed that all five of them were steadily inching closer to the speaker.

"Yes we speak the English, but you notice our...hm...talk sound different than yours." He waited a moment to see if they laughed at his joke. When they didn't, he continued. "This make us have the ability—"

He cut off as another sasquatch entered the room. The captain was pretty sure she hadn't seen this one before. He spoke immediately upon entering. "Sp'atung, the Xruhnituhm Siem is ready. You please bring the sen' to the Great Hall."

Sp'atung traced a circle in the air with his hand that apparently told the messenger that he understood and would be there shortly. Unwilling to miss out on this information a second time, Captain Smith grabbed his shoulder and pressed him, "Finish what you were telling us! Before we go to the Great Hall!"

Looking more nervous than before, sp'atung again spoke in a hushed tone. "We make a...how you say...'loud voice'?"

Sp'atung noticed that all five of the humans were looking askance at him. He thought for a moment, realizing that he needed to hurry and get his charges to their destination. Finally he said, "We make sound with voices and those who not sasquatch get dizzy and sleepy."

Smith noticed an abrupt change come over Sarah. With realization in her eyes she blurted, "That's what happened to me!" She looked at all of her companions and, due to her excitement, found it marginally difficult to speak coherently. "I get it now! That night I first saw one of the Enemy." She looked at Captain Smith and said, "It was a few days before you arrived at the camp. I woke up all dizzy and I found it hard to think about anything. Apparently I had been exposed to this 'loud voice'!"

"Yes!" sp'atung replied. He too was getting excited as well. "I do the Voice to you. I saw Tarantula going to you and so do Voice and make Tarantula dizzy. It worked." He was grinning now, a massive, optimistic smile splitting his face.

"So," Captain Smith continued slowly, trying to understand what she was hearing, "this 'loud voice' is some kind of a...sonic blast?"

Looking even more excited, sp'atung interjected, "Yes! That is it. Those are words I mean. Sasquatch able to make sonic blast (his pronunciation of the words was more garbled than normal) and make others dizzy or sleep. We do it to most animals, mainly sen'."

Smith was grateful she had pressed him to provide this explanation. *What a revelation! This could be very useful information indeed. The military has tried for years to make an effective DEW (directed energy weapon) that emits an incapacitating sonic blast. And here we apparently have what we need in these animals.* She sat back continuing her train of thought. *No wonder we've never found the sasquatch before. Everytime we see one, the sighted sasquatch sends a sonic blast at the person and that person's thoughts get all jumbled and can't remember a thing.* Smith looked up just in time to get a drop of water in her eye. Caring not a whit for it she looked at sp'atung with a mixture of scientific curiosity and military supremacy. *Amazing!*

At this point in the discussion, one of the two sasquatch outside the room poked his head in and told them in a gruff, rock-chewing voice that it was time to go. As they walked back toward the Great Hall, Smith directed half her attention to verifying she remembered the path correctly. However, she was also pondering the strategic power of this new weapon–the sonic blast. *I need to learn the range of this weapon and how effective it is at varying distances.*

They continued walking through earthen corridors past mounted torches and saw very few other sasquatch. *They must be at the Great Hall already,* Captain Smith figured.

Too bad the sonic blast isn't lethal, she thought as she resumed considering this revelation. *Or perhaps it is under certain circumstances. I guess we'll just have to field-test it to know for sure.*

Then, just as they were entering the Great Hall, Smith paused in midstride, as a new thought came into her mind. She had an idea of how they might be able to use this new weapon against the Enemy. *It could turn the tide. I need to get to my superiors and make them aware of this new information.*

The rest of her entourage saw her stop and figured she was responding to the room full of sasquatch. She caught Jack's pleasant but wary eye and knew that he <u>wasn't</u> thinking that. He seemed to be trying to read her thoughts. She ignored him, giving her entire focus to the task at hand–getting the sasquatch to aid them in the War.

They were led to the position in the middle of the room that they had occupied previously. Again, they were surrounded. This time they weren't quite as nervous or worried. They knew a little more about what was going on and what they were facing. Following sp'atung's example, the five humans directed their attention to one particular part of the room. They were looking right at the three members of the Xruhnituhm Siem. Though they were not adorned with any raiment to cause them to stand out and they were not seated on thrones, it was clear to all five humans that these three individuals were in charge.

Without preamble tuhngiqr, the bright white haired sasquatch, began speaking. "We think on these things. We know it important we make right choice about let you go or no." She paused for nearly a minute and Smith noticed that none of the sasquatch seemed to find the ensuing silence to be uncomfortable. On the contrary, their various visages seemed to relax a bit. Continuing, tuhngiqr decreed, "We <u>not</u> decide have talk with sen'again. Maybe we do with another sun, but not this sun." She paused, perhaps for dramatic emphasis.

Smith looked over at Sarah and the boys and noticed that they looked a little bit crestfallen. *It sure sounded like they're not going to let us go.*

Tuhngiqr continued her marble-speak address, seeming to speak only to the humans, "We not mean creatures. We can kill, but we live peaceful with our nature so we no want kill to solve this problem of you know our home and where we live." She seemed to resume speaking to the entire room again, her voice like gravel, "We no can let you go or more sen' come and kill us. Unless—" At this point she paused and looked over at a male sasquatch standing next to her. "My fellow Lat', steek'eew, say we make you make oath. So, it decision of Xruhnituhm Siem that you promise never show cave to any one, ever." The room had become dreadfully silent. "If say yes, you can leave."

Smith's first thought was, *Excellent. I can swear to that. I can tell my superiors about these creatures, just not about their location.* She grinned and thought, *Sometimes I love working with naïve people.*

Aloud, Captain Smith proclaimed, "We accept your terms and thank you for your gracious hospitality." That last part she said through gritted teeth, but she figured their hosts wouldn't understand the subtle human inflection.

With Smith agreeing to take the oath, steek'eew said, "Place your palms on your foreheads and say, 'I swear by power of my life that I no tell where sasquatch live." After the five humans had taken the oath, the mood of the sasquatch around the room relaxed considerably.

However, Smith wasn't done. "Also mighty tuhngiqr, we would like to ask for your permission to stay here just a little longer among your beautiful people and perhaps learn of your ways from them." Smith pretended not to notice her four companions subtly looking at her like she'd gone crazy.

Tuhngiqr looked at the other two Lat', steek'eew and tsin'tsun'tsan, and upon seeing the two both hold forth a similar looking black rock announced, "That is good. You keep two guides with you so you not get lost. You go where you like in our home."

Smith craftily thought to herself, *Excellent!*

CHAPTER 14
Upgrades

He couldn't believe he'd survived. That battle had been one of the worst that he'd ever been in–and he'd been in quite a few. It wasn't only the ferocity of the battle that moved him so much, it was also the sheer decimation of his forces. As far as Major Garrison knew, the handful of survivors who had made it out with him were the *only* survivors.

He was in one of the new Scorpion-class military helicopters. It was truly impressive—comfortable and unparalleled in its deadliness—and it had an amazing range of travel. When the attack had begun, a conscientious radio operator had quickly sent a message to Garrison's superiors and alerted them of the situation—*just* before the equipment had been destroyed. The chopper was one of four vehicles that had been sent for support. Instead of providing support the only function they were able to serve was that of ferrying out the injured and wounded. Unfortunately, only one of the four choppers had been needed.

He didn't know where he was heading. That didn't surprise him. In his line of work, he knew that a man was sometimes whisked away to heaven knows where. It was, of course, based on a need to know, and right now, he didn't need to know. *Doesn't matter. I'll know soon enough,* he sighed.

He leaned back in his chair and tried to determine there their destination. He didn't really care. He just wanted to keep his mind on something safe so the gut-wrenching, nightmare images of the recent battle of Oscar-Romeo-17 didn't fill his conscious mind. *I'm probably heading for a court martial. The Army tends to frown on getting nearly all of your men killed in a single conflict.*

He let his glance slowly slide across the faces of the few men who'd made it out alive and unscathed with him.

There were only five.

They were all loyal and strong, but so many others were just as good as these and they'd been brutally cut down. He tried figuring out their location again.

After a few hours, the major noticed that the motion of the chopper was changing. He realized at that moment that he had been able to finally get some sleep that had been surprisingly devoid of nightmares. As he realized that, he felt guilty. *It hasn't been that long since the battle took place. I was the leader. I don't deserve to sleep without my demons. Not yet.* He sighed again and thought, *perhaps not ever.*

Steady and sure, the chopper descended and touched down. Garrison and his men looked out the windows of the large craft and noticed that they were obviously at a military base. It didn't look familiar to him but then, there were a lot of bases. *At least there were before the War,* he silently brooded.

He exited the aircraft, walking with a measured and sure gait. He knew he might be a free man for only a few more moments of his life but he was determined to show a good example to the few remaining men under his command. They followed him and they were all escorted to a bunker at the edge of the airfield.

They were lead through the only visible door and immediately began descending stairs. After a few flights of stairs, Garrison was surprised how deep they had already gone. He was also surprised that their escort didn't seem to be guarding them, but simply escorting them. *Looks can be deceiving,* the major thought.

As they descended his mind wandered onto many things. The one thing that he couldn't help but consider was the battle he'd so recently survived. He was terribly disappointed and overwrought by the thoughts and memories of so many of his friends and comrades having died so recently. He was especially despondent about the death of Sarah Scott. *I should've found a way to get her out of there!* he thought with unforced sadness.

After what must've been enough stairs to have passed at least ten floors, they exited at one of the landings. They passed into a long, white hallway that had a lingering scent of concrete. The walls were all bare and the hallway itself also seemed to be devoid of any foot traffic. Garrison chanced a glance behind him and noticed that they had no escort following them. Both of their guides were in front.

They continued walking down the corridor, making occasional turns here and there. It was a labyrinth of doors, passageways and invisible ducts. Garrison couldn't help thinking the same thing his men were thinking as they all moved along silently. *This is one big underground installation! Where are we?*

Finally, they entered an anteroom and were instructed to take a seat. Garrison and the five remaining men under his command– they were beginning to refer to themselves as the 'five horsemen of the apocalypse'–all felt a little odd since they were quite dirty and no longer clean shaven. It had been at least a couple of days since they'd had a chance to really get cleaned up. What with all that had happened in such a short time, it was difficult to remember how long it had been since they'd had a real shower.

They hadn't been in the room more than five minutes before a woman entered. They could tell by her lieutenant's bars that she was most likely not the person they were there to see. "Good evening. My name is Lieutenant Malistair. I work directly under General Martin."

Major Garrison and his five companions all began to feel a profound sense of curiosity. Various thoughts began to race through their minds.

General Martin? He's the Chairman of the Joint Chiefs of Staff. What's the CJCS want with us?

He must be ready to pull his hair out, and ours, after what happened at 17.

If this is a court marshal, at least we'll have a chance to hash it out with the big cheese.

Lieutenant Malistair continued. "As you're undoubtedly aware, the six of you are in a somewhat unique situation. You're the only known survivors of the latest attack by the Enemy." She began to pace around the room. It didn't seem to Major Garrison that she did so out of nervousness. Rather, it appeared to just be her way of collecting her thoughts. "The truly interesting part of your situation is that you are the survivors of the only attack the Enemy has propagated against us that was in an environment that was completely rural." She chuckled briefly and then said, "And you've got to admit, Oscar-Romeo-17 was as rural as you can get."

Though she obviously didn't mean any offense by it, that one word 'was' stung Major Garrison like the knife wound he'd earned in a small battle a few years back. He continued to sit impassively before speaking. "Ma'am, with all due respect, what's going on? We've been given no information whatsoever, and to be honest, we've been pretty patient." He sighed and tried not to let his fatigue show. "To be blunt, we're exhausted and my men could sure use a little down time and a place to get cleaned up rather than sitting here listening to you discuss what we already know." He tried to say it casually and without causing a provocation, but it was a little difficult to do at that point.

It was then that Malistair allowed herself to take her first good look at the men before her. Some of them had torn clothes. Some of them had dark patches of color, most likely someone's blood—or something's. One of them had his arm in a sling. Another had a patch of his hair burned away. They really did look exhausted. However, she knew that they were exactly what the general was hoping to find.

After looking them over, the lieutenant finally said, "Your presence is requested in a meeting that will begin shortly."

After several moments a small indicator light on the room's only desk silently came alive and Malistair immediately stood up. "They'll see you now."

The six men stood and followed their guide into the adjoining room. It was spacious and elegant, or at least as elegant as anything could be under the given conditions. Garrison was surprised that he noticed a Mr. Coffee noisily whirring somewhere within the room, and that reminded him just how hungry he was. The main feature of the room that grabbed their attention however, was the presence of dozens of men and women, most of whom had an awed look in their eyes. Garrison wasn't sure why everyone was staring at them, but he wasn't particularly interested in being dragged about like a show-pony. For the moment, he went along with it until he could figure out what was going on.

After they entered, a woman stood up at the front of the room and bade them sit. She appeared to be the one running the meeting and, after the major and his men had a chance to take a seat, she spoke. "Thank you very much for coming on such short notice, and under such strict security conditions." She stepped around the podium so that there was nothing between her and her audience when she said, "I expect you have a question or two. They will be answered in due course and—"

Barely able to contain his frustration any longer, Garrison interrupted, "Ma'am, like I told the lieutenant, with all due respect, my men could either use answers or food and rest right about now. Preferably the latter." As soon as he'd said it he knew he'd made a tactical error and wished he could take it back.

The woman he addressed took on a look that could only be described as seething. Everyone in the room saw it and understood it for what it was. It was most assuredly not lost on Major Garrison, but at that point, he was too tired to care and he felt too jerked around to worry about caring very much. It took her several moments to make certain she was composed before she spoke. When she did it was with slow, measured words. "Major, I know you've had some challenges recently. So have we. Unless you'd like a demotion right now," Garrison could feel the heat coming into her words, "you'll keep silent and only speak when you're spoken to!"

Major Garrison stared at her carefully. He was certainly not intimidated. He'd survived a battle that was a thousand-fold more feral than this lady's remarks. Though his expression didn't betray his thoughts, he thought to himself, *What a small person.* Aloud he calmly stated, "Ma'am, I apologize if I gave offense." That seemed to begin to placate her. *Or stroke her ego. Whatever works.* "I thought you were the Secretary of the Interior."

Though the woman was certainly more placid than she had been a moment before, she seemed to swell with power as she proclaimed, "I am President Griffith and your commander-in-chief."

The room became quiet. The president enjoyed the silence. Major Garrison, bone-weary and rarely impressed by posturing, was disappointed that his new president seemed so petty and undisciplined. Of course, he didn't let his feelings show on his face. Instead he allowed himself to automatically shift into standard military protocol mode. He stood and executed a smart salute to President Griffith and said, "Madame President, inasmuch as I spoke insubordinately to my superior, I submit myself for discipline."

The president was immediately taken aback. To her credit, she quickly shored up her facial expression so that very little of her thoughts and emotions were put on display. She considered the man before her and again the room was quiet except for the Mr. Coffee and a humming noise coming from an adjacent room. After several moments of the president and the major staring at one another, she smiled a friendly, gracious smile that did not reach her eyes. At last she said, "No need for that, Major. What with all the recent changes in the government, it's not your fault you were *ignorant* of who your commander-in-chief was."

Major Garrison wasn't the only one in the room to notice that the olive branch the president had just extended seemed to be laced with barbs. Nevertheless, he took it with all the grace he could muster. "Thank you, Ma'am. I look forward to serving under your able leadership." Then he sat down.

Had Garrison been able to see his five men behind him, he would've seen five soldiers doing their best not to look astonished. He also would've seen loyalty in their eyes—loyalty to him.

With Washington D.C. having been sacked just so recently, it wasn't any wonder that Garrison or anyone not around the president might be unaware that the late President Mark Wagner had died and that he'd been replaced by his Secretary of the Interior—Gwyneth Griffith.

His sitting down seemed to somewhat thaw the frosty mood the room had just possessed moments before. Everyone knew that it was time to move on. Some knew that Major Garrison had just made an eternal enemy out of the president. All eyes returned to President Griffith in mute expectation of what was next on the meeting's agenda.

"Well, we've had a chance to meet the heroes of the battle of Oscar-Romeo-17," she said. Garrison wasn't certain whether he'd heard a bit of sarcasm injected into the word 'heroes' but he let it pass, knowing it was completely irrelevant and unimportant. They had a war to win and interpersonal conflicts and bickering were not going to help make that happen.

The president continued, "Before we continue with our agenda, I would like a report on the battle at Oscar-Romeo-17." She turned back to Major Garrison and nearly barked, "Major."

Garrison stood and slowly moved toward the front of the room. He knew he looked like he'd been run over by a dump truck, or close enough to it. The looks that were sent his way proved it. He ignored them, focusing on the next task at hand—getting through a report to a group of politicians.

Standing at the microphone he finally had a chance to see the whole group in attendance. He took a few seconds to size up the group. He told himself that he was unfortunately right. *This is a big group of politicians.* He saw General Martin off to the side. The general was seemed to be continuing to form his first impression of Garrison.

The major gave a brief summary of what had transpired. He made sure he stuck to details that were pertinent and did not offer any theories or hypotheses. He purposefully left out any mention of Sarah Scott or Captain Sonya Smith—each for different reasons.

He provided the barest information regarding their preparations. He spent most of his time reviewing the battle, the weapons used, their effectiveness, the tactics employed by the Enemy and other topics that he knew his audience would wish to hear.

When he was finished he politely turned and looked at the president. She nodded to him which he understood to mean that she was satisfied with his report. Turning back to his audience, he asked if there were any questions. Having been clear and succinct, there weren't many.

The first question came from a mature man with a Brazilian accent. "Major, based on your experience, do you think that the Enemy will attack small, rural populations in the future?"

"I am not yet able to form a conclusion regarding that," Garrison replied.

Another person asked, "Major Garrison, did this attack seem to be more..." The man paused, searching for the right word. "...vicious than other attacks you've experienced?"

He immediately responded, "Vicious? I don't think so. Aggressive? Yes. I've never seen the Spiders push that hard on such an insignificant target."

The same man followed up, asking, "And why do you think that is?"

A quiet snort of derision could be heard across the room in the vicinity of CIA director Cheryl Rodriguez.

Ignoring it, Garrison replied, "It seemed very out of character for the Enemy to attack the way they did. I suspect something, from their perspective, is changing in the War." Almost under his breath, he indulged himself upon adding, "And I'll bet that can't be good."

Surprisingly, the next question came from General Martin. "Why do you think such a small pond was attacked? After all, there've been almost no such attacks in the past."

The major reached for a glass of water that had been placed near him. He took that moment to consider why General Martin would ask that question. In the space of a heartbeat he concluded that the general was testing him. *Testing me for what? To see if I can stand up to the pressure? To see if I can intelligently analyze a situation?* Finally Garrison replied, "I would conjecture that the Enemy is attempting to engage in a sort of mopping-up exercise around a primary target, perhaps Portland. Once the small groups of soldiers surrounding the area have been subdued or eliminated," he was impressed with himself, that his voice didn't waver, "then moving onto the larger target would be attempted."

Garrison noted that the general did not look impressed. *Well, I gave the safest and most obvious answer.* Before anyone else spoke Garrison thought he'd add a little more to see if the general might show his hand. "Then again, there's much we don't know about the Enemy. Who knows. Perhaps they go out into the forest to hunt us the way we hunt deer and elk." He noticed the general begin to look more interested in what he had to say. *In for a penny,* he thought. "Or maybe they see it as a chance to engage in live-fire war games."

He ceased speaking and saw that there was now a gleam of approval in the general's eye that hadn't been there before. Garrison noticed the man's grandfatherly smile. He was proud that he could impress his commanding officer. He'd heard good things about the general.

"I'd say the only thing more ridiculous than some of those theories is that General Martin over there seems to actually agree." It was Nicolai Reznikov who spoke. For most people in the room, that was the first they'd known that he was there. Immediately there were hushed whispers snaking their way through the room.

"What's he doing here?"

"I figured he'd be in the stockade by now."

"I agree with him."

"Worthless excuse for a human being, masquerading as a geologist."

"Are we safe with him wandering around?"

"The Butcher of Bryanskaya!"

Major Garrison stood and turned, looking at the man who'd spoken and didn't recognize him, but from the rash of table-talk that had spontaneously broken out, he knew that the man was known, and not well liked.

Garrison saw that the man was dressed in a very contemporary outfit and appeared to be fashionably in vogue, despite his large, white beard. Garrison saw that the man had an amiable smile on his faced that his eyes belied most vehemently. Garrison always tried to give people the benefit of the doubt and in this case he was immediately experiencing an excess of doubt. He summarized his first impression of his assailant as he thought to himself, *I'd better keep an eye on this guy. He looks like the kind who stirs up trouble wherever he goes.*

Upon making a momentary assessment of the man with the beard, Major Garrison turned back to the audience and waited for another question. When none came he looked back at the president who extended her hand to suggest that he might take his seat. He did so, but kept a wary eye on the bearded man.

The president resumed the podium and asked General Martin to give a report on the recent sorties against the Enemy's mining operations. The CJCS stood and began to address those assembled in the room. The man's medals stood out on his uniform. How he managed to keep it clean and pressed in that environment was a minor mystery at Camp Dodge. Though he primarily had bad news, the look in his eyes said that he was absolutely certain that mankind would win in the end. When he spoke, the same spirit and attitude came through. Garrison figured he wasn't the only person in the room who thought that the wrong person was president.

"Ladies and gentlemen," General Martin began somewhat formally. "As some of you already know, we have news about our various operations we've been conducting at some of the mining facilities that the Enemy has taken over." He looked around the room, perhaps to gauge the mood, perhaps to assess how much bad news they could handle. "Due to our more recent intel regarding what we believe to be the Enemy's intentions for resupplying their orbital bombardment resources, we've sent in three large teams to assault three of their mining facilities–one team for each mine." A look of sadness passed across his face like a cold, fleeting breeze. Pete Garrison wasn't certain he'd even seen it. "All three delta teams suffered severe casualties. Very few of our personnel returned." He paused and noted the looks of sincere melancholy that were spreading across the room in a contagious way. "Based on the reports that have come in from the handful of survivors, all three missions were a wash. At only one mine did we do appreciable damage but it wasn't enough to make a lasting difference of any kind." He shook his head in disappointment and then cast a hard look back at his audience. "My people are working hard to figure out a better way to stop the Enemy at the mines. I would love to hear your suggestions at this time."

He paused to let everyone in the room know that he was not speaking rhetorically. For a moment, everyone seemed to hope that someone else would speak. Finally, someone did.

Tugging on his right ear, Phil Johnson, the secretary of commerce, said, "Is there some way we might be able to, you know, lure them out into the open? Away from the protection of the mines and away from their Directed Energy Weapons?"

"That's a great idea," the general rejoined. "We've considered that and have not yet come up with a way to make that happen. We've even thought about mining some of the minerals they want and leaving them out some place they're sure to find them. Of course, why would they come after it if they're already getting what they need from the safety of their mines?"

After a few moments of silence, Cheryl Rodriguez, the CIA director, stood looking characteristically paranoid. "What about tanks? We roll in, hard and fast, and blast away from practically point-blank range so their DEWs won't be able to help them!"

Martin began to look as tired as everyone felt. He hesitated only a moment before replying, "If we get that close, they'll just launch that green and red sludge they use. It'll melt right through our tanks and there's little assurance that we'd do enough damage to warrant the losses we'd undoubtedly incur since the mines go deep underground and would be protected from our tanks."

Someone asked, "Sir, *red* sludge? What kind of weapon is that?"

Martin looked at the man and replied off-handedly, "We've only recently learned about the red stuff. It's more viscous than that jello-like green slime. Instead of burning like acid, it explodes where it lands in a small radius emitting shrapnel in all directions." All eyes were on the general. He looked up and concluded, "It would make a nasty mess of any fishing hole."

With that, the room became silent again–and remained silent. It was an incredibly depressing moment for most of the people there. Some of them felt like they were in quicksand and every time they struggled they sank deeper.

After several long moments of nearly everyone staring at their shoes, Secretary of State Michaels stood and bellowed, "Since we have no idea how to stop them at their work, I have another question. How come—I'll say it out loud—the Butcher of Bryanskaya is here and not in the brig—or the chair?" The cold vehemence that frosted his eyes over was mirrored in the faces of many others in the room. General Martin looked at Michaels and nodded his head in silent approval. Surprisingly, there appeared to be a look of mild amusement that emanated from the eyes of the bearded man. He was most certainly composed and did not look as though he felt uncomfortable or trapped in any way. Rather, it seemed to Garrison that the man was all too familiar with these circumstances–and relished them.

Before anyone else could speak, the president rose to her feet almost too quickly. Without taking the time to position herself behind the podium, she immediately began to speak. "My friends, I am fully aware of Mr. Reznikov's past. I am also aware of his more recent personal history. I give you my assurance, as president of the United States of America that he has done what he can to atone for the atrocities in which he was mixed up those many decades ago."

The looks of cold disdain around the room were giving way to disbelief and incredulity.

"I know that keeping Mr. Reznikov around does seem rather anathema to our purposes and principles. However, after considerable evaluation I am convinced that this man has changed and possesses the...people skills...that we'll need for an upcoming project."

Upon hearing about the Butcher's 'people skills', the ghosts of years gone by flashed before the collective mind's eye of those in the room. They remembered not only the man's sadistic and wanton destruction for 'The Higher Calling', they also remembered how he had manipulated–almost hypnotized–the masses in a way that had not been seen since the days of Adolph Hitler.

But there was an undercurrent in the maelstrom of emotion that was ebbing and flowing in the minds and hearts of those present. Major Garrison could sense it. It wasn't just Reznikov, it was something more. Something *bigger that was stirring the souls of them all.* He thought, *Without a functioning congress, decisions are being made by this president in an increasingly unilateral way. Choices need to be made and put into effect, but I don't think this nation is a republic any more. It certainly doesn't seem to have a representative government.* He shuddered inwardly.

The president continued, "As I know you're aware, our neighbor and one of our main allies, Canada, is experiencing increasing difficulty in her fight against the Enemy. I don't know if you've seen the reports but over the last six months a large portion of their military has been completely annihilated. They are desperate." The looks of incredulity were turning again. This time to confusion. Without waiting for a response, the president steam-rolled ahead. "What with Canada's vast areas of unpopulated land, the Enemy is finding easy opportunities to 'set up shop' as it were." Some in the room were beginning to wonder if the president was mentally coherent. "So, in order to protect our northern flank and at the same time assist our ally, I have decided to send what military resources we can into Canada to assist them."

Now the looks on the faces in the room all said the same thing.

Is she insane?

Why didn't she consult us?

How can we possibly help the Canadians in a significant way while still protecting ourselves?

We're already spread out as thin as thread.

If the president noticed the obvious looks of horror on the faces of her audience, she gave no sign of it. "I've already spoken with the prime minister of Canada and he has consented to allow us to set up our base of operations in Montreal."

Garrison had been certain that the denizens in the room couldn't look more crestfallen and upset—but he was wrong. He bewilderedly thought, *What's going on here? This doesn't make sense! This is insanity!*

A long and lengthy discussion ensued. It was heated most of the time with words like 'foreign occupation' and 'totalitarianism' emerging like raw sewage, but the president was persuasive and she eloquently reminded them that "desperate times call for desperate measures." In the end she won enough support from the group—barely—that she was finally willing to unveil her last surprise.

"Of course," she continued, after the debate had ended, "we'll need someone to head this…delegation. I've been thinking about it since this all began and, after extremely careful consideration and not a little sagacious advice, I believe the person we'll send to lead the operation will be Nicolai Reznikov."

That was the rebar that broke the camel's back. Before Reznikov could stand and express his gratitude to this supposedly unexpected turn for him, the room erupted in an uproar that made the previous one seem tame. This time there were people in the room who were very near violence. It was then that Garrison noticed for the first time just how strategically placed the Camp Dodge soldiers in the room were. He carefully and quietly eyed the situation, the soldiers with weapons ready, the president standing before everyone like a blazing sun that seared and destroyed whatever she touched rather than give light for others to see. He looked over at his five companions and they all quietly shared a look that said, *This isn't right. Something needs to be done.*

Then something happened. Amidst the chaos and perhaps near dissolution of the government itself, a loud, piercing whistle cut through the cacophony and everyone, including the president, turned and looked at the deliverer of the shrill blast. General Martin stood like a knight in shining armor. Composed and poised, ever ready to win the war, even if he had to lose a battle or two. His visage said he hadn't given up and he was going to fight whoever he had to in order to best serve the people of America. He looked deathly serious. When all was finally quiet, he spoke in a cold, calculating voice. "Madame President, undoubtedly you can see that sending Reznikov to lead our forces into Canada to...assist them would be completely unpopular. However, I offer an alternative plan, one that I suspect you'll be able to get more people behind. Send Reznikov if you want–to blazes with him!–but send Major Garrison to lead the group."

Major Garrison was stunned and taken completely by surprise. *Was this a spur of the moment decision by the general or had he caught wind of what might happen here and prepared this in advance?* He looked over at his men and they looked as surprised as he felt. He knew he couldn't leave these men behind. He trusted them and he was seeing more and more that having people around him he could trust would be a truly rare and valuable commodity.

Unlike the president's proposal, Martin's did not promote chaos. There were thoughtful looks around the room. Everyone quietly looked into the eyes of others around them. With only a few minutes of discussion a general consensus seemed to be reached that Martin's idea would be acceptable.

Seeing the response from the general's remarks, President Griffith reluctantly replied, "That would be...agreeable." That last word seemed to be dragged out of her like an impacted molar with only half an aspirin for killing the pain. Then she surprised everyone and continued, "Except that he is only a major." Her feral smile seemed to find its place again on her mask-like face. "The Canadians would see it as an insult if we didn't send a general, or at least a colonel." She began looking around the room when she said, "I'll assist in the selection of just such a person. We'll find that woman or man as soon as possible and get things moving." Some in the room thought that Martin had just hung himself, that the president would send him and finally get him out of her political hair or select someone more in line with her own ideas of how things should be done.

While basking in yet another personal victory, the president was gently interrupted by the general. "Ma'am, I agree with you. It would be insulting. Therefore, I am hereby granting a promotion to Major Pete Garrison. Major step forward!"

Woodenly, Garrison arose and again walked to the front of the room to stand before General Martin. He saluted and the general returned the gesture. The general spoke. "Major Garrison, I hereby promote you to the rank of Colonel with all the rights and privileges of such rank." They shook hands and Garrison, dumbfounded and numb, didn't know what to do. So he quietly returned to his seat.

Before the president had a chance to 'take up the conch' again, Martin resumed his speech. "Madame President, we now have a colonel who is ready to do this job and do it well. The people of this room are behind him. When were you hoping for our forces to move out and occupy...er...assist in Montreal?"

General Martin stood looking at Griffith as if he were a naïve, wide-eyed boy. With words almost literally dripping with an acid-like contempt, she replied, "Very well. They'll move out within the week."

CHAPTER 15
Poisoning the Well

After the Xruhnituhm Siem decided to allow the humans to stay, the five guests spent the next few days getting to know a little bit about the sasquatch and their ways. The small group recognized that this was likely an unprecedented event and, despite the War raging on around them throughout the world, at least they were able to learn about and experience something simple and good.

They learned that the sasquatch prefer to eat their meat raw. The sasquatch however knew that the humans probably wouldn't enjoy that so they made sure that the meat they brought to their guests was always cooked. Usually, very over-done. The sasquatch couldn't understand why the humans preferred their meat that way. It helped their understanding when Sarah volunteered, after two days of a diet of 'burnt offerings', that although they liked their food cooked, they enjoyed eating it much more when it was not cooked quite so much. She volunteered to show their sasquatch chef what she meant. One or two of the sasquatch tried this new version and were impressed. They said it was actually edible that way. Of course, their comrades thought they were insane. So, very few of the sasquatch ever tried or enjoyed the humans' way of cooking their meat.

Through this experience, Smith and the others realized that the sasquatch had not always lived entirely apart from humans. Hundreds of years ago, the sasquatch had had minor relations with the Salish tribes of American Indians that used to inhabit that region of North America.

On the third evening of their stay, Jack was sitting outside the cave with sp'atung, watching the stars. They sat there like they'd grown up together all their lives. At one point Jack casually asked sp'atung what he thought of his people referring to the sasquatch as "bigfoot." The only reply he received was a long, loud roar of laughter from the smoky gray sp'atung.

On the fourth day in the cave, Sergeant Jameson found that the sasquatch kept sheaves of paper on which they write. Jameson was surprised to find that they knew how to make a simple form of paper. He was not only excited to tell his companions about this discovery but that the sasquatch used a charcoal-type pencil to write on the papers. They weren't very interested in writing books or scientific discoveries. They mainly used it to record their own history. While learning about this, Jameson noticed that in the sasquatch histories that he was shown, names of individuals were never capitalized. When he realized this he asked his host why that was. The sasquatch replied, "We not like put us above another. This why we no make big letters for our names. It one thing we do keep mi'tuhng happy."

Jameson had also been surprised to find that much of their histories were written in their semi-broken English. He asked about that and was told that once the sasquatch had picked up English, they'd quickly learned that it was an easier language to use for the purpose of writing a complete record and more fully describing what they wanted to say.

Sarah explored other aspects of this new culture. She was genuinely impressed and pleased to find that the parents of a sasquatch truly loved their children and took care of them. However, once an offspring was about five years old–an adolescent–it was understood that it would be on its own and need to provide for itself. That responsibility included that new adolescent sasquatch digging its own quarters in the cave to have a place to house itself. Having learned that, Sarah wasn't surprised to find that the cave turned out to be a veritable honeycomb of paths and rooms.

Of course Smith was interested in other things. She had attached herself to tuhngiqr and tried to spend as much time with the Lat' as she could. She asked her sasquatch benefactor all kinds of questions about their laws and protocols. Although she found it quite mentally stimulating, she was more interested in her objective–defeating the Enemy. She saw in the sasquatch a tremendous weapon that just might have the power and capability of assisting the military in defeating their foe, and if a few sasquatch died along the way, so be it.

Day after day Smith and tuhngiqr conversed about a multitude of subjects. They discussed history, philosophy, politics and more. At times their discussions brought them nearly to blows. At other times they found they and their societies had more in common than either of them would have suspected. Despite the variety of their discourse, Captain Smith was always vigilant in making certain that their topics of conversation ended up, at some point, showing the virtues of the sasquatch aiding humans, or at least the reasons for the human race being preserved. It was work that was different for Smith compared to her normal assignments. This one was entirely diplomatic.

Smith was, of course, very aware of the clock as well. She knew that what she was doing could potentially have very positive effects on the War. She also knew that her work with the sasquatch would need time to develop and bear fruit, but she was reluctant to spend any more time with them than was necessary. She needed to report her findings to the top brass as soon as possible so that the U.S. military could deploy this new weapon as quickly and effectively as possible.

On one of the occasions in which she was talking with the white pelt leader, she mentioned the War. "Tuhngiqr, the War is going rather poorly." With a practiced look of sincerity and confidence, Smith looked up at tuhngiqr and continued. "Many of our soldiers aren't even aware of this fact, but I know I can trust *you.*"

Tuhngiqr didn't notice the slightest hint of a mocking grin. Instead she pleasantly rejoined, "Thank you. I like talk with you. I think I start trust you too."

There were times when they simply sat outside the cave and watched an owl or a martin in a nearby tree moving about. A couple of times they watched little sasquatch children run around in the room they were occupying. Smith found that the sasquatch were not only good listeners, they were also very good at quietly watching something, whether it was exciting and dynamic or slow and dull. She thought they would make good analysts.

On another occasion they were sitting and talking together with some other sasquatch. They were visiting about the cooler weather they were expecting and how it would affect them. They were very concerned about too much rain creating landslides, a prolonged cold-snap causing a significant decline in the plants they eat, and other issues that would affect them individually and as a group.

A couple of days later, the fiery haired Smith decided the time was right to push tuhngiqr a little further. When they were quietly eating together, the human looked at the sasquatch and said, "Tuhngiqr, you've seen the Enemy running through your forest...er jungle, right?"

Quick—and solemn—was the reply, "Yes."

"Then I propose that we work together to rid our lands and jungles of these destructive creatures." Smith paused a moment, since doing so was the sasquatch way. When she resumed speaking she chose her words very carefully. "I'm sure you've seen the change they've brought to your jungle: the reduction in animal life around you so there's less to hunt, the wanton destruction they cause wherever they go. And like I've said before," at this point Smith perfectly took on the image of someone who's worried about a friend, "once they destroy we humans, they'll come after you. I'm certain of it!" Almost as an afterthought she added, "I've spoken about this with sp'atung and he agrees that something must be done."

This was far from the first time that the two of them had discussed this topic. Smith had directed tuhngiqr's attention to the War, the Enemy, and a possible alliance before—but never this directly. The reduction in subtlety wasn't lost on the hulking female. Slowly, perhaps slow even for a sasquatch, she finally replied, "I think you make sense. I agree now with you, but what can we do? We are few and I no want hunt and have my mi'tuhng get killed."

Smith's heart thrilled. Again, she treaded very carefully. "The only participation we would need from your people is to accompany our soldiers, perhaps one of your people for each of our teams, and use that sonic blast thing that you do to incapacitate the Enemy. Once that's accomplished, the odds won't be in the Enemy's favor nearly as much." With a conspiratorially wry grin she continued, "And the odds might even swing our way a whole lot."

Seeing Smith's grin, tuhngiqr smiled back in either agreement or acknowledgement. Then she stopped smiling and turned away. She looked off into the distance at a wall of the cave. There wasn't anything special about that section of dirt wall, but Smith was getting used to the sasquatch taking extended periods of time to quietly think. Finally the chief Lat' spoke. "I think this is good. But, I only one Lat' on Xruhnituhm Siem. There two others, and for choice to be make, two Lat' must be agree."

Undaunted and seeing the proverbial light at the end of the tunnel, the captain gently inquired, "Which of the other two do you think would be more likely to...see things as you do?"

Again, the sasquatch remained quiet for several minutes. At last she replied, "I no think steek'eew agree with us—not for many suns, maybe many rounds. Tsin'tsun'tsan maybe agree." She paused to look around the room and the outer corridor. It appeared to Smith that tuhngiqr looked surprisingly nervous, as if cloak-and-dagger discussions of this nature were quite foreign to her. She scratched at her neck and flicked away a bug that had gotten into her pelt. "I not know if he agree, but he make choice quick."

"Then let's go talk to him," Smith enthusiastically replied.

The next day, they went to speak with tsin'tsun'tsan. Part of Smith's first impression of the Lat' was that he was flighty in his thoughts. He had a thick, beautiful pelt that was so green it was like new leaves in early spring. Though his movements and motions were not particularly quick or overly skittish, his conversation bore out Smith's impression.

"Yes, we speak now. What about? You want bracken tea?" He spoke to them as if he'd known both of them all his long life. That was certainly true of tuhngiqr but not Smith. "It is big having sen' here. Where you from?"

"The east," Captain Smith replied cordially.

They continually worked at bringing tsin'tsun'tsan's focus back to the discussion at hand. Smith watched as tuhngiqr sort of 'handled' the other.

When they'd been speaking, discussing, explaining and debating for a few hours tsin'tsun'tsan suddenly declared, "I see what you think. I vote with you, tuhngiqr." Before the captain could fully experience the elation that was immediately coursing through her, she heard the male sasquatch continue. "This all very strange."

"What do you mean?" tuhngiqr replied, sincerely interested in her friend's thoughts.

Tsin'tsun'tsan replied in his marble-chewing voice, "You come me to talk issue for Xruhnituhm Siem. We always talk things more slow—mainly things that not yet talked about with Xruhnituhm Siem." He sighed a loud sasquatch sigh and then said, "I not think anything wrong with you come here to talk in secret. But it feels...wrong. Like cow lilies that been picked and left out too long before eat."

The two visitors looked askance at their host. He seemed to be more nervous and skittish than normal. Smith suspected that this second Lat' was beginning to experience the feeling that he had perhaps made an overly hasty and poor decision. She quickly spoke up, "Tsin'tsun'tsan, I know that this is all a little irregular, but then, so is the War. Aliens from outer space coming to completely destroy we humans and then you and your people. It's so different from anything <u>any</u> of us have ever experienced." Smith gave a practiced sigh and concluded, "I'm just glad that you're using your authority as a Lat' to help your people, and mine." She looked at the male sasquatch closely and thought that she needed to add just a little more. "Remember that when times are desperate, it's often the case that the ends justify the means."

Looking up as if he just awoke from some sort of pleasant dream that had to end eventually, tsin'tsun'tsan asked, "What that mean, 'the ends justify the means'? I not know those words."

"It means that sometimes, what we face is so big and terrible that it doesn't matter what methods we use to overcome it. Because if we don't overcome that challenge, our principles and doctrines won't matter." With a tone of finality, she amended, "They'll die with us." Smith took a moment to think and then added, "Whether you want to get into this War or not, the War is coming to *you*. And if you choose not to fight, then instead of a few of your people getting killed in combat, they'll all get wiped out eventually."

Smith sat back and got quiet, allowing her words to dig their way into the hearts of her two companions and strengthen their budding resolves.

Several long minutes passed before tsin'tsun'tsan finally looked at his pair of visitors. When he did his countenance was changed and he had the look of firm resolution in his eye. All he said was, "I agree."

Releasing a breath she didn't know she'd been holding, tuhngiqr exhaled deeply and relaxed. Without wasting time she said, "It is good. We is ready to meet Xruhnituhm Siem and make choice." Not having a calendar, tuhngiqr didn't bother looking at any wall in particular. Instead the narrow-faced sasquatch just sat for a moment, staring at nothing for a few seconds, and then proclaimed, "We meet with next sun. I give words to steek'eew so he know we meet. Tsin'tsun'tsan, share the words to all sasquatch that they know we meet with next sun in Great Hall at high sun." Looking at tsin'tsun'tsan she asked, "How that sound?"

"It is good," the other sasquatch replied. With that, the junior Lat' took his leave and departed.

They quickly dispersed, tuhngiqr to visit with steek'eew and tsin'tsun'tsan to speak with everyone else.

Smith figured she'd better mill about amidst the cave's denizens and keep her ear to the ground to do her best at quelling any dissensions that might arise before the meeting in the Great Hall the next day. She overheard conversations about the recent harvest and about the antics the children had been creating. She heard some discussing the humans and others talking about their children moving out and digging out their own rooms in the communal cave.

As the day wore on she heard more and more discussions regarding the meeting of the Xruhnituhm Siem on the next day. Most were surprised and, instead of being suspicious of the secrecy of the meeting's topic, they were simply very curious and a little bit confused. As she listened in, the main thread that seemed to permeate all the discussions was, 'We have never had a meeting like this, in which we did not have a clue regarding its purpose. What is going on?'

At last the meeting arrived at noon on the next day. Due to sheer curiosity there was a greater gathering of sasquatch than was normal. Everyone wanted to know what it was all about. The mood in the room was nearly electric and there was an air of excitement...and concern.

Smith saw her four human companions standing together looking as confused as the rest of the group.

Smith made sure that she stood apart from any of the Lat', especially tuhngiqr. She didn't want the trail back to her to be too obvious. She knew that this would all work better and garner more popular support from the sasquatch if it appeared that this idea— this vote—was spawned from their own kind. *Everyone likes to think that what they do was their own idea in the first place,* she reflected.

As is customary with the sasquatch, the meeting began quickly, without any pomp or flare. All those present simply got quiet when it was time to begin and then waited for someone of authority to speak. Tsin'tsun'tsan stood forward and, before he began to speak, Smith thought, *Have someone else host the meeting, tuhngiqr. Nice touch. You're catching on.*

Upon looking at everyone in the room with one brief, cursory glance tsin'tsun'tsan spoke. "Thank you for come. The

Xruhnituhm Siem learn of something—a need." All ears in the room seemed to prick up even more than they already were. "Our jungle has Tarantulas. Gets killed by Tarantulas. They hunt and kill our plants and animals." Some heads began to nod in agreement—but not all. "More and more plants are hurt or killed." A few more heads joined the chorus of nods. "It not safe for children outside cave." Smith was surprised that she found his rock munching voice mildly soothing. Tsin'tsun'tsan's last statement got more attention from the audience, and more nods. Smith could see that he was beginning to get the audience behind him. He definitely didn't have the whole group, but it appeared that he now had nearly enough of the sasquatch agreeing with him so that the Xruhnituhm Siem's upcoming decision wouldn't be stricken down by a popular uprising, or whatever passed for one in the sasquatch culture. "I have speaked with the sen' and learn of weapons Tarantulas have. If Tarantulas come to cave they kill *many* of us and we not able to live in cave again! So we talk and make choice to maybe work with the sen' get rid of Tarantulas."

He stopped speaking, providing a typical sasquatch break in the "conversation." For various reasons, neighbor shared fearful look with neighbor. The sasquatch looked at each other in confusion and doubt. Only a very few looked on with something akin to uncertainty. As a people the sasquatch were similar in their response to that which had been tsin'tsun'tsan's. He too had felt very odd about the speed of these proceedings and the sheer magnitude of it all. So it was with so many of the sasquatch at that very moment. They were confused and unsure, but wanting to help themselves and others. They knew the Enemy were out there and would never be their allies. It was just too much coming at them too quickly. The speed with which events were spiraling out of control was totally foreign to their quiet minds.

Once tsin'tsun'tsan finished speaking, another Lat' spoke, steek'eew. Smith remembered all too well that this was the only Lat' out of the three who was not on board with her. She figured that he would do his best to thwart her efforts with the next few words he would speak.

Steek'eew didn't disappoint her. His old eyes held plenty of caution. His deep black pelt with a single off-white patch on his back looked regal on him.

"My friends. I knew not what think when one Lat' come give words with me with last sun. She give me know we have this meet." Steek'eew looked around the Great Hall and, for the first time, didn't seem to be seeing the people. It was as if he was viewing their great history and heritage back through the ages. He seemed to almost be able to see the many rounds of harmonious tradition crumbling away before his very eyes!

With a tear in his eye steek'eew resumed his speech. "I never see this kind of thing in my rounds. I not *hear* of such words before!" Though he was full of emotion, the humans were surprised that his voice wasn't riddled with contempt, but rather sadness and disappointment. "I think tuhngiqr and tsin'tsun'tsan make choice alone, without me, to make...alliance so they can have their choice made law on this sun." He paused to allow the catch in his throat to pass which was just as well. It gave the audience the chance to reconsider what they'd heard and try to understand what it all meant. When steek'eew resumed speaking he seemed to do so with greater earnestness and sincerity than before. Much more. "I no can choose how other two Lat' will vote, so I ask you help them know we need do things as we have done for many rounds. This how we be people we are."

There was a loud rumbling of voices beginning to erupt from hundreds of throats. It wasn't riotous. Yet to those present, it felt that way since they'd never had anything like a riot before.

"Friends! Friends!" steek'eew continued, trying to make himself heard again. His voice that sounded like grinding gravel grew in volume. "Dear friends! Please! Listen!" The crowd slowly quieted down, ready to listen again. "I not had time to think of what been said, not even some breaths. *You* not have time too! Maybe we come agree with tuhngiqr and tsin'tsun'tsan, but we need time think so we make good choice."

Smith noticed that the crowd was definitely swaying toward steek'eew. She caught tuhngiqr's eye, which was getting more worried by the moment. When their eyes met, she let the sasquatch know that it wasn't over, they could still win. With a glance she communicated to the other that time was of the essence and they needed to press on–now!

When steek'eew finished his brief speech, tuhngiqr stepped forward and the Great Hall became as silent as a tomb. Doing a fair job of hiding her nervousness and trepidation, she spoke again.

"I know we always do things one way, but desperate times call for desperate measures." Though she said Smith's words clearly, it was obvious that she was less familiar with them.

Despite the mood in the room, tuhngiqr pressed on. "We need do <u>now</u> something, before we killed! Remember, our law say we <u>must</u> vote on this thing, because we together as Xruhnituhm Siem."

All eyes in the room looked at her as if she'd grown a third eye, or was possessed with a demon. It seemed to some that they were seeing tuhngiqr for the first time, despite the many decades they'd all lived together. Notwithstanding the great trust they'd all had in her judgment up until a few minutes ago many of their hearts were filled with great concern. Perhaps the sasquatch who looked the most dumbfounded was steek'eew.

After what seemed an eternity, steek'eew slowly turned back toward the crowd, away from tuhngiqr, and quietly said, "We follow our law, if not tradition." Though he spoke quietly, his voice was heard in every ear for the silence in the Great Hall was truly palpable. "We vote!" he said. The other two Lat' turned to move into an adjacent room where the three of them would customarily discuss the issue further and then anonymously cast their votes. However, before they took a handful of steps, steek'eew bellowed for all to hear, "Stop! Our *law* not make us vote in secret. Only *tradition* demand that. We vote here for all see."

Shamefacedly tuhngiqr and tsin'tsun'tsan looked at each other, too nervous to speak. Woodenly, they moved back toward steek'eew. Without further preamble, steek'eew spoke to the other two Lat', but plainly he wanted all in the room to hear. Still full to capacity, the Great Hall was filled with sasquatch who wanted to witness the vote that would soon be carried out by the Xruhnituhm Siem. "We hear words for help the sen' against the Tarantulas and we hear words against." Then, speaking to his two fellow Lat' so all in the cavernous room could hear, "We now make choice of will we do these words by tsin'tsun'tsan to help the sen'." Steek'eew paused and then concluded, "Xruhnituhm Siem, hold forth your rocks." As with all meetings in the Great Hall, each of the three Lat' had come to the meeting prepared. Each one carried a pair of ceremonial rocks–one white and one black. The black rocks were to be held aloft to signify a vote in favor of the proposition. A white rock would be a dissenting vote. With his back to the other two,

Steek'eew did not immediately see what he already knew would happen. He shamelessly held aloft the only polished, white rock.

Meanwhile, Colonel Garrison was traveling to Montreal with his surprisingly massive convoy. The story had been that he'd be leading a team to aid the Canadians but something didn't quite wash.

He was in one of many helicopters that had been assigned to him. He was just fine with not being in the same one as Reznikov, the 'co-leader' the president had assigned to work with him. *Or is it the other way around? I still don't fully understand the chain of command. Reznikov is supposed to run the diplomatic and political side of things while I run the military side. We're supposed to be equals, but every time the president explained it to me, it sounded like I'll eventually end up taking my orders from him.*

Sitting there quietly in the large chopper he looked up at his five horsemen and knew that he needed to finally share some of his thoughts with them. "Men, you know I've been behaving a little differently since I was promoted to colonel." Their heads bobbed in acknowledgement. "It's not because of the promotion. It has to do with the fact that I feel like I'm being used as a pawn in some game of power." They began to listen more attentively. "General Martin pulled me aside back at Camp Dodge and told me how he thought the president was trying to make a power grab or something. Just before we left the president spoke to me and sort of suggested that there were people in the government who could not be trusted and would do anything to seize the government. I couldn't help but think that she was mainly suggesting the general." He paused to let what he'd said sink in to his audience. "So, I need to tell you. I believe you're the *only* people I can absolutely trust right now." He looked out the window of the craft, hating the position he'd been put in and added, "Hopefully that'll change. Hopefully things won't turn out to be as bad as they look but for now, you men are my entire inner circle."

The five men Colonel Garrison had recently caused to be promoted to lieutenant responded with different expressions ranging from surprise to pride. Finally one of them queried, "Are you sure?"

Garrison ran his hand through his hair and said, "I'm not sure about anything. I just know that there's an awful lot of mistrust surrounding Camp Dodge and the president and what with this war, it seems pretty insane." He turned away from the window and continued, "The way this convoy was essentially ready to go as soon as the president announced we'd be helping the Canadians, the president using the Butcher of Bryanskaya as her ambassador, some secret meeting that the general supposedly overheard and a whole host of other things I've heard from the president and from Martin. It just has my head swimming and, like I said before, I don't know who to trust." Silently he wondered, *Is the president trying to play me, or is it General Martin? Or both? Or neither?*

The convoy continued to move on.

CHAPTER 16
Sunset

Jack sat alongside the stream that ran near one of the mouths of the sasquatch cave. He was idly relaxing, allowing his thoughts to wander. After a short time, Sarah appeared and sat down next to him in a huff. He could feel the energy coming off her and he was certain it wasn't happy.

Sarah immediately began to speak. "I can't believe the sasquatch are going to work with the military!"

Jack smiled disarmingly and carefully replied, "I understand, but perhaps it will be what we need to beat back the Spiders."

Sarah glared at him but he knew it wasn't really directed at him, or perhaps even any one person. Except maybe for Captain Smith.

Trying to distract her, Jack said, "The Celeset was sure nice."

Though Sarah knew exactly what he was trying to do, she replied, "Yes. I never would've suspected that they would have a room set aside for where they make covenants and commitments to each other. Husbands and wives promising to be dedicated to each other. Parents and children. It was beautiful and so serene."

"To be honest, I especially liked the sasquatch kansel who we met in there." Chuckling he added, "She was even more placid than the typical sasquatch. She reminds me of my grandmother."

Totally surprised at Jack's rare reference to his past, Sarah couldn't help but laugh.

Jack thought to himself, *It was so...peaceful. This is the peace I've been seeking in the woods all these years.*

As they sat quietly, they saw tuhngiqr walking and talking with tsin'tsun'tsan. That reminded Sarah of what she'd been saying. "It's not like I think the sasquatch shouldn't mingle with our people, I just think that starting with our military in a warzone might not be the best way to begin." Exasperatedly she added, "I feel like the Xruhnituhm Siem, mainly tuhngiqr and tsin'tsun'tsan, are turning into Smith's lapdogs."

It was then that sp'atung appeared and sat down by them. Jack and Sarah weren't surprised when he invited himself into their discussion without being asked and sat close enough to Sarah for her to be aware of her "personal space." However, she ignored those feelings and welcomed her new friend and his sasquatch culture.

"How are you sp'atung?"

"Very well, Soruh." His gravel crunching voice was still struggling to pronounce Sarah's name. "I feel good as wind in trees."

They all sat quietly for a minute when Sarah asked, "Sp'atung, I know you originally brought us to your home to encourage your own people in taking a role in eliminating the threat from the Spiders but what do you think about the way things are happening?"

"I think it good is and I want meet more sen'." He said it with such an honest, optimistic smile that Sarah didn't know what to say. Jack did. Seeing the excited and naïve smile on sp'atung's face caused a bittersweet feeling to course through Jack's heart. Brushing away one stray tear from his eye he simply noted, "We humans are all different. Some will give you the shirt off their back. Others will try to take it from you for no reason at all."

The resultant silence that emerged felt like an impossibly icy cold blanket over Jack's heart, but to sp'atung, it was a cloud of confusion. *He'll learn,* Jack said to himself. *Through painful experience, he'll learn.* Jack's silent lamentation was like a stale, colorless sunset ending a bright, beautiful day.

CHAPTER 17
A Cup of Coffee

Everything is going according to plan, Captain Smith grinned to herself. *Too bad I have to continually make sure tuhngiqr and tsin'tsun'tsan aren't losing their nerve. I hate playing politics.* What with her frustration with the two sasquatch, she had to make a conscious effort not to spit. She was, after all, in the middle of a discussion with those two sasquatch as well as a few others.

Tsin'tsun'tsan was saying, "I am no sure that send any sasquatch to meet sen' warriors be good idea. No yet." Some nodded their heads in agreement, or at least in acknowledgement of a point worth considering. As the only human present, Smith looked around the group, sizing them up. She knew that the two members of the Xruhnituhm Siem were on board with her plan to take at least one sasquatch with her to a military base, however reluctant they may be. The rest of those present had learned of that idea one way or another. Smith wasn't particularly worried about that. Through her various encouragements, reasonings and cajolings she had made sure this—oversight committee?—was entirely populated by sasquatch who, in some degree, favored the decision made by their leaders.

We NEED their help! she thought.

Though at a passing glance Smith looked like a dwarf compared to the others present at this meeting, her efforts, vision and sheer force of will made her appear as a giant in their eyes. She had pushed and manipulated individuals and groups of sasquatch into going along with the Xruhnituhm Siem's decision to work with humans. For a moment she reflected, *I can't wait to get back to battling the Enemy on the battlefield. This diplomacy and politics stuff is frustrating and exhausting.*

Out of the thirteen sasquatch present, only three of them were not yet towing the line to the extent that Smith would've been satisfied. They'd all talked back and forth, discussing pros and cons as much as discussing their own families and, of course, the mi'tuhng. Had Smith had an inkling of interest in anthropology, she would've been content to stay and just listen until the end of time. However, being a soldier at heart, she grew increasingly frustrated with the calm, pleasant, incessant dialogues.

Knowing that she needed to control her temper and handle these creatures in a way that would encourage them to see things her way, she waited until they took a break from speaking. With that she stood, trying to garner every last inch of respect and obedience from them. Seeing that she was about to speak, they were a little surprised since the current break in conversation was understood by them to be a brief pause during which all could think before speaking. Smith also knew that but was tired of waiting. "My friends," the captain nearly grated. "The Enemy is attacking us on all sides. As we've said before, once we humans are destroyed it will only be a matter of time before you're hunted down...and exterminated. The longer we wait around here the less my people are going to be able to work with and help you."

They all sat quietly, looking on. She felt their stares on her. She wouldn't have described them as cold. Rather, they seemed to be heavily laced with concern and trepidation. Uncertain of how to proceed in the face of this response, Smith sat down and merely stared at them with a blank face.

Tuhngiqr, seeing that it was up to her to say something, finally spoke. "Smith Captain, thank you for your good words. But you must know. Change hard for us. We no do change well. This big change for us. Biggest in all our rounds. We know what do, it just take time to make big change."

Satisfied by this entreaty, Smith smiled a genuine smile. She knew she had their help. She now knew the sasquatch *would* help the humans defeat the Enemy. Smith nodded her head in acquiescence.

However, she was still wanting to get things moving and therefore asked, "When do you think—"

Surprisingly, one of the larger sasquatch present cut her off. He stood and said, "I go with you, Smith Captain. I will be the sasquatch that go with you." He sounded like machine chewing up metal and looked twice as strong. By the time he finished his brief speech, he was now no longer looking at Smith. Instead his gaze had slid over to tuhngiqr and tsin'tsun'tsan, the two members of the Xruhnituhm Siem who were present. His name was xtela. Smith noticed his striking blood-red pelt. Perhaps what she noticed most about him, however was his eyes. They were a strange mixture of typical sasquatch kindness and aggressiveness. Tsin'tsun'tsan spoke up immediately proclaiming, "Thank you this for, xtela. Tuhngiqr and I speak you alone before leave you."

While this dialogue was unfolding, Smith was carefully peering at xtela, and tsin'tsun'tsan. *I think this xtela and I are going to get along pretty well. He looks like a warrior willing to do whatever it takes to get the job done.* Ending her appraisal she concluded, *Only time will tell.* The eager look in his eyes matched his dark red pelt.

The meeting quickly dwindled away after xtela volunteered to go. Before it ended completely, tuhngiqr said, "I think we just need choose when go you." She was looking at xtela, not Smith.

Fearing that any other discussion might serve as another roadblock in making things happen, Smith spoke up before anyone else had a chance to do so. "We will need to leave no later than tomorrow...to help our two peoples as much as possible." No one else spoke. She knew this was tremendously faster than they would've preferred. *Who knows. Maybe they figure they need to provide some sort of ceremonial going-away-party before he leaves.*

Smith wasn't surprised that all eyes were on her. Nor that they all seemed to say the same thing, *This is not our way!* However, she knew they were close enough to capitulating. What she didn't know was how the War was going. Like a woman going to the doctor, unsure if she has a life-threatening disease, she thought to herself, *I have no idea how the War has been progressing these last few days. This War has moved so quickly, anything could've happened.* She shuddered involuntarily.

Correctly figuring that the people of the Earth desperately needed any advantage that could be mustered, she pressed on. "I know this is hard for you but people are dying out there and the sooner we *actively* begin working together, the fewer dead sasquatch there will be!" Smith tried to be civil, but she knew that wasn't her strong suit. Instead she did what she knew best— advance. "Xtela, will you be ready tomorrow morning?"

All eyes turned to him and, though he was large and powerful for a sasquatch, there was a hint of intimidation in his eyes for a moment, and then it passed. In a clear voice that resonated with confidence and surety he replied, "Black bears! I be ready go with you, Smith Captain."

Though xtela's exclamation was strange to her, Captain Smith managed to hide the release of the breath she'd been holding.

She'd succeeded! *We're finally going to get moving and get back to civilization.* She wryly thought to herself, *If the Enemy hasn't destroyed it all.*

All eyes were still on her and xtela. There was disbelief painted in some of their expressions. Some were pictures of a disappointment they themselves did not understand. However, one of their culture's pillars was that, when the decision was made, discussion was done. Yet this time, the decision didn't feel like it had been made by a governing body, and so they felt uncertain.

Nevertheless, even the sasquatch knew they couldn't just sit there indefinitely so, one by one, they rose and left. Smith made certain she was the last. She didn't want any of them continuing the discussion without her. She knew they were upset and felt something akin to betrayal but her focus was on winning the War and the survival of the human race. She needed these creatures that she'd been fortuitous enough to discover.

Late that night, the captain finally came to bed in the little room she shared with the other four humans. She saw the four lumps on the ground and moved cat-like amidst them till she found the two soldiers. She gently woke them, trying to be careful not to disturb the two civilians, and then spoke. "We leave in the morning."

Early the next morning, before the sun was up, Captain Smith was waking Jameson and Stansbury. Though she hadn't slept more than a brief handful of hours, she was ready, and very eager, to move out. It wasn't a desire to return home that drew her away, rather it was her insatiable interest in winning the War, and of course, she preferred associating herself with military personnel over civilians, to say nothing of wild animals that could speak. *It's like something out of some cheap science fiction movie around here,* she thought.

Xtela made some hasty goodbyes and then Smith, Stansbury, Jameson and xtela departed the safety of the cave, the sasquatch home. Smith knew that they should be able to keep up a good pace so as to arrive in Drain, Oregon in less than a week. She left Jack and the sandy blond-haired Sarah at the cave. Being civilians, they didn't have clearance to go with her to a military base. Besides, they weren't ready to leave. *Tree hugging fools!* Smith thought of them. *At least I'll never have to see those two yokels again.* She smiled at this thought.

It was a strange procession that made its way across the raw, untamed Oregon backcountry. Being sasquatch, xtela didn't mind the quiet and certainly didn't interpret it as anything having to do with their collective sociality. Smith on the other hand enjoyed the quiet because she found that when people weren't talking, she wasn't having to listen to "so much asinine gibberish."

Every few hours, one of the two enlisted men would ask xtela a question about the sasquatch and their culture. The answers were always readily available and devoid of "an angle." During one such instance Stansbury asked, "How old do you sasquatch get?"

Xtela replied simply, "Two hundred rounds."

That brought a slow, thoughtful whistle from Jameson. *They live for two hundred years!*

They continued on their journey, some semi-mutely enjoying their surroundings, others stoically focusing on the mission.

The second day came and with it, a light drizzle of typically cold Oregon rainfall. Undaunted and uninterested in taking longer than she supposed was necessary, Smith pressed on. The two men under her command silently, and sometimes morosely, plodded on after her. Xtela followed suit but the rain didn't seem to bother him or affect his spirits. His thick, shaggy pelt seemed to have a natural oil to it that not only had an odd smell, but served as an effective water-proofing agent. His three companions noticed the smooth, powerful movements of his muscles beneath his blood-red pelt.

A pair of hours after lunch xtela stopped short. Smith in the lead did not notice at first. However, sensing the sudden tenseness of the hairy creature, she stopped as well and cocked her weapon. Following their leader's example, Stansbury and Jameson did the same. They instinctively formed a circle, backs to the center. Meticulously they scanned the surrounding forest for any hint of movement or danger. After more than a minute of statue-like vigil, they began to think they were jumping at shadows. Then they heard it. The telltale soft mewling sound that the Enemy made. It was their own form of vocal communication. It sounded like a soft whimper whispering through the trees. Smith realized that she'd better say something or this might unnerve her companions.

She spoke quietly, "Steady, boys. Just take it easy. Relax and pick your targets carefully and quickly." She spared herself a very brief glance at the others and added, "We can do this!"

Wondering if they were being hunted in some sort of premeditated way or if they were just in the wrong place at the wrong time, Smith mutely motioned to the three individuals with her to get down low to hopefully avoid detection.

A moment later, several bursts of the Enemy's green sludge came blasting out of the foliage. The SPAWNs made their telltale *wump* sounds. The first few acidic compounds landed all around them in a buckshot pattern. One of the globules took Private Stansbury. He never had a chance.

Seeing from whence it came, Smith and Jameson fired a barrage into the underbrush. They were rewarded with the sight of some Enemy blood leaking out from behind a bush. *Too bad there wasn't more,* Smith considered. *That much blood means we probably only got one of them.*

The three of them crouched tense and ready, focusing on where they had fired, but doing their best to divert as much attention as they dared to the remainder of the compass. Smith, still on one knee, looked confident and ready to fight to the last. Jameson looked shaken up, but resigned to his duty. His hands shook only a little as he mentally prepared to meet his end. Xtela, the hunter, looked eager as if ready to finally test his skills on such a worthy opponent.

After several tense seconds they all heard the sound the Enemy always seemed to make just before making a charge. Smith knew it was them speaking and coordinating with each other. She knew there was little chance of any of them coming away unharmed or even alive. *And what of the War?* Smith wondered. *I have what the world needs to fight these monsters. If I don't make them aware of the sasquatch and their unique abilities—.*

She stopped, realizing she had what she needed right there in xtela. *As good a time as any for a field test,* she thought desperately. Aloud she said, "Xtela! Do that...er...loud, screechy thing you sasquatch do!" She had not yet heard the sasquatch Voice so she wasn't sure how to describe it.

For a precious handful of heartbeats, xtela looked askance at Smith, uncertain what she meant. Smith and Stansbury covered their ears. Then, as understanding dawned on him, he turned to face the now visibly approaching Enemy. He let out a loud, piercing bellow just like Sarah heard those many days ago. Almost instantly, every Enemy—and human—collapsed to the ground, stunned. Fortunately for the humans, they'd been covering their ears and the blast was aimed elsewhere, at the Enemy. However, that fact didn't help that much, and due to the different physiologies, the Enemy were back up on their feet after only a dozen seconds or so. The Spiders quickly began cutting down the distance between them and their quarry.

Regaining her senses by sheer force of will, Smith saw their impending doom. She saw Stansbury lying their dead and Jameson lying on the ground, immobile due to xtela's sonic blast. A little blood was leaking out his nose, but Smith's instincts told her that his condition wasn't critical. She dropped her rifle, cupping both hands over her ears as tightly as she could. She looked at a startled xtela and painfully struggled to command him to do it again, but this time with more power and a longer blast. Xtela nodded and took a deep breath. During that breath, Smith couldn't help but notice how close the Enemy all were. They couldn't have been more than forty meters away. She could see one of them swinging a SPAWN around from one hairy arm to another, similar to how a theatrical cowboy might spin his six-shooter. Right then, xtela let loose a sonic boom like few had ever heard.

The blast that erupted from his mouth and vocal cords was truly awesome! It slammed into the Enemy soldiers like a ton of bricks. They all fell in a heap wherever they were. Most of them were moving so fast that they rolled and skidded to a stop. One of them nearest the front was even bleeding a little.

Captain Smith, thoroughly dazed by the second blast, though not as much as she would have been had she not covered her ears so completely, slowly put her left hand on the ground to support herself. She noticed how slippery her thoughts were. She knew it was urgent that she remember whatever it was she needed to do. So she kept her eyes on the Enemy combatants that littered the surrounding forest floor. That gave her the constant reminder of what she was supposed to be doing right then. Worse than any inebriation she'd ever experienced, she raggedly groped for her rifle with her right hand, feeling like the hand was all numb. After a couple of attempts, she was able to scoop it up. She saw that one or two of the Enemy creatures were beginning to stir. She had no idea how much time had passed since the second blast. Five seconds? Thirty seconds?

Smith lethargically drew her weapon up. It all felt so slow, like watching a single hair falling through honey. She did her best to sight along the barrel, but between the dizziness in her head and the difficulty of holding onto the weapon, she just aimed at the nearest dark smudge in her vision and fired. She heard the thuds that provided acknowledgement that she'd hit her target.

A stray, peripheral thought told the captain she had to work fast. She knew she wouldn't be able to withstand another sonic blast, no matter how tightly she covered her ears. She found another fuzzy bit of darkness somewhere across her temporarily impaired vision and fired again. Again she was rewarded with proof that she'd hit the mark.

Rough though her vision was, she was able to make out that her remaining targets were beginning to stir. She tried to hang on to the insanely slippery thought that she had to move faster, get them all before they had a chance to be on the move again. She staggered a little but caught herself before she went down, knowing that for some reason she needed to stay upright, that if she didn't something terrible would happen. Allowing her anger at the situation to seep back into her, she found just enough focus to resume her work. Amidst her oily thoughts she plugged two more of the Spiders that were near each other and moving a little more than the others.

She could just barely notice that her thoughts were becoming less greasy in her mind. They were beginning to solidify and find more traction. Unfortunately, her eyes told her the same thing was happening for the few Spiders that still lived. She ignored the gun sight and just quickly aimed for anything that looked like an extraterrestrial. She heard several more reassuring thuds as she expertly discharged her weapon. The few remaining Enemies were just about ready to get on their feet again. Smith was trying to hurry, certain that, like a polar bear coming off a tranquilizer, her Enemy would come out of the effects of the sonic blast more quickly than she. Her sight was like rain streaking down a window, blurring her vision. She had lost track of which of the dark shapes she'd shot and which ones she hadn't. She fired again, certain some of her shots hit the mark, but having no way of knowing if what she hit had already been killed. Sluggishly her mind thought, *They're stirring. They'll be up and coming this way again any second.* She fired a few more rounds, her vision clearing up only a little more.

Smith blinked and the remaining Enemies were on their feet and eating up the remaining distance like lightning. She fired again and winged one of them. Injured as it was, it kept moving. She fired another barrage at the same creature and finished it off. There were still two of the vermin remaining and she knew they would be upon her in an instant. She lifted her rifle to fire at one of them, as a fleeting thought raced across her mind with depressing finality, *I only have time to fire at one of them.*

Captain Smith made a quick aim and fired. Normally, the Enemy aberration would've dodged but it was *so* close, and probably still feeling some effects from the sonic blasts, it didn't have time. An instant after destroying the creature Smith thought, *There's no way I'll get the last one. It's only three meters away.* Right at that moment, a massive fist pounded the creature into the ground. Xtela had finally been able to execute an attack with the Enemy at hand-to-hand combat distance. Though shaken and damaged, the amazingly robust creature stood and advanced again. This time xtela used his fangs and the already stunned and injured monster was ripped and shredded until it ceased its movements. When it was over, the mighty sasquatch exclaimed, "Great Lakes! They strong for so small."

It was all over so quickly, even the battle-hardened captain found it hard to believe the skirmish had ended already, to say nothing of having survived. Smith and xtela stared at the carnage all around them. Dumbfounded, they spent a few seconds trying to make sense of what had just happened. For the still dizzy Smith it went further than that. *Out of all the battles I've fought, I never thought I wouldn't survive. Until this one.* No tears escaped her eyes nor did a look of fear cross her face. Nevertheless, she felt the gravity of the moment very poignantly and in a manner she'd never experienced before.

Almost as if they had planned it, they simultaneously looked over at the fallen forms of their comrades. One of them dead, the other incapacitated to a degree they did not yet know. Xtela stood peering down at the limp form of Jameson, unsure what to do. With a sense of duty and responsibility, Smith knelt down next to the fallen sergeant and assessed his condition. He was certainly still breathing and didn't appear to have received any wounds from SPAWNs or the Enemy themselves. She assumed that he was merely driven to some sort of painful unconsciousness by xtela's sonic blasts.

Unable to do anything more for him, Smith set to work burying Stansbury. Since the sasquatch don't bury their dead, it took xtela a few moments to figure out why Smith was digging a large hole in the ground. Once he understood, he voluntarily joined in and soon they had a hole large enough for Stansbury's body.

The only words spoken as they dug were by the captain. "We need to hurry. We don't know if there will be more of them coming."

They laid the body of the young private in his fresh grave and Smith was pleased that the hole appeared to be deep enough that wild animals would not be inclined to dig him up.

Xtela picked up the still unconscious Jameson and easily slung him over his large, hairy shoulder. They moved out quietly, continuing their somber sojourn to the small town of Drain. As they trudged on, the beauty around them was somehow strange and foreign considering the short battle they'd just survived.

Eventually, Sergeant Jameson awoke; it was later that same day, after the trio had moved across several miles of raw countryside. They were taking a break and he began to stir. Finally, he opened his eyes. It appeared that it took a lot of effort on his part. He still looked thoroughly exhausted.

Upon seeing a sign of life from the young sergeant, Smith walked over to him from the tree stump on which she'd been sitting. "Jameson. Are you okay?"

Quite unsure of what had happened, especially in light of the fact that his last memory was of intense pain in his head while the Enemy bore down on them, he numbly responded, "I'm okay. I guess." He began to breathe more evenly and then tried speaking again. "What happened?"

The captain filled him in on how the battle had transpired. She included how Stansbury had died and been interred. For security reasons, she glossed over and downplayed xtela's part in the battle. When she was done with her tale, Jameson mutely nodded in acknowledgement. The movement of his head made him wince in pain. She knew that he and Stansbury were becoming good friends over the many days since the battle of Oscar-Romeo-17 and that he would take it a lot harder than she would. *I never really knew the kid*, she thought with a hint of emotion.

They rested for another half hour. The break would've been shorter but now that Jameson was conscious, he insisted on moving on his own power. Xtela used that half hour to quickly fashion a crutch for the sergeant. The young man wasn't physically damaged with a broken leg or even a pulled muscle, but they knew that the effects of the sonic blasts would leave him at weakened till at least the end of the day. So, as they resumed their march, the mourning and subdued Jameson used the crutch for balance. Smith thought with scientific consideration, *After being hit by the first blast, xtela's second sonic blast must've hit him especially hard.* She looked ahead of herself at him. *I guess it would've been like cutting into a raw, open wound with a rusty chainsaw.*

Despite the inherent solemnity of the battle, more especially the death of one of her comrades, she could not keep a smile from maneuvering its way across her face. *Instead of all four of us being completely obliterated, we only lost one man.* Smith continued hiking and then paused again so as not to overrun Jameson. Then a wicked gleam emanated from her piercing eyes. *As far as I can tell, though they ambushed us, we wiped out every last one of the worthless creatures in that sortie.* The strategic importance and value of the situation was not lost on the captain.

That night they made camp next to a large boulder in the midst of a thicket of trees. It was defensible and reasonably well hidden. They made no fire for they wanted to avoid the attention of any Spiders that might be passing through the area. Jameson still hadn't said much of anything and just seemed to be going through the motions of walking and eating like some kind of machine, devoid of a soul. He lay down after he ate a little and was soon asleep.

Smith and xtela were still awake. Smith had volunteered for the first watch and xtela smiled, finding the need for a 'watch' to be humorous. Before Smith took up her position, she asked the sasquatch, "What do your kind do when someone dies?" A human would've easily recognized Smith's flat tone to be possessed with emotion—and pain.

However, xtela was not yet familiar with the various inflections, timbres and intonations of human speech. So he replied simply, "I give you the words with next sun."

Smith mulled xtela's brief words in her mind as she took up the first watch. She wondered why he hadn't told her right away. *I suppose it is something very special to them.*

The night past blessedly uneventfully. In the morning they resumed their trek.   Walking past a truly majestic waterfall, xtela replied in a reverent, yet no nonsense way. "It very sacred to us." His churning voice seemed to smoothly merge with the sounds of the waterfall. He paused as Smith looked askance at xtela, unsure what he was getting at. Jameson made no outward response. Smith waited patiently as the three of them continued along their path. "When sasquatch dies, we take body to water." He paused again, perhaps trying to decide if he should continue. "We take body to good place of water deep." Xtela looked around at the surrounding woods and peered at a porcupine that was eating at some bit of stuff a dozen or so meters away. "At water other sasquatch Speak about dead sasquatch. Speaking take till high sun, but sometime it longer." A wry chuckle of amusement erupted amidst his words. "One mi'tuhng leader truly loved die. When he die, the Speaking go three suns!"

Smith looked on, perhaps a bit cynically, but after her experiences with the sasquatch civilization she knew that xtela probably wasn't exaggerating at all. Upon thinking on what he'd said for a minute or two, a question entered her mind. "Wait a minute. What happens after the...Speaking? Do you cremate or bury or what?"

Wresting his attention back to the discussion, xtela exclaimed, "Black bears! Oh, yes. I forget. After the Speaking, body is made heavy and go under water in part deep of water so body there stay."

"And that's it?" Smith asked, feeling like she was missing something.

With a look of surprise xtela responded, "Yes, that it. Why?"

Becoming nearly red-faced with exasperation, Smith said, "You just leave the body in the water where the fish will eat it up and destroy it?"

Looking slightly amused xtela said, "Yes. It not matter. Fish eat. Worms eat. It same. This way, body of sasquatch be food for dirt, plants and animals for place he love much."

Smith was ready to reply in an almost acid like fashion. However, just before speaking, she checked her tongue and thought about what her large, ferocious looking companion had said. *In a way, that goes against everything I've never known or believed,* she thought in a somber way, *but it makes sense.* Perhaps the biggest surprise to Smith was the thought—or was it an emotion—that was slowly creeping into her soul. She was beginning to see xtela as something other than an animal or tool. She couldn't put her finger on it. All she knew was that this confusing, ethereal revelation made her uncomfortable.

The next day Smith said to her two traveling companions, "We'll probably hit the small town of Drain today. I don't know what time but we'll see it before we're there. There's hills all around it and so as we come off of one of them, we'll see it."

In the distance the humans could barely hear the powerful waterfall behind them, thrashing and burbling.

Late that afternoon, the three weary companions crested a beautiful hill to the south and finally saw their destination. They had been seeing increasing numbers of civilization during the last few miles of their hike before seeing the small town of Drain, Oregon. From Mount Yoncalla, their trail lead them past Sheep Hill and then Bear Hill. Knowing they were getting close, they stayed to the trees to avoid any locals seeing xtela. Once they were in sight of the town, Smith issued orders. "I'll go into town alone. You two stay here and sit tight."

Xtela didn't care one way or another so he sat at the base of a large pacific dogwood tree.

After ten minutes, Captain Smith reached the edge of town. Standing on the first pavement under her feet in weeks, her automatic thought was, *This place has no strategic value.*

Despite her rigid disinterest in the town that she viewed as a 'backwater village', she found herself becoming interested in some of the things she saw. A cross along the side of the road where someone had died. A large pile of firewood in a front yard. She saw the 'Welcome to Drain' sign just before a solitary sidewalk began on the east side of the street. She looked up and saw that the name of the street she was walking was Cedar Street. In her fiercely patriotic fashion she thought to herself, *That's almost as American as apple pie.* For the first time in a long time, a smile crept onto her face that had nothing to do with winning the War.

Moving steadily toward what appeared to be the center of town, Smith ignored the quizzical looks that her ragged appearance prompted. After several locals stopped and stared, she realized it wasn't just the fact that she was carrying a high-powered, government issued firearm. Her clothes were tattered with dirt, blood, and who knew what else–and more than a few holes. *I must look a sight.*

Perhaps the only thing that kept the local denizens from reacting more fearfully was what all that living off the land and with the sasquatch couldn't cover up. She was still a fire-haired beauty and, though her eyes might've said otherwise, no amount of dirt was going to hide that.

She ignored everyone, of course. She merely kept hiking toward what appeared to be her destination, some type of coffee shop wherein she'd hopefully be able to make contact with her superiors. With luck, she'd be able to quickly get a hold of General Martin himself. That would get the ball rolling.

Continuing her northward bearing, she walked past a defunct mini-storage and didn't notice the name. Soon she walked across a simple bridge and saw her destination–Uncle John's Great Coffee. She had to restrain herself from double-timing it the rest of the way. She wanted to get back to the only family she'd ever known, or at least the only one she could remember–the military.

She strode into Uncle John's like she'd been there a thousand times. The locals seated at various booths and barstools knew better. Sarah's town of Drain wasn't all that big. Smith asked the man behind the counter to use his phone. Normally he would've said "no" to a stranger since phone service was a highly coveted commodity that seldom worked, but Captain Smith was no ordinary stranger. He merely said, "We only got two phones and one shortwave in this town." He paused and then added, "Here's one of the phones. Go easy on it. It's a precious to us here."

The conversations and chatter didn't completely stop, but they all became very subdued. Certainly Smith was the center of everyone's attention. After pressing every button on the phone at least three times each, she began speaking. That's when everyone else became completely silent except for one little girl playing with an old doll.

"Alpha-Mike—Niner-November-Foxtrot," was all she said at first. A very brief barrage of whispering was heard throughout the establishment. Then she was heard to say, as if in response to a pair of questions, "Affirmative...affirmative."

Several tense seconds ticked by and then a few people pretending to be paying attention to something other than Smith and her phone call jumped in surprise as she piped up again, "Eight-six-zero-zero-niner-two-four." A few more moments passed and she spoke yet again. "This is Captain Smith of Oscar-Romeo-

17. Request immediate evac. Pickup site is two miles north of Drain, Oregon. Be prepared to airlift four...no, make that the equivalent of five adults." She paused a moment only, everyone in the diner on the edges of their seats except for the doll-playing girl. "Understood."

Smith hung up the phone and there was a collective sigh exhaled by nearly everyone present. They knew almost nothing more than they had before Smith had walked into their lives five minutes prior, but they would surely have plenty to discuss with friends and family that night.

The man behind the counter said, "Ma'am, you look like you could use a cup of coffee." She gratefully accepted it. Drinking it slowly, part of her mind rebelled against the claim that it was a "great" cup of coffee. However, after what she'd been through those last few weeks, and where she'd been, the rest of her mind won out insisting it tasted like the best thing she'd ever eaten as she savored every last drop.

CHAPTER 18
A New Hope

"General Martin!" It was Lieutenant Malistair, Martin's primary aide. She rarely came whirling into her boss's office, or anywhere else, and never without good reason.

The general looked up at her slowly, flashing his grandfatherly smile, trying to project an air of calm that he suspected she needed right then. "What's on the end of your line, Lieutenant?"

Familiar with his angling lingo, Malistair didn't skip a beat. "Sir, it's Oscar-Romeo-17."

Taking a moment to recall the camp, his eyes quickly took on a gleam of recognition. "Oh, yes. *Colonel* Garrison's old camp in Oregon. What about it?"

Malistair's posture drew her focus to a point at eye level on the wall across the room from her. By chance, it happened to be of a picture of the general fishing somewhere in Idaho with a friend of his. She recalled that the general never spoke of that picture, despite repeated attempts to learn about it from various junior officers. She'd certainly learned nothing of the man standing next to him in the photograph. The only thing she could discern was that it was taken a long time ago. The two of them couldn't have been thirty years old in the picture.

The lieutenant averted her gaze from the photo she knew from memory and looked down at the general before speaking again. "Two more survivors have been recovered."

Martin leaned back in his spartan office chair and looked up at the low ceiling as he let out a quiet whistle of surprise. *After all this time, more survivors from that debacle have been found*, he pondered. *But why are they emerging now? Why not weeks ago? Where have they been? What have they been up to?*

Aloud he said, "That's good news. Where are they now."

Before Malistair replied, she took on a very uncharacteristic look, something between confusion and sheepishness. "That's the strange thing. They're on their way *here* right now. They've been airlifted from a small town called Drain, Oregon. Apparently they made their way there after the battle."

Curious about this new revelation, he immediately turned to his desk computer and began looking up Oscar-Romeo-17 and Drain, Oregon. When the requested information came up on the search engine, he raised a single eyebrow in surprise and turned back to his aide. "It's been weeks. The distance between the two locations is no more than a few dozen miles." Pausing to consider this, he stared at his desk for a moment. "Are either of them injured? Perhaps that would have slowed them down."

"I have no report as to their physical condition. However, I would add that there was no indication, subtle or otherwise, to suggest that the two survivors were injured in any way."

He asked, "Estimated time of arrival?"

"One hour, seventeen minutes," came the brisk reply.

Martin thought again. *Something's...off here. Something doesn't feel quite right.* Aloud he pressed, "Who knows about this so far?"

For just an instant, a knowing look washed over Malistair's face before she replied, "You, the comm officer who received the communique and myself." She allowed a rare smile to play over her pretty features before continuing. "Fortunately, I was nearby when the message was received. Knowing that you might have your own reasons for wanting to be the first to know, I issued orders, in your name, for the comm officer to share this information with no one."

General Martin smiled that warm, grandpa smile that was only one of the reasons men followed him. "Thank you. Thank you very much." With a conspiratorial twinkle in his eye he said, "I don't see any reason to bother the president with this. For now, make sure as few people find out about this as possible. At least until we know how big a fish were frying. There's something strange about this. Something just doesn't add up."

Malistair replied simply with, "Acknowledged." With that, she turned smartly and exited the small office.

A cogitating General Martin was left to sit and wonder about these new proceedings. After several minutes of considering various scenarios and possible ways of putting the few pieces together that he had, he decided he could use his time more wisely by plowing through some of the reports on his desk that were beginning to take on the shape of a mountain.

An hour and seventeen minutes later, a newly developed AH-45X Mongoose attack-and-transport helicopter came rumbling through the sky toward the deceptively docile-looking Camp Dodge. General Martin would've referred to the massive machine as a 'flying fortress' if the B-17 heavy bomber hadn't already claimed the title. Its personnel capacity not only edged out the Russian Mil Mi-26, its armament and armor earned it the nickname, The Flying Battleship. Under optimal conditions, it was practically unbeatable. General Martin silently wished he had a few more of those at his disposal. He thought, *If wishes were fishes...* Unfortunately, most of the few that they'd built had already been destroyed in the War, before they really knew what they were up against.

The general joined Lieutenant Malistair on an obscure and isolated over-sized landing pad at one end of the Camp. It felt strange to him to be standing there, waiting to welcome soldiers back from such a harrowing experience, and only have a two-man parade to greet them. By now the feeling in his gut that something odd was going on had subsided. He wanted to believe they had a perfectly legitimate reason for not coming into communication sooner. Perhaps one or both of them had been presumed dead by Garrison as well as the Enemy and left for dead under so much rubble after the battle. One of them may have had a broken leg or some such thing. That would certainly explain things.

Amidst his strategic reverie, the titanic helicopter touched down gently, as if it were a civilian vehicle and didn't have a care in the world. The general allowed himself a handful of seconds to look around and see the old outbuildings behind him. He took in the greater beauty of what little he could see of Big Creek State Park across the lake. *Before the War,* he silently mused for the hundredth time, *that area would've been full of weekend vacationers much of the year. Now it's all but deserted. Hopefully our world can someday get back to the way things used be.* He paused in his reverie before admitting to himself, *If things ever do get back to 'normal', it probably won't be for another hundred years.*

As the helicopter's rotors were just beginning to slow down, a squad of tense soldiers spilled out of the amazing craft. To Martin's experienced eye, it seemed odd that these soldiers appeared to be on such a heightened sense of alert. They were only returning a pair of soldiers back to base for a debriefing. The public would've called it "a hero's welcome."

Following the small group of armed soldiers dismounting the mighty aircraft, a young man exited. Even from Martin's distance, the youthful looking sergeant looked something akin to shell-shocked. That didn't surprise the general, he just hated seeing the agonies of war take their toll on his men.

On the sergeant's heals trailed a beautiful, fiery-haired woman. *Definitely not shell-shocked, that one*, Martin quietly thought, as he sized her up as well. She was obviously the one in charge, and Martin didn't need to see her captain's bars to know it. Her whole demeanor and countenance seemed to exude self-assuredness and command.

And strength.

Upon seeing the second of the two survivors depart the helicopter, General Martin began walking over to welcome them to Camp Dodge, hoping in the pit of his gut that these survivors had learned *something* that might help turn the tide in this insane War. He only got a few steps under his feet before he saw something that nearly made his eyes dangle from their sockets. Emerging from the interior of the helicopter lumbered out a creature that was like something out of a movie. Or a nightmare. It stood around eight feet tall and probably weighed upwards of two hundred fifty kilograms. It was as hairy as anything he'd ever seen before. Yet it walked upright, like a man. It's bloodred pelt seemed to match the woman's hair in some otherworldly way. A skilled career soldier, Martin immediately noticed the rippling muscle all over its body as well as the short but powerful looking fangs. Undoubtedly, they promised tremendous violence if given the proper motivation.

Trusting the people under his command, Martin resumed his gait to the mass of people who had exited the helicopter. He took confidence in knowing that, despite being in such close proximity to this creature—this unknown quantity—his people were still alive and apparently interacting with it.

As the general approached the group he consciously stiffened his backbone and spoke in a carefully measured voice. "Welcome back, Captain." Pausing only a moment he resumed, "I'm General Martin." He paused and, while carefully glancing at the creature, added, "It would appear that introductions are in order." Martin was proud of himself for getting the words out without stammering at all. It was hard what with that behemoth towering over him like an avalanche.

The captain stepped forward and spoke briskly, all calm, self-assurance. "General." She saluted smartly and continued. "My name is Captain Sonya Smith. I was sent to Oscar-Romeo-17 just before the attack. In that capacity, my commanding officer was a Major Garrison."

Upon hearing that name, Martin smiled and wryly said, "Yes, I've met *Colonel* Garrison. Good man."

Startled by this revelation, she continued with the utmost poise. "This is Sergeant Jameson," she said, turning to the young man at her eight o'clock. Martin noted that Jameson barely acknowledged his introduction–or anyone present for that matter. Martin reflexively thought, *That fish has been out of the water a little too long.*

Turning only a little to her right, Smith extended a hand, indicating the hulking creature next to her. "And this is xtela."

Perhaps more surprised than initially seeing the animal was Martin's astonishment when he heard xtela offer, "Hello, Martin General?"

Despite his years of experience and even his recent adventures battling extraterrestrials, General Martin still found himself gaping wide enough to drive a truck into his mouth. As if the creature's appearance wasn't strange enough, its voice was unmistakably foreign. It reminded Martin of a cement mixer rolling gravelly material around.

"It okay," xtela continued. "I feel same when meet sen'." As he looked at Smith and Jameson, Martin assumed the word sen' meant them. Now that Martin had a moment to analyze xtela more closely, he couldn't help but notice his fierce visage. "Smith Captain try help me know about...this," he waved a mighty arm around to indicate human civilization.

Regaining his composure–and presence of mind, General Martin quickly began ushering his three guests toward the nearest hangar a mere fifty yards away.

The hangar was massive. With a two-hundred-sixty foot mouth, it could've housed a double-decker 747. Upon entering the building, the general took full control. Speaking to the guards who had come with his three distinguished guests, he said, "Men, these people are top secret. You never saw them. You've never heard of them. You certainly never escorted them." Taking on an even more austere countenance he concluded with, "As far as you know, you know *absolutely* nothing about them. Understood?"

In unison they responded with a hearty, "Yes, Sir!"

Continuing their walk, Martin finally stopped them at a floor hatch that could be accessed for the purpose of conducting repairs that may require getting below a low-lying vehicle. Martin figured it was seldom used and was rewarded with a view under the hatch that bespoke of little or no operations. Before entering he turned and, speaking to the guards he said, "You men, we'll be okay down here." From his peripheral vision, Martin caught an appraising eye from Smith. *She's impressed at how much I appear to feel at ease with this...creature.* "Just lounge around the hangar, keep people away, and if anyone asks about your authorization, it came *directly* from me."

Again, the familiar "Yes, Sir!" was repeated.

Dust everywhere and old, spotty mechanical liquid residue, the general and his three new companions stepped down into the darkness. Martin found a light, punched the switch to turn it on, and then lead the rest of the group down into the vacant "cellar." Finally away from prying eyes, they found some buckets to sit on and tried to get comfortable. None of them were able to, especially the huge xtela. On the other hand, Jameson appeared to be almost entirely oblivious to their surroundings and lack of comforts. *That kid's mind might never recover,* the general thought sadly.

Turning his attention back to the proverbial elephant in the room, Martin did not wait for any type of preamble. "All right, Smith. What's going on? I want the whole story."

Unflinchingly, she held his gaze. He was impressed. Nevertheless, she immediately dove into all the relevant details regarding what had happened to her since the battle of Oscar-Romeo-17. She didn't mention Sarah or Jack, but she did relate how Stansbury had died. She told a little of what she knew about the sasquatch culture and then concluded with, "Sir, the sasquatch could end up being the very ally we need to take the fight to the Enemy and turn the tide."

Mutely, the CJCS sat, staring at Smith and xtela. Calculating and considering the value of his new assets and how best to utilize them, his thoughts swirled within his mind. He sat like that for nearly two minutes. Smith's training as a soldier kept her from interrupting. Xtela's culture raised him to find such breaks in conversation to be pleasant. Jameson sat quietly.

Finally, General Martin spoke. "Xtela, I would like to organize a raid on a known Enemy stronghold. Are you willing to work with us to make that happen?"

Xtela replied, "That why I here. I tired of Tarantulas kill my jungle." Then, with an incredibly blood-thirsty look in his eyes, xtela summarized with, "Great lakes, I ready to hunt!"

Taken aback by xtela's sheer ferocity, Martin didn't notice at first a sound at the end of the pit. However, Smith did. Like lightning, she apprehended and hauled a young soldier who'd been behind some barrels of coolant.

Even before any of them had a chance to ask him any questions, he blurted, "I don't believe it. At first I saw the creature," staring wildly at xtela, "but it can talk to! What is it!?!"

Smith turned to her senior officer to take her cue from him. Martin didn't wait for anyone else to speak. In the dim light he said, "Son, what's your name?"

"Fetch, Sir." He was beginning to tremble. Perhaps shock was setting in. If it was, no one was offering him a blanket or help with elevating his legs. "Private Arthur Fetch." A belated "Sir" followed shortly thereafter. All present noticed that Private Fetch was short and lanky with a smear of oil on his face. It seemed that he was probably perpetually disheveled looking.

Martin looked at the young man, then at Smith, then back at the Private. "Son, you've just joined my general staff. All of you have." A look of pained confusion flew across Fetch's face. Smith merely looked concerned. "We need to keep this buttoned up tight. The fewer people who know about this fishing pond, the easier it will be to keep it secret so we can attack the Enemy most effectively."

Looking directly at Captain Smith he continued, "Smith, for now, you're one of my main aides. You will report directly to me and NO ONE else. You will be directly responsible for keeping this secret and keeping all who know about it in line. If word gets out, you're responsible. Understood?"

With a sour expression that quickly evaporated, Smith forcefully replied, "Yes, Sir."

"Excellent. Now, let's talk about where we go from here." The old General Martin was back as he began organizing and planning the bare bones of a strategy involving the sasquatch. "I seem to remember we have an old, unused utility building near the southwest corner of the base. For now, we'll put xtela in there to keep him out of sight. Once we—"

Xtela didn't waste time speaking up, which made Private Fetch nearly swoon. In his deep, rumbly voice he said, "Stop. I not understand a thing. Why you want hide me?"

The general took on a sad look generated by a lifetime of experience with other humans. In a hushed tone he nearly whispered. "It's a little hard to explain. Please trust me."

Martin couldn't have known it but asking xtela to trust him was the best thing he could've done. Captain Smith permitted a knowing look of understanding to overshadow her features for a moment. Perhaps she recognized the nearly blind trust that the sasquatch had in the Xruhnituhm Siem and other sasquatch.

Whatever was passing through the minds of those present, Martin could tell everyone was on board. *It's enough.*

Without any detectable expression, xtela replied simply by saying, "I stay there, in the...owbilling." Like all sasquatch, the sound of him chewing on his words was a little unusual. The sound of him pronouncing the word 'outbuilding' for the first time was strange to say the least. Xtela had obviously never heard the word "outbuilding." His initial pronunciation was even rougher coming off his tongue than most other words.

With obviously genuine gratitude tingeing his voice, Martin said, "Thank you. Now, I'd like you all to stay here until night. Smith will orchestrate the moving of xtela under cover of darkness. Will that be a problem?"

Knowing the question was directed at her, Smith simply replied, "No, Sir. I'll take care of it. He won't be seen."

Smiling, General Martin retorted, "Good. I'll have a plan ready to go by tomorrow. Captain, given your experience and intimate knowledge in this situation, I'd like your input on that plan."

"Yes, Sir."

Martin was only slightly surprised that she didn't give any indication of gratitude. *Most people in her position would*, he thought. *I'll definitely need to pull her file later today and see what I can learn.*

With that, the general departed and headed back for his office. On the way over he allowed a brief thought to move across his mind. *Should I inform Malistair about all this and bring her up to speed?* He paused in his tracks for only a moment as he quickly considered the answer. *No. Secrets have a way of getting out when too many people know them, no matter how trustworthy they are.*

Back in the mechanic pit, Smith immediately took control. She moved out of the pit to ground level and signaled all the guards who had come with her. "I'm Captain Smith. As per General Martin's orders, you now report to me. Understood?"

The sheer audacity, conviction, and certainty with which she spoke seemed to suppress all questions they might have had. Instead they simply replied in unison, "Yes, Ma'am."

Without smiling, she continued, "From now on, you will discuss what you've seen and heard here today with absolutely *no one*. Not even with each other."

"Yes, Ma'am," came the repeated response.

In her typically clipped tone, she continued her instructions, "You five will guard this hangar. No one comes in, except the general or myself, and no one goes out. Period! Understood?"

"Yes, Ma'am!"

"I'll return in a few minutes." Peering at them more intently, she sized up the group and selected the most serious looking one. "Sergeant, what's your name?"

Looking only a little shaken at being singled out, the man in question replied, "Sergeant Franks, Ma'am." He saluted unnecessarily but Smith was pleased at how quickly she was making a forbidding impression. *They'll be more likely to tow the line if they see me as some kind of bull barreling toward them.*

"Franks, you'll be in charge of your men here and the people down in that pit," she said as she pointed a thumb from where she'd recently emerged. "Anything goes wrong, it's your baby."

Paling only slightly, the brave, young man made an effort to give a solid, "Yes, Ma'am!"

Satisfied that security would be maintained during her brief absence, Smith left the hangar for a few minutes. She soon hurried back to the hangar where her new command was awaiting her return. She made sure everyone sat tight, despite being uncomfortable.

That night at 02:30, General Martin came to them alone and quietly escorted the nine-man entourage to the outbuilding mentioned earlier in the day. "We shouldn't have any problem avoiding being spotted by anyone."

They soon found that xtela certainly wouldn't slow them down. His long legs quickly ate up the ground and the rest of the group ended up jogging to keep up to his walk.

Without incident, they reached their destination and settled in. They were grateful to find that during the day, the general had some 'surplus furniture' sent to their outbuilding. They each had a bed to sleep on and were truly grateful for the sleeping conditions. Despite the general being present, Smith took command of her men. "Franks, nice work earlier today. You five will continue to maintain an around-the-clock watch."

Franks immediately made as if to issue an order to assign one of his men to stand guard outside. Before he could utter a word, Smith continued, "Single-man ought to be enough. After all, we are on one of our own military bases. However, the man on watch ought to be inside. He can conduct his surveillance of the surrounding area from the windows. That way we won't attract any undue attention."

Feeling a little more comfortable with his new superior officer, he merely nodded in acknowledgement and began issuing orders to the four men under his command. General Martin reflected, *She's good, just like her file says.* Sitting down, all eyes turned to the general. "I have a plan devised but in the interest of security, I've not yet been able to run it by anyone else as of yet. You nine will need to be my advisors on this one and let me know where the holes in the plan are."

Though no one said anything, most of them looked eager and pleased at the trust the Commander of the Joint Chiefs of Staff was placing in them. "One of the many places that the Enemy is holding up is in a mine. It's the Degtyarskoye mine located in the Urals." The general noticed that the sasquatch was obviously not comprehending the given location. He added, "It's in a country called Russia." Knowing that description probably didn't help much he also provided, "It's a place on the other side of the world. It's a long way from here."

Xtela smiled and said, "Thank you Martin General." Martin still found the creature's voice strangely like a person talking with their mouth full.

Martin replied with his own grandfatherly smile and then continued with his briefing. "With the exception of xtela's contribution, it will be a standard search-and-destroy mission. We fly all of you in with a team of Rangers on a couple of Mi-17 choppers. You'll land behind a ridge about two miles out. You move in, wipe out as many as you can, and then blow the mine with the C-4 you'll be issued. Questions."

Xtela immediately spoke in his gravelly voice, "This strange jungle."

Martin smiled, assuming he referred to the concrete and lack of trees.

Then surprisingly, it was the mechanic, Private Fetch, who spoke. "Sir, I know C-4 is a lot of fun to play with," he said as he began to look around nervously, beginning to think it might be better to choose his words more carefully, "but I don't know that we can carry enough C-4 to take down a whole mine. At least, not in a timely manner."

"The RDX in *this* batch of C-4 is of a different sort. It's much more concentrated and provides a *much* bigger blast radius. On the other hand, you'll need to be extra careful as you carry it." The general winked at them as he spoke.

After a brief pause Smith asked, "Sir, as I told you earlier today, I've felt what happens when xtela's blast hits you. It's not only down right painful, but it's also incapacitating. What do you have planned for handling that?"

The general got a smile on his face and a gleam in his eye. "Not only are you going in with night-vision goggles, but we're going to be giving you some enhanced ear muffs. They'll be similar to what you wear at the shooting range, but they use an ultra-dense, poly-dungaree to do an amazing job of suppressing incoming sound."

For the first time in days, Jameson spoke. As he did so, all eyes turned to him with rapt attention. Even Smith showed surprise on her normally wooden face. "General, you obviously haven't had a chance to test the muffs out yet. Were you planning on doing that before the mission begins?"

Martin replied, "Actually, I'm glad you asked. We'll be testing them out tomorrow. I'll have a truck waiting and one of you can back it right up to the door of this building." He looked around the room as if to emphasize his meaning. "We'll then load up and head out to a remote site where we can do a test." After pausing, the general looked around at the people in the room and asked, "Anything else?"

Several seconds ticked by and Franks nearly blurted out, "Yes. When do we leave for this raid!"

By the next night, they'd conducted their test and found the muffs to be sufficiently effective against a sasquatch's sonic blast. Smith was especially pleased, having endured it twice before without any such protection. She still found it a little disorienting, but only slightly. *Nothing we can't handle*, she thought. She dutifully mentioned her marginal mental confusion at the sonic blast test to General Martin. Since no one else reported having the same response, they concluded that she was more susceptible due to her previous experience hearing the blast.

After the test, they all loaded up in the trucks they'd used to get to the remote test site, xtela well under cover in the back of a cargo truck. Sitting in the cab, Smith served as the general's driver. For the first few minutes, the two of them spent the return trip in silence. However, the general, wanting to become more familiar with his newest staff member, struck up a conversation.

"That must've been really weird seeing the sasquatch for the first time and living with them."

Taking the hint, the normally morose Smith replied, "That's for certain. They definitely do things differently than we do. Maybe the strangest thing of all wasn't that they speak a language that we knew, but that they speak it so well." She turned her head to look for oncoming traffic at an upcoming intersection in the dirt roads.

Surprisingly, she volunteered more information. "It was...pleasant, I suppose. Maybe the only real downer was a couple of yokel civilians that we somehow hooked up with." She shook her head in a way that seemed to say "What a couple of buffoons!"

Interested, the general pressed her. "Really? Where did they come from? What were they doing there?"

"It's a long story," she replied with her characteristic absence of humor.

"Well, I've got some time and I'm up for a good story."

Between the resultant silence enduring longer than is ordinarily comfortable in just such a situation and the friendly grin on the general's face, Smith finally gave in and told a little more of what had happened between Oscar-Romeo-17 and Camp Dodge. "Well, when I first arrived at Garrison's camp, there was a young woman there. I don't know why she was there. She was from a nearby town."

"Do you know which one?" Martin interrupted.

"Drain. Same place the chopper picked us up," Smith answered. "Like I said, I don't know why she was there. We had that nasty fight with the Enemy and somehow she got out and survived in one piece. I'll admit this, I was completely surprised and a little impressed when we found her alive a day or two later."

"What was her name?"

"Scott. Sarah Scott." Smith paused and then added, "So, I lead her and the other two enlisted men toward Drain. On our way there, but before we met the first sasquatch, we bumped into some strange old hermit named Jack."

At that, the relaxed manner the general had donned seemed to wash away like a flashflood. In its wake was a stony-faced man who seemed completely devoid of the more pleasant emotions he had exhibited only moments before. Trying to sound casual again he asked, "Does this Jack have a last name?"

"Armstrong."

Martin merely stared straight ahead, seemingly no longer aware of his surroundings. Noticing this obvious change in his countenance, Smith asked, "I take it you know him?"

In a throaty voice, halfway between a whisper and a gasp, Martin replied, "Yes, I know him."

The rest of the ride back was quiet which suited both of them just fine.

As they pulled back into camp, General Martin looked over at Captain Smith and said, "I trust you and your team will be ready to move out first thing in the morning." It was not a question.

"Yes, Sir," Smith replied, completely confident in her abilities and desiring nothing more than to sock it to the Enemy. "We'll be ready to head out for the Degtyarskoye, Russia mine at 05:00.

"Good," he replied, still somewhat subdued from their earlier conversation. However, he felt the need to add, "How many more people do you want on your team for this mission?"

She quickly replied, "Another dozen."

"You got it. I'll send them over to you within the hour." Pointing to a particular building Martin said, "You can let me off here." Smith pulled the truck up to the building and stopped. As Martin disembarked, he looked back at her and said, "Captain, we *need* this raid to be a success." Captain Smith was struck by the emphasis placed on the word 'need' as well as how thick his voice was with raw emotion. She understood that the word 'we' meant all of humanity.

Feeling a carnivorous sort of patriotism welling up within her, she replied, "We *will* succeed!"

Martin smiled and walked toward the building and disappeared.

CHAPTER 19
By the Pricking of My Thumbs...

Late that same night, about fifty miles away from Camp Dodge in a small town of only about fifteen thousand people, three uncharacteristically newer, clean cars drove into Indianola. They didn't all arrive at the same time, but they all had the same destination. None of the three persons of interest had any desire to be anywhere near their normal bases of operations, instead wanting complete secrecy, or as close as they could get to it.

Folks in town looked on the newcomers with only a hint of interest, shell-shocked by the War into a state of near ambivalence. Nevertheless, some did note with a mild kind of awe the impressive states of repair the three vehicles boasted.

Driving into town, the first to arrive was a shiny, black Lincoln Continental. Perhaps it made the passenger feel more like JFK—a symbol to some of a better, bygone age. With zero fanfare, it made its way along Front Street to the town's only surviving place of lodging, a Super 8 motel. The main passenger in the vehicle noticed with less than casual interest the now defunct Pay Day Loan Center and the Pizza Ranch that couched the motel. *Perfectly anonymous*, she reflected as she sat in the back of her chauffeured vehicle. She was dressed in a pair of jeans and an 'I ♥ New York' t-shirt. Her sneakers were in good repair and she wore a ball cap that did a good job of covering her face without seeming obvious. When she arrived at the motel, she went to her room and waited with her armed and heavily muscled chauffeur.

Only a few minutes behind her was the second person coming to the meeting. Alone, he drove himself in a steel-blue Ford Mustang. Though dressed in a suit, he did not wear a tie and the top button of his white Armani shirt was undone. His Gucci loafers completed his ensemble. Looking at him, no one would suspect his incredibly humble origins. He pulled into the motel parking lot and parked his car. Exiting the vehicle, he noticed that the roof of the motel was still somewhat damaged from an early sortie in the War. There were parts of the composite shingle roof that were charred. Ignoring the sight, he entered the building. With obvious disdain in his eyes, he walked right past the seventeen year old kid standing at the front counter without speaking. The young man at the desk nearly wilted before the presence of the other, not to mention the fact that it was rare that such well-dressed people came to his town, to say nothing of his motel. Overflowing with confidence, 'Armani' briskly walked to the room where 'New York' was waiting. When he arrived, he knew it would be suicidal to just walk in unannounced. Instead, he knocked on the door and awaited a response. He heard the barely audible tell-tale sound of a Glock 40 being cocked. Rather than becoming nervous, he relaxed knowing that he was at the right place. The door opened and New York's chauffeur admitted him. New York stood and greeted Armani.

"Thanks for coming."

"Let's get down to business," Armani said, taking a seat. "I trust your man here already swept the room for bugs?" he said, pointing a thumb at the chauffeur behind him.

"Of course," she replied. A quiet yet annoyed grunt was heard behind Armani from the chauffeur. He ignored it, knowing the man was professional and would "stay in his place." Not waiting for Armani to speak again, New York continued wearily, knowing her next words would not bring a pleasant response. "We'll begin when we're all here."

With obvious fury only partially in check, Armani nearly exploded, "What? You didn't notify me about bringing someone else on board?" It was not his style to get violent which saved his life from the chauffeur who obviously doubled as a bodyguard. Nevertheless, his voice did increase in volume and intensity.

Trying to stave off the explosion that was already coming forth, New York said, "Look, we need this guy and, without us, he's nothing. Better yet," she said with a conspiratorial gleam in her eyes, "he knows it." She added, "And he has valuable skills we can use."

In a rare act of contrition, genuine or false, Armani replied, "I'm sorry. I know you want this to succeed as much as I do. I'm getting anxious."

"I'd be lying if I said I wasn't," she replied. "Between the audacity of this operation and my suspicions that people are beginning to ferret out some of our plans—including General Martin—I have trouble sleeping at night. Occasionally."

"Martin? What's he got to do with anything?"

Slowly she told him, "I think someone was listening in on one of our conversations back at Camp Dodge. I suspect it just may have been the good general."

"You have any plans for...the good general?" he asked, smiling. His smile was anything but humorous. More like murderous, the way a bird eyes a struggling worm.

"Not yet. We'll see. Time is still on our side." Looking at her watch, New York proclaimed, "Speaking of time, the last member of our company should be here any moment."

Armani asked, "Who is it? Anyone I know?"

"Oh, yes," came the immediate reply.

For the first time since the interview began, Armani began feeling nervous. He couldn't quite put a finger on why, but he knew trusting anyone implicitly would quickly lead to his death.

So, he waited and kept his eyes open.

New York and Armani didn't have long to wait. Within one minute, a knock at the door was heard. The chauffeur answered the door just as he had when Armani had arrived. An old, bearded man stood in the doorway. Besides recognizing him, the first thing that Armani acknowledged was the intense—slightly maniacal—look in his eyes. Armani wasn't intimidated in the least, but he did notice the newcomer's eyes seemed to say, "I know something you don't, and because of that, I'll be the last man standing." The second thing Armani noticed was the newcomer's very full, white beard. 'Beard' entered the room without preamble and sat down on one of the two queen-sized beds since there were no more available chairs in the tiny motel room. He wore a stylish white polo shirt that didn't seem to suit him but rather suggested that he, unlike most people, was able to luxuriate in good clothing. He smiled a respectful smile at New York, a wicked one at Armani. In a thick accent he asked, "What have I missed?"

Deflecting a potential argument, New York spoke up immediately. "Nothing. We were just getting ready to begin." With a diplomatic smile she continued. "How are we doing up north?"

Beard answered with the smoldering fire that never left his eyes. "Things are moving ahead on schedule. Though our forces are not claiming any new ground, we have been successful at retaining nearly all the land that was in our possession a month ago."

Not knowing whether to be pleased or disappointed by the report New York rejoined, "In any other war, that would be unacceptable, but this... It's about the best news we've had in a while." Looking him in the eye anew she said, "Continue."

Beard scratched at his facial hair as he resumed his report. "We're only a little behind schedule in spreading out our forces to claim those areas for ourselves. When the time comes, we'll be ready."

In mild exasperation, New York retorted, "Timing is everything. We can't get behind schedule!"

Placatingly, but without sincerity, Beard held his hands up as if to say I'm doing my best. Aloud he said, "I'll get us back on schedule, but that boy scout I'm shackled to," he said in disgust, "is proving to be more competent than any of us suspected." Looking away he added, "and difficult to infiltrate with my spies."

"Just get the job done on time!" was the only sympathy he received. Turning to Armani, New York continued. "How are we doing on your end of things?"

Brandishing a self-satisfied smile, Armani began his report. "I'm still moving ahead to have a Central Bank set up for each state with each one directly tied to the Federal Reserve." Before New York could ask any of the obvious questions, he answered them. "I'm still on schedule," he said as he favored Beard with a triumphant sneer, "and I've begun laying the groundwork for tying us in to have *the* dominant position in the global banking system after the War."

Satisfied, New York merely nodded her head, but Armani wasn't done. With his ire returning he pressed, "I don't know about him," he said poking a thumb toward Beard, "but why are we here? None of this information is sensitive enough that we couldn't have communicated through cryptic means *without* meeting in this backwater town." He finished his sentence with open disgust. "I know I don't have to remind you that meeting like this has the potential of revealing our plans." Armani let his last words hang in the air. He peered at his two comrades, certain of the mission but uncertain of their qualifications and competence.

New York picked up the conversation. Smiling condescendingly she lectured, "Talking about our fundamental plans was not my primary reason for inviting you here." With renewed interest, Armani and Beard leaned forward to hear what she had to say. With her audience mildly intrigued, she revealed, "I set up this meeting on such short notice because I only just found out about a new development in the War."

Beard leaned back on the bed, letting her words sink in, subconsciously aware that her next words would be surprising and significant. Armani merely blinked and continued his penetrating stare at his host.

"General Martin has been made aware of a new weapon that just might turn the tide in this War," she continued. "He has met with a representative of a culture we would call...sasquatch."

New York paused to let that sink in. Her two conspirators both looked at her incredulously. Armani was the first to speak. "Are you insane? What kind of nonsense is this? Why did you really invite us hear?"

Not to be outdone, Beard chimed in, "Ma'am, I must admit. This is ridiculous. I've heard and seen many things in my long life but this pushes the bounds of reason."

The two men made as if to stand to leave. Half way between sitting and standing New York resumed. "I didn't believe it either when my informant contacted me. I would've laughed it off but this particular informant is very thorough and *not* inclined at all to making fantastic speculations." She looked down at her hands, hanging between her knees and sighed. Before looking back up she continued speaking. "Before I called you all, I confirmed her story."

"How?" the two men rejoined in unison.

"That doesn't matter. What does matter is not that the story is true but the implications of that truth."

Armani and Beard both took on a knowing look in their eyes. For the former, it was a look tinged with a lust for power. For the latter, a desire to unlock secrets.

New York looked up from her hands and held their eyes with a rock-steady gaze whose sincerity could not be denied. "First, these sasquatch are massive, humanoid creatures that speak English. I don't yet know how they know English, but they do."

Beard was the first to ask a question, his thick accent coming through. "When you say 'massive', what are we talking about?" The puzzle-solving look in his eyes was quickly being overshadowed by Armani's power-lust visage.

"The one I saw was about seven or eight feet tall and with a mountain of muscle to back it up." She experienced a mirthless chuckle and said, "Either of you ever see those old comic books of The Hulk?" Neither of her companions being from America, they both replied in the negative. "Well, it looks like a hairy version of The Hulk—and a lot less green."

Armani and Beard had no idea what she was talking about and so they just shrugged and impatiently waited for her to continue. "By themselves, they aren't significant, but they apparently have a certain ability. They're able to make some sort of sonic pulse. It causes a kind of temporary incapacitation of whoever—or whatever—hears it."

Simultaneously, a knowing gleam of intelligence entered the eyes of both men. This time it was Armani who responded first. He carefully asked, "I trust you are suggesting that this sonic pulse will also incapacitate the Enemy?"

"That is correct. It was field-tested shortly before the creature came to us."

"Where is it now?" Beard quickly asked, his breathing coming a little faster.

With only a small flicker of annoyance creeping into her voice, New York replied, "Don't worry about it. I'm keeping a close eye on things." Then, toning down her voice again, she resumed saying, "The sonic pulse is apparently effective enough that using it in battle could make all the difference. No more Enemy combatants scampering about, avoiding most of our ordnance. No more making fools of our military and weapons. With these sasquatch going into battle with us, we *will* prevail."

In his characteristically callous way, Beard interjected, "So, we have a disposable resource that we can use to turn the tide! Excellent!" He rubbed his hands together greedily—maniacally— and then added, "Then we'll definitely be able to put our plans into effect!"

Backing things up a little, New York responded, "I don't know if I'd necessarily call them resources, but they're definitely no more than tools. That much is certain; and after a tool is used up and broken, it's discarded."

Armani quickly asked, "But what about this sonic pulse thing? Is it really all that effective at doing...whatever it does?"

New York turned to him with an air of superiority and replied, "I don't know if its devastating effect is due to it being so loud or maybe it possesses some special sonic frequency. The point is, it works. That's a fact."

Beard spoke up saying, "Once they're tame, I could use them in my neck of the woods up north to help 'tame the land'." He couldn't help saying it with a wide smile that emerged from behind his full beard like some sort of snake coming out of its den to strike. "Once they're trained, we could begin stationing them all over to help hold...'strategic locations'." The other two nodded in agreement. "We could even use shock collars on them to keep them in line," he added, laughing under his breath.

New York replied, "That's not a bad idea."

Armani, recognizing the power of the sasquatch, said, "We could use this new tool against any threats—foreign or domestic."

All three gave various versions of the same knowing smile, chuckling slightly yet humorously.

Despite the positive mood of all present, New York stood up and began slowly pacing around the small room. She could only walk a few steps before having to turn around. Armani almost spoke but, taking an ever so subtle hint from her mood, he changed his mind. He could tell something important was eating at her. So he gave her a little space and did what he did best. He waited.

After a couple of minutes of listening to the sound of New York's shoes quietly gliding across the old, dirty carpet, she finally stopped and turned to the other two and said, "There's one more thing. General Martin is about to send out a team with this particular sasquatch. They're going to conduct a raid on some Enemy encampment. Apparently he wants to conduct his own field test. I can't say I blame him." Instead of smiling, or even scowling, she sighed and continued. "The point is he's doing this raid supposedly without my knowledge. He's going behind my back and trying to keep the prize for himself."

Beard and Armani were surprised at the sudden fire that flared up in her eyes. "He will learn what it means to betray me. These sasquatch will be *my* pets and *my* tools. They will obey <u>me</u> and grind Martin, and anyone else who opposes me, under my boot!"

A day later, in Montreal, Canada, Garrison silently brooded. His thoughts were focused on a meeting he'd had with Reznikov earlier that evening. They had met in Mount Royal Park and it had come out that Reznikov had gone behind Garrison's back to acquire more troops to push the perimeter they'd set up around Quebec to encompass more Canadian land. Garrison had been extremely upset and was still very frustrated. He stared at the wall, not seeing it, lost in his tempest of thoughts. *Then*, he thought, *that worthless Russian also went behind my back and brokered the deal with the Canadian prime minister.*

Garrison stood and began pacing within his small office. *And if that hadn't been bad enough*, he relived for the hundredth time that evening, *A Spider had come barreling out of the bushes!* He knew he'd been lucky to survive the encounter. Though he'd had a full clip in his Beretta M9, he'd only wounded the creature as it had charged. *If that sniper hadn't finished him off, Reznikov and I would be dead right now.*

He paused in his pacing and looked out a window. *But who was that sniper? Why did he just happen to be there? Where did he disappear to after he'd shot the creature? It couldn't have all just been luck.* He was certain about his conclusion, yet he didn't have any answers, only more questions.

Uncertain what else to do, Garrison went to the office of one of his 'five horsemen', Lieutenant Garner. When he arrived at the man's office he came right to the point. "Garner, I've got a problem. I need to meet with you and my other four lieutenants. Let them know I'll need to see them tonight at Notre-Dame Basilica at 21:00."

"You got it," came the loyal reply.

That night they all met and went inside the church. They sat down on the pews for a moment before they began. Garrison filled them in on what had happened earlier that day with Reznikov and the Spider. Having had several hours to ponder the events of the day Garrison said, "Gentlemen, I'm a soldier and I follow orders to the best of my ability, but I have to admit, something feels very...wrong about what's happening here. I don't understand what it is I'm getting at, but I know when my gut tells me something's fishy, and I'll bet you dollars to loonies that we're smack in the middle of whatever is wrong."

He then added, "Also, I'm getting the impression that more and more of our servicemen and women under my command are actually loyal to Reznikov. Again, I can't prove it."

Seeing the questions and comments immediately rising in the eyes of his listeners he continued before they had a chance to give voice to their thoughts. "I hardly believe that every soldier who came with us is willing to betray me at the whims of Reznikov, or anyone else. However, I'll say this." He paused and looked even more somber than before. "You five men are the only people in this armada who I *know* I can trust. I'm going to need you more than ever. If I need a message sent privately, I'm going to need you guys to be the couriers. If I need intel on something and it's crucial, I'll definitely be calling on you. Understood?"

With a mixture of trepidation and pride in their eyes, they responded as one, "Yes, Sir."

A clergyman walking by heard their unusually loud response and shushed them gently. Shaw and Driggs looked sheepish; the others ignored him.

After the minister was out of earshot, Rodriguez earnestly queried, "Is it really as bad as all that?"

Taking on a wistful look that spoke to his shaky optimism, Garrison replied, "Let me put it to you this way. I spoke with the prime minister of Canada *and* the president today. They both had a lot of fancy things to say. After hanging up with each of them, I had a chance to think about what they said." He looked around the holy structure, perhaps in paranoia, perhaps out of a desire for greater inspiration. "The president said the same thing presidents always seem to say: meaningless political jargon. On the other hand, the PM sounded like he would like to have said, 'this deal keeps getting worse all the time'."

They all sat quietly for several moments, allowing the potential implications of the news to sink in. When the silence was beginning to drag on, the ever-steady Lieutenant Garner changed the subject saying, "Pete, you said that when you spoke to Reznikov, he said we'd be getting more men to beef up security?"

"That's right."

"I admit, I'm surprised you're not more bent out of shape about this change. I mean about stationing extra men at strategic points throughout eastern provinces: Nova Scotia, PEI, Newfoundland and New Brunswick, since that takes men from more important locations."

Colonel Garrison's head whipped around. "Where did you hear this, about stationing men in provinces outside of Quebec?"

Garner rejoined, "At a bar. I overheard one of the officers talking about it."

Garrison took a long, calming breath. *Who's pulling the strings and to what end? The right hand doesn't know what the left hand is doing.*

And I'm the right hand.

He suddenly looked as tired as he felt. Looking each of his men in the eye he added, "I don't know if I'm reading a whole lot of extra stuff into it or not but I'll tell you this. I think I'm beginning to understand why the president named this mission "Double-Edged Sword.""

CHAPTER 20
In for a Penny

General Martin sat down at one of the few remaining diners near Camp Dodge–Cactus Bob's Bbq Corral. The War had made a mess of things nearly everywhere. *I suppose about the only places that have gone relatively unscathed have been backwater, third-world areas. The Enemy never saw them as a threat.* He waved at a waitress to get her attention and thought, *And even some of those have had terrible encounters with the Enemy.*

He hadn't been reading his menu more than a pair of minutes before a fiery red-haired woman arrived. Smith immediately sat down. By her posture, he knew she would rather eat somewhere else. Perhaps at a 'high class' restaurant. *Well, if they hadn't all been destroyed or run out of business by the War, we could be eating there, but I'd take Cactus Bob's over one of those fancy places any day.* He smiled as he thought that for now, she'd have to put up with his more rural habits.

Picking up her menu, she asked, "What are you having?"

Having eaten there before, Martin already knew what he wanted, but he pretended to peruse the menu. *Perhaps there's something new,* he thought without conviction. When the waitress returned he said, "I think I'll have the Sloppy Bob and a little bit of Chuck's Smoke Pit Beans to wash it down."

"Very good, Sir. For you Miss?"

"Coffee."

Not to be deterred, or denied a larger tip, the waitress offered, "I can suggest the The Big Pig, our Texas Toothpicks, or our world famous Beef Jerky!"

Without looking up, but making up for it with a mild amount of teeth grating, Smith replied in her same monotone voice, "Coffee."

Finally the waitress departed to place the general's order with the chef and Martin couldn't help but smile at Smith. *Well this world takes all kinds I suppose.*

Knowing that the captain would get antsy if he didn't talk business pretty soon, he said, "Well Smith, where are we at?"

Her eyes lit up and she said, "Sir, we conducted the raid with xtela as per your orders." She subconsciously rubbed the cut that crested her forehead. General Martin noted that it hadn't been there before the raid. "We came in low, landing the choppers on the other side of a small mountain near the Degtyarskoye mine in the Ural Mountains in Russia. From there we went on foot the rest of the short distance, arriving at the mine precisely at 23:00. We encountered no resistance at first which allowed us to get close to one of the entrances."

Her coffee arrived and she immediately took a drink. She arched a single eyebrow, apparently surprised with the quality. "At that point, we encountered a lone sentinel. We eliminated the Spider and moved inside. Though we had studied the blueprints of the mine, I knew it would be suicide to get creative with our route." She took another drink and continued. "We entered the main area, had it out with them, and departed like wraiths."

The general's food arrived and he immediately attacked it with gusto. He listened to the captain catalog more of the events from the preceding evening. When she ended her report, he leaned back and took a break from eating. Pointing at her forehead he asked, "How did you get that?"

As if the gash were of no consequence she responded, "I'm really not sure. I believe it was during the running firefight on our way out of the mine."

"And how hard did they try to follow you after you left the mine?"

"I expect they gave every effort," Smith replied. "But on our way in, we had set our C-4 explosives at the mouth of the mine. So, on our way out..." She made a small gesture with her hands to suggest an explosion.

"Nicely done," came the reply. Pretending to be impatient, the general said, "You've obviously saved the best for last." He gave her an encouraging gesture to get her to add more. When she responded with an equally mute look that bespoke of incomprehension, he blurted, "Tell me about the sasquatch! How did he do?"

"Well, considering that we only lost one man in the raid, I'd say his contribution was *most* helpful." Smith allowed a smile to play across her stony face. "He's a born hunter. He relished the opportunity to engage in some 'hand-to-hand' combat, and he's just as strong as he looks—maybe stronger! When he went up against one of the Enemy, it didn't know what hit it." She laughed a mirthless, yet satisfying chuckle.

General Thomas Q. Martin let out a long whistle. "I hate for any of my men to die but that is by far the absolute best we've ever done when going up against the Enemy. Especially in their own pond. Congratulations, Captain!"

"Thank you, Sir."

The waitress came back and refilled Smith's cup. She asked if the general would like anything else and he declined.

"What about the sonic blast? Did he use it?" The general was beginning to get worried. He wanted to know just how effective the sasquatch Voice really was. *That could be our secret weapon, or it could be a dead end. That's the main reason I ordered this raid.*

After another sip of her drink, Smith answered, "The first time he tried it, we had just entered the primary cavern where we expected to find more Enemy combatants." Again she absently, yet gingerly, rubbed the small laceration on her forehead. "I gave him the sign to proceed with the blast. The rest of us already had our ear protection set up with the comm-system built in so we could still communicate." She paused for only a moment to look out the window and watch an old Model T Ford drive by. "He let it out for all he was worth. I confess, it was amazing how much more pleasant the experience was *with* the earmuffs." Neither of them laughed. "A couple of our men got just a little dizzy, but not bad. Most of the Enemy within the cavern were stunned immediately. Of course, I had briefed everyone that it wouldn't last long. We immediately opened fire and wiped out most of them."

"Like shooting fish in a barrel," Martin interrupted.

"The few that were not stunned either rushed us or fled. We found out about a minute later they were going for reinforcements elsewhere in the mine. That was about the time we began beating our retreat."

"And?"

"Xtela used his sonic blast a couple more times. We mainly used it to stay ahead of the Enemy. They were pouring out so fast, we would've all been cut to pieces as quick as that," she snapped her fingers, "if not for his help, and even then, it got pretty touch-and-go."

Martin looked again at the cut her forehead boasted and then took on a somber caste. "The man who died, when did it happen?"

Without skipping a beat she replied, "On the way out. Like I said, even with xtela's help it still got awfully dicey at times. When that young soldier went down, there was no way to get his body." Though she hadn't ever gotten to know the dead soldier, she shuddered involuntarily.

They sat silently for a few minutes, digesting the intel and emotions that were roiling through their hearts and minds. Recognizing the success of the mission and the far reaching possibilities that it suggested, General Martin felt a surge of exultation. On its heels, he immediately felt guilty. The young man that died needed to be remembered for at least a moment before moving on with the War. *I'll contact his family and make sure they know their son not only died for something, but in making manifest what might just be the key in liberating the planet and avoiding extermination.* He involuntarily suppressed his emotions before thinking, *He died a hero.*

Instead of commenting directly on the obvious success of the mission and Smith's personal success in leading the raid, he said, "It'll sure be nice when this War is over." He sighed tiredly. "What with so many major cities around the world destroyed and so many people killed, it's been a while since I really had the deep-seated conviction that we would win."

After a few moments, Martin snapped out of his brief bout of melancholy and turned a smile at his junior officer, a smile that spoke of confidence and optimism. "So, the raid was a success but, the way I see it the Enemy has too many strongholds for us to send your team in everywhere all over the world."

"Sir, approximately how many of these Enemy held sites are there around the globe?"

The general took on a quirky smile. "Tell you the truth, I don't have an exact number, but intel suggests the number is at the very least in the hundreds."

For the first time in their conversation, Smith showed concern. Speaking slowly she voiced, "Sir, I agree. I don't think it's realistic for my team to hit them all."

"Precisely," Martin exclaimed. "If we hit them piecemeal, one site at a time, they'll be able to regroup and determine a much more effective plan for defense. We've got to hit them hard and all over the world. I don't think we'll have enough raiding parties to hit them at every site simultaneously, to say nothing of choppers, supplies,—"

"—and sasquatch. Again, in order for these raids to work, we've got to have *at least* one sasquatch with every group. I don't know how many we can get. Certainly some, but I can assure you many of them are not going to be particularly keen on joining the U.S. military. Also, based on my recent experience, some of these raids are going to yield not only dead soldiers, but dead sasquatch."

Martin looked down at the table in contemplation. "Then we need to talk to them face to face and get them to understand."

Smith took on a concerned look and said, "Sir, perhaps now would be a good time to let you know that I gave them my word that I would not lead anyone to their cave." Martin looked frustrated, but like he understood. Smith then added, "Don't get me wrong. I want to win this War and push those disgusting, nine-legged monsters all the way back outside of our solar system but I did give them my word as an officer."

The general smiled an almost grandfatherly grin and replied, "Don't worry. We'll just do something different. Something that won't betray your oath." He used his spoon to play with the few bits of food remaining on his plate when he finally said, "You could take us to within a few miles of their home and then we could send xtela in to talk to them and get some of them to come to us."

Smith chewed on his words for a moment before announcing that that would be satisfactory.

"Great," Martin concluded. "When we get back to town, you tell xtela we'll be flying out tomorrow to meet with his people. If he needs extra convincing, let me know and I'll come over and have a man to...man talk with him."

"Yes, Sir," came the ever circumspect reply.

Early the next morning, General Martin emerged into a guarded hangar at Camp Dodge. The men guarding the hangar were the men he'd recruited when he'd formed Smith's team. It seemed like a life time ago but he knew it had been only a few days. Assisting the hangar's guards were some of the other men from the raid. They necessarily learned of the existence and capability of the sasquatch so Martin had pulled them into his 'inner circle' as well.

The general strode across the hangar, alone. He walked right up to the V-25 Buzzard aircraft that had the ability to rotate between 'helicopter mode' for hovering and 'forward flight mode' to create a relatively rapid forward movement.

The mechanic assigned to Smith's team, Private Fetch, popped his head outside the vehicle's portside hatch and gave a sloppy salute to the general. Martin let it pass, knowing that minor infractions in military protocol were of no importance on a day like this. Instead he asked, "Fetch, everything ready to go?"

"Yes, Sir," came the swift reply.

"Everyone inside?"

"Everyone except the prison guards," he rejoined, casually waving his hand in the general direction of the men guarding the hangar.

Though he decided to let that additional breach of protocol pass as well, Martin found himself grinding his teeth. *That kid is going to get himself in trouble in this man's army.* Then he silently chuckled to himself and thought, *That's probably why he's still a buck private.*

"They're not coming," Martin retorted. "Let's roll."

The general climbed inside and looked around the passenger cargo area. He saw Smith, xtela, some of his newly formed personal guard, the pilot and, of course, Private Fetch. "Take us out," General Martin barked.

They were soon traveling at a satisfying clip of over six hundred kilometers per hour. They stopped halfway to their destination at the semi-defunct Hill Air Force Base in Utah to refuel. From there, they departed and headed for a remote place south of Drain, Oregon.

Five hours after their quiet exit from Camp Dodge, they found themselves approaching Drain. Smith took over the navigation and instructed the pilot where to set down, about five kilometers south of the small town.

Upon landing, everyone except the pilot disembarked the aircraft. Xtela had been more quiet than usual during the flight, but his hiatus from speaking was at an end. He turned and walked over to where General Martin was standing and, looming over him, said, "Martin General, I go find my mi'tuhng and bring back with me. I try get back before moon come, but maybe next sun."

Martin replied, "Thanks for *all* your help, xtela. I look forward to meeting more sasquatch."

The powerful sasquatch with blood red pelt surprised them all by leaving the area on his arms *and* legs. Apparently, he was faster on all fours than on just his legs. Minutes after xtela made off toward his cave, the dull silence was broken by Smith. "General, permission to speak freely."

"Granted," came the simple reply.

"Sir, I have to admit that all of this 'sasquatch stuff' seems to be under the table. I'm not entirely certain I'm comfortable with that."

Martin smiled and said, "Captain, I could go into lengthy detail about my reasons but it comes down to this. President Griffith is not exactly what I would call 'trustworthy'." He smiled and added, "I wouldn't trust her any farther than I could kick xtela."

Smith immediately understood that the conversation was over. Throughout the rest of the day, she considered his words.

After a blessedly uneventful night, they arose expectantly, eager to see the sasquatch, if they should come. After a few hours, they heard a rustling in the dense foliage nearby. Immediately, rifles were cocked and pulled into shoulders, most being aimed from whence the sound came. One or two others were pointed in other directions in the unlikely chance the sound they'd heard was some sort of diversion. Moments later, three sasquatch emerged from the surrounding forest. Despite the fact that General Martin had already seen and interacted with xtela, he still found it to be amazing and exciting to look up into the faces of three of the mighty woodland creatures at once!

To his untrained eyes the creatures appeared to range in size very little. Like xtela, they were huge compared to him. Perhaps the thing that he noticed most was their eyes. Their eyes did not appear to him to be at all aggressive. He walked up to them to greet them but before he could, more sasquatch walked out of the brush. It was xtela and another one. There were a few more that appeared, trailing immediately behind them as well. Martin quickly eyed his own troops to make sure they weren't getting skittish. Of course, Smith was completely fine with so many sasquatch around, but Martin was pleasantly surprised to find the others to be at least marginally relaxed.

The general moved as if to make a second go at welcoming all those who had come when he heard more rustling from the nearby bushes. First, a young woman came forth. She had sandy blond hair and sky blue eyes. She smiled but the general noticed that her smile lost some of its luster as her eyes passed across Smith. Smith returned the look, but otherwise ignored her.

On the young woman's heals, the last person to arrive was the last person in the world General Martin expected to ever see again. Upon seeing each other, Martin and Armstrong both stiffened only slightly and then visibly composed themselves, purposely ignoring each other.

Finally, Martin extended a hand to the three sasquatch. He was impressed that one of the three understood and carefully took his hand and shook it. The same creature immediately spoke. In the now familiar rock-chewing voice she said, "Welcome Martin General. May your jungle ever run free." She gave an appraising look at Captain Smith. "I tuhngiqr Lat'. You call me tuhngiqr." Then, pointing to the other two who flanked her she said, "This steek'eew Lat' and tsin'tsun'tsan Lat'."

She paused for more than a moment and Martin took it to mean that she expected him to introduce some of his people. "I believe you already know Captain Smith." They nodded in acknowledgement. He made the rest of his introductions and then looked expectantly at them.

Instead of beginning to speak about the purpose of their meeting, tuhngiqr finished her introductions. "This sp'atung." She turned and pointed, "and xtela you know." Turning to face the two humans who had accompanied them, tuhngiqr said, "I think some you know each other. This Sarah Scott and Jack Armstrong." The way tuhngiqr labored over the pronunciation of the two human names was mildly humor to the general. *I imagine we sound the same to them.*

The general gave a polite, gentlemanly nod of the head to Sarah. At the mention of Jack's name he merely stared at the other. Jack reciprocated in kind. The look they shared was stiff and tinged with sadness.

Seemingly oblivious to the social interplay taking place around them, the sasquatch sat down on the rich, green grass that carpeted the forest floor. The humans followed the example and waited for one of the sasquatch to speak. They said nothing at first, just sitting and looking pensive. After a few uncomfortable moments of that, General Martin made as if to speak. Smith, sitting next to him, put a hand on his shoulder. It only took the span of half a heartbeat for him to understand that he should wait. Immediately thereafter he correctly deduced that sasquatch welcome lulls in conversation.

After a minute or so of listening to the nearby stream burble along, steek'eew spoke. "Xtela has tell of his doings with you. We thanks he been safe and you respect him. We also pleased you do job good." Though steek'eew sounded, of course, like he was speaking with marbles in his mouth, the sound was strangely melodic. He finished by saying, "We sad your sen' die."

Martin was utterly pleasantly surprised by this sincere admission.

"Martin General, xtela also tell what you want. We bring all Xruhnituhm Siem to make choice." With that, steek'eew leaned back to listen.

Martin was only a little taken aback by the almost complete absence of preamble but he found it a refreshing change from how large meetings were conducted back at Camp Dodge. Taking only a moment to collect his thoughts, he said. "Which of you constitute this governing body, the Xronitone Seeim?" Xtela was the only sasquatch who showed any sign that the general did a poor job of pronouncing the name of their government.

"We three," tuhngiqr proclaimed, waving her white-pelted hand toward herself and her two companions. "We Xruhnituhm Siem. We called Lat'." With a docile expression on her narrow face she added, "We are three leaders our mi'tuhng. We no have more power than other two." Her proclamation came with pride in their way of life and governance. Martin noticed that he was becoming familiar with their accent and catching more of the words they were saying.

Without waiting for a response, she continued. "Martin General, xtela try give us know you not leader of your people. This true?"

Confident that he should play it straight with these creatures who he hoped would become their allies he replied, "Yes, that's correct. I am a high ranking leader among my people, but not the highest."

Looking mildly perturbed the excitable tsin'tsun'tsan queried, "Why you here? Has leader sent you?"

"My friends," he replied. "I'll be honest with you. My leader-we call her 'president'—has not sent me here to talk with you." Martin noticed that the three Xruhnituhm Siem, as well as the other sasquatch present, began squirming in an odd way that he suspected meant they were uncomfortable with the ramifications of what he had said. "As a leader of my people, my job is to command the military and make sure we're able to defeat our enemies. Up until we met you, we've had a pretty rough time against the Spiders." Pausing to take a breath, Martin could hear some of the sasquatch whisper words like "Tarantulas" and "evil."

Continuing he said, "We've been kicked around and bloodied up pretty well, and though I hate to admit it, I've got to tell you that the fish on the end of our line has nearly pulled us in and we've been losing during most of the War."

Hoping they understood his idiomatic phrases, he paused again to see if they had any comments. He noticed Jack smile at the 'fish talk'. When the sasquatch continued to stare at him rather intently he decided to remain silent as well and let them make the next move. He remembered the old salesman's axiom: He who speaks first loses the argument.

Finally, steek'eew spoke up. "Martin General, xtela teach us that attack you make on Tarantulas was good. How much xtela help? He help much?"

Smiling wryly, Martin opened his mouth to speak but Smith beat him to it. "Absolutely! We haven't had a battle or raid go half as successfully in a long time. One of the main problems we have is that the Enemy is not just incredibly numerous but they move like lightning, bobbing and weaving like Mohamed Ali on speed." She realized they would have no idea who the boxer was, or even what boxing is. General Martin looked at her appraisingly with one eyebrow raised in interest. "The point is," she continued, "xtela's sonic blast was just enough to stun the Enemy so we could kill them off. That doesn't mean there wasn't any challenge to the situation, but the raid was still an unprecedented success. Based on my experience, I can almost guarantee *none* of us would have come back alive had it not been for xtela's help!"

Martin turned from the captain back toward the Xruhnituhm Siem. The smile on his lips had not diminished.

"Does Smith Captain speak your words?" was all steek'eew replied.

"I stand by what she has said," the general replied.

Looking a little disappointed, steek'eew simply said, "Very well," as he turned to the other two Lat'. His manner seemed to say, *What questions do you have?*

Or perhaps there was more to it than that, General Martin thought. It almost seemed like there was some friction there.

Tsin'tsun'tsan spoke up, "Martin General, we not sure of all this. We not sure about War. We know of need hunt Tarantulas, but we afraid how might sasquatch hurt."

Martin waited a moment for additional clarification. When none was forthcoming he cleared his throat and replied, "When you say hurt, what exactly do you mean?"

Before tsin'tsun'tsan could answer, steek'eew rushed into an explanation. "He mean other things happen, not just sasquatch die. We now have talk with sen'. We have sen' live with us. This all strange." He paused and looked at a nearby mighty oak that appeared to be rotting from the inside out. "Things changing. They changing too fastly and we no know what best for us." He ended by flicking a beetle out of his pelt.

A kindly smile spread across Martin's face as he proclaimed, "I know it's hard. I know that change hurts. I've felt the pain of hard choices that you can never take back." He looked over toward Jack for the barest fraction of a glance as he said that. Then his eyes were again on the three Lat' before him. "I also know that some things simply *must* be done. Fighting side by side to expunge the Earth of these vermin *must* be done. Any other choice is a choice to be overrun and destroyed. Or worse–subjugated."

It was tuhngiqr's turn to speak saying, "Your words strong—we listen and think—but send one sasquatch," she said, looking at xtela, "help you few suns not same as many sasquatch help for many suns or moons and get sasquatch killed." Her powerfully, rumbly voice ceased and the forest went quiet.

Surprisingly, the young woman who'd been introduced as Sarah began to speak. "Members of the Xruhnituhm Siem, my friends," she began. Martin noticed Smith tense almost imperceptibly and wondered at the friction between the two of them. "Not too long ago, I had a negative opinion of these people and their methods," Sarah said, pointing at all the human soldiers present. "But I've come to work with them and get to know some of them." Before she said more, she looked General Martin straight in the eye and used all her mental faculties to attempt to size him up as a leader. Then she turned her gaze back on the three Lat' and with conviction said, "I believe these are people you can trust in many things. I would work with them to help defeat the Enemy."

Still looking uncomfortable, steek'eew spoke slowly and carefully saying, "Jack, you seem know Martin General. This true?"

"Yes," came the emotionless reply.

"What you think of him? He good sen'? We him trust?"

Jack's and Martin's eyes locked like the horns of a couple of large mountain sheep. They stared at each other and it seemed a lifetime of memories, good and bad, seemed to rush across the void that separated them. Neither of them so much as twitched a muscle and yet, to those present, it seemed a mighty struggle of some sort was transpiring. At last, Jack replied simply, "Yes. He is an honorable man."

A powerful silence ensued as all present continued looking at Armstrong and Martin. Finally, the three members of the Xruhnituhm Siem moved away a stone's throw to confer with each other in a small triangle and in hushed tones. Minutes passed before they broke apart and looked at General Martin. Tuhngiqr said, "We work with you and send more sasquatch help hunt Tarantulas."

Martin visibly relaxed and let go of a breath he did not know he'd been holding. Then tuhngiqr spoke again.

"We need send a sasquatch make sure all sasquatch good treated. We send sp'atung go you for us. He make choices like Xruhnituhm Siem is there."

The tenseness began to return to Martin's shoulders and back but he had to admit that things were going better than he had any right to have hoped.

"That's asking a lot," was all the general said at first. All eyes were on him to see if negotiations would fall apart or continue. "But I have to admit that we're asking a lot of you." He smiled his grandfather's smile and added, "I can live with sp'atung and the power you'd vest in him but I must insist that a human be his...counterpart. The two of them would work together in everything."

Before anything further could be said, tsin'tsun'tsan abruptly blurted, "It is good. *We* make choose which sen'." Turning, he looked at one of the two humans who'd come with them from their cave. In a strong voice he said, "We choose Jack."

Martin blinked in surprise at the suddenness of the statement. However, his astonishment was more profoundly felt at knowing that he'd be working with Jack.

Again.

Out of the corner of his eye he caught Smith shaking her head, side to side, almost imperceptibly. *I guess Jack rubbed her the wrong way,* he thought with a chuckle. *That would've been fun to see.* Sighing, he said aloud, "Agreed."

With that, Jack stepped forward to speak to all present, but especially General Martin. "Tom, you know I'm getting old. I'm going to need someone to help me out if I'm going to be able to do this."

Martin thought he heard Smith sputter in surprise and he wondered, *What are you up to, Jack?* Instead, he replied, "I can live with that, but who did you have in mind?"

Armstrong turned, put an arm around Sarah's shoulders, and ushered her forward a handful of steps. "Ms. Sarah Scott." This time Martin was certain that Smith was sputtering in indignation. "Just like Captain Smith there, I've gotten to know her." This time Smith didn't respond. Rather, her eyes were daggers. Flaming daggers that seemed intent on excavating a hole through Jack's forehead. He continued saying, "During our time living with the sasquatch she's been incredibly helpful. I want her to stay on with me."

Martin noticed that Jack seemed to be ignoring the look of surprise on Sarah's face that exceeded the look of anger that Smith harbored. *Some day, I've got to find out what happened between these three.* The general thought for a moment about all that he knew about Jack and the barest fraction of knowledge that he had about Ms. Scott. He looked away from everyone and seemed to seek inspiration from the clouds above. *Webs within webs,* he pondered. At last he turned back to the group and said, "Deal, but remember this, Jack. She's a civilian and she's your responsibility. Make sure she stays out of trouble and learns how things are done."

As if he had not just been given a subtly veiled ultimatum–or was it a threat–Jack smiled as though he hadn't a care in the world and replied, "Great, let's get going."

CHAPTER 21
Return And Report

Sarah was greatly impressed by the V-25 Buzzard tiltrotor aircraft that gave her, Jack, Martin's company and twenty sasquatch a ride out of the area. It was a smooth trip and, despite the number of personnel inside the vehicle, she found it to be less crowded than she had originally anticipated. However, with all those sasquatch together in an enclosed space, the humans within couldn't help notice a mild smell that permeated the air they were breathing.

At first, the passengers were all mostly quiet as the journey coursed over the mountains and fertile landscapes below. The sasquatch quietly talked amongst themselves of their astonishment at being in the air so high above their jungle. Sarah was beginning to find the telltale sound of them chewing on their words to be something of a comfort. She had to remind herself that, for them, flying wasn't just a new experience. It was completely beyond their previous experiences and their wildest expectations. Sarah hadn't been in an aircraft since the War began—few civilians had—but the highest the sasquatch had likely ever been in the air probably came from climbing a tree.

Sarah did notice that some of the sasquatch were talking amongst themselves, causing a wave of loud rumblings to wash over her. Others were playing a game that involved their hands and a lot of noise. All of them frequently looked out the windows at the world below them.

Moving along at a steady clip of just under six hundred kilometers per hour they advanced toward their destination toward the northeast. After about an hour, Sarah walked through the cargo bay to where General Martin sat reading.

"Excuse me, Sir," she uttered in a loud voice to be heard over the powerful engines.

Martin looked up and, as if seeing her for the first time, said, "Yes, Ma'am. What can I do for you?"

His smile warmed her and made her feel comfortable. "Where exactly are we headed?"

Looking back down at his book he'd been reading he absently replied, "Fairchild."

Puzzling over his response for a moment, she finally followed up with, "Fairchild? Is that a town in Oregon?"

Smiling again, as if in reflex, General Martin responded, "It's an air force base. It's near Spokane."

In mute reply, Sarah mouthed, "Oh." Silently she asked herself, *Am I ever going home again?*

Sarah sat down where she was and allowed her thoughts to meander across the fabric of her feelings. Home. *When will I return? Will the Enemy have killed everyone off before I get back? Will I survive to someday get back?* It was surprisingly overwhelming and she rested her tired head in her hands.

Then another line of thinking wriggled its way into to her mind. *Where is home? Is it really Drain? Or is it somewhere else?* She continued to sit quietly, pondering her thoughts, feelings and recent experiences. *Maybe it's in the cave with the sasquatch? Maybe it's wherever my friends are.* She casually looked around the Buzzard's cargo bay. *Perhaps with people like sp'atung and Jack.*

Sarah and Martin sat next to each other for another pair of minutes before Sarah's curiosity and need to be 'doing something' got the better of her. With only a hint of impatience she queried, "What's this base like? I've been to Spokane but it's been a long time."

The general looked up toward the Buzzard's cowling, idly peering at the gear stored above, as he replied, "I don't know. I've never been there."

Surprised by this, the general's temporary interrogator followed up with, "Really. Then where were you coming from?"

Knowing that he should share only what information was necessary regarding the location of the country's government, he evasively replied, "Just east of the Rockies."

"That's rather general." Then, in a belated effort to be cordial, she added, "General."

"True, but that's the best I can give you right now."

Again, a blanket of quiet passed over them, allowing both of them to be safely tucked away in the worlds of their own thoughts. However, Sarah found she had more questions and 'needed' to ask them.

"Why aren't we heading back to 'east of the Rockies'?"

The general was silent for longer than Sarah had expected. He didn't look uncomfortable or unsure about anything. *In fact,* she noted, *his face is rather inscrutable.*

Finally, he said, "Security."

He turned away, and she found herself a little frustrated with his response. As if reading her thoughts, he added, "I know that's not what you wanted to hear. Just more 'military babble', as you might call it, but it would be inappropriate for me to tell you more." He sighed and then wearily added, "Sometimes it's hard to know who to trust."

Sarah nodded slowly, grateful for the answer she'd received.

Like an arrow speeding toward an alternate target, the Buzzard continued along its path.

After about an hour the Buzzard came in for a landing at Fairchild AFB nearly fifteen kilometers southwest of Spokane. Coming into the area, Sarah noted that Spokane didn't look nearly as decimated as many cities did. *Not being one of the bigger cities seems to have saved it,* she quietly pondered. Then she added, *For now.*

The tiltrotor came into Fairchild for a landing and all around was the characteristic beauty of the Pacific Northwest woodlands. The multi-hued greens that ranged across the light spectrum found their only competition in gorgeous shades of blue that the sky presented amidst a mass of clouds dotting the atmosphere above.

The craft landed easily and the bay doors opened. Everyone quickly marched out of the vehicle and followed General Martin. As one, they walked by the nearest building and Sarah felt a perverse sense of irony as she read the sign on the structure that read 'Survival School.' She hoped this plan of Martin's worked. Otherwise, she didn't have much confidence that humans as a species would survive.

On the way to Fairchild she'd been briefed about the mission and that they were fighting the clock every step of the way. So, she was no longer in the dark regarding the fact that if they didn't hurry and do something to thwart the Enemy, those ships in the sky would soon have the materials they needed to resume their orbital bombardments and finish off all of humanity.

The entire group quickly marched into the Survival School and congregated in the main room. General Martin didn't waste any time. Without medals dangling from his chest he strode to the front of the room. From across the chamber Sarah watched Jack watch the general. He looked as calm and composed as he ever did but somehow she knew that his cool exterior was thinner than usual. There was something about his eyes that had a wealth of knowledge and a lifetime of stories to tell.

And somehow she knew that they were definitely not all happy memories.

Too big for the chairs, the sasquatch sat on the cool floor. This turned out to work well inasmuch as that put their heads at eye level with the rest of the company. Sarah had to remember that for nearly all the sasquatch–all but xtela–being in that thoroughly human environment was utterly foreign. For their sakes she was grateful that xtela had talked with his brethren about human environments during the ride to Fairchild AFB. Nevertheless, It was obvious to her that they definitely felt out of their element. What with their fidgeting and constant peering about, they looked something like a duck out of water, or a sasquatch out of his jungle.

Standing before the entire group of a few dozen, General Martin signaled everyone to give him their attention. Upon hearing the group quiet down, he began.

"I know I don't have to tell you how dire the situation is for us and everyone on this planet, sasquatch and human alike. Captain Smith and I have worked up a plan of how to best utilize you sasquatch in as effective a way as we can without compromising your safety any more than is needed." Turning to Smith he extended a hand toward her to signal she had the floor.

Already standing behind and to the side of her commanding officer, the beautiful and fiery red-haired captain stepped forward and wasted no time with pleasantries. "We know that the Enemy is able to communicate reasonably effectively between the various places where they are holed up, namely mines around the world. We also know that within those mines they are acquiring the materials they need to be able to finish the work they've begun." She paused a moment or two, perhaps for dramatic emphasis, and then added, "Our annihilation." The words came out like she'd been chewing on something bitter.

Upon hearing those words, spines stiffened and eyes took on a feral caste. No one in that room had any desire to back down but every intention of taking the fight to the Enemy.

"So, we recognize that we *have* to hit the Enemy and we *have* to do it soon, before the Enemy has finished its mining and resumes its orbital bombardments on our cities."

One hand went up by a soldier near the rear of the room, his uniform in good repair but dirty and soiled from his recent time in the forest near Drain. "Captain, how much time do we have? I mean, before the Enemy is ready to strike again with the orbital bombardments?"

Her reply came like the practiced attack of a sword master. "We don't know. It could be today, tomorrow, or in a month. All we know is we can't wait. You've already seen how much damage they can do when their orbital ships are armed for planetary bombardments. D.C., gone. New York City, gone. Los Angeles, gone. Beijing, gone. Paris, gone. And the list goes on."

A hushed and reverent silence stole across the room. One could've heard and felt a stray hair hit the ground. Finally, Smith broke the morbid quiet, continuing her report. "General Martin and I also acknowledge that in these dire circumstances, when we make a strong attack, wiping out the Enemy combatants at one particular mine, word of our use of the sasquatch and their powerful contribution will more than likely get out. In that event, future missions would likely be fraught with significantly more danger, and casualties, than otherwise." She paused to take a quick drink from a canteen she had stashed away somewhere.

Another young soldier raised a hand and asked, "Regarding that first mine raid with xtela," he seemed to have difficulty pronouncing the name of the sasquatch, trying it out on his tongue like some kind of new flavor. "Wouldn't that have alerted the Spiders to our new strategy?"

The captain smiled in satisfaction as she replied, "I'm highly confident that the few Spiders that survived our assault won't yet have enough information to piece together what exactly the sasquatch are contributing. After the next assault, that will probably no longer be the case."

Smith looked around the room only mildly impatiently as she continued laying out the battle plan. "Therefore, the plan is to execute ten major strike operations–raids if you will–against ten different Enemy strongholds/mines. Simultaneously."

Sarah found herself getting wrapped up in the intensity of Smith's manner and words. The captain knew what she was talking about and obviously wanted to do what she could to destroy the Enemy and liberate planet Earth. After a few minutes of listening to Smith, Sarah suddenly became acutely aware of who she was listening to and tried to clear her head and end the trance she'd unknowingly entered. With a knee-jerk reaction like a politician raising taxes, she reminded herself of her resentment of the other woman. Yet even then she was beginning to taste the first drops of forgetfulness, not remembering clearly why she had ever disliked the other woman who had come parachuting into her life like an MX-missile. Sarah thought, *I'm glad she's on our side.*

"As you all know, we can't just bomb the mines. First, we'd destroy the DEWs (directed energy weapons) that the Enemy have positioned therein and we wouldn't have an effective weapon against their orbiting ships. And let's face it, those ships are the main threat. Second, we've already tried that in the past and every time we attempt to destroy a mine, and all the Spiders inside, they simply use their DEWs to destroy our incoming missiles and bombs."

Getting back to the strategy of the raids, she continued. "So, since we're going to hit ten mines simultaneously, you can see why we insisted on twenty different sasquatch, two for each team." There was more buzz, but it quieted itself down rapidly. "Each raiding party will have *two* sasquatch assigned to it. That should give each group the strength and flexibility needed to successfully complete its operation."

Upon hearing that, Sarah could see looks of optimism sprouting on faces around the room.

"Each of the ten teams will be organized today. Each team will have three days to train together and get prepared for the mission."

In approximate imitation of the inquisitive young soldier, a sasquatch raised her hand. Smith gave her the floor and she asked in her marble-chewing voice, "Smith Captain, why three suns?" Some of the humans in the room squinted their eyes as if trying to understand the garbled sasquatch voice more clearly.

She replied, "Although we have no certainty regarding when the Enemy will resume orbital bombardments, upon discussing it together, General Martin and I agree that we can't wait any longer. If the Enemy gets its ships' weapons sufficiently supplied...we're done."

Again, the room became as quiet as a tomb, but Smith didn't wait for a 'moment of silence' and didn't mind stepping on anyone's feelings. "Before you leave the room, I'll give you your team assignments and immediately thereafter, you'll meet up with the rest of your team." She paused and added, "Remember, we're not going in to destroy the mines. We want to get control of those DEWs that the Enemy has set up to protect the mines. If we're going to ultimately beat the Spiders, we're going to need to have every weapon and advantage we can muster. That will make the missions that much more dangerous, but the payoff that much greater."

A few moments later the meeting ended and team assignments were quickly distributed. Sarah noted with optimistic appraisal at how quickly the ten various teams were coming together. She knew that not all the team members were present. Others were elsewhere on base, but from those persons present, each team was coming to a preliminary head count of about five people. The other personnel for each team would join them in a few minutes.

Before the ten teams separated, Smith assigned team leaders and gave special instructions to them. Then each team moved out to its respective location wherein it would meet the remainder of its members and begin to train. Soon, Sarah found that she was nearly alone in the Survival School. Jack, the smoky gray haired sp'atung, and General Martin were her only remaining company. Shortly after the last of the teams departed, the general began moving across the room to exit. His eyes were a practiced mask, ignoring his elephant in the room—Jack Armstrong. Jack, in his own way, was doing the same. Perhaps it was fate, but somehow their eyes met and a spark of recognition flared up between them again. Sarah couldn't tell if that spark quickly turned to anger, admiration, or just simple acknowledgement.

The general departed and the three remaining individuals came together. Jack looked at sp'atung and, after a brief pause of contemplation, he said, "Sp'atung, my friend. I guess it's time we get to work."

"It is good. I ready to move river. What you think we do first?"

Jack took on his country smile and, looking in the direction everyone else had gone said, "I've got some ideas."

That night, at 21:00 sharp, Sarah found herself arriving at the quarters that Jack had been assigned. They weren't hard to find, they were just down the hall from her own. When the door opened, she noticed that sp'atung was already there. His massive frame occupied a large part of the small quarters. He sat atop the bed, taking up nearly the whole thing. Jack offered the only chair to Sarah. She took it graciously, sat down, and immediately withdrew her notes from a satchel.

Jack wasted no time getting started. "Let's get going. Sarah, how did things go for you today as you monitored the three teams you were assigned?" It seemed to Sarah that he was all too familiar with this type of return-and-report meeting, and being in charge.

She replied, "I've got to be honest. I kind of suspected that I'd see some problems, that some of our soldiers might've caused some sort of a ruckus but, from what I saw, things went pretty well. I saw the occasional friction between human and sasquatch, but it didn't seem to me to be anything more than I've seen countless times between any pair of humans."

Peering over his steepled fingers at her, Jack squinted for a moment, perhaps attempting to ferret out of her words anything she may have omitted intentionally or otherwise. At last he nodded woodenly in acknowledgement. Then he gestured with his hand for sp'atung to relay how his day had transpired. The mountainous sasquatch, still unfamiliar with many human mannerisms, wasn't sure at first what Jack meant.

It took him only a moment to get his meaning and then he discussed what he'd seen. "I think it good. Some sasquatch seem unsure about this. Everything new like new sun."

Immediately, Sarah was grateful that sp'atung was assigned to this task. Though Sarah recognized she knew more about the sasquatch than perhaps anyone else alive, she also acknowledged the fact that she didn't understand them nearly as well as would one of their own, like sp'atung.

The hairy giant continued with the telltale chewing of his words. As always, it sounded a bit like he was grinding up gravel while speaking. "Some look sort of...er...I not know word. It feel miss where come from."

"Homesick," Sarah quickly volunteered.

"Homesick," sp'atung slowly replied. He quickly became familiar with how to pronounce it. "Some sasquatch...homesick, but no many," he added hastily. "It good none alone." He beamed an optimistic smile that seemed to promise to be able to fill the whole outdoors.

"Anything else from either of you?" Jack pressed.

Sarah and sp'atung took turns describing how the manmade DEWs, which were pathetic compared to the Enemy's, worked. They discussed how the human operators looked a little fearful during the training exercises in which the sasquatch charged the DEWs with a ferocity they'd never seen before. They also talked about the 'cave training' that had been done in blacked out buildings, to better simulate the mines they'd soon enter.

At last Jack said, "Well, that's about what I expected. Our military people are highly trained professionals. Regarding the sasquatch, after getting to know them, I felt confident of their decorum and willingness to get along."

Suddenly, quite unexpectedly, Jack began to chuckle. It started out small and quickly began to grow. "I just remembered something." He extinguished his laughter just enough so he could speak. "When I was watching Team 9 at the Enemy Combat station, where they train to fight the Spiders in close quarters, one of the men, a corporal I believe..." He began to laugh again, "...took it into his head that the sasquatch on his Team were just dumb animals." By this time, Jack was wiping tears from his eyes because of his full-body laughter. "The kid...began talking...to the sasquatch...really slowly and so everyone could hear him...and to suggest the sasquatch...were slow mentally. The kid asked him, 'Where are you from?' The sasquatch, obviously catching on that something peculiar was going on quickly replied, 'I come from sundown side, past big mountains. You not see this from plane?' Everyone started laughing at the corporal. Then the sasquatch, I don't remember his name, added icing to the cake. He said, 'You learn more from one your books.' At this point, everyone—except that corporal—was almost rolling on the floor laughing."

By this time, Sarah was laughing heartily as well. Even sp'atung was catching on to this new variety of humor and joining in the mirth.

They decided to continue the next day as before. The meeting soon broke up and sp'atung and Sarah retired to their quarters.

Over the next two days, the training continued, and so did the oversight by Jack, sp'atung and Sarah.

When the ten raids were only half a day away, Martin went to visit the president and make her aware of the sasquatch and his plans. Though he gave her his reasons for keeping her in the dark, primarily issues of security, she still had to work to hold her temper in check throughout their discussion. He knew she was furious about him working on this project without her supposed knowledge. When their brief interview was coming to a close she said, "General, the world owes you its thanks. When the War is over, I'm certain you'll be rewarded appropriately and get what's coming to you."

Martin noticed that her smile never reached her eyes.

CHAPTER 22
Ten Places To See Before You Die

Sinyukhinskoye, Russia Mine

Captain Nick Sparks calmly drew forth his compact binoculars and peered through them from behind a ridge overlooking the Sinyukhinskoye mine northwest of Moscow, Russia. Slowly and carefully he surveyed the landscape of the surrounding area. An experienced soldier, he scanned the topography for Enemy combatants, potential ambush points, and possible routes of escape if things didn't go according to plan.

Sparks was in his mid-thirties without a hint of gray in his fine shock of hair. He boasted a strong chin like a movie star and hailed from Arizona. He never did seem to get used to cooler environments, especially if they weren't devoid of moisture in the air. Like this one.

Satisfied, he finally slid along the dirt on his belly back to the rest of his unit. He looked at the men and women under his command and was proud of them. However, he didn't know if he'd ever be able to root out the uneasy feeling he got when he thought of the two sasquatch in the company. Of course, he'd trained with them back at Fairchild AFB, but that had only been for three days.

But he knew that wasn't really what concerned him. Just a few high-speed days before he never would've believed that Bigfoot was real. *Now I'm leading two of them into combat. This man's army is getting stranger and stranger by the day.*

They all knew the mission and how it was supposed to go down. Sparks also knew that they were all aware of the sense of urgency that seemed to permeate their every movement, thought and word. The War had been mostly one-sided and everyone knew it. Even though his entire team understood the gravity of the situation and how important their success was, he still wanted to say something just to make sure they were all on the same page.

"Before we move in," he began, "I want you to remember, when it gets tough in there, don't forget why we're fighting." He took off his cap that was devoid of any insignia, the one he wore when going into combat. He subconsciously wiped his beaded forehead with the back of one hand and continued in a subdued tone. "We're not a bunch of war junkies. We're fighting for our families, our country and...our world." He paused briefly, as if his previous words were a crescendo for the rest. With growing intensity he proclaimed, "Let's get in there and kill every one of those worthless creatures. This is *our* world and they're not welcome!"

Sparks was surprised to note that even the pair of sasquatch were getting caught up in the emotional fervor. With the end of his brief speech, Captain Sparks nodded to his team in mute signal to move out.

Thirty minutes later they had made their way to a ridge that was adjacent to the mine, but a few hundred meters behind the entrance. It was the only clear way to approach the front door, the only door into the mine. Of course, the entrance was heavily guarded, just as they knew it would be. The team silently made the short trek through the trees to their destination. Sparks was pleasantly surprised to find that the two sasquatch moved as quietly as a gentle breeze through a jungle. *Of course they're quiet,* he silently chided himself.

The captain was glad that the two sasquatch who were assigned to his unit were significantly different in appearance. That first day he'd seen all twenty of them—was it only four days ago?—he had to admit that, to him, they all looked alike. The two assigned to work with him, celewiltx and memimen, were mercifully different in appearance. The female, celewiltx, was obviously more aggressive than some of the other sasquatch, and she had a luxurious brown pelt streaked with vicious looking jagged grey stripes. Sparks found it a little challenging to not feel intimidated when talking with her.

The other, memimen, was a young male sasquatch a few inches shorter than celewiltx with jet black hair. During the training he'd seemed more docile than his female counterpart.

The unit of soldiers moved silently through the trees like wraiths through a graveyard.

Clad in darkness, Sparks was grateful to be assigned to head up one of the Russian raids. Since two of the ten raids that were transpiring simultaneously were in Russia, it had been decided that those two would take place at night, giving as many teams as possible as much advantage as they could, while having all ten teams strike simultaneously. To help the other teams as well, the plan was for Sparks' team to begin their raid at 04:00.

He heard a twig snap on his five o'clock. Instinctively he cranked his head around to determine the source of the small, night-shattering sound. He found it immediately, a young corporal with a sheepish look on his face. Out of the corner of his eye, Sparks could see the memimen silently making gestures to celewiltx. Though celewiltx seemed disinterested in what the younger sasquatch had to say, Captain Sparks had the strangest feeling that those two were sharing some sort of private joke. *They probably find it amusing how noisy we humans are. Well, if that's what it takes for the men to be more careful, so be it.*

They moved on.

Minutes later, they found themselves on a ridge above the entrance to the mine. Sparks having already made sure everyone knew the plan, signaled with his hands for half the squad to move out to approach the entrance from the east side while the other half covered the west side. Celewiltx would go with the 'east group' and memimen would go with the 'west.'

Grateful for the new moon and the darkness it brought with it, Sparks tapped the top of his head before everyone moved out to take up their positions. His men understood all too well what he meant: *Put on your ear protectors!*

They began fanning out, Sparks with celewiltx and the 'east group' and, ten minutes later, they were in position to start the raid. He allowed for another five minutes to account for any potentially unforeseen obstacles. Knowing that the leader of the 'west group' would be doing the same thing with memimen, at the fifteen-minute mark exactly, Sparks tapped the elevated shoulder of celewiltx in signal for her to begin with the sonic blast.

Immediately a throbbing pulse of sonic energy emanated from the two sasquatch, climaxing in between them, right where the Enemy was guarding the entrance to the mine. It took less than one painful heartbeat for Sparks to recognize that the two sasquatch were much more emotionally cranked up now that they were going into battle. The power of their sonic blasts was intense! He couldn't imagine how it would've been without the ear protection. He remembered hearing the scuttlebutt a couple of days ago about how Captain Smith had actually endured a blast without ear muffs and stayed conscious. At that exact moment in time, he couldn't imagine *anyone* being able to pull off such a feat.

As previously arranged, they immediately began moving in, having been formerly briefed that the Enemy would recover quickly, more so than humans deprived of ear protection.

Each man was wearing a pair of infrared goggles, allowing them to clearly see the heat signatures of any and all living objects along their lines of sight. Figuring that with the sonic blasts of the sasquatch there wouldn't be much point in using silencers on their weapons, the two teams converged on the stunned Enemy soldiers in a V-formation, automatic weapons making a huge, but brief cacophony.

In a matter of seconds, the small melee was over. The two teams came together again as a single group and began making their way into the mine. Sparks took the point up front with celewiltx right behind him. Memimen was placed near the rear of the column that soon found itself snaking its way through the tunnels and caverns of the Sinyukhinskoye mine.

Because the passages of the mine were, by their very nature, narrow, they found that for the moment they needed the sasquatch very little. Notwithstanding the incredible speed and agility of the Enemy, it was still reminiscent of shooting fish in a barrel.

They moved quickly through the tunnels, being extremely careful to keep track of where they were. Coming up on a large fork in the path, Sparks expressed a prayer of silent gratitude for the maps they'd received to get them through the maze. At that main fork, he used two fingers to signal the 'west group' to take the left tunnel while his own group would take the right. If all went well, they'd bump into most of the Enemy soldiers and mow them down as they moved. Sparks figured it would take at least thirty minutes for the two teams to reunite in the main chamber. A veteran of the War, he knew it was risky, but necessary to complete their vital mission.

The two teams split up and began making their way through the tunnels. Sparks again offered a silent prayer in gratitude for the IR goggles they were using. He was certain he was not the only one who felt that way. Without them, he was sure they would be sitting ducks and have absolutely no chance of making it out alive.

The captain spared himself a split second to look back at his team and couldn't help but notice the massive thunderhead trailing him. Celewiltx was following like some otherworldly sentinel of death. He knew he didn't know much about sasquatch, but he could tell that, in combat, this one would be incredibly powerful. He also wondered how well she was doing in the darkness without IR goggles. Someone had told him that the creatures lived in caves. If that was true, he supposed they would be just fine the way they were.

They came around a bend in the path and, as he caught a glimpse of some Enemy combatants ahead, he instantly heard the powerful sonic boom coming from immediately behind him. The few Enemy soldiers that became incapacitated never had a chance. Despite the headache that Sparks was beginning to develop from repeated exposure to the sasquatch 'Voice,' he had to admit that plowing through Enemy soldiers in this way beat the alternative any day of the week.

After quickly cutting down the few adversaries before them, they moved on. Sparks knew that they were getting close to the main chamber where they were likely to meet up with many more Spiders. *How many will there be?* he wondered for only a moment. *A dozen? Four dozen?* No one had ever gone into a den of destruction like this before and come back to report.

However, that wasn't his main concern. He figured that, at some point in this incursion, they would get surrounded and have to really begin to fight for their lives, and sasquatch or no, he knew it was likely to get pretty scrappy. He knew this mission was different from the one Captain Smith had recently conducted. Hers had been to test the sasquatch Voice. The ten missions transpiring today were all about retaking mines and completely eliminating any and all resistance therein by the Spiders.

After a handful of minutes Sparks had to suppress the distinct impression that, as he moved down the tunnel, he was being squeezed through a tube of toothpaste. *Heck of a time to find out I'm claustrophobic,* he thought.

Shortly thereafter they came around another bend in the tunnel and he couldn't believe what he was seeing. There were Spiders everywhere! Off the cuff, he guessed there must've been at least three hundred.

At about that same moment when they entered the reasonably well-lit chamber, he and his men peered around and beheld the horrors before them. There was a moment of stunned silence—the Enemy not anticipating such an audacious and successful attack and the humans aghast at the hornet's nest they'd just walked into.

The silence lasted only a moment before projectile weapons began being discharged. High powered machine guns with hollow-point rounds and the multi-colored SPAWNs used by the Enemy were being fired with reckless abandon. Through it all rang out the sound of celewiltx using her sasquatch sonic blast for all she was worth!

Sparks quickly noted that, due to the temperamental, below-ground environment, the Enemy was being marginally careful with their red-sludge weapons. Yet the exploding characteristics of the red material had a small blast radius and was therefore still used without too much concern of cave-ins. He was also subconsciously aware that the Enemy soldiers were breaking up into groups, as if they had some sort of military organization reminiscent of squads and companies, like humans. *Who would've thought.*

The captain and his men tried to take cover behind any little rock or mound of earth that could be found nearby. They huddled primarily around the mouth of the chamber through which they'd made their entrance. Standing next to Sparks, Celewiltx stood bellowing her incapacitating blasts and reminded him of the Tarzan books he'd read as a child. The female sasquatch looked dazzlingly terrifying! The strength of her repeated sonic booms were definitely taking their toll on the nine-legged monstrosities. More and more of them were collapsing where they stood.

Some of them upon earthen shelves were falling to the chamber floor below. Sparks noted between headache inducing blasts that the fall certainly wasn't killing the aliens, but it was definitely doing its part to help stun them.

The humans were picking their targets and laying waste almost as fast as they could squeeze their triggers. Each man quickly lost count of how many Enemies he'd hit. The stench was already becoming mercilessly pungent.

Then, amidst their success, something shattered the moment with horrifying abruptness. One of his men began screaming. Sparks turned to look at the young man and saw that some of the flesh on his arm was melting. Recognizing the still-burning chemical, he knew that the intelligent Spiders had changed up their tactics. He quickly pulled a small packet of powder out of a pocket and began applying it to the man's wounded arm. The chemicals in the powder immediately began to neutralize the green sludge, ending the burning. The man gratefully looked up at Sparks.

Bringing his mind back to the battle, Sparks yelled, "They're staying further back and firing their SPAWNs from the rear of the chamber!" A splash of red material landed nearby, causing an eruption of earth as the stuff emitted its telltale explosion. He and his men were thrown back. One of them stared vacantly up at the cavern's ceiling. The man wasn't dead, but severely stunned. Probably in shock.

With the terrans beginning to take a beating, Sparks looked around at his increasingly battered company and then back at the Enemy batteries. *I've got to do something and it needs to be now!*

As if in answer to his silent petition, the 'west' group emerged from another portal leading into the chamber. They were immediately firing everything they had at the SPAWN-wielding Enemy soldiers. However, the alien menace that had shown on countless occasions its ability to move and fire rapidly, proved its acumen to adjust its strategy to be of equal capacity. Almost as if they were working by telepathy, the Enemy soldiers broke up into three groups. One group continued its assault on Sparks' east group while a second formation focused on the newly arrived west group. Both of these two assault teams were doing what they could with their red and green SPAWNs. The Enemy was clearly losing but they were counting on the only advantage they seemed to have for the moment—their overwhelming numbers. Deftly they handled their SPAWNs in their hairy, grotesque appendages.

Sparks noticed that there was a third group that was hanging back and though he wasn't sure how they fit into the Enemy's strategy, he began to get a churning feeling in the pit of his guts. Between salvos made from his own personal weapon, he wondered, *What are you guys up to?*

The east group and the west group had both come in on roughly the same side of the cavern, at opposite corners, but as the mole burrows, they were separated by approximately fifty yards from each other with little or no cover between them—just the face of the cavern wall. Though it was touch-and-go the first couple of minutes, Sparks was pleased that the two groups didn't really need to converge. They were both doing sufficiently well at holding their own.

The two sasquatch kept bellowing within the echo chamber and the automatic weapons kept firing. The cacophony was insistent and the humans were unspeakably grateful for their ear protectors, despite the certainty they had that they would have splitting headaches for who knew how long. The assault continued and just as Sparks noticed that the Spiders were on the verge of formational collapse, he saw something that caused the queasy feeling in his guts to rise up like bubbles in a putrid swamp. The third group of Spiders was missing! *Perhaps that group disbanded to move into buoy up the other two groups in support?*

Though he knew it was a responsible and useful tactic in warfare, something told him that those creatures had gone somewhere else.

Hoping memimen in the 'west group' would be able to cover the large chamber with his sonic blasts by himself, he immediately signaled celewiltx and half his men to follow him back the way they'd come in case the Enemy had decided on sending the third group in the back way to attack from behind.

At first, nothing happened. Having moved a short way down the tunnel, it was relatively quiet. Even celewiltx was pleased with the break that was being afforded her. Sparks looked up at her terrifyingly vicious face and saw her trying to catch her breath and massage her throat with one large, hairy hand.

A whole minute passed in which the only sounds to be heard were the muffled noises of combat down the tunnel.

Sparks knew he was moving those around him into a potential ambush. However, he also knew that the job had to be done. Moments before the Enemy was upon them in the twisting, turning, tortuous tunnels, Sparks realized the error of his split second decision of where to post up his men. He and his men were perched at a position in the pathway just before a corner. The Enemy combatants from the third group swung around that corner with essentially no warning.

Before they were even aware that the Enemy was upon them, a green globule of burning jello scorched the two men flanking Sparks. They never had a chance.

The terran response was immediate. The bullets flooding the corridor and celewiltx's Voice unitedly bowled over the Spiders.

Through the pain of losing two more of his men, Sparks was surprised and even allowed himself to feel a little pleased at how quickly and malevolently the rearguard opposition they faced was cut down. However, the elation of success was short lived as he looked down at the slowly melting remains of his two friends.

Sparks cursed himself for leading his men into such a situation. *I shouldn't have positioned them right in front of a turn in the path,* he silently chastised himself. *Our IR goggles were next to worthless with the tunnel wall between us and those accursed creatures.*

Shortly after finishing off the Enemy's third group, Sparks led his small group team to the main body in the large chamber. On their way back, they could hear the sounds of battle gradually slacken. When they arrived the sight that greeted them was grisly. Dead Spiders carpeted the chamber floor. Though some of his men had been killed, the captain was immensely impressed by the power of the sasquatch, namely their mighty Voice.

He knew war was never a complete success, but against this Enemy, he felt at that moment that the skirmish had been as near completely successful as they were going to get. *Without the sasquatch,* he solemnly considered, *we would've been cut to pieces in a matter of seconds! And though it boils my bile to think it we only lost a quarter of our force.*

His men knew how things tended to shape up in the War and so he didn't find it difficult to read in their faces the mix of emotions that they felt. The elation of success and the pain of lost comrades was evident in their countenances as well. However, they were good men and professional soldiers so they didn't waste time blubbering. Yet the anguish of not only seeing their dead friends nearby, but knowing that what remained of their bodies made it essentially impossible to return home with their corpses.

With a single look back at the scene of destruction and massacre, they contacted Fairchild AFB. Sparks thought, *If the other nine raids go this well, we just might have a chance at winning this War.*

Albert Silver Mine, South Africa

Located nearly as close to Johannesburg, South Africa as the Sinyukhinskoye, Russia mine was from Moscow, the Albert Silver Mine was located in northern South Africa. Whereas the Russian mine was northwest of Moscow, the Albert Silver Mine was northeast of Johannesburg.

The team that had been prepping for 'Albert' was led by an extremely focused and intense woman named Major Amanda Cautrail. The two sasquatch assigned to her unit were leqi and cqiqen.

Cqiqen was pleased that they would be beginning their assault at 02:00. He loved the middle of the night. After all, it was the best time to pull a prank on someone. However, he knew that this night would be totally unlike any night he'd spent before. It would not be a night for dropping a snake around the neck of a friend or sprinkling the juice from under ripe blackberries on the food of another. Nor would it be a time to be anything less than serious and somber. He knew he never had any kind of interest in being serious or somber, but he also knew that his antics and jocularity needed to be put away for just one evening.

As the CV-22 Osprey military helicopter finished its flight toward their destination, cqiqen was surprised to find that he was less intrigued about his human teammates and more interested in the other sasquatch accompanying them. To be certain, he somehow found the whole situation of being in a fighting unit with humans quite humorous, but leqi was another matter altogether.

He'd known her all their lives but he'd never gotten to really know her. Yet that wasn't really the rub. Although he'd always been told that she wasn't deadpan stupid, he had a hard time believing it. Growing up, cqiqen had always seen leqi as being rather unaware of her surroundings and almost entirely oblivious to anything that was not of interest to her. However, he had to admit she was pretty. She had a pelt of greenish blue with swirls of white peppered occasionally throughout.

Oh, well, cqiqen thought casually. *I just hope I don't have to babysit her during this whole...thing. I'm going to have my hands full with these humans.* He laughed to himself. Some of his mirth must've spilled out onto his face for Major Cautrail's cool exterior was slightly ruffled as she noticed cqiqen. Seeing a sasquatch laugh was even more unusual to the major than the creatures themselves.

They soon landed at the extreme northeast 'corner' of the Bronkhorstspruit Municipal Nature Preserve near Johannesburg, South Africa. Due to the open terrain surrounding the Albert Mine, it had been decided that their landing site would be about 4 kilometers out.

Just before moving out for the mine on foot, cqiqen noted the beautiful nearby lake that sat on the Earth like some sort of glassy paint stroke etched by a god. He saw the tall grasses swaying in the breeze in hypnotic rhythm. His keen sasquatch nighttime vision showed him a wandering gazelle loping by in the distance and the gently rolling hills it traversed with leisure skill. Moments later, it was time to move out.

With very little discussion or fanfare the team disembarked the aircraft and began their silent trek toward the nearby mine. Of course, each human had his IR goggles and ear muffs securely in place and the sasquatch wore nothing.

The four-kilometer march to the Albert Mine took a mere forty minutes. When they arrived the exterior of the mine appeared to be deserted. Sequestered amidst some tall African grass just under a hundred meters from the mine entrance, the party laid down to determine their next move.

Major Cautrail looked at her team, all of them laying prone nearby. "It's strange that there's no one out there guarding the front door. It could be a trap." She subconsciously wiped a precariously hanging bead of sweat from her brow. "But who knows how those monsters think." She turned away from her team and continued speaking while again surveying the mine entrance. "So, here's how we're going to play it. We'll go in fast and stay as low as we can until we're inside. From there, we'll proceed just as we trained. Any questions?"

The deathly silence of the night was the only reply she received. "Good. Let's move."

It took them only one incident-free minute to enter the mine. Cqiqen, who had done his share of hunting, was surprised that he didn't smell much of anything emanating from the mine. At least, nothing particularly unusual. He was assigned to the group's rearguard while leqi moved near the front. Moving through the mine's corridors, cqiqen couldn't help but wonder if there were snakes down there. He figured there were and hoped they bump into some. *Any kind of snake is awfully tasty,* he quietly thought as his stomach growled.

Despite the dark and the multitude of potential opportunities for the Spiders to ambush them, Cautrail moved quickly through the tunnels, knowing full well just how vital her part of the ten-pronged mission was at that very moment. Like everyone else involved with the ten raids, she knew that they had to hit the Enemy simultaneously and hit them *hard!*

They moved on through the inkwell tunnel, following a memorized route. None of them wanted to have to look down at a map any more than they needed. *Taking your eye off the ball was a good way to get yourself and your comrades killed,* the major told herself.

Moving through the death-at-any-moment corridors, they looked like a group of bug-eyed creatures walking erect, all except the two sasquatch in the unit. They moved with surety and confidence. After a few minutes of winding through the maze of pathways within the mine, cqiqen suddenly realized that he had not yet smelled or heard anything that was likely to be the Tarantulas. Ordinarily, he would've shrugged it off and ignored the thought. However, given the potentially perilous circumstances in which he found himself, he wondered at this.

Moments later he ghosted to the front of the procession and tapped Cautrail on the shoulder. She raised one fist to signal everyone to halt. Cqiqen immediately began to relay his curious thoughts. The major focusing all her mental energy to understand the sasquatch accent. "Cautrail Major, I think about something," he began. Though he tried to speak quietly, his words still came out like a moderately loud mashing of rocks.

Raising one eyebrow, she replied in a hushed whisper. "Don't worry. We'll take care of you."

Thinking she had made a joke, cqiqen stifled a laugh. After a moment of forcing himself to be quiet he continued. "No, it not that. Something be missing."

Allowing a look of impatience to cross her face she replied, "What is it?"

"I no hear or smell nothing."

"What do you mean?" came the more interested response.

"Tarantulas stay here. So, I should smell or hear them."

Cautrail froze in place for a moment as realization dawned. A few moments later, she nodded to cqiqen in acknowledgement and gratitude. She immediately passed the word along the train to be extra wary of an ambush.

At last, they arrived at the main chamber where the miners had originally stored large equipment and had room to conduct many of their planning activities.

It was empty.

They searched the tomb-like room carefully and found nothing but a few sheddings from one or more of the Spiders. At last, Cautrail huddled them all together and spoke hurriedly in a raspy, quiet breath. "This feels like an ambush or some kind of trap." She noticed the others nodding their heads in ascent. "But if this is a trap, when will it get sprung?" She thought for a moment and then finished with, "I don't see any reason to stay here any longer. Let's head back."

They resumed their batting order as they cautiously made their way back the way they had come. At this point, each member of the party was only partially surprised to find a complete lack of Spiders on their way out.

Upon exiting the mine Cautrail huddled everyone together and, notwithstanding the apparent absence of danger, she woodenly whispered to everyone, "Let's head back to the Osprey and report in so we can get some other people here to hold the mine. Then we'll head back home."

Everyone turned toward the southwest, toward the safety of their aircraft a mere four kilometers distant. Cqiqen immediately heard the discharge of a SPAWN. *WUMP!* With a split second decision cqiqen yelled "Down!" as he endeavored to tackle as many in the group as he could.

The surprised looks on the faces around him turned ashen as they saw the effects of the incoming red goop splatter and the resultant shrapnel on those soldiers who had been outside the reach of the mighty sasquatch.

Major Cautrail pushed, or at least tried to push, cqiqen off of her. She looked about and her soldier's instincts kicked in immediately, ignoring those around her who were dead or for whom there could be no help. "Everyone, behind that boulder on my nine o'clock!" she bellowed in a way that would make a sasquatch proud.

When they had all quickly scurried to the safety of the wall-like rock, Cautrail passed an appraising eye upon those persons who were still alive. She was pleased to note that there were no other casualties beyond the initial six men and women who had bought it on the first salvo. Before she had a chance to issue any further orders cqiqen and leqi began emitting their terribly frightening sonic blasts.

Again, the humans' training kicked in immediately. Upon hearing the sasquatch fire away with their Voice, they whipped their firearms around to begin lacing the Enemy with lead poisoning. Most of the weapons that flashed to life were M4 Carbines, but there were one or two other types. Cautrail herself extended the bipod on her M240 7.62 mm machine gun and began to fire on any and all Spiders that entered her sights.

She noticed that one of her men was writhing on the ground. For an instant she wondered at that and then noticed that his ear protection was on the ground next to him. He was getting the full force of the sasquatch blasts. She quickly put his ear muffs back on him and then resumed her station.

Strangely, the battle seemed to be over in moments. With no discernible targets moving around, Cautrail split her people up into groups of three and fanned them out to look for surviving Enemy combatants. The two sasquatch remained in the center of the ad hoc compound, just outside the mine. They stood ready for action, ready for anything that might happen at a moment's notice. Cqiqen noticed that, at least for the moment, leqi appeared to be fully aware of her surroundings and not at all glassy eyed. He considered that and thought, *Maybe I misjudged her.*

As the various trios moved out, sporadic gunfire was heard every so often. Team members finishing off any stragglers that hadn't yet had the decency to die.

A few minutes later, all the teams slowly came back together, fairly certain there were no more threats in the immediate vicinity. Before moving out for the Osprey, Cautrail turned to cqiqen and leqi and with enough gratitude to fill a sasquatch cave she simply said, "Thank you."

The other eight mine raids were conducted at the same time. Each one was successful, except for the raid on the Copper Basin Mine in Tennessee. On that raid, only one person survived. It had been a wiry and scrappy warrior sasquatch named lec'. The rest of his team, including the sasquatch who'd been with him, had all been killed.

CHAPTER 23
Progress

Two Weeks Later

Sp'atung and Sarah sat together in a cafeteria at Camp Dodge. It was their lunch break and they were taking a much needed respite from their constant work.

Sp'atung said, "It still strange for I that we sasquatch work with sen' for a moon. Other jungle people no leave homes for so long."

"I know," Sarah replied. "It feels like it's been months."

The pair looked casually around the large room and noticed just how different the people were. "Everyone seems happier and more optimistic," Sarah mused.

"Yes, I see it," sp'atung replied. "We hunt Tarantulas good. It make us happy."

They sat quietly for a minute or two before sp'atung inquired, "I know there is speak of hunt Tarantula ships in sky, but when you think it go?"

Despite all the optimism that was contagiously filling the corridors of Camp Dodge, Sarah still wasn't entirely certain that they would be able to effectively attack the orbiting ships and win the War. Not wanting to ruin sp'atung's mood, she replied, "Any day now, I'm sure."

Sarah sat pensively considering the enormous amount of death and destruction that had taken place around the globe. She wanted to believe that they could win but it was difficult to fathom. *So many have died, like Pete Garrison. I wish I could've gotten to know him better.*

Wanting to think about something else, Sarah said, "Sp'atung, I've noticed your people adopting human ways here and there. How do you feel about that?"

"What you mean?"

Sarah paused for a moment or two before responding. "I've seen how some of the sasquatch have said things more like how a human would, or made hand gestures that are very human-like?"

Sp'atung thought for several long moments and said, "I think it good. I see sasquatch brethren be with sen', make new friends. It is good. It good we learn what other animals do and think." Then he added, "I see things too. I see sen' do, say things like sasquatch." He offered a genuine smile. Then his smile turned to sadness as he

said, "It sad. Some sasquatch, my friends, die in mines." Sarah scarcely noticed the tell-tale sasquatch accent, like sp'atung was sucking on a large piece of meat. His eyes began to water before he added, "We knew what happen before
we make choose to help sen'. It hurt to lose friends."

Sarah looked earnestly at the other and said, "Sp'atung, I hope you know you're one of my best friends. You're very special to me."

"I know. Thank you."

They both picked at their food for a couple of minutes before sp'atung suddenly blurted out, "Strange thing happen me this morning."

"What's that?" Sarah queried.

"Griffith President invite me dinner at low sun!"

"Oh, that's wonderful," Sarah said.

"Yes, but feel strange about it."

"Why's that?"

The sasquatch fidgeted for a moment, perhaps seeking the right words. "I see Griffith President many times. It seem like accident, but happen many times."

"That's nice. What do you talk about?"

"She ask about sasquatch, my mi'tuhng. How old we live, about Xruhnituhm Siem, how strong we are. Lots more."

"It sounds like she's just interested in getting to know the neighbors."

In exasperation, sp'atung nearly spat, "Yes, but now she inviting me big, special dinner and also many other sasquatch."

Sarah didn't see any harm in any of it, but she did find it odd that the president seemed to be giving the sasquatch so much VIP treatment compared to everyone else. However, there were always many more important things to consider and so the thought was soon out of her head.

The next day found Sarah working with three different teams. She had gotten good at coordinating them and enjoyed the job. She realized it wasn't just being able to work with the sasquatch. That would've been incentive enough to do the job and do her best. Not surprisingly, she also found it invigorating and rewarding to be working with so many other people who were so professional and good at what they did for the purpose of protecting her family, her people, their way of life and their very existence.

She was in the middle of debriefing a pair of sasquatch that had just gotten back from patrol when sp'atung materialized, knocking on her office door. Sarah turned to her friend and inquired, "What's up, sp'atung? I'm in the middle of a meeting but I can visit with you later."

Undeterred, the other replied, "I need talk you *now!*"

Something about the exaggerated seriousness in his voice made Sarah do a double-take. Instead of acquiescing immediately she said, "Tell you what. I'll finish up here real quick and be with you in about five minutes."

Reminiscent of an impatient child waiting to go to the park, sp'atung opened his mouth as if to make a rebuttal. Sarah cut him off with a single finger held up in the air between them as she quipped, "Five minutes."

Sp'atung inquiringly replied, "But you hold up only one finger." With a look from Sarah, he gave over and quietly closed the door behind him.

Seven and a half minutes later, Sarah and her two interviewees emerged from the small room into the adjoining corridor where sp'atung awaited with baited breath.

Sarah couldn't help but smiling a little. Her friend always looked rather comical when he got like this.

"What is it?" she asked, as she continued filing her notes into a folder.

"The dinner!" sp'atung excitedly replied in the loudest whisper Sarah had ever heard. It sounded reminiscent of an avalanche.

"What are you talking about? Dinner isn't for several hours yet."

Looking two parts flummoxed and three parts nervous he spat, "No! Dinner last night. With Griffith President!" Trying to whisper was making his normally rocky voice sound more like boulders moving through a gravel crusher.

"Oh, yeah. How'd that go? Was the food all right?"

"Food?" sp'atung nearly choked on his words. "Food fine. That not what I mean."

Enjoying the lather that he was working himself into, Sarah blithely replied, "Well, what pray tell is the point?"

"During meal, she talk all us about sasquatch. That okay. I not surprise by this." He seemed to be getting a grip on his emotions, if only a little.

Good heavens, Sarah thought. *If he doesn't settle down he's going to start...I don't know. Foaming at the mouth?*

"She also ask we stay here, after War end." Sarah raised an eyebrow at that.

Not noticing her response, sp'atung plowed on, "I make talk with her more than other sasquatch, so I ask how long." His breathing was beginning to get more shallow and Sarah wondered if it was the beginning of some sort of sasquatch seizure. "She say she not sure, but we help much after War. 'After all,' she say, 'there will be pockets of Enemy soldiers holding out around the globe even after the War is over'." Sarah could tell that he struggled to repeat her words exactly, what with the difference in grammar.

Sarah scratched at her head a little and finally said, "Well, I guess that makes sense. There are so many of those little stinkers that we're undoubtedly going to miss some of them the first time through."

Looking exasperated and impatient all at once, sp'atung stated, "That what I think. Then she say take words to Xruhnituhm Siem ask for *all* us stay for long time after War. Maybe moons."

Sarah thought for a moment and said, "Hmm, that's strange. I wonder why she'd be so interested in keeping you guys around after the War."

Then sp'atung delivered a bombshell when he nearly yelled, "There more. She ask me be one who give words from sen' to sasquatch!"

Astonished at the news, Sarah could only half-heartedly say, "An ambassador? Congratulations!"

They sat quietly for a couple of minutes when sp'atung finally said, "I no want be ambissadour for her or other. I want be me. Sasquatch no should be gone from cave too many suns."

Sarah said, "Listen. You're a good man...er, sasquatch. I have no doubt that you'll do a great job representing your people."

A handful of quiet moments passed by and Sarah couldn't help but reopening this recent 'wound' incurred by her friend. "So, why didn't you say 'no'?"

The sasquatch's eyes rolled back in his head for a moment before answering. "How I do that? She your president. And I get my mi'tuhng into this. I need be here help."

Turning serious, Sarah interjected, "Well, if you're going to be ambassador, you're going to have to learn to not roll over whenever she speaks."

"I not roll. I stay on feet when we make words." Sarah explained what she meant and sp'atung replied wearily, "I know." He was looking quite somber.

Still they sat there in the concrete shrouded room. Both of them gave silent audience to the sundry thoughts that paraded across their minds' eyes.

"There other thing she say," the sasquatch added. "She say it small, like it not big words, so I think other sasquatch not hear."

"What did she say?"

"She say 'When the War is over, things would probably remain rather fragile for a while. What with all the destruction and loss of key personnel, I'm not sure how I'll be able to hold things together. And I'm not sure who I can trust'." Sarah noticed the way sp'atung seemed to labor over the contractions the president had used.

Notwithstanding speech patterns, Sarah wasn't sure what the president meant by all that, but she did know one thing. Her friend needed cheering up at that moment and so Sarah offered, "Be that as it may, I think you'll do great. Besides, how bad can it be to be ambassador?"

Sp'atung's eyes narrowed and when he spoke, the quiet tone that edged his words seemed to belie the energy and concern hidden beneath. "I not know. I have bad feeling for this. It feel like being in snake home."

Moments later the intercom that is wired throughout the base came alive. The disembodied voice sounded entirely disinterested in the message it delivered. "All top clearance personnel please report to the main conference room in thirty minutes. That is all."

Sarah and sp'atung looked at each, knowing that they both needed to attend the meeting. "Probably just another briefing before another raid," Sarah voiced. She stretched and added, "Well, let's get it over with."

Minutes later, the main conference room was quickly filling up. The president was there and her cabinet. Several other sasquatch were there by the time sp'atung arrived with Sarah in tow. All told there were a few dozen individuals present when the thirty minutes had elapsed. The inevitable dull roar of multiple conversations around the room began to subside when President Griffith stood.

She began to speak and the last vestiges of noise were quickly extinguished.

"My friends," she began. "It's late and time is of the essence so I won't give a frivolous speech." That was met by some guarded smiles and muted laughter. "General Martin and I, and a very few other select individuals, have discussed the situation regarding the War and where we are. We recognize that our very existence was on the line for quite a while. It still is. Granted, the raids over the last few weeks have been incredibly successful, due in large part to our sasquatch brethren." She gave a small bow and a warm smile to each of the sasquatch present. "Nevertheless, we definitely still have not 'won the day'. These raids have kept the hammer from irrevocably pounding us into oblivion." She paused for emphasis. "But the hammer still hangs over our heads." A collection of brief, yet quiet, bubbles of discussion erupted in various pockets around the room.

"Therefore," she said, "we have a plan to not only tip the scale back in our favor but to perhaps win the War in one swift stroke!"

The discussions that broke out this time made the previous ones seem quiet by comparison. Not daring to believe such words of hope, Sarah thought to herself, *Is it possible? Can it be? Could this War really end without us all dying?*

The president concluded, "To discuss the plan we've devised I'll let General Martin have the floor."

President Griffith stood off to one side, away from the podium and microphone, and the general stepped forward, somberly. He stared out at everyone and there was a sense of deep emotion in his eyes. It was as if his silence was a signal to all in the room to do the same, and to remember their fallen comrades. It didn't take long and the mood in the room was totally different. With President Griffith, the people in the room were a respectful and interested audience. With General Martin, the audience had turned into a team, or perhaps even a family.

At last he broke the silence.

"My friends. Our time is at hand." His voice steadily grew in volume and intensity. "The time is *now* to show the Spiders that we can not only take the fight to them but rid our planet of them and destroy them once and for all." By the end of this brief speech, the room spontaneously exploded into applause and cheering. They weren't cheering for him so much, but for themselves and countrymen and world. It felt great to everyone present. Despite the recent weeks of success, it had been a long time since any of them had really felt such whole-hearted optimism.

It was a day few would forget.

At last he raised his hands to signal that he needed some quiet to continue his message. "My friends, our plan is this. We know that our missiles are shot down every time we attempt to fire them at the Enemy's orbiting ships and the DEWs that we've made are too primitive and weak to do the job." His grandfatherly smile snuck across his face as he said, "Now, I don't have to tell you that the key to us winning this War is to get rid of those orbiting ships and so far everything we've tried has done exactly nothing."

The mood in the room was beginning to grow somber again as Martin resumed.

"Well, you know the old saying. 'If you can't beat them, join them'." That drew some half-hearted smiles but mainly curiosity. "So, what we're going to do is conduct another simultaneous attack on the Enemy, just like we did a few weeks ago." He paused for only a moment. "At the various mines around the world that we've recaptured, that still have operational DEWs that the Enemy left behind, we're going to strike back. We're going to take those DEWs and fire away at the orbiting spacecraft. Since their directed energy weapons are far superior to ours, the energy beams emitted should have enough strength and concentration to destroy their orbiting ships!"

This time the applause was truly thunderous. Sarah began to wonder if the very walls were going to cave in. Her gaze swept over the exultant masses within the room and noted the president. She seemed to be the only one who was less than ecstatic. *She must've eaten something that didn't agree with her. Around here, that's not very difficult.*

Finally, the sound died down again to something resembling a freight train. Speaking directly into the microphone, Martin continued. "As you know, many of the Enemy's mines and bases are now in our possession. So gaining control of the particular DEWs we need has already been done. At least, it has in most cases." He paused again and most people in the room took the hint and quieted down. "To win this War, we need to make a simultaneous attack on all of the orbiting ships. If we don't, the surviving ships will quickly catch wind of our plan and just move further out into space, far enough away so that their DEWs being used against them will have no effect. There's a slight kink in this plan, however. There are two ships in orbit that we simply won't be able to hit from the *captured* bases." His words got heavier. "The Spiders still possess bases on the ground that are right below those ships. We will need to send in a team to each of those bases to *quickly* knock out the garrisons posted there and then use the DEWs therein to assist in our well-timed assault on their ships."

He paused but did not falter. "Here's the kicker. They now know how we operate and many of our tactics, especially our various uses of the sasquatch. So, I figure they're going to be ready for us this time. More than any of the other raids, I fully expect them to be well prepared and ready to inflict an awful lot of casualties on us—and to target the sasquatch."

"Now, we have our own plans," Martin continued, with a twinkle in his eye. "You'll become privy to them just as soon as assignments are given to each of the two groups going to those mines."

Secretary of State Carmine Michaels inquired, "When is this worldwide assault supposed to happen?"

Martin replied swiftly, "We attack in two days."

Muffled gasps broke out around the room. It was clear to Sarah that a lot of people present thought that wouldn't be near enough time to coordinate the effort.

Martin quieted everyone down. "Work has already begun on the preparations and logistics of the assault. The teams will move out tomorrow." He looked around the room, perhaps challenging anyone else to speak against him. "Remember that these men and women we're sending in, namely to the two Enemy held mines, are field tested and battle hardened. They're ready to go at a moment's notice, and don't forget this. Although the Spiders are not yet ready to begin a bombing on us that will finish us off as a species, they have been rebuilding their arsenal for some time. They are likely to be ready at any moment to rain death on us again—and finish us off. The president and I agree that waiting any longer is simply a risk we cannot take."

Someone asked, "How many men are going in to these heavily fortified bases?"

"Two entire companies EACH rather than just the standard platoon. So, eight times more men than usual. And eight sasquatch for each mine."

That drew a few pleased looks and some whistles signifying that most people were impressed. The few sasquatch who were in the room automatically began chanting powerfully, "Siqa Laka Qa!" over and over.

When things got quiet again, Martin added, "I know I don't have to tell you that by doing this, the die is cast. The War has bled us, and every other nation, of vital resources of every kind, especially military resources. This will likely be our last attempt at a large scale strike. We're throwing nearly all we have at them. If we lose, there won't be much of anything left." He paused to take a breath to compose himself. "If this fails, it's over."

Not surprisingly, the mood in the room became heavily somber.

The intelligent Secretary of Veteran's affairs, John Dillon, spoke out. "Where are these mines?"

"As you know, most of the mines we'll be using for this worldwide assault on the orbiting ships are already back in our possession." He paused briefly, perhaps not wanting to relive the deaths of so many brave men, women and sasquatch. "The two mines we need for this attack that are not currently in our possession are the Rimbaba mine in Bohemia and the Uchucchacua Mine in Peru."

CHAPTER 24
Uchucchacua Mine, Peru

Colonel Damon Knight stood over the shoulders of the pilots guiding his Blackhawk helicopter. They were staying in perfect formation with the two dozen other powerful aircraft of like model. More importantly, they were sticking to the colonel's plan.

Knight stood like a typical war hero. Six foot two with gray smoothly overtaking his dark hair, a confident smile never seemed far from his lips.

To a man, nearly every person in the team was aware of the colonel's sometimes—perhaps oft times—creative style and flamboyant ways. Generals had frequently shaken their heads in disappointment at the colonel and his methods. His lack of political correctness made him just a bit of a live wire in times of peace.

In times of war, he was an ace in the hole. It seemed that no matter how tough things got, he would always deliver.

The pilots and the rest of the team were grateful, honored and excited about being a part of one of his missions—including this one which was likely to be his most dangerous and challenging one yet.

Seven minutes out from the mine he tapped the copilot on the shoulder. The man reached over to his communication system and *pinged* the entire squadron in signal. Immediately the fleet of attack helicopters broke off in pairs. Each group descended to nearly treetop level with a pair of aircraft on either side of the formation flying away from the main group. Their job was to be available to hit the mine from the flanks and eat away at any resistance as needed. Meanwhile, the bulk of the fleet continued straight on toward the mine. The colonel's superiors had balked at his plan, feeling that a massive, overwhelming frontal assault would work best. As was typical with Colonel Knight, he ignored their advice.

For the first stage of the operation, Knight was all too aware of the DEW that would be guarding the mine. He didn't want to get any closer to it with Blackhawks than he had to. However, he also knew that time was a key factor. So, he knew they needed to land as close as he could get them. *That's going to be tricky,* he mused, *but nothing worse than the battle in Honduras last week.* He smiled outwardly.

As they approached the last few kilometers to the mine, the colonel and his men were grateful for the rough topography of the surrounding area. They knew it would make it much easier to sneak up on the Enemy without being targeted by their main weapon, the DEW housed at the mine which they needed to seize intact. He was fully aware that they desperately needed to use the "DEW's wave energy against the Enemy. He could not help but see in his mind's eye what once was a majestic layer of flora and fauna nearby known as Machu Pichu. Now, much of it was devastated by the War. By the Enemy. Their DEW located at the mine had seen to that.

In less than a handful of minutes they came in for a landing. As they approached their landing site, the convoy noticed that the landscape had been decimated to make what Knight and his people were doing have a difficult time finding cover. Nevertheless, they did have the advantage of the twisting, winding valleys of earth that lead to and surrounded their target. Those meandering crevasses provided a lot of cover–until one got really close.

Colonel Knight had judiciously determined to use the steep hills to his advantage. Therefore, he had chosen a place to set down a mere kilometer away from the entrance to the mine but just behind a wall of earth. *Just out of sight of any DEWs guarding the front door*, Knight thought.

Moments after landing, they moved out toward the mine. On the valley floor, once they came around the ravine wall that was protecting their helicopters, they fanned out knowing the Enemy would be after them despite the lack of an invitation.

The Spiders did not disappoint. They crashed the party with everything they had. In moments, the base's DEW was firing volley after volley into the oncoming attackers. Enemy foot soldiers began firing their green and red SPAWNs as soon as the terrans were within range. Too far away to do much good, the sasquatch held off from engaging in their debilitating bellowings. The sheer ferocity of all kinds of weapons thrown against the humans and sasquatch was almost overwhelming. The powerful sounds of weapons discharge were everywhere, drowning out all but the most determined voices. Great heaps of earth were thrown about as raw power from the energy waves emitted by the DEW swept over the ground as well as some of the soldiers.

A paltry two minutes into the battle, a massive number of Enemy troops had piled out of the mine and were advancing and firing on the woefully outnumbered earthlings. Knight knew that if his aces didn't show up, they'd be destroyed in a matter of minutes.

Out of the corner of his eye the colonel saw one of his eight sasquatch go down. Knowing of the importance of the hairy creatures, he immediately spread the word to his men to protect the sasquatch at all costs.

When are those blasted flyboys going to get here! Knight cursed.

As if on cue, two Blackhawks screamed through the mountain pass into the battle area on the Enemy's left flank. Seeing the massive press of Enemy soldiers making their way toward their comrades, the two aircraft both opened up with the newly designed twin M7 50-caliber machine guns. Unlike the old fifties, these air-cooled arms were able to fire a staggering one thousand rounds per minute. Although the sun was definitely still up, Knight had to admit that the light show put on by the guns' tracers was spectacularly reminiscent of something he would expect to see in a high budget sci-fi movie.

The 50-caliber rounds emanating from the pair of Blackhawks washed over the battlefield near the mine entrance where the Enemy was piled up. The Spiders tried to turn a portion of their anti-personnel red and green SPAWNs on the attacking choppers but this wasn't the first rodeo for these pilots. They made sure they kept well out of range. However, the massive directed energy weapon had a range of twenty-five hundred kilometers and the pilots were fully aware that being hit by its beam would more than likely prove fatal. As the DEW was methodically, yet quickly, turning away from the oncoming ground assault and toward the choppers, the pilots made sure to back off and quickly retreat behind a nearby chasm wall.

Moments before reaching the comparative safety of the gigantic mound of earth, a DEW blast was fired in their general direction. The second chopper to have wound its way around the hill experienced minor damage as some of its power systems hiccupped and temporarily went offline. A hasty landing was executed and repairs were immediately begun.

Nevertheless, as the DEW was attempting to pummel the helicopters on its left flank, the pair of choppers Knight had assigned to the right flank emerged. With the DEW aimed directly away from the battle's new arrivals, the as yet unscathed pair of Blackhawks began to rain down destruction and general mayhem on the Enemy combatants who, by now, were *really* scrambling around. At least, the live ones were.

The DEW turned, eager to sink its feral energy into the new pair of threats. These choppers didn't wait around. As the directed energy weapon turned, they high-tailed it out and made a clean getaway.

However, for the Enemy, the damage had been done. Their assault against the earthlings had been broken.

During the 50-caliber surprise, Knight and his men had moved up the field and were now a pittance of distance away from the mine entrance. With the Enemy quickly retreating like lightning, and the DEW unable to hit them near the mine's entrance due to its elevated position, the men and sasquatch soon had command of the area outside the mine.

Knowing they were on a strict timetable, Colonel Knight rapidly assessed the situation and his men and began forming them up for the hardest part of all, entering the mine that he knew was certainly a death trap. He noticed that several of his men and women were injured and being treated for burns, or dead. What bothered him most was that they had already lost three out of their eight sasquatch.

At least we got rid of a whole lot of them, he considered. *That will sure help when we get inside.* He turned and looked at his men. *It just might make the difference between success and failure.*

With men, women and sasquatch now ready to head into the mine he couldn't help but ponder on how slowly the Enemy on the ground had moved and responded when the Blackhawks came in and worked their flanking maneuvers. Though he was of course pleased with that, he couldn't help but feel like something was...off. *I've never seen them respond that slowly,* he marveled. *They move slower when the sasquatch are blasting away at them, but other than that, they've never been at all lethargic. It was like they didn't hear the choppers coming until they were nearly here.* Knowing there was nothing he could do about it right now, Knight pushed the thought out of his mind.

He and his men moved out. All the humans present affixed their ear muffs and IR-goggles over their eyes after they'd traversed the first few steps into the Peruvian mine. If it hadn't been for the goggles, it would've felt like being dipped in ink. Even with the eye wear, it was still disconcerting what with the peripheral limitations of the goggles.

Typical of the sasquatch, they didn't wear any IR-goggles even though the military had offered to make some their size. Yet having grown up in caves, they didn't need the goggles and especially didn't want to sacrifice their peripheral vision.

As they first entered the mine, moods were overly tense. Everyone seemed to be on pins and needles, continually wary of the inevitable attacks that they knew the Enemy would soon send. It wasn't a question of *if* the Spiders would attempt to ambush them, rather it was a question of whether they would be able to endure the repeated series of impending assaults. They all felt a little bit like they were playing Russian roulette and staring down the barrel of the gun.

However, a handful of minutes passed without incident and, one by one, members of the team began to relax, if only slightly. No one allowed his guard to drop, but each person's nerves began to be less taut.

Though Knight couldn't be certain, he figured *these* Spiders were all too aware of the power the sasquatch were able to emit through their vocal chords. He therefore made sure they were all located in the center of the group, safely tucked away.

At least I hope they're safe, he thought with only a portion of his usual optimism.

The colonel made sure that their weapons were trained ahead and behind and that they stayed close together. Soldiers in the front and rear of the column held the new SPAWN shields that would be able to endure a couple of salvos of the sludge emitted by the Spiders' weapons. Similar to riot gear used by police, he'd been excited to see them put into action. He recalled an irascible Captain Roger Stevens commenting, "Too bad they're not round with a target on them."

Onward they plodded down another midnight tunnel, the only sound was their steady breathing and the quiet scraping of boots along the earthen floor. The sasquatch made no noise.

Then something happened. One moment all was quiet and dark. The next there was a blinding flash which illuminated the cavern. Immediately chaos erupted.

A contingent of Spiders appeared ahead of the group from just around a corner. Another hit them from behind. They wasted no time launching the green sludge from their SPAWNs. Their spider-like claws deftly held and manipulated the weapons like a ballerina performing on stage. They all materialized, attempting to spray the large group of men, women and sasquatch with their burning acid projectiles.

Perhaps it would've been a more frightening sight except that the initial flash temporarily disturbed every person's eyesight. However, the effect was most pronounced for the humans. Each of them was wearing infrared goggles and so any and all heat signatures were displayed to their eyes, including the hot, blinding flash in the cave.

The blinding affect was short-lived but the Enemy rapidly made the most of the opportunity. Despite the shields being used, some of the personnel located at the front and rear of the column were hit. Those not injured quickly brought their weapons to bear and fired down the tunnels, half-seeing. Within the tight confines of the mine's tunnel the sound quickly became deafening. The sasquatch instantly chimed in and began their chorus of disorientation and lethargy, but Colonel Knight noticed that it wasn't affecting the Spiders as much as it had on previous raids. Seconds after the grand cacophony began, it was over. The Spiders had retreated to their holes in the earth from which they had sprung their trap, biding their time for the next one.

In the ensuing silence, Knight and his men took stock of the situation. Clearly, some people would not be continuing on—from both sides.

Fortunately, none of the five sasquatch who had entered the mine had been injured at all. The humans had, of course, not gotten off so well. Their numbers were steadily decreasing. It didn't take much imagination for Knight and the other officers to realize that at this rate they would soon be down to half-strength.

He shook his head in wonder and, in a strained voice, quietly added, "It's almost as if the sasquatch Voice didn't do very much." Though he'd never admit it, he began to have a sinking feeling in his gut.

More than a pair of flash-bomb attacks later, the men under the command of the ever optimistic and creative Knight were getting worn down by the constant pummeling they were taking. Though they had the utmost trust and confidence in his leadership, they were slowly coming to believe that their current endeavor was impossible.

They knew they were getting close to their objective—the Enemy's DEW located on an open-cover freight elevator that could quickly raise the machine to the surface to repel any and all attacks. Knight made sure that everyone else knew about how close they were to succeeding. He knew that if they lost hope and panicked, they would all be gone in a matter of minutes.

I just wish we could have an idea of how many of those blasted Spiders are left, Knight thought grimly.

Knight peered down at his less than fancy ten dollar watch and noticed that they really didn't have time for a break. They needed to continue on toward their objective—the DEW. The worldwide assault on the orbiting ships would begin soon and every directed energy weapon that was to be employed absolutely needed to be ready to go.

With that thought, Knight hurriedly moved his people forward toward their goal. He knew they were close but he also knew they were getting dangerously low on men.

Peering down at the map with one of his lieutenants and a sasquatch, Knight could see through the grainy green light of the goggles that they were nearly at their destination. He didn't have to say what everyone already knew. There would be a reception awaiting them at the main chamber where the DEW was housed. He couldn't help but know with certainty that it was going to be painful. Despite his ever-persistent optimism, he had to admit to himself that he would consider this mission a success if even one person survived to activate the DEW and knock out the orbiting Enemy ship above them. It was a painful realization, but that was his reality.

They walked along carefully, ever attempting to sense an attack before it could be sprung. In the midst of the dark, foreboding path some of those present absently noticed the dank smell of rot and moisture. The sasquatch occasionally wrinkled their noses at the odors that seemed bent on assaulting their olfactory senses.

Ignoring what their sense of smell told them, they moved on, determined to survive.

CHAPTER 25
Rimbaba Mine, Bohemia

Nick Sparks was a rising star in the U.S. military. Ever since the first raid that he led in Sinyukhinskoye, Russia he had been piling up a sizable stack of successes in the field. As a result, he'd recently been promoted from captain to major. He was settling into his new duties and wasn't particularly surprised when he found that he had been chosen to lead one of the two teams going in to take over yet another Enemy mine, as well as quickly getting the DEW therein under human control and firing up at orbiting Enemy ships.

His crew flew in toward the mine in a small fleet of retrofitted Chinook helicopters. The calm skies over the Czech Republic, which promised peace and solace, teased the men in the choppers. It was a promise Sparks and his men knew would not come to fruition on that day. The twin rotors, fore and aft, tore up the air around them in a powerful wash of air. The vehicles had been modified with M7 50-caliber machine guns just like the Blackhawks in Peru. Major Sparks wasn't interested in going into this particular combat environment with anything less.

Having previously examined the available maps for the area around the mine, the new major wasn't surprised to find that the surrounding landscape was almost entirely devoid of any appreciable topography. However, the tradeoff was that his men would be able to go in at night, clad in their typically effective IR-goggles. He'd used them before in raids and had become very good at employing them to his advantage. Of course, he had no doubts that the mission would be the toughest challenge yet since they had begun raiding Enemy bases and mines.

At ten kilometers out, he gave the signal for the choppers to descend as low as they could above the trees. Since the ground was nearly entirely flat, it wouldn't be difficult for his men to fly in low, but then, the landscape wouldn't provide much cover.

At five kilometers out, all personnel affixed Infrared goggles as the cabin lights and all others winked out. Setting down about two kilometers out, the safest place to do so was behind a *slight* rise in the terrain. Depending on the height of the Enemy DEW, the rise just might be tall enough to protect their vehicles. Maybe. Sparks wasn't counting on it but he also knew that going home from this mission was secondary after successfully doing his part to best the

Spiders at this particular base and knock a ship or two in orbit out of the sky.

The choppers landed forming a straight line, each one doing the best it could to take advantage of the small amount of cover the nearby knoll provided. Everyone quickly moved out as per their previously arranged assignments and tasks. Fully aware of the power of the Enemy DEW, Sparks had assigned his men to fan out in groups of ten with a single sasquatch in eight of the twenty-nine groups. If a group got hit by a DEW–or something else–he didn't want all the sasquatch getting taken out. That would be disastrous once they got into the mine.

A sasquatch walked up to him. Sparks didn't recognize the creature though he was finally beginning to be able to tell them apart a little better. "Sparks Major, I in team yours. We ready to hunt."

Nodding, the major walked alongside the massive creature. He quickly jogged his memory, trying to place the name of his powerful yet wiry companion. Now he remembered. "Lec', you ready for this?"

"Yes, Sparks Major. I ready," came the immediate and sure reply in the bass voice that rumbled its way out of the speaker's throat.

Sparks was surprised to find a measure of comfort in that. *Am I getting soft*, he mutely queried. *Or maybe it's just that this guy, lec', was the only one to live to tell the tale in that Tennessee mine raid. He must be one tough beast.* Aloud he said, "All right then. Let's move out."

Orders were issued and the various teams moved out along their prescribed routes. At first, everything was eerily silent. Sparks had hoped that he'd catch the Enemy flat-footed, but he'd never really believed that it would work out that way. The absence of anything more than the sounds of nearby crickets and the occasional hoot of an owl unnerved him as he continued to lead his men toward the giant hole in the ground, a hole that was currently as quiet as a tomb.

Each group continued to move forward and the major had to suppress a desire to talk with lec' or any of his other men about what they should expect. They were closing in on the mine in a semi-circular formation with a diameter of about three hundred meters and closing. At half a kilometer out everyone could see the entrance, no matter their various positions around the area. Due primarily to the distance, not even their IR-goggles could penetrate the inky blackness therein.

And then it happened.

The sky began to quickly grow a faint glimmer that was reminiscent of a painter's palette. Myriad colors were forming and developing—and getting larger!

Sparks understood what it was an instant before anyone else. Immediately he split the quiet of the night with a yell. "Incoming!" In the next instant, he knew he had to make a decision. He did. Instead of instructing the people under his command to take cover he chose, "Head for the mine!"

Less than a handful of heartbeats later, multi-colored shelling came down and lit up the area. Men were tossed about as the ordnance rained down upon them. The light of the Enemy's shelling illuminated the ground.

Shouts could be heard from all over.

"What   is   it?"
"Take cover!"
"Where's it coming from?"
"Where's my team?"
"I'm hit!"
"Somebody help me!"

Major Sparks knew the origin of the rainbow shelling that came from above. An Enemy ship in orbit. In fact, the ship that was *their* ultimate target. It was bombarding the compound as a means of protecting their own kind within the mine. He also knew that if he didn't take command immediately, this attack was going to fall apart very quickly.

Amidst the deafening sounds surrounding him and having to dodge around the plasma missiles the major lead his small team toward the entrance. Since he wasn't able to communicate effectively with the other teams, he hoped they would see his team moving as a coherent unit and follow suit. It took a few moments but, one by one, the other teams made their way in his direction.

The scene around them was completely nightmarish, probably worse. The ship so many miles above and out of view, callously sent down salvo after salvo.

The mayhem was intense. Yet somehow all the teams but one reported in as they arrived near the mine entrance. They were astonished that one team came out of the attack unscathed.

As Sparks had assumed, the precision bombardments were not taking place right next to the entrance. *They don't want to harm their own people, just slow us down and soften us up.* So, at the mine entrance, they were able to catch their breath. He quickly reorganized the remaining men, women and sasquatch under his command. Though their losses were already significant, he understood the point of the mission and knew that if it took every one of them to complete the assignment, the price would still be small by comparison.

After a quick five-minute break to catch their collective breath they headed inside. Sparks noticed many of his people were not there, but had been killed. He also noticed many others being treated as best they could for wounds sustained during the aerial bombardment. Perhaps the thing that unnerved him most was when he looked at the sasquatch. From his original eight, he was down to only three!

Several tense minutes later found Major Sparks leading his men into the inky, dark maw of the mine and away from the orbital bombardment outside. Although he knew the Spiders would likely set traps and attempt to repeatedly ambush them, he chose a strategy based almost entirely on speed. He figured that if they could keep moving quickly to the site where the DEW was housed, they would have their greatest chance of success.

So they kept on the move, their pace eating up the ground rapidly. They were all aware, of course, that traversing the caverns so quickly would possibly sacrifice some of their ability to perceive danger before it struck, but Sparks knew that they needed to hurry. After ten blessedly uneventful minutes many in the group were beginning to believe that their strategy just might work.

Then, a cry was heard in the darkness. It came from the very rear of the column. Everyone turned.

Just at that moment, two more cries were heard from the head of the column. Everyone had instinctively, yet unwisely, turned to face the first attack at the rear. No one saw the pair of Enemy creatures waft in from the darkness like smoke. A fleeting glimpse of the retreating shapes was barely seen before they disappeared around a corner in the darkness. Their multitude of sinewy legs moving in a repulsive manner reminded everyone of the terrible danger in which they still found themselves.

Sparks looked around at his already pummeled force and, despite the blurred view through his goggles, saw in their eyes a fear welling up that would certainly destroy them. He also looked at the sasquatch. He couldn't be certain but he thought that even they showed minute signs of stress. However, they still appeared quite stoic. He pulled lec' aside and asked, "How are you and the others doing?"

From his more than seven feet of height, lec' peered down at Sparks and replied, "We think we die soon, but we are fine."

Sparks tried not to stare back in awe and confusion at this unusual response. *Well, unusual for humans*, he thought. "Listen, I know it's going to get worse before it gets better." The major took a moment to look around and make sure nothing else was happening. "I'm sure that we're going to all need to count on you and your two sasquatch brethren before this is over."

Lec' replied simply, "Sparks Major, you ask me something?"

Without emotion, Sparks replied, "Just stay safe. We need you!"

The only response that lec' provided was nodding his head in acknowledgement.

Allowing his thoughts to shift back to the twin attacks that had just taken place, the major thought to himself, *They're learning.* He peered around the cave, searching for a clue that was not there, a clue that would tell them from where the next strike would emanate. *They strike and fade so quickly that our sasquatch aren't able to assist us.* He swallowed hard and concluded, *They plan to slowly pick us off, keeping the sasquatch out of the game as much as possible.*

Making sure that the sasquatch with them were located in the center of the group, with everyone else aiming their weapons outward, he gave a brief speech to buoy up their spirits and get the fight back into his people.

Then they moved on down the dark tunnel.

After a short time, Sparks looked at his watch and swore under his breath. The clock was ticking and they were rapidly running out of time. He understood how important it was that they all synchronize their attacks on the orbiting ships. *We've got to get to that DEW soon or it's not going to matter*, he silently quipped.

He looked at his men and, despite their losses, they were still ready to move forward and get the job done.

Then, through the grainy light of his IR-goggles, Sparks saw something he'd not seen before. A pair of Enemy soldiers just around a corner in the dark path fired their SPAWNs at them. The sludge that the Spiders launched toward him and his men wasn't green or red. It was purple. An instant before it struck he realized that it was some new material. He groaned inwardly, not wanting to learn what this new menace was. At first, nothing happened and a few of the people at the front of the column figured—or perhaps hoped—that it was either red or green slime that had gone inert. Their hope was in vain. After a pair of heartbeats, the purple material began to hiss as it quickly transformed into some type of gas. It didn't take long for those around the purplish substance to realize that the gas was toxic in nature. Everyone around the stuff began to cough and sputter.

Losing no time, Sparks immediately pulled his shirt up over his nose and mouth to serve as an impromptu gas mask. He tried to get the attention of those around him to do the same. Most did but a few weren't fast enough. More humans and sasquatch would not be moving on.

As did the rest of his men, Sparks cursed himself for not having brought gas masks. He knew there was no way they could have predicted this particular play by the Enemy but he still wished he could've done more to help them!

Major Sparks got his team moving forward again at a steady clip and quickly spread the word about the new weapon the Enemy had chosen to employ as well as to prepare any kind of breathing filter they could.

He didn't have to do the math. He knew just by looking at his team that they were definitely below half-strength. Perhaps more disturbing to him was the realization that they were now down to a single sasquatch, lec'. He recognized that their prospects were looking bad. They needed to find that blasted DEW soon or there wouldn't be any of them left to find it!

CHAPTER 26
DEW Chambers

At Camp Dodge the mood was tense. The Command Center that had been used to coordinate countless other military operations was a large, white, cement room. Simple and plain, it looked like nearly every other room at Dodge. It was full of personnel as the more than two dozen DEW-carrying mines were under surveillance. Everyone present knew the score. They were all perfectly aware that they had to make a decisive and synchronized blow against all of the Enemy ships in orbit or their species could very well be destroyed, and soon.

The radio operators monitoring the signals emanating from the human-held mines knew that their jobs were, for the moment, window dressing. The mines previously held by the Spiders had been secured and swept clean of the alien vermin and the DEWs had all been made operational and ready for battle days ago.

However, off to one side of the room, the intensity was triple thick, like moving-and sinking—through quicksand. No one had to be told which mines they were monitoring. The radio men and women monitoring the mines currently being stormed by Major Sparks and Colonel Knight were anything but relaxed. They were receiving bits and pieces of information–almost nothing–from the few soldiers who'd been left behind at the aircraft rather than going inside the mines. Just about all they could offer after the initial fighting had begun was to make mention of any Enemy stragglers that exited the mine (and were quickly dealt with) or the muffled sounds of gunfire and explosions emanating from the mines' points of egress.

President Griffith paced the floor, eager for any new information. Equally concerned, General Martin stood resolute in the midst of what just might—and perhaps likely would—turn to sudden chaos. He listened and considered, but did little else, knowing that he would just be getting in the way. Besides, nearly all the information that was coming in was being displayed on multiple, electronic kiosks.

Sarah and sp'atung stood off to the side, also trying to not be in the way. Sarah was surprised that she didn't already have an ulcer, what with her continual desire to be doing something to help but knowing she should stand still and be quiet and let the people in the room do their jobs. Occasionally, when a report would come in, especially if it involved a sasquatch, she would look up into sp'atung's eyes and an unspoken pair of concerned looks would harmonize in an emotional medley.

At last, sp'atung put a hand on Sarah's shoulder and ushered her out of the room for a moment. Sarah didn't really mind since it was getting a bit stuffy in there. When they were outside, sp'atung inquired, "Sarah, you okay?"

Sarah didn't know what to say. The fate of the world was in the hands of a few brave souls and though the Command Center was now receiving precious few reports of what was happening, Sarah knew with complete certainty that soldiers–their people–were in those mines and dying right at that moment. It gnawed at her guts and she felt once again that she just might lose her lunch. Looking into the peaceful eyes of the sasquatch who was quickly becoming one of her closest friends, she finally replied, "If this doesn't work, can I come live with your people in the cave?" She hesitated as sp'atung returned a rare look of surprise. Now she began speaking faster. "If we don't get rid of those monstrous creatures, I don't think any 'human place' will be safe *anywhere* on the Earth!"

Sp'atung took her into a warm, friendly embrace and held her for a few moments, knowing that humans find it comforting in times of emotional stress. At last he replied, "I no think you need do that." She moved away from him a little and looked up again with the hint of a smile. Then sp'atung solemnly added, "But if so, you live with mi'tuhng til we all dead."

Sarah's moment of hope was just that. A single moment.

Away from the battles currently being waged against the Spiders in the two notorious mines, Captain Rex Murphy was eager to take the fight back to the Enemy. His blocky build that resembled a bulldozer was as imposing as ever, not to mention how it had helped him survive various encounters with the Enemy. Ever since his miraculous escape from the notorious battle of Oscar-Romeo-17, he had wanted payback and his appetite for retribution seemed insatiable.

He was the new commander of the strategically located Sinyukhinskoye mine in Russia that had been retaken from the Enemy when the sasquatch had first begun giving their assistance.

He'd read the report of how Captain Sparks–now Major Sparks–had led the assault to take back the mine and keep the Spiders from using it against them. Captain Murphy was absolutely determined the Enemy would *not* regain the mine. Not on his watch!

As the final minutes before their assault on the orbital ship above them continued to tick away, Murphy walked over to the radar scope on which others were intensely searching for any indication that there might be some kind–any kind–of Enemy movement in his vicinity. He was almost disappointed that there wasn't any activity.

However, after the devastating experience of Oscar-Romeo-17, he knew just how effective the Spiders were. Thinking about the past reminded him of the present, of the man sitting next to him.

Corporal Cornwall had been there in that battle. He'd seen the same horrors, the same battleground. They'd worked together to get out of that scrape after it had become apparent that there was nothing left to protect. Cornwall had gotten away relatively unscathed. He'd only lost his left hand.

Perhaps that was what drove Murphy to an almost obsessive desire to meet and eliminate any Enemy soldiers he could. Every time he looked at that kid, he remembered. He remembered it all.

Mentally brushing away the ghosts that never truly ceased to haunt his days and nights, he turned toward the other person standing near. Her name was celewiltx. She'd been there with Sparks when the man had liberated the mine from the accursed Enemy. Celewiltx had never left and Murphy had come to find her assistance to be most beneficial. He was surprised just how much he was coming to rely on her.

"Cornwall," Captain Murphy asked for the twenty-seventh time that night. "Any sign of the Spiders in our area?"

"No, Sir," came the sure reply. There was a time when Cornwall might have shifted in his seat due to nervousness around such an imposing senior officer, but he had become familiar with Captain Murphy and had moved past his previously trepid responses.

The captain turned and asked, "Celewiltx, any activity on your end?"

The mighty sasquatch was an appropriate counterpart to Murphy. Even for her species she was strong and powerfully built. If Murphy was a bulldozer, she was like a mine truck that could drive over a car without noticing it. Her brown pelt with jagged, grey streaks reminded Murphy of a thundering avalanche tearing down a mountain. He had to admit, her ferocity in battle matched her appearance. "Murphy Captain, my sasquatch team hunts the jungle." Her deep, gravelly voice spoke of raw power and strength. "Our...beefed up," she stumbled over the human idiom, "hunters find no Tarantulas."

Murphy looked up into her face and replied, "Good."

The three of them remained in place, unmoving for several moments longer, Cornwall hunched over the radar with celewiltx and Murphy staring at a larger computer monitor.

After several moments of silence, Murphy asked, "Celewiltx, do you believe the Spiders will be back before the time to fire the DEW?"

The aggressive reply was not slow in coming. "No! They cowards."

They both stood silently before she spoke again, "If they back come..." As she paused midsentence, Murphy heard her chuckle. It was a surprisingly terrifying sound. She finished with, "...that good!"

Xtela, the first sasquatch to work with the humans, ran like the wind through the forests surrounding the recently recovered Zyryanovsk mine in Russia. His blood red pelt led several of his sasquatch brethren through the woods, attempting to detect what the human radar and other detection systems might not. They passed through the midst of towering pines. They ran and searched past mighty firs. Onward they ran, enjoying the sheer exhilaration of speed through a jungle of trees. Nevertheless, they were continually vigilant to detect any trace of the Tarantulas.

Although it still felt odd to him, he wore a heavy belt that carried a small two-way radio so that he could quickly communicate with his base of operations within the mine. His belt also held a Glock 22. Whenever he held the diminutive weapon in his hand he felt foolish. Perhaps some of the other sasquatch quietly agreed. What with his massive, hairy hand holding the relatively small handgun, it almost looked like a child's toy. Fire arms had not yet been built to accommodate the larger hands of the sasquatch, but there were rumors that they were coming.

Of course, the trigger guard had been meticulously removed via hacksaw and file; otherwise xtela wouldn't have been able to get his large, sausage-like finger over the trigger to actually discharge the weapon.

However, it wasn't the Glock that he scooped up. He needed to check in again with his senior officer, Captain Nishomoto. Calling the mine on his radio, he waited for a response. Nishomoto's familiar voice broke the silence of the forest.

"Nishomoto here. Xtela, are you seeing anything on your end?"

"Nishomoto, Captain. No," came the reply, with a belated, "Sir." Xtela was still getting used to some of the simple human protocols. "We have run...er, patrolled sun down side of jungle. We not anything find."

There was a slight pause from the other end of the line of communication, Captain Nishomoto considering what to do next. Though the man was precise and efficient, ever since he had rescued Nicolai Reznikov in Nicaragua all those weeks ago, he was still suffering occasional bouts of guilt and doubt from inadvertently helping such a despicable criminal. The captain blinked and recovered his focus. "That's okay. I wasn't expecting anything out there anyway. But, better safe than sorry."

Xtela replied simply, "Yes, Sir. You want I take my team hunt more?"

Nishomoto paused only a moment in thought before replying, "No. Bring it in. When you get here you and I can talk further and discuss final preparations for making our assault on the orbiting ship above us."

"How much time till hunt ships in sky?"

Nishomoto needlessly looked at his watch. He'd been paying *very* close attention to the time all day. "Only a couple of hours. Then we'll see if we can destroy all those blasted ships in orbit!"

With only a touch of concern tingeing his voice, xtela inquired further, "You think other mines make hunt on sky ships?"

Without skipping a beat, Nishomoto said, "I have no doubt they'll be successful and fire their DEWs on time." He swallowed and felt a shiver run down his spine. "It's those two DEWs that still need to be taken from the Enemy that worry me a little. I hope they can pull it off."

He wiped away the sweat that was quickly accumulating on his brow.

Colonel Knight and his men were pinned down just inside the massive primary chamber where the DEW was found in the Peruvian mine. They were taking refuge behind a wall of mining supplies left behind by the company that had run the place before the Enemy's invasion. The heavy supplies of piping, huge steel gears and more were affording them good protection, but Knight and his men knew that it was only a matter of time before they were routed.

And time was a commodity they knew they didn't have.

There was a slight lull in the exchange of weapon's fire and the colonel decided to take stock of the situation. He noticed that few of the original team were still with him.

A glob of purple sludge found its way over the tall pile of machinery and spare parts that were quickly turning into a misshapen slag heap. Having already experienced this new weapon more than once in the last hour, he knew he didn't need to say it. However, his training got the better of him.

"Gas!"

Over the sounds of battle, everyone heard and instantly placed their makeshift gasmasks over their noses and mouths. Only one young soldier got caught by the noxious, purple fumes.

With a wet piece of cloth covering his face, the ever-resourceful Colonel Knight looked around, searching for some way to fulfill his mission. Like all those he led, he had long since realized that the advantage the sasquatch were providing on this particular mission was inexplicably diminished. Firing another quick burst, and missing the elusive target, he wondered why that might be. *Could it be a problem with the sasquatch?* he asked himself. *I doubt it. They sound the same to me.*

He ducked back behind the mine equipment as a salvo of red and green sailed swiftly passed him. He hoped it didn't find its mark. Spinning around the makeshift blockade, he fired again. This time he hit his target. However, during the instant he stood there, he saw as much as any reconnaissance team might have told him. The Spiders were still seemingly everywhere. There was still an enormous host of them. He saw there was absolutely no way that they would be able to make it to the DEW and fulfill their mission unless something drastic was done.

And if we don't complete our mission, he thought while struggling to find a solution, *it just might spell the end of the human race.*

Ducking back behind the cover afforded by the rapidly disintegrating mine equipment, Knight looked around him. He saw the people under his command. They were painfully few in number. He saw the weapons they carried. He looked at the surrounding cave and its features, searching for something—anything—that might be used as a veritable *deus ex machina*.

Then, from the back of his mind, he remembered something—a piece of equipment—but it was back at the choppers. There was no way to get it and bring it back quick enough. None of them could run that quickly.

Then the colonel's view turned to the one, lone sasquatch remaining. Wasting no time, he moved over to her. "Leqi, are you injured?"

"No, Knight Colonel," came the quick but characteristically dreamy reply.

"Good." Knight looked around him again to see if the Enemy had begun trying to flank them. Not an easy task in the confines of the chamber, but he needed to be continually aware of how the battle was changing. "I have an assignment for you. I'm guessing that all of the Spiders are in this chamber. So, what I need you to do is leave the way we came. Can you remember the way back to the mine entrance?"

Leqi's continually relaxed countenance was quickly replaced by a look of confusion. However, she answered with a simple, "Yes."

"All right. I need you to run as fast as you can until you get to the choppers. I need you to get a weapon we brought. It's an experimental weapon so some of the men out there might not be aware of it. It's called a *thermo-bolt.* It's a long, heavy rifle. It's silver and has a large canister attached to it. I need you to run like the wind, grab it, and bring it back." Knight blinked only once and then concluded, "I suppose I don't need to remind you that if you don't hurry, there likely won't be any of us left when you return. Understood?"

"Yes," came the reply. This time it was devoid of any dreaminess. Her senses were alert and focused.

"We'll give you cover-fire and when we do, you run like the devil himself is chasing you!" Though leqi didn't understand the reference to 'the devil', she had no doubt what the colonel meant.

Knight spread the word to his dwindling unit and, on his signal, gave a quick but effective salvo of covering fire.

Leqi was gone like a shot and out of the large chamber in less than a handful of seconds.

Impressed by her speed, Knight thought to himself, *Who knows. That plan just might work.*

As he saw her sprint off like lightning, his mind immediately began working on a backup plan. He decided it was time to use their store of grenades. He knew it was an imperfect plan, but he was running out of options.

Ten minutes after leqi's departure back to the choppers, Knight and his men were attempting to make good use of their explosives. However, it took only a pair of the grenades to realize that the Enemy recognized the devices from previous encounters and were very adept at scrambling out of the blast radius. Consequently, the colonel and his men were finding it disconcertingly challenging to make good use of the things. Then they tried switching things up a bit with their tactics. One person would throw a grenade off to the side of a larger group of Enemy soldiers, causing the creatures to move off away from it. A split second after the first grenade was thrown, a second one would land where it was anticipated the Spiders would go. It didn't work every time, but it bought them some time, and they were able to get rid of more of the nine-legged aliens.

However, the strategy was flawed and Knight knew it. It was clear to him that, although it was proving more effective than just trading rounds of gunfire and multi-hued goop, it would ultimately fail for three reasons. First, they still weren't defeating the Enemy fast enough. Second, the Enemy was getting wise to their strategy and deploying their flash-bombs whenever they saw a grenade. That made it hard to aim and do any mopping up necessary after the grenades were thrown. Lastly, they would run out of grenades long before they could finish the job.

His mind whirling, desperate to pull another rabbit out of his hat, but suspecting that for the first time in his life he would not have 'another trick', Colonel Knight saw the impossible. An obviously exhausted leqi roared in through the tunnel with the *thermo-bolt* and collapsed in a heap next to him. Her pelt was completely soddened with sweat. She lay on the ground, every muscle in her body heaving from the incredible exertion. Knight was amazed. Notwithstanding the tremendously impressive physical abilities of the sasquatch, he knew it must've been no mean feat for her to have run about two miles back to the chopper and then carry the heavy weapon another two miles back in ten minutes!

With his team ridiculously close to extinction, Knight didn't ponder on the Olympic ramifications of the female sasquatch. Instead, he grabbed the heavy weapon with both hands, checked the pressure gauge to verify that it was ready to go and then told his men to get behind him. The painfully few people remaining obediently moved to his six o'clock, continuing to fire on the merciless Spiders.

Standing up from behind his small boulder, Knight rested the long, silver barrel on his protective rock and, without preamble, pulled the trigger. Knight had pulled the stock of the weapon into his shoulder nice and tight. He'd never personally used the thing and so he wanted to be ready. To his dismay, nothing happened. He pulled the trigger again. Still nothing. Disheartened and thoroughly disillusioned, he began to curse at the sleek rifle which boasted so much and delivered so little. In the midst of his cursings, he absent-mindedly pulled the trigger in frustration and held it.

Surprisingly, he began to hear something. It sounded like a low hum. With his earmuffs on to protect his ears from the sasquatch bellowings, he wasn't sure of the origin of the sound. However, the sound grew louder and louder. Soon he knew exactly from whence it came. It was the *thermo-bolt*! He realized he was still holding the trigger. For an instant, he almost obeyed his instinct to release the trigger so as not to allow it to explode in his face. Yet the next thought, close on the heels of the first was, *What do we have to lose?*

It took only about ten seconds of humming and the *thermo-bolt* suddenly sprang to life, spewing forth a storm of electricity and miniature lightning bolts! Hanging onto the thing for dear life, Knight was surprised that his IR-goggles weren't blinding him with the flashes of lightning arcing before him. Then he remembered briefly reading the specs on the *thermo-bolt* several weeks before. An experimental weapon, it used cold fusion to create a strange electrical storm. The bolts and arcs of charged particles were uncharacteristically cold instead of hot. He didn't understand the science behind it and didn't care. Instead, he stood in the dark cavern like a Greek god brandishing electricity from his personal Mount Olympus. The electricity snaked out before him approximately in the shape of a cone, about sixty degrees wide. The bolts slithered and struck Spider after Spider in an unparalleled light show. The sharp, crackling sound of the *thermo-bolt* reverberated off the cavern walls like a child's rubber ball striking a wall and bouncing off. Like a Tesla coil randomly lancing out with cords of otherworldly energy, the *thermo-bolt* created round after round of cold, electric currents that seized, stunned and eliminated nearly all the Enemy combatants in the cave.

Knight and some of his men removed their IR-goggles. The *thermo-bolt* was doing a great job of illuminating the chamber all on its own and it felt surprisingly refreshing to use their "own eyes."

As Colonel Knight continued to strafe the alien abominations, he saw the curving arcs of nuclear power snake out and find the Enemy hiding in the clefts of rocks and behind ridges. Knight continued to use his cold fist of electricity until every last one of the vermin was stopped moving.

And then, as quick as it had begun, it was over. Knowing that he'd hit them all, Knight shut down the weapon. He was surprised to find that he was sweating and even shaking a little. He wasn't sure if it was due to an adrenaline surge or a byproduct of using the *thermo-bolt*. Either way, he was glad they'd won the day.

Setting the weapon down, he pulled his IR-goggles back over his face and looked at his men. Out of the original two hundred eighty-eight, there were only eight that remained. They just stood there in silence, sharing the moment of solemnity. After the loud, ongoing firefight and the crackling sounds of the *thermo-bolt*, the subsequent silence was strangely peaceful.

One somber minute later, one of the men spoke up, perhaps feeling uncomfortable with the serious silence. "Sir, why didn't we just use that thing in the first place?"

A moment or two passed and everyone began to laugh. When the moment of mirth passed, Knight replied, "I'll tell you. It's an experimental weapon and the tests done on it were extremely unreliable." He paused, turning to look at the carnage all around him, the soft, grainy, green glow of warm objects fading away on the recently deceased humans and Enemies. "In one trial, the lightning went everywhere and the operator and his crew were all killed. In another, the fuel cell couldn't take the stress and exploded. Again, the operator died." He turned back toward them and, offering a lopsided smile, concluded, "So, it was sort of a weapon of last resort."

The eight men and leqi all began to laugh again, surprised that they never did doubt their commanding officer would win the day.

Deep within the Bohemian mine, Lec' was surprised that he could hear Sparks over the cacophony of battle. Like many others, he quickly turned to look at his senior officer. The Major was yelling and pointing toward the DEW located toward the rear of the massive chamber. Lec' turned his focus toward the machine and quickly ducked out of the way of a blast of the Enemy's green scum that would certainly have given him a nasty head ache. He bellowed some more and wondered at the ineffectiveness of his sonic blasts. Nevertheless, without a projectile weapon, there was little else he could do.

Peeking around a large rock that was providing adequate protection, he peered at the DEW across the massive room. At first, he couldn't tell what Sparks had been all worked up about. Then he saw it. Less than a handful of Spiders had broken off from their defensive formation and begun hitting the directed energy weapon with some kinds of metal tools. Having seen humans work on jeeps and other kinds of machines he figured they might be engaging in some kind of repair job so as to use the weapon against the sasquatch and humans. Unable to do much else, he continued to watch and then he realized the rest of what Sparks had seen.

They weren't repairing it. They were sabotaging it!

He saw a Tarantula take aim at an unsuspecting human soldier. Without thinking, he grabbed a large rock the size of a cantaloupe and hurled it at the leggy abomination with a speed and accuracy that would make a Major League pitcher immensely jealous. The rock struck home and, though its intended target still lived, lec' knew that particular Spider wouldn't be causing them more problems any time soon. The soldier turned to the whipcord sasquatch and offered him a brief salute of gratitude.

With a few blessedly free moments available, lec' did what he could to spread the word that they needed to hurry and get to that directed energy weapon. The tide was certainly flowing in favor of the terrans, but it didn't seem like they would have enough time to finish off the Enemy soldiers in the mine before those otherworldly abominations could complete an irreparable sabotage.

Meanwhile, lec' moved from rock to rock, doing his best to keep himself behind cover until he reached Sparks. With his unique size and appearance, he realized he stood out like a sore thumb. It seemed that every Enemy combatant was taking aim at him as he moved about. Fortunately, he gained his destination with his messy orange pelt getting only a little singed.

In his deep, marbley sasquatch voice lec' quickly asked, "Sparks Major, what the plan?"

Sparks fired another burst of gunfire and was pleased to see that he winged one of the loathsome creatures. As it ran it was spun around by Sparks' salvo.

Without turning to look at the other he replied, "We've got to get to that DEW and we need to do it *now*!"

"Agreed." Lec' didn't bother asking again what his commander's specific instructions were. He knew they would be forthcoming and soon.

Had he been human, he wouldn't have been disappointed. As a sasquatch, waiting for an answer wasn't an issue. "We need to send a squad of men, about a dozen, along the left side of the cavern." Sparks barked his orders at the top of his lungs so that he could be heard over the din of battle. Although he knew the ears of a sasquatch could hear him much better than a human's ears, he knew it would feel weird to him if he spoke any quieter than a full roar. Another burst of sludge flashed between them and both lec' and the major instantly ducked down behind their respective boulders. The globular projectile passed so fast and close to them that they could scarcely determine the color.

Continuing, Major Sparks added, "Round up a group of men and take them over along that wall. I want you to set up a crossfire so we can finish off these worthless vermin before they can do very much damage to that DEW. Go!"

Keeping his head down, lec' loped away with the speed of a gazelle. His muscular, wiry form seemed untouchable as he nimbly moved amidst the bullets and sludge plastering the walls. It took less than a minute and he had a team together. Staying low and creeping between rock formations, lec's team quickly made its way to the left side of the enormous chamber. As they began making their way forward to set up for the crossfire, it became quickly apparent that the Enemy was wise to their plan and began diverting a significant amount of their attention to this second prong of attack.

Lec' and his men immediately took cover and returned fire as best they could. However, the area where they'd taken up shelter was quickly inundated in a deluge of red and green slime—a veritable rainbow nightmare. One of his men went down, but lec' could see that the man would recover.

The sasquatch returned his attention back to the battle and noticed that things had changed in the moments his focus had been diverted. With a significant amount of the Enemy's attention and salvos focusing on lec' and his small team, Sparks and the main group were feeling a lot less pressure from the Enemy. With guns blazing they'd begun knocking out the Enemy in earnest.

Lec' carefully peered around a small boulder just in time to witness the beginning of the end of the Tarantulas. The few that were remaining took shelter in a small enclosure in the rock wall that gave them partial cover from both forces.

Not wanting to risk a catastrophic cave-in so close to victory, no one lobbed grenades into the temporary, yet effective, shelter being used by the Tarantulas. However, they didn't want to give their foes any more respite than was necessary. Sparks quickly determined they should charge in after the leggy creatures with guns blazing.

Sparks gave a prearranged signal and all of his men charged in after them. The formation was reminiscent of a net collapsing in on a single target. The two groups would meet at an approximately ninety degree angle and everyone who could walk joined the charge.

Carried away by the excitement, lec' accidentally allowed himself to outpace the men in his small force. When everyone was getting close, the two remaining Tarantulas lunged out of their rocky cove and sprung toward the mighty sasquatch. The dark, loathsome creatures slammed into lec' simultaneously. Between his surprise and their momentum, they knocked him to the floor and all three of them went down in a heap.

However, the Tarantulas were quick and each was immediately on its nine feet again. With fangs dripping and dark eyes glaring malevolently, they wasted no time in their efforts to strike. No one present allowed himself to be fooled by the diminutive stature of the aliens. At three to four feet tall, nature had crafted an amazing amount of strength in those small, black bodies.

And yet, the lean and muscular Iec' was no slower than his two opponents and, spinning on a knee, came up ready for combat.

The three of them were so close and moving so fast that none of the humans felt comfortable attempting to shoot and kill the two Enemies. Having done all they could for the moment, they stood mutely, watching the free-for-all melee ensue. Tarantula fangs slashed and sasquatch teeth tore. Arms and legs flailed, striking, missing, hitting true. All the while, Iec' bellowed his debilitating sasquatch sonic blast. Every human present, and certainly Iec' as well, were amazed at how little the sasquatch bellows were affecting the aliens.

On they continued, moving, dodging, weaving, searching for an advantage. None of the humans dared enter the fray, knowing they wouldn't last a heartbeat. Each person aimed his weapon at the tangle of bodies. How Iec' was able to move that quickly and keep going against his two quicksilver Enemies was amazing. On he fought, always causing the two Enemy combatants to just miss his vital organs and fail to strike a killing blow against him.

Though the three of them still fought with tremendous ferocity, they all began to show signs of ever-increasing fatigue. Those watching couldn't help but see the similarity between what they were witnessing and some kind of ultimate wrestling cage match.

Finally, after what seemed an eternity, the cut and bleeding Iec' managed to get a good grip on one of the gesticulating legs of an opponent. Instantly, he swung the surprised creature with all his considerable strength into its brother. The one that was thrown knocked the other off balance, landing several feet away. With the one Tarantula having cleared the melee, more than two dozen automatic weapons simultaneously opened fire on the creature.

With only one opponent remaining, the surrounding soldiers began to take heart, firmly believing that Iec' would be the one to survive. However, his fatigue was now being put on full display for the tiring Spider to see. Knowing that stepping away from the nearly exhausted sasquatch would yield a quick death by the surrounding soldiers, the nine-legged abomination gave no quarter and stayed close to the large sasquatch, wrestling with legs and dagger fangs.

They continued their struggle and the Tarantula continued to refuse to step even half a meter away from lec'. Both of them were now running out of steam, lec' the more so. He had cuts, scratches and bruises everywhere. His fur shined wetly with sweat. Everyone watching knew that he could've easily taken the creature if he hadn't already been worn down with lacerations and fatigue from having had to battle a two-Tarantula team all at once.

Every time the Spider's mouth went in for a crucial bite, lec' would somehow push the creature's fangs away. Each time they came, they snatched at a vital body part that managed to dodge again and again. Each time the fangs came closer to causing a mortal wound.

How long had they been at it? The noble sasquatch continued to fight for his life, knowing that he must end the battle soon or he would not be the victor. His movements and responses came a fraction slower each time. His waning strength and energy, though still impressive, were rapidly losing the magnanimity they had known only minutes before.

The alien Tarantula lunged again, this time finding its mark. Though lec' was able to push the fangs to the side again, they sank into his shoulder. He howled in pain as the twin dagger-like teeth caused his shoulder to sing with agony and his muscles to protest.

However, lec' didn't waste the opportunity that he saw. With the Tarantula's fangs sunk into him, that placed his own head right next to the mouth and body of the repugnant creature. Without thinking, lec' somehow managed to use his own teeth. Using his surprisingly lightning-like reflexes, the exhausted sasquatch leaned his head toward the Enemy and plunged his mouthful of teeth into the face of the other. He bit and pulled away. Now it was the alien creature's turn to howl in pain. Totally unprepared for such a feral attack, it momentarily forgot its strategy of staying close to the sasquatch. It fell back away from lec' in anguish and horror. In that instant, when it was away from the tired and bleeding sasquatch, the chorus of automatic weapons erupted in unison once again. The otherworldly monster instantly became just another casualty.

In exhaustion, lec' collapsed on the ground, knowing he'd won. Though the brief battle had only taken a couple of minutes, it had felt like hours for everyone present.

The instant the battle between lec' and the last two Spiders was over, Sparks sprinted to the side of his friend. He was worried, though he unsuccessfully tried not to let it show. With the battle over, he could now see how his comrade had fared.

Of course, his eyes were drawn to the twin holes in lec's left shoulder. The bleeding from the fang-strikes was abating, but the holes promised internal, muscular damage. His mighty chest was still heaving, sucking in the stuffy mine air. Sparks allowed his gaze to pass over the full length of the huge creature before him. He couldn't find a place on lec's body that was devoid of injury. Most of the damage the sasquatch had taken was cuts and slashes that weren't deep. However, they all added up, including a large knot that was beginning to make itself manifest above lec's right eye. Sparks figured that the knot was coming in purple, but he couldn't tell what with all the hair and matted blood on the jungle creature.

Sparks and his men did what they could to dress the wounds and help stop the bleedings. Having done this, lec' finally felt ready to speak. Showing experience with humans and their idioms, he said simply, "Let us not do that again."

At first, a corporal attending to a nasty cut on lec's left foot began to laugh. Then, one by one they all joined in until their sides hurt. Despite his pain and injuries, it made lec' want to join in, but of course, it just made the pain throughout his frame swell all the more.

The only one who didn't laugh was Captain Jones. Sparks noticed that the kid looked pretty shaken up. *Who wouldn't be after that battle?*

When the laughter was over, Sparks sat down next to his friend and looking past him said, "My friend, you are amazing! I have never seen anything like that." He paused and then added, "I'm not sure I want to ever again."

A bit of laughter followed this and lec' merely nodded his head a fraction. The effort made him grunt in pain from one of many wounds and so he didn't repeat the gesture. Instead he spoke. "I learn."

Surprised at the statement, Sparks replied, "What are you talking about?"

"My Voice no stop Tarantulas. I learn why."

A look of professional interest overcame Sparks as he eagerly waited for the reason. His men felt the same way, each one huddling closer to their wounded comrade.

"During hunt with these two creatures, I see something in them I no seen before. It like-" He paused to think of the right word. "It like heavy mud. It in ear holes. It stop most of my Voice so they not slow down." He paused again to rest before continuing. "I know the smell of it. Silktassel."

Sparks and his men all looked on with confused eyes so lec' elaborated in his rock-chewing accent. "It big bush grows in my jungle in what you call Oregon. I think they eat plant and it make strange stuff come up in ears.

Sparks was quickly catching on. "So, just like we humans get hay fever and our noses fill up with mucus, the Spiders purposely generated an allergic reaction thereby filling their ear holes with..."

The man who'd been first to laugh supplied, "Snot! They had snot in their ears!"

Everyone rolled their eyes but smiled good-naturedly.

"So that's how they did it. I was beginning to wonder," Sparks exclaimed.

"I too," lec' said.

Having attended to their champion, Sparks and some of his men finally moved over to their goal—the DEW.

The machine was a massive, blocky, metallic machine with a large barrel jutting out from the top. It was also obviously damaged and sabotaged by the Enemy during the battle. He and his men got to work immediately, trying to determine the scope of the damage and learn the new technology all at the same time. It was a ridiculously daunting task but they all knew that there was very little time remaining before they needed to fire on the ship in orbit above them.

After fifteen precious minutes, the most mechanically inclined soldier declared, "Sir, I've got some good news and some bad news."

Sparks sighed heavily, but not hopelessly, and said, "Let's hear it."

"The good news is that the platform that raises the DEW up through the hole out the top of the mine works just fine. So, we still have a clear shot at the ship in space."

Closing his eyes in defiance of harsh reality Sparks asked, "And the bad news?" He was pretty sure he already knew what it would be.

The young mechanic wiped some oil off his hands onto his pants. "The bad news is that those blasted Spiders damaged the DEW to the point that we're not going to get it operational for several days."

"Days!" Sparks nearly screamed in frustration.

Before his commanding officer could continue with his tirade that was springing like a leak in a boat, the mechanic added, "And that's only if I have the tools I need and a team of people working with me. Not to mention I'd probably need a machinist to build replacement parts from scratch."

At the end of the brief speech that sounded more like a death knell for the human race, they all sat down on the barren, earthen floor and allowed a mood of despondency to overtake them.

CHAPTER 27
Final Preparations

"Time to fire?"

Within the bowels of the Zyryanovsk mine in Russia, Xtela peered over at the anxious Captain Nishomoto and thought, *If he keep talk this way, he even make me nervous.* Aloud he voiced, "Three minutes, Nishomoto Captain." His rock-sucking voice still struggled with the new word 'minutes'. Marginally proud of himself that he was quickly adapting to human customs, he allowed himself to beam inside. On the exterior he looked characteristically placid and calm, as a sasquatch should.

After having been with humans for several weeks, the battle-hardened xtela was surprised to find that the humans around him weren't scurrying about like a stirred up ant hill. However, he had to admit, there wasn't much to do for the moment. Yet having survived numerous battles he knew that once the fighting began in just three minutes, there would be much that needed doing.

The blood-red-haired sasquatch moved over near his commanding officer, Captain Nishomoto, and tried to provide an air of calm and confidence for the much younger human.

Xtela was already just over one hundred years old–middle age for a sasquatch–so he was still in his prime. Though the young captain was considered experienced by human standards, xtela knew that he could provide timely wisdom to the senior officer. *Maybe*, xtela thought, *I be leader of place like this.* A moment later he added to himself, *If Xruhnituhm Siem agree.*

With less than a handful of minutes remaining before what everyone hoped would be the final battle to end the War with the Enemy, xtela looked around at the precision, intelligence, and order surrounding him and concluded he could definitely lead just such a team with great success.

Celewiltx could feel her brown and grey pelt moving less smoothly. She knew she needed to clean herself but she didn't care. The battle was only moments away. She and Captain Murphy stood poised, ready for battle. *In few breaths, Murphy Captain give order and we hunt and kill Tarantulas in sky,* she thought savagely.

Though she knew that Murphy's lust to kill the abominable creatures was equal to her own, she still saw it as some sort of personal vendetta. Upon being assigned to the original team to take back the Sinyukhinskoye, Russia mine, she'd felt an instant sense of camaraderie with her fellow soldiers, sasquatch and human alike. When many of them had died and she'd seen the grotesque creatures that had come to her Russian jungle and commenced such a work of death, she had been deeply affected. She'd surrounded her heart with a wall of revenge that might never be torn down, and so she drove herself on, always seeking, always searching for more of the detestable Tarantulas that didn't belong in her jungle.

Thinking about those recent memories and allowing her mind to drift elsewhere, Captain Murphy must have noticed the vacant, glossy eyed stare she offered. "Celewiltx. You all right?"

Yanking her attention back to the present tasks at hand, she answered in the affirmative, "Yes, Murphy Captain."

"Good. Cause I'm going to need you an awful lot before this day is through."

The two warriors took on twin expressions of grim enthusiasm.

The DEW platform finished elevating to the surface above the mine. Still within the mine Knight, the brilliant tactician, looked up at the DEW now positioned above him. He looked down at his watch and saw that there were only two minutes to go before the battle began. He barked out some unnecessary last minute orders and he heard the comforting sound of boots striking earth.

Standing within the mine, he knew they were ready. Though precious few of his men had survived, he was all too aware of just how lucky they'd been to do as well as they had. *By rights we should've all died long before we made it to the DEW-chamber.*

The salt-and-pepper haired man looked up the shaft at the sky in an obviously vain attempt to see their quarry—the four ships in orbit above their position. He'd seen the orders for all the mines. He knew this mine in Uchucchacua, Peru was unique since it was the only mine that had multiple targets to shoot down. All the others had just one ship in the skies above. However, for some reason the Enemy had chosen to have four ships harbored in a geosynchronous orbit above Uchucchacua.

Colonel Knight had gone back and forth in his mind about what strategy he should attempt to employ. With multiple targets, all of which were mobile, and only one weapon in his arsenal—and stationary no less—he still hadn't concluded what might be their best plan of attack. *Looks like we'll just have to play it by ear,* he thought with his usual optimism.

Knowing that the last seconds were quickly ticking away before the battle would begin, he turned to his men and addressed them. "I know you boys are all ready for this turkey shoot."

He heard some quiet snickering and let it pass.

"This is very likely going to get really messy." He added to himself, *As if it hasn't already.* "I'm going to need each of you to stay at your posts and carry out my orders."

He paused and then, with an unintended tone of finality, added, "No matter what."

The somber caste to his words did not go unnoticed by his small, but captive audience.

"Well, I guess that's it," one of Sparks' men gave up with a sigh. "With this machine busted, we're out of the game." Like everyone else, the man was staring at the sabotaged DEW.

Another soldier took up the rant, "And the human race along with it." She paused and added, "Everyone we know—slaughtered like animals."

Major Sparks felt the same and, for a moment, allowed himself the luxury of not commanding. However, his instincts and sense of duty kicked in anew and he began to rally his few remaining troops. "How much time till we're supposed to fire on that ship in space?"

"Twenty-five minutes," came an anonymous, hollow reply.

"Then we're not out of the game yet," announced the major with an optimism that belied what he was really feeling.

Dejected, exhausted and thoroughly spent, everyone turned to look at Sparks. Amidst the plethora of bodies that now populated the surrounding killing field, he stood slowly and surveyed the people under his command. The group was painfully smaller than it had been earlier that day when they'd first flown in on the Chinook helicopters what seemed forever ago. Doing his best to galvanize his troops, and himself, he carefully said, "Listen up! We're not dead and as long as I have breath in my body, I'm not going to give up. I don't care what the odds are and I couldn't care less what those worthless Spiders have in store for me. We've lost a lot of good people today. They fought hard and died for this world and the people living on it now and in the future."

One young man had a pregnant wife at home and unashamedly let a tear slide down his face. It collected dirt as it made its way toward his chin.

Sparks continued. "We need to get our act together and solve this problem." He had begun pacing. His mood was improving. "I know we don't have much time, but that just means we need to hurry and come up with a solution that much faster."

The group's attitude was getting better. The major ceased his pacing and slowly turned toward his audience. As he turned, his countenance quickly changed, taking on a terribly menacing and determined air. After pausing for a few seconds to allow the mood in the vast cavern to crescendo, he finally exclaimed in a quiet, powerful voice, "As far as I'm concerned, those worthless vermin can have this planet when they pry it from my cold, dead fingers." His strong chin added to the impressive image that he cut.

His speech did the trick. Sparks' people, even the sasquatch, erupted into a cheer that must've resounded throughout the entire mine.

With that, the major quickly issued assignments ranging from working on the DEW, to foraging for other supplies, to communicating with Camp Dodge to alert them of the situation. He knew he had to keep them busy or the euphoria would wear off as quick as his people had been cut down.

After Sparks and his men communicated their situation with Dodge, they set their minds to solving their impossible problem. They all knew they were running out of time and fast. Sparks couldn't help but keep repeating to himself, *There's something we should be able to do. We've got to find some way to knock that ship out of the sky!*

Moments later, he heard a strange sound, a sound he'd scarcely heard in what seemed an eternity. It was the sound of cheerful excitement. Everyone turned toward a side alcove in the large chamber and saw a pair from their team emerge exultantly. "Sir, we've found something. You're definitely going to want to see this!"

Lead by Sparks' two discoverers, he shortly arrived in an earthen room just off the main chamber. It measured about twenty feet square and was entirely nondescript except for the object in the room. It was a large machine, even larger than the DEW on the platform in the main room. It looked impressive and reminiscent of the DEW but different in some ways. Instead of a large housing used to convert raw energy into battering waves of sound, electromagnetism, or some other kind of energy, its appearance looked more like—

"A SPAWN?" Sparks marveled.

"Yes, Sir," came the hasty reply.

"So, you're telling me those disgusting creatures made a *giant* SPAWN?"

When the two men again confirmed his suspicion, he exclaimed, "That thing is huge! Much bigger than the weapons they carried around. Bigger than those platform-based DEWs!" Allowing himself to feel a glimmer of hope again, he rubbed at his quickly forming beard. Ignoring his whiskers for the moment he said, "How far do you think it will shoot?"

The two soldiers looked at each other and finally one of them replied, "There's no way to tell, Sir, but if the size of that reservoir and motor are any indication, I imagine it just might be able to hit the atmosphere." The young man had a twinkle in his eye as he knew he was delivering good news that was as good to hear as it was unexpected.

Allowing a grim smile to envelop his face, Sparks stated grandly, "Then let's get this thing ready to start blasting away at those accursed ships."

Before a pair of seconds could pass, the other young man politely coughed. "Sir, there is a problem, of course. This machine is pretty heavy and we can't shoot at orbiting ships from this room." The three of them grew silent before he added, "Sir, we need to get this weapon on the platform, raise it up out of the mine and *then* fire it."

With disappointment and depression threatening to wash over them again, the first young soldier offered, "Maybe we could just blast a hole through the roof of the mine and then we could hit the ships in orbit?" His words were ludicrous and his two listeners heard the lack of faith in the statement. They all knew the obvious. If they tried blasting through the ceiling and countless tons of rock, all they would accomplish is a massive cave-in and nothing else.

Sparks ran a hand through his thick shock of dark hair. His eyes never lost their gleam as he said, "I need you two to go up on that platform and signal one of the choppers. I've got an idea."

Five minutes later, Sparks and his men were working like the well-oiled machine their training guaranteed. With one of the powerful Chinook helicopters hovering above the mine–more specifically, the platform shaft–the men inside the mine were hustling to run a strong, thick cable from the chopper, down through the shaft, to the grotesquely oversized SPAWN. When the cable was secured to the new weapon, they signaled the Chinook.

The powerful twin rotors groaned and pulled. At first, nothing happened except the cable going taut as the chopper pulled in the slack. The injured lec' resting nearby watched it all play out in front of him. He wanted to help but he knew he was too injured. He wished that his sasquatch brethren who had entered the mine with him were still alive. Together, they might've been able to move the massive SPAWN.

With the cable holding taut, lec' could see the weapon moving almost imperceptibly slowly. Despite their position deep in the mine, he could still clearly hear the protestings of the Chinook's pair of turboshaft engines. Nevertheless, the large weapon continued to slowly creep across the floor of the mine. First, it made its way out of the side room where it was found. Then, it inched along the floor of the main chamber. As it moved, every available man stood behind the machine and to the sides, attempting to steer it and provide what little force they could.

With time so short and every second counting, Sparks assigned a pair of his men to looking over the machine as it moved to try to determine what they could about how it functioned.

It took only ten minutes to move the untested weapon. Everyone present knew that had to be a record that would never be broken. However, they all knew that left them only about five minutes until they needed to fire the thing.

With the cable removed and the Chinook landing a few dozen yards from the top of the platform shaft, they used the platform to raise the weapon. Even while it quickly moved up through the cavity of rock and dirt on the lift, Sparks and his men continued to determine how to use it.

When they and the weapon emerged through the shaft at the top of the mine, one of the people desperately attempting to decipher what they saw turned to Sparks and said, "Sir, as far as I can tell, this thing works. However, I don't think it's ever been fired. It must be a prototype weapon. That would explain why we never saw it in action."

Keeping an eye on the seconds quickly ticking away like the infrequent heartbeats of a dying man, Sparks exclaimed, "Fine. Let's fire it up."

The other man looked like he wanted to be able to tell his commanding officer something different than what he had to offer, but to no avail. Instead he told it straight. "Since this weapon hasn't been fired before, that means it hasn't been calibrated. If I'm right, we're going to need to do that before we start shooting down Enemy ships."

After having overcome so much already that day, Major Sparks couldn't believe it. This time, instead of feeling crestfallen, he could only laugh.

President Griffith paced the floor of Camp Dodge's Command Center from which she and other government officials were monitoring the battle. She slowly, almost meticulously, carved a path into the floor with her measured gait. She paused occasionally to look at the clock on the wall. Each time she did, she tried not to allow a worried caste to envelop her face. With the fate of the human race likely hinging on this gamble of a worldwide battle, she had reason to be concerned. Although she had never been in complete agreement with General Martin about the strategy, she figured it was their best shot.

She saw sp'atung and Sarah standing below the clock. She nodded to them, mainly to sp'atung. She didn't hold Sarah Scott in particularly high regard. The young woman was some kind of upstart who didn't belong in this world of power and influence.

Moments later a sound was heard through the stagnant buzz of voices and equipment. It was a warning klaxon notifying everyone on base that the attack was scheduled to begin in exactly one minute. Everyone stood stock still, including President Griffith. She turned to face Martin across the room. He noticed and looked at her in turn. They shared a look that said, *It's now or never.* Griffith noticed Martin's lackey, Lieutenant Malistair hand him some kind of report. Martin held the president's glance a moment longer and then looked down at the paper.

When he looked up, his face was a mixture of grim determination and ashen disillusionment. He stood stock still for a pair of seconds and then began moving across the room to the president. Griffith watched him the whole way, certain she would not like what she was about to hear.

When Martin had finished the trek he handed the paper in his hand to Griffith. Without waiting for her to read it, in a quiet voice he told her straight out. "Madame President, we have a problem. Our team from Bohemia has made contact." He paused only long enough to take a breath. "The team led by Major Sparks."

She remembered Sparks and thought he was a good soldier. She thought he might even be worthy of a higher post eventually. She nodded for him to continue.

"They've run into a bit of a snag." Martin pursed his lips and looked around the room. He wasn't struggling with having to report bad news to his superior, he just didn't like the news. "Although his team has secured the mine, they've run into a problem."

President Griffith waited for the sucker-punch.

"Before they were able to completely overcome the Enemy in the mine, the Spiders did manage to...sabotage the DEW." Martin looked at the president through a furrowed brow that was weary with responsibility and concern.

Another klaxon sounded. Thirty seconds.

Pointing at the paper in her hand, he continued, "This report says that although they're not going to be able to get it operational in time, they are working on an alternate plan."

Martin paused again and President Griffith took the moment to look down at the report for further details. She quickly realized why the general did not provide additional information. There was none.

With seconds to go before the battle was to begin, she couldn't fathom how Sparks and his team in Bohemia might somehow pull a rabbit out of their hats and blast that orbiting ship to smithereens.

Just as a third klaxon shrilly blared in unmistakable certainty, Griffith looked at the clock. Zero hour.

Around the globe, the final battle for Earth was coming to a close.

CHAPTER 28
The Quick And The Dead

Captain Murphy and the vicious celewiltx stood over opposite shoulders of the appreciated, yet relatively diminutive form of Corporal Cornwall. The corporal operated the foreign console that controlled the DEW housed in the Sinyukhinskoye, Russia mine. With both alphas pressing him to do it their way, he couldn't help but allow his characteristically mischievous look to fill his eyes. The man and sasquatch behind him both pushed and prodded him good-naturedly to follow their own strategies. However, Cornwall knew he was competent and so he fired away at the orbiting ship in his own way.

Despite having only his right hand, he still manipulated the machine's controls as deftly as anyone. When one blast of unbridled energy came particularly close to the target, Cornwall tuned out his two coaches even more and fired again. This time, he chanced holding a steady stream of energy that he used to sweep the sky in an attempt to take out the orbiting ship and its crew.

To his satisfaction, he immediately heard the captain and the sasquatch proclaim the foolhardiness of his actions, that he would surely overheat the DEW. Ignoring their protests, he swept the beam of disrupting energy across the far reaches of the atmosphere. In seconds, he struck the ship and watched the radar scope with pleasure as their quarry soon devolved into multiple pieces.

Murphy and celewiltx immediately became silent, but only for a moment. When it was clear the ship had been destroyed, the various people and sasquatch around the control room cheered. Celewiltx and Murphy, however began yelling at him about what a crazy gamble it had been. Then they began yelling at each other. Smiling inwardly at their perpetual banter, Corporal Cornwall sat back and finally relaxed.

Operating the mechanism that controlled the DEW, the blood red-haired xtela fired repeatedly, each blast of raw energy coming closer to hitting its mark.

In the Zyryanovsk mine in Russia, several people around him were giving him advice in a veritable flood of information. He found their suggestions to be less than useful. Instead of listening, he focused on his task in his calm, sasquatch way.

Having spent several weeks with humans, the all-warrior xtela had become surprisingly familiar with their machines and computers. Though far from an expert, he had readily grasped the gist of how things worked. So, watching the small radar screen built into the DEW's control module, he saw that each salvo he discharged was closer to the target than the previous shot. "Great lakes!" xtela exclaimed. "This like hunt flying bird."

To the men and women around him, it seemed as though an eternity was transpiring as they breathlessly waited for the sasquatch to hit and destroy the target. Though one or two people present were feeling they could do a better job than 'the hairball', they dared not give voice to their thoughts. They knew that their commanding officer, Captain Nishomoto, had a very favorable opinion of their new allies—especially this particular sasquatch. Also, they weren't particularly interested in incurring the wrath of a larger than average sasquatch who had already proved himself in combat after vicious combat.

Soon, even the naysayers ceased giving voice to their negative thoughts toward the hairy creature who dwarfed the console he operated. One shot, though a miss, was particularly close. Taking only an instant to re-aim the directed energy weapon, xtela quickly snapped off another shot. Not having time to maneuver evasively between the two successive salvos, the Enemy vessel took the invisible blast of energy right through the bow of the ship. Instantly, it lost control, and began its rapid descent toward Earth, cartwheeling the whole way down.

Immediately the men, women and sasquatch in the Russian mine let out a deafening cry of victory. Congratulations were offered all around, but the most ardent felicitations were reserved for xtela and Captain Nishomoto. To the people present, they were the true heroes.

With less than a minute remaining before it was time to fire the DEW in Peru, Colonel Knight addressed Private Jackson, an artillery specialist, who was manning the DEW's controls.

"Son, I know I don't have to tell you that we have to hit them hard and fast. With four ships up there, we're going to be hard-pressed to get them all before they're out of range." Then, looking directly into the younger man's eyes, he added, "Make *every* shot count."

Moments later they heard the person keeping an eye on the time announce, "Ten seconds till battle commences." Then, "Five, four, three, two, one."

On 'one' the DEW roared to life, lancing out a pulse of energy that slashed right through the aft section of the biggest of the four ships. For an instant the group in the mine was in danger of erupting into a distracting celebration—but only for a moment. The first ship quickly deteriorated into an explosive ball of fire and debris.

Shortly after the first blast, another erupted from the powerful directed energy weapon. The second shot narrowly grazed its target. The Enemies in the sky were already beginning evasive maneuvers. However, the second ship to be hit was lagging, moving slowly. It began to list to the north. A proverbial sitting duck, Jackson opened fire again, sending a shock of pure energy tearing through the Enemy vessel.

With two down, and the element of surprise expended, Knight knew that the battle was going as well as they could've hoped. He also knew that the two remaining ships would prove to be much more difficult to destroy than their two friends had been.

"Keep firing," Knight commanded to Private Jackson. "We need to get them before they're out of range of the DEW!"

Attempting to line up his next shot to knock down one of the two remaining elusive craft, Jackson broke in, "Sir, I don't think you're going to have to worry about that."

"What? Why? What are you talking about?"

Jackson swallowed hard and said, "Because they're not moving off. In fact, I think they're preparing to attack!"

Knight paused for only a moment as the information sunk in. This changed everything. The strategy he was using was no longer valid, and yet, it also changed nothing. Either way, they knew they had to take out those ships quickly.

Immediately, Colonel Knight's many years of tactical and strategic experience kicked into high gear. *So, they want to play chicken, do they.*

Aloud he ordered, "Jackson, keep firing. I need you to keep those two off balance. Make it hard for them to set up for a clean shot." Wiping away some of the quickly accumulating sweat from his mine dusted forehead he added, "If we lose the DEW, we're out of the game. *All* of us." Colonel Knight knew that he didn't need to elaborate on what he meant by "all."

Moments later, they all began to hear the telltale whistle of an incoming projectile. When it struck, the earth shook and dust began to fall from the ceiling. Tucked away within the bowels of the mine, Knight and his men needed to rely almost entirely on what the radar was telling them. They also knew that the protection the mine afforded could very quickly become their tomb.

Jackson fired again at the larger ship. He was building a rhythm. He would snap off a shot at whichever of the ships was moving slower. They made easier targets but he also knew that as they slowed down, they were setting up for a clean shot. So far, he'd been successful in depriving them of those shots.

However, between their evasive maneuvers and the fact that he had to hold two of them at bay, he hadn't hit anything since the first two he'd downed at the beginning of the battle.

Knight knew if they didn't take out *both* of those ships, it was only a matter of time before those alien craft caused a cave-in and buried him and his men. He knew that, ultimately, the Enemy wouldn't need a clean shot, just a lot of salvos that landed close enough to destabilize the mine ceiling and bring it down.

The colonel could hear—and feel—the detonations of ordnance taking place around the mine. Some were farther away than others. Nearly all of them were *close.*

One incoming projectile rattled the entire mine. The walls shook and the floor seemed to buckle. Somewhere down a corridor, wooden supports could be heard collapsing. Everyone was certain that particular shot was going to bring the roof down on them. Or at the very least, knock out the DEW. However, the DEW on its elevated platform continued to deal out shot after shot, distracting the Enemy and keeping them off balance.

All around them the battle raged on.

Then suddenly, Jackson let out a *whoop* of delight that immediately turned to disappointment. He thought they'd knocked out one of the two remaining Enemy ships that were pulverizing the landscape around them. Instead, he'd barely winged it. As far as he could tell, it hadn't made a difference in the way that ship bobbed and weaved or, more especially, the way it slung shot after shot at the sitting-duck mine.

The sweat was beginning to come off his forehead in increasingly large amounts. The pivotal nature of the moment was not lost on him and the stress on his face was evidence of that fact.

Again and again the ships in the sky traded salvos with the DEW on the ground. Neither force made headway and both continued to attempt to best the other. The ships, miles away in the sky, flew in the midst of powerful slices of energy, cutting the sky in pieces around them. The men on the ground played the deadly game of cat-and-mouse surrounded by an environment as dangerous and explosive as an otherworldly, volcanic landscape.

As the two opposing sides continued trading shots, Jackson began to notice that the ship he thought he'd hit was slowing down. It was still adding to the barrage but its movements were less clean, less evasive.

Realizing he had in fact previously damaged the ship and seeing his opportunity to finish the job, he lined up a shot to hit the damaged craft and quietly exclaimed, "I have you now."

He fired a single shot that lanced through the engines in the rear of the large vessel. With death raining down all around the mine and shaking the living daylights out of everyone therein, he was only aware of the success of his shot as he saw, on his radar screen, the single ship momentarily transformed into two separate entities. Then, as Earth's gravitational pull grasped both pieces in her merciless clutches, the two pieces quickly dissolved as the friction of reentry took its toll.

With only one ship remaining, the victory was all but certain and everyone in the mine knew it. They figured the creatures in the Enemy ship above must've known it as well, but instead of retreating or trying to get low on the deck so as to get under the DEW's trajectories, it began to attack with an increased ferocity.

The way the ship moved and attacked, Jackson figured that the person flying the ship was *not* the same person working the weapons. The shots were getting closer to the DEW and the whole mine was now rattling and shaking. Certain that their demise was imminent, and with earth, timbers and electrical wires collapsing around them, Knight, leqi and everyone else who could stand worked furiously to use the fallen beams to make a triangular shelter over and around Jackson and his station. Within the triangle, dust fell and rubble dislodged. There was scarcely any light and what illumination it provided showed a host of filthy and desperate looking soldiers hovering around Jackson in a very enclosed space.

Still the DEW fired, and still the last, lone ship above juked and danced to the rhythm set by Jackson. The dance of death was certain to end soon. The only question was who would stay alive to dance to the same tune on another day—and who would dance no more.

With dust, dirt and rock now continually falling down around them, Jackson tried to keep the dirt out of his eyes as his comrades did their best to keep he and his station functioning. The mayhem surrounding the poor private was almost as maddening as it was deafening.

Then, an instant after Private Jackson let loose another volley of destructive energy, a strangely loud explosion rocked the surface of the mine. As an even greater deluge of rocks and debris came down around the lone sasquatch and the exhausted men, they all knew what had caused the destruction.

The Enemy had detonated the DEW. It was now out of commission.

In that instant, a terrible feeling of inevitability overtook the worn out men. Despite all their efforts, and the loss of so many friends, they still hadn't managed to knock out the Enemy. Now at least one ship would escape. At least one Enemy vessel might just depart and rearm elsewhere and then come back to finish the job. The heartache was nearly overwhelming.

Nevertheless, a single second after the DEW had been totally destroyed, the last shot that Jackson had gotten off could be seen on the radar to rip through a single wing of the ship above. It didn't seem to do much, but it definitely made contact with their quarry.

Despite the cave-in taking place around them, they all watched the radar screen with baited breath and rapt fascination as the one ship above began to veer off in a parabolic path. Its trajectory seemed to be controlled and so it was difficult for Knight and his men to determine just how much damage the last ship had sustained. After several seconds, the ship's trajectory began to degrade and become less stable. With all eyes glued to the radar, they saw its flight path seemed to shimmy and shake. It no longer followed its parabolic trail to regain the outer atmosphere. Instead, like a great beast struggling to breathe its few remaining breaths it continued to do all it could to escape the terrible, inexorable pull of gravity to which its sister-ship had so recently succumbed.

In mute anticipation that slowly turned to wild celebration, they watched the last of the four ships plummet to the surface of the Earth, never to fly again.

Major Sparks could hear one of his men cry out, "Time!" On that signal, the major and all of his team knew that the battle was beginning.

And they weren't ready to fire the gargantuan SPAWN they'd found within the Bohemian mine.

Sweat dripping from their foreheads due to exertion, but mainly due to stress, they furiously worked at puzzling out how to calibrate the weapon so that it would fire properly. Every few seconds, someone would say something like, "I think I've got it!" and then would quickly follow up with one more acknowledgement of failure.

While attempting to decipher the symbols and functional controls on the large weapon, Sparks would occasionally bark, "Time!"

Each time the response was more and more disheartening.

"Time plus thirty seconds."

"Time plus one minute."

"Time plus two minutes!"

Anxiously they worked, desperate to rapidly figure out the weapon and fire on the ship in orbit above.

All the while one older soldier, Sergeant Vince Kovar, kept his eyes on the sky. The man's hair was kept extremely short, presumably to avoid attention being drawn to his balding features. Even looking through a pair of Steiner military-grade binoculars, he could barely see their target. Two minutes after the attack was to commence, Kovar announced in his typically mature way, "Sir, I can't be certain but–"

"What is it?" Sparks demanded.

"Sir, if I'm right, that ship up there is beginning to move off. I can't tell yet if it's moving away from Earth or just sliding along the atmosphere to set up a new geosynchronous orbit."

Still working, everyone grimaced at the depressing turn of events that they had all been expecting.

Unbidden, Kovar offered, "Either way, it's going to be out of range in seconds."

At least it took those blasted Spiders two minutes to get moving, Sparks thought in the back of his mind as he continued to try to find a solution of how to operate the weapon. *Who knows, maybe that'll be just the time we need.*

Though he continued to work, he felt the situation had become hopeless.

As they stayed focused on the task at hand, the mood around the colossal SPAWN was going from bad to worse. Sparks and his men didn't seem to be getting any closer than they had been at finding out how to properly operate the machine. Nerves were frayed and some members of the team were snapping at each other.

In the midst of the depressing mood that was clutching their hearts with an icy hand Kovar, with his binoculars, stoically announced, "That big sucker is now out of range."

Hearing the death knell of their efforts, and their world, a couple people stopped working. Not impervious to the prevailing attitude, Sparks barked at them to continue.

Moments later, Kovar took his eyes from the high powered binoculars and looked at the SPAWN. He cocked his head to one side and looked more relaxed than anyone else around.

At last he cut in, "Major Sparks, we've seen the Enemy use SPAWNs on us in the past. We've got an idea of how those work. Wouldn't this probably operate in about the same way?"

Everyone stopped, wanting to believe that the sergeant just might be on to something, but could it be that simple? Standing up in a minor state of nervous agitation, Sparks looked at the man and then back at the machine. "Maybe you're right. Maybe we're over-thinking this."

Sparks' men all turned toward him. Hiding his dejection he announced, "What have we got to lose? If it goes wide or blows up in our faces, it can't really get any worse." Then, with more of his typical conviction he pronounced, "Let's fire this thing up!"

With eyes glued to the skies through his binoculars, Sergeant Kovar breathlessly searched for the tiny spot in the sky that was the orbiting ship. He knew it was moving off and so he also knew he might not be able to find it. *It might be out of range of my eyes as well as of the SPAWN-cannon,* he thought.

After several quickly eroding seconds, he announced, "I see it! It's just barely in view. It must be nearly twice as far as a DEW's known range."

Quickly, but without much conviction, Sparks commanded, "Start it up."

An odd sounding motor immediately began to fire up. It had a strangely static-like sound. It reminded them of the sound of glass shattering.

Satisfied it was working properly, Sparks looked over at Kovar and beckoned, "What's your trajectory?"

The newest feature to the Steiner binoculars was that they had a vectoring GPS feature built in. So, Sergeant Kovar merely had to press a black button on top to lock in the angle at which he was looking through the device.

"Seventy-two degrees from the horizontal plane," came the reply. Sparks and his men made the necessary adjustment.

"Eighteen degrees, seventeen minutes west of true north." Again, the men operating the gigantic SPAWN carefully made the adjustment, rotating the weapon until it matched the indicated angle.

Looking like he'd spent the last twenty minutes gargling his own bile, Sparks asked, "Kovar, are you sure about the trajectory? I doubt we're going to get more than one shot at that thing." He didn't bother giving voice to his added thoughts, *If we can even hit it now. Who knows. This thing may only fire a mile or so.*

"Yes, I'm certain," came the experienced reply. "But don't take your time. I can barely see it. In a few moments, if it changes course, I won't know where it is."

While this brief conversation was taking place, another man got in contact with Camp Dodge to hopefully be able to use their significantly enhanced telemetry. Dodge would, of course, be able to see the ship much better than they, and be able to tell if it were hit by their prototype SPAWN-cannon.

An instant after Kovar confirmed his measurements, Sparks bellowed, "Fire!"

The sound the SPAWN emitted was reminiscent of the portable SPAWNs to which they had all become accustomed. The *wump* sound it made was deeper and sounded tremendously more powerful. Everyone around noticed that the weapon also seemed to draw in all the surrounding air around it for an instant. Sparks and his men all felt, for a moment, like they were in a pressurized container.

But if they felt disconcerted, they almost didn't notice. At first, all eyes were on the massive, green, semi-viscous globule that shot out of the weapon, quite literally, like a cannonball. In less than three seconds it was beyond the scope of the naked eye. With that, all eyes turned to Kovar as he attempted to keep his eyes on the ship. A moment later, he brought the binoculars down from his eyes and said, "I'm sorry. I can't see the ship any more. I'm pretty sure it's out of range of even these babies," he said, patting the eyewear.

They all stared at the ground in exhausted disappointment. One man even sunk to his knees. The feeling of ultimate failure was almost unbearable. The human race as they knew it would be destroyed.

On the radio, a static-filled crackle broke the silence. The man with the radio replied to the incoming signal. A moment later everyone heard the unthinkable, "Major Sparks, this is Camp Dodge. Do you read?"

Lifelessly, the major took the radio and replied, "Yes, Dodge this is Sparks. Over."

"Son, this is General Martin. What kind of weapon did you fire at that ship?"

Not recognizing the general's growing excitement, Sparks replied in a defeated, monotone voice, "Just some prototype weapon we found in the mine. It looks like a giant SPAWN."

"Well, I've got to hand it to you. That thing works like a charm! It just ripped through the ship that was moving away from your position!"

Sparks slowly looked up at the radio he held. "Sir, would you please repeat that?"

With a grandfatherly smile that clearly came through the radio, General Martin replied, "That salvo you launched didn't leave much behind. The whole ship was instantly incinerated."

Immediately, cheers once again erupted around the haggard Major Sparks, merging with the cheers that could be heard in the background at Camp Dodge.

Stepping out of character, Sparks inquired, "Are you sure?" He quickly added a belated, "Sir".

The general either didn't notice the breach of protocol or didn't care. Instead he said, "Are you kidding? I'll bet the range on that weapon is at least twice as far as what you just mustered! Great job!"

A tired, elated smile slowly overtook the major's face. Looking over at Kovar, he gave a thumbs-up. Together, they were victorious.

When President Griffith, General Martin, and the other personnel with them in the Command Center at Camp Dodge saw the last ship blown apart by Sparks and his team, an exultant cry went up that seemed to rival the shout that took down Jericho's walls.

A plethora of hand-wringing and backslapping broke out between friends and colleagues. Even President Griffith extended a warm hand to General Martin.

"We did it. I can't believe it but we did it!" she exclaimed, her tan pants suit impeccably clean.

Martin replied, "I knew we'd make it. I'm just glad it didn't take any longer than this."

Near the back of the room, Sarah gave sp'atung a hug that she'd been holding in for many months. Happy and relieved at their success, she was glad that she could be there with such a close friend. Sp'atung peered down at her from his great height and from behind his deep, placid eyes said, "We do it. Hunt was good. We no more like hurt birds on ground."

As the cheers continued, communiqués began to come in from the mines around the world. Status reports began trickling in as the various teams started telling the story, by radio, of what the victory had cost.

General Martin took the first few reports from the fiery-haired Captain Smith and soon commenced disseminating the information. A strikingly somber mood soon prevailed over the room. Hundreds of men, women and sasquatch had been killed. Though everyone knew the steep price was worth it, it still stung their hearts to know that the vast majority of the people they'd sent out would not be coming back.

The emotion in the room was palpable and for several seconds, nobody spoke. Gradually, the sounds of life and routine resumed. More reports came in and each team confirmed what the satellites had told them. Their victory was complete. They'd destroyed *every* ship in orbit.

CHAPTER 29
Reunion

Less than a week after what was already coming to be known as the Battle of Liberation, a large gathering of dignitaries, soldiers and any other 'important' people available was taking place at Camp Dodge in Iowa.

It was a celebration and, though resources were limited, President Griffith intended that the event go off in high fashion. There would be awards and medals and accolades all around. Of course, since the existence of the sasquatch was still a guarded secret, only authorized personnel were allowed to enjoy the festivities.

The event began in a large, outdoor training area. A stage had been erected for President Griffith, General Martin and a few other prominent persons. There were simple streamers hung from the stage but little else. Most of the desired decorations simply weren't readily available.

Below the stage, the several hundred invited guests milled about, talking, drinking and eating. There were command personnel who helped direct the Battle of Liberation and the War. There were technicians, pilots, sasquatch and, of course, the people who had survived the raids on the last three mines. The mood was as cheerful and upbeat as the world's mood had been dour and depressed for so long.

One speaker after another spoke on the stage about the time since the War began and the terrible heartache and pain that everyone had endured. Each made particular mention of heroic deeds executed by the living and those who had passed on. It was a truly tear-jerking and therapeutic experience for all present. Each person, in his own way, reflected on the friends and family they would never see again because of the destruction the War had brought to them. Even the sasquatch had lost many comrades and felt the loss. They too felt and recognized how much this victory had cost.

Finally, President Griffith stood and spoke. Her comments were uncharacteristically tender. She pulled on the heartstrings that had already been stretched that day. She made reference to the teamwork that had taken place. She briefly discussed the grand alliance between sasquatch and human and how each side had been able to derive great value from that relationship.

At last, she concluded by quickly making reference to the undeniable fact that there would still be pockets of Enemy resistance here and there around the globe. She expressed the need to deal with them as she proclaimed, "For only a short while longer, we will need to continue to maintain martial law."

A few hums and murmurs were heard to make their way through pockets of listeners, but the people had already lived under martial law for so long that they figured a little longer wouldn't be a problem.

Continuing, she said, "Along with rebuilding our great society, we will make it a priority to flush out and destroy the few remaining vermin left on *our* planet as quickly as possible." She paused for a moment and then at last stated, "Then we will be able to truly get things back to normal. Again, congratulations to us all!" A thunderous applause burst forth from all quarters.

With the speeches concluded, there was nothing left to do but talk, reminisce, dance, and celebrate being alive.

Some of the humans present had had very little interaction with the sasquatch and so visiting with them was at a premium. Small throngs of people surrounded nearly every one of them, especially each of the three members of the Xruhnituhm Siem. Flown in by chopper, tuhngiqr, tsin'tsun'tsan, and steek'eew were present as well.

Amidst the well-wishing and celebrations, several people who'd never met ended up together. Colonel Damon Knight, leqi, Major Nick Sparks, lec' and even Captain Franklin Jones. Perhaps it was inevitable that the conquerors of the last two mines would come together. They talked and traded stories, each person trying to keep the mood light in the face of obviously morbid and painful memories. They eyed the medals they'd each been given by the president only moments before. At least one person in the exclusive group noticed how the stress of the mission was etched so painfully on the face of Captain Jones.

Elsewhere amidst the throng, Sarah Scott stood alone in the middle of hundreds of people and sasquatch. She would've been with sp'atung, but he'd sought out his wife and countrymen, eager to renew old ties. Jack's company would've been appreciated but he was being aloof. So, there she stood. Alone, but happy. She was happy that the War was over, that they could all finally settle down. She was happy that no more of her friends would die needlessly to those otherworldly creatures. Yet through it all, she couldn't help but feel a sense of loss. Of course she'd felt like part of her had been cut out every time someone she knew had been killed in the ongoing War, but this was somehow different. Not necessarily deeper or more profound, just different. She pondered on the many people she'd met since her travels had begun. She'd liked most of the people she'd met, some she'd disliked. Others were somewhere in between.

She reflected on her time at Oscar-Romeo-17 when she'd begun to change. *I was so certain of so many things before I made some friends at that camp*, she silently contemplated, as people laughed and hustled by. *Life has gotten a lot harder since that day I ended up there.* Thinking back on that experience had a very different effect on her now. Now it made her laugh, but she couldn't help but think about the people she'd known in that camp who she would never see again. The people who'd died. *Everyone but me, Jameson, Stansbury and, of course, Captain Smith.* When she thought of the fiery red-haired woman, this time she didn't sneer or wish to lace the woman's bed with leaches or itching powder.

Amidst all of her thoughts and feelings that seemed to fill her up, for some reason she *truly* felt painfully alone. She thought it was silly, but she felt as though she just might cry right there. Then a miracle happened.

Looking up from the pit of her problems she saw a man walking toward her rather deliberately. A pair of tears obscured her vision so she wasn't sure who he was. It was like looking through a stain glass window. As the man drew closer, he began to look familiar to her. He took a few more steps and she could've sworn she'd seen that hair before. A few more steps were traversed and she knew.

It was Pete Garrison. Overwhelmed by the moment and the intensity of her feelings, she ran toward him and embraced him. A little sheepishly, he hugged her back. Her tears of relief that another friend had survived began to flow freely. After several seconds, Garrison finally offered a polite cough. Sarah didn't get the hint and so he said, "I have to admit. The first time we met, I never would've seen this scene playing out quite like this."

She laughed at herself and moved back a pair of steps. She looked up into his piercing gray eyes and saw an even greater measure of maturity than had been there before. *Well, wherever he's been, he's undoubtedly had some crazy experiences. Like everyone else.*

When her mouth finally worked, all she could say was, "How? When?" Realizing she wasn't making sense, she paused for a moment and then asked, "What happened?"

"I presume you mean back at OR-17?" She nodded and he told her of his escape with his five horsemen. He didn't dwell on the more sordid and painful details from his memory. They were both grateful for that. They'd both lived through the nightmare in horrifying relief. When he finished his brief story he added, "Sarah, I must admit. You weren't the only one without complete intel. *I* thought *you* were dead. Until a few moments ago, I had no idea you were alive and well and working here at Camp Dodge!" Almost belatedly he added, "I missed you."

She blushed and replied in turn, "I missed you too." They both stood quietly for a few moments before she asked, "I've got to ask, where in the world have you been?"

Without making it into a long story he told her, "After the battle I got promoted to colonel." She raised a playful eyebrow in a mock display of being worshipfully impressed. He laughed and continued. "Shortly thereafter I was sent on assignment to Canada to take command of our forces that were there to...er... assist the Canadians in the fight against the Enemy." He looked over toward the stage, where the president had spoken minutes before. "Of course, now that the War is over, I expect we'll all be coming home soon." He didn't look like he believed it.

Sarah couldn't help but notice that there was a shadow over the man before her, a shadow that had not been there before. She couldn't quite put her finger on it, but if she had to guess she figured it meant that Pete Garrison's life was somehow less simple and black and white than it had been when she'd last seen him. She let it pass, knowing he'd talk about it if he wanted to.

After a few minutes their conversation began to come more easily and they talked and reminisced about this and that, always trying to steer clear of the more obviously painful parts of their jobs and lives. He described to her the beauties he'd seen in the somewhat war-ravaged Montreal and the rest of Quebec. The parks and grasslands, the artwork of Carole Spandau and horse drawn carriage rides.

He ended his soliloquy with, "Je vous ai manqué." He smiled for a moment and said, "I learned a little French while I was there."

"What does it mean?"

"It means 'I missed you'."

She blushed again.

Then, for a few moments, they both stood quietly, allowing an increasingly uncomfortable silence to evolve. At last, Garrison said, "So what have you been up to?"

"Well, since you're here, you must know about the sasquatch."

He nodded in acknowledgement.

"My job is to serve as a sort of liaison between the sasquatch we have working with us and we humans."

She looked proud of herself and he had no doubt that what she was doing was important. Upon reflection he had to admit that his job in Quebec probably had a few similarities. Nevertheless, he did have one question. Speaking slowly and carefully he asked, "That's great. It sounds important, but why did they pick you?"

The old fire came back into her eyes and he found himself enjoying the sight of it. It was like some kind of long, lost friend from a simpler age. He raised his hands, palms forward, placatingly and wasted no time adding, "I don't mean you're not the right person for the job. I just meant that this is a government installation and last I checked, you weren't exactly at the top of the totem pole when it came to classified information." He ended with a smile and she dropped her guard.

Smiling, she responded, "Well, after the battle, I ended up meeting a sasquatch. His name is sp'atung."

Garrison replied, "Sp'atung? Odd name. Sounds like something from an Indian language."

She gave an approving look. "That's right. In fact, the word comes from the Salish language. Look for the sasquatch with the smoky gray pelt."

When he didn't say anything she continued. "Jameson, Smith and Stansbury were with me when—"

"You ended up with Captain Smith? That is too funny." She began to scowl at him but he knew she didn't mean it. "As I recall, the two of you weren't exactly planning on sending each other Christmas cards any time soon."

"True, but circumstances brought us together."

"This story just keeps getting better and better," he beamed with arms crossed. "Please continue," he added with only a hint of mock fascination, his posture suggesting rapt attention.

She ignored the playful gesture and said, "We stayed with the sasquatch for a while and then Smith got them to agree to form some sort of alliance. So, General Martin came to meet 'the neighbors' at their home in the jungle and formalized the agreement. Part of the pact was that sp'atung would serve the sasquatch as an ambassador to us. Martin agreed on the condition that Jack be his assistant."

When Garrison showed confusion on his face, Sarah added, "Jack's a guy we met a day or so before meeting sp'atung."

"I guess I was right before when I said this story gets better and better." Cocking an eye, Pete asked, "So you just found some wild man living in the forest?"

Not interested in digressing too much she simply said, "Yes."

The two of them laughed and she continued, "Once Jack was on board, he said he'd need someone youthful—and beautiful, I might add—to assist him."

This time, when Pete cocked an eye at her, he only looked amused, not incredulous.

"Okay," Sarah corrected. "Maybe he didn't say 'beautiful', but I knew darn well that he didn't need me. He just wanted to have someone else around him he knew he could trust."

The expression on the colonel's face darkened in the twinkling of an eye. It surprised Sarah and this time she had to ask, "Pete, what is it?"

He clearly measured each word and subtle nuance before he spoke. "I've certainly had my own issues with who I can trust."

Looking nervous and a little unsure of her personal standing with her friend, she asked, "What do you mean?"

And just like that the thundercloud that covered the man's features was gone. "Oh, don't worry. I wasn't talking about you. In fact, I have to tell you that I trust you a lot more than a few other people around here who I'm *supposed* to trust."

Though relief flooded into her heart and mind, Sarah was still concerned. Nevertheless, she didn't press the issue. She vowed to herself that she would investigate later.

As the two of them continued to get caught up and enjoy the other's company, elsewhere amidst the festivities, President Griffith in a mauve pants suit had managed to bump into the red-haired beauty, Captain Sonya Smith. The president and the captain spoke of this and that, procedures and protocols, the ongoing mopping up after the War and other significant events. At last, the president said, "Smith, how long has it been since you made captain?"

"Three years, Ma'am."

"Three years," the president responded. "With a track record of successes like yours, that seems like a long time without promotion."

"I suppose," came the bland reply.

"How do you like working with General Martin?" Griffith continued.

"I can't complain."

Griffith hid a wince. "Well, that's good to hear." Her tone wasn't entirely convincing. "I've read your file. I can't wait to see you promoted some day and take on more responsibilities. You're someone I know I can count on." Then, trying to offer some strange sort of praise, she added, "You're a valued commodity. I look forward to continuing to see you around here."

Smith allowed her eyes to squint, almost imperceptibly, in consideration of the words she was hearing. She didn't know exactly what the president was driving at, but she was certain that there was more to it than what she had initially heard.

President Griffith then said, "Well, I'll let you get back to the party. You certainly wouldn't want to listen to the dry ramblings of the president, day in and day out." With that, the president smiled and allowed herself to be caught away in the flow of people.

Smith was thoughtful. The president's smile had been so multifaceted. It held charm, something akin to warmth, and yet so much more. She wasn't quite sure what had just happened, but she was certain that she should file away what she'd seen and heard and then ponder on it later. She had a new puzzle to solve.

Just outside the parade ground, while the festivities were in full swing, a pair of unlikely people met up. General Martin called out, "Jack!"

Jack turned slowly, casually. Upon turning, he stood stock still, allowing the general to approach him. Martin didn't walk wearily, just tiredly.

At last, Martin carefully spoke, "It's been a long time." A short pause ensued that dragged on.

"Yeah, I suppose so," Jack replied in his easy way.

Martin looked up at the sky as if to search for the right words. When they didn't come, he advanced anyway. "I must admit, I was surprised to see you that day when I first met the sasquatch."

Despite the uncomfortably somber mood that prevailed, Jack said in reply, "You should've seen *my* first experience with them. Now, *that* was...astonishing."

The general knew the other man too well to believe that his casual manner of speech suggested that the ice between them was broken. He also knew that the icy chasm between them had somehow been forged from both directions. Instead he replied, "Well, I can see why you like them. Those sasquatch are good people."

Rather than respond, Jack merely plunged his hands in his pockets and looked about him at the surrounding military installation that had been dutifully serving as the center of government.

Martin wished that Jack would say more but he understood the man's reasons. His own were essentially the same. Yet, despite those reasons, he couldn't let the opportunity to talk to the other pass him by. The chance might never return.

At last, the general made a gamble and asked, "You still think about her?"

Martin didn't need to say who he meant by 'her', and they both knew it. Though Jack had no desire to respond in any way to that exact question, he figured twenty years might just be enough to get him to answer. He replied, "Jessica? Yeah, every worthless day." Though he made the statement without venom, Martin was still taken aback, perhaps because of the unguarded, hollowness that came through in the reply.

The conversation over, Jack continued to walk away, never looking back. With tears in his eyes, Martin stood there watching him turn a corner past a building and wondered if Jack was shedding a tear as well.

When Jack was gone from view, he slowly turned back toward the celebration. Part of him wanted to go after the other man, but he knew it was not to be. So he slowly and contemplatively sauntered back toward the joy and revelry at the parade ground. With a heavy heart that was increasingly lifted with each step he took, General Martin returned and joined in the hand-wringings, congratulations and general merriment. For the moment, the only thing in his mind and world was the unequivocal victory over the Enemy.

EPILOGUE
Peace Is Not Enough

Deep in the bowels of Camp Dodge, a solitary and seldom used room sat at the end of a rarely used corridor. The room was dusty and musty from a lack of use. It caused the occupants to cough occasionally. The people conducting the meeting were not interested in careless or prying eyes witnessing the event. They also desired that their attendees recognize how secret they wished the contents of the meeting to be.

Bathed in dim light, they sat in plush chairs in a circle. President Griffith sat at one point along the circle, with a clear view of the single door leading into the near lifeless room. Except for two other individuals, the remainder of the solemn circle was populated with a host of sasquatch. Xtela with his blood red pelt sat prominently, the first of the sasquatch to fight alongside humans. Celewiltx, with her jagged stripes and vicious eyes, proudly perched on her seat, another hero from multiple battles waged against the hated Enemy. The dreamy leqi who had made the incredible run to recover the *thermo-bolt* for Colonel Knight and lec' who had battled a pair of Tarantulas were also present in the circle, two of the most prominent heroes from the Battle of Liberation. There were several others including the small but scrappy memimen, one of the first twenty sasquatch to be recruited by General Martin. Also present from the original twenty was cqiqen, his joking style always seeming at odds with how sedate humans frequently thought "a sasquatch should be." A busy sasquatch with light brown fur named axllwis was also present. It seemed that nearly every sasquatch on base was in attendance.

In all, there were about fifty sasquatch present.

Some of those sasquatch noticed with surprise that not one Lat' was present. Some wondered at that. Surprisingly, sp'atung was also absent.

They had all been told in advance that this assembly was not to be on record. Yet trust was in their hearts as they sat together, looking at the leader of the sen', a species with whom they had thus far worked so well. Eagerly, they waited to know the reason for the gathering.

The last two people in attendance were, by their sizes, obviously humans. They sat outside the circle in dark corners opposite each other. The lone light bulb suspended from a thin electrical cord in the center of the ceiling failed to illuminate their faces.

When all were present and seated, President Griffith began to speak.

With kindly, yet determined, eyes she began, "My friends. Thank you for coming to this meeting. I hope you will all feel comfortable as we progress. I also encourage each of you to add what you will while we are here together."

Being sasquatch, they didn't clap or nod their heads in agreement. They merely sat quietly and expectantly.

"The reason I've invited you each here this day is not only because each of you as individuals have shown repeatedly that you are competent and capable but also because you are trustworthy. Let me remind you at this time that this meeting is not to be discussed in any way with anyone outside this room."

A few heads bobbed slightly in ascent, in imitation of their human colleagues. *Good,* Griffith thought. *They can keep a secret.*

Continuing she said, "Let me tell you a little story. Most of it you already know. The most important parts, as it relates to our meeting here today, will likely be new to you."

She coughed once on the dust in the dank room and pressed on. "Not long ago, an extraterrestrial life form came to Earth. We referred to them as the Enemy, or the Spiders. You called them Tarantulas. They invaded and they destroyed. The War broke out and erupted throughout the Earth. Many millions of people died and we were forced to fight back. Humans and sasquatch forged an alliance and combined their strengths to vanquish the Enemy."

Griffith could see some of her listeners begin to sit up straighter. A couple leaned forward in eagerness and pride.

She then said, "However, while all this was taking place, there were people with power who wanted something else as well." She took on a look of breathless anticipation and allowed the mood in the room to crescendo. "They wanted to use the War for their own aims and to amass power for themselves. They were selfish and not as helpful to the cause as they might've been."

Some of the sasquatch looked confused, others looked concerned. Still others looked resolute and ready to resist these people being described to them.

"Sure, they did their part in helping to take down and destroy the Enemy, but now that the Spiders have been beaten," she said as her voice became tinged with concern, "I fear they may direct their efforts elsewhere—at grabbing what bits and pieces of power they can. If this were to happen the successes we've won and shared together would come crumbling down." Her voice became more impassioned and her speech seemed to take on a life of its own. "We need to stand together! We need to work together, united against these people who would stand in the way of progress and peace."

Then, she finally made her gamble. "So I ask you, my friends, will you stand by me and assist me in stamping out this cancer that has begun to grow within our ranks? Will you work with me to keep peace and harmony afloat in this maelstrom of deception and intrigue? Will you serve as my personal guards, assistants and protectors, reporting only to me so that together we can right the wrongs that have been waged against us all?"

The cheer that exploded from the sasquatch throats was deafening and resembled a roar more than a cheer.

With the die cast, Griffith and the other two humans present known as 'Armani' and 'Beard' smiled.

The End

LIST OF CHARACTERS

Armstrong, Jack
Older man who is some sort of easy going woodsman

axllwis [ak-s*uh*l-wis]
A sasquatch who has a tendency to digress when she speaks

Bates, George
Leader of the Drain, Oregon tribe

celewiltx [sel-uh-**wilt**-uhks]
A sasquatch warrior, she is strong, fierce and intense

Cornwall, Simon
Corporal; A competent yet playfully mischievous soldier assigned to Oscar-Romeo-17

cqiqen [suh-**kee**-ken]
A girthy sasquatch who's a bit of a joker

Dillon, John
Competent Secretary of Veterans Affairs

Driggs, William
Sergeant; One of Garrison's five horsemen, he never seemed to learn to joke around

Fergurson, Mitchell
A sour member of the Drain, Oregon tribe

Fetch, Arthur
Private; A whiz mechanic but has a tough time doing things "the Army way"

Garner, Amos
Private; One of Garrison's five horsemen, he's a solid soldier

Garrison, Pete
Major; Newly assigned leader of the Oscar-Romeo-17 camp

Griffith, Gwyneth
New president of the United States of America

Jackson, William
Private; An artilleryman

Jameson, Oliver
Sergeant; A stiff and formal soldier assigned to Oscar-Romeo-17

Johnson, Mary
Former Vice President of the United States of America

Johnson, Phil
Secretary of Commerce

Jones, Franklin
Captain; A good officer with a good sense of humor

kansel [kawn-s*uh*l]
She is a pleasant, thoughtful sasquatch

Knight, Damon
Colonel; A dynamic soldier who doesn't do things by the book, his methods for successfully completing missions are often creative

Kovar, Vince
Sergeant; An older, steady soldier
lec' [lek]
A noble, wiry sasquatch whipcord

leqi [le-kee]
A very distracted sasquatch

Malistair, Grace
Lieutenant; General Martin's primary aide

Marquez, Jose
President of Brazil

Martin, Thomas Q.
General; Current Chairman of the Joint Chiefs of Staff

memimen [mem-i-men]
A smaller sasquatch but gutsy and scrappy

Michaels, Carmine
Oily Secretary of State

Moreau, Jean
Prime Minister of Canada

Murphy, Rex
Captain; A man who works closely with Major Pete Garrison at Oscar-Romeo-17, he is built like a tank

Nishomoto, Jackson
Captain; Good soldier who leads a delta team on a reconnaissance mission, later to work in other important capacities

Reznikov, Nicolai
A Russian geologist who has been out of the public eye for 20 years and whose skills go well beyond earth science

Rideout, Carl
Private; One of Garrison's five horsemen, he's outspoken and loves to pull pranks on others

Rodriguez, Cheryl
De facto head of the CIA

Rodriguez, Elio
Sergeant; One of Garrison's five horsemen, he's a bit of a hothead

Scott, Sarah
A woman residing in Drain, Oregon

Shaw; Henry
Corporal; One of Garrison's five horsemen, he prefers to stay in the background

skatut [skuh-**tut**]
A sasquatch who is a little slow but not stupid

Smith, Abe
Secretary of Agriculture

Smith, Sonya
Captain; An extremely tough soldier with firey red hair, she is initially assigned to be Major Garrison's new first officer

Sparks, Nick
Captain; A crack commando who is very certain of his abilities and of his personal success on any mission

sp'atung [spuh-**toong**]
First sasquatch to appear

sqece [**ske**-ke]
A sasquatch warrior

Stansbury, John
Private; A thoughtful soldier assigned to Oscar-Romeo-17

steek'eew [steek **oo**]
One of the three Lat' in the sasquatch governing body known as the Xruhnituhm Siem

thi'thuhl [**thi**-thool]
Wife of sp'atung

Tremayne, Roger
Secretary of the Treasury

tsin'tsun'tsan [tseen-**tsoon**-tsawn]
One of the three Lat' in the sasquatch governing body known as the Xruhnituhm Siem

tuhngiqr [toon-**gik**-ur]
One of the three Lat' in the sasquatch governing body known as
the Xruhnituhm Siem

Wagner, Mark S.
Former president of the United States of America

Xruhnituhm Siem [zuh-**roon**-i-toom seem]
The three-person governing body used by the sasquatch

xtela [zuh-**tel**-uh]
A powerful sasquatch warrior, he is the first one to try new things

Printed in Great Britain
by Amazon

19273668R00185